Sometimes we don't get all the answers.
Sometimes the bad guys win.

Copyright

Cover Image designed by Hart & Bailey

Chapter One

I twisted the solid gold band on my wedding ring finger; three turns, it was a ritual. It had been our ritual. Whenever she had held my hand, it's what she did. Why three, I had no idea. Three seemed to be her number. She wanted three children, we didn't get beyond the one that I sat watching sleep.

I smoothed a piece of hair from my daughter's face, she murmured a little before settling back into what I hoped was a dreamless sleep. Night after night I sat and soothed her, chasing away the nightmares that plagued her. My baby was only five-years-old and had seen the stuff of horror movies. She had been locked in a bathroom while her mother was murdered.

The house was cold, empty, and full of memories as I walked from room to room. I stood at the end of my bed and stared, willing my wife to return to us. I wanted to picture her naked, her perfect body lying prone, waiting for me. Instead what I saw was blood and dead eyes wide with fright. My stomach recoiled and I clamped a hand over my mouth. Maybe it was a mistake to stay here. Maybe I should have done what my parents had advised and moved out immediately after, but I was torn. I wanted my daughter safe. I wanted her to be free of her nightmares and to be as far away from the source of them as possible. Until I found who had taken my wife, her mother, I was paralyzed into staying.

Did that make me a bad father? Probably. Was everything I did focused on my own agenda? Maybe. I was going to find the man who had murdered my wife, who had inflicted such insufferable pain and anguish, and I'd make him pay. That was a promise I'd made to my wife as we laid her body to rest, no more than a few months prior, and a promise I intended to keep.

The local police were about useless. They'd already decided it was a failed burglary, an opportunist who had been disturbed by my wife returning home early. Someone who was passing through, because there couldn't be anyone who resided in our Hicksville town so deranged as to want to murder the local schoolteacher. I believed they just wanted the case closed, they didn't want to have the thought there was a killer on the loose.

However, nothing had been taken. There had been plenty of mess left. Drawers and cupboards had been upended, as if someone was looking for something, but jewelry and electronics were all left behind. I'd argued over and over that it wasn't a burglary; any fool could see that. I'd wanted the FBI called in, someone with an ounce of sense to investigate; my pleas fell on deaf ears. So it was up to me to solve the crime. It was up to me to rid the world of the scum that had made a child motherless, a husband a widower, a classroom of five-year-olds, teacherless.

It was up to me to avenge the beautiful Sierra, a woman without a mean bone in her body. A woman who had loved me despite my past. A woman that had given birth to something so precious my heart ached every time I looked at our daughter. It was up to me to right the wrong. Bringing the culprit to justice wasn't my plan. It should have been, it was the right thing to do, but I needed to know whoever had destroyed my family was going to suffer. There would be no chance of a cozy jail cell, or a fucking lawyer to defend their actions. Oh no. An eye for an eye the Bible taught us. I intended to crucify the man.

I scrubbed my hands over my face with exasperation. I was trying to stay calm.

"Baby girl, we have five minutes to get to school. Can you please tell me where you put your shoe?" I asked.

Taylor was sitting on the first step of the stairs. She had one shoe in her hand, and we were missing the other. I hadn't gotten a lot of sleep the previous night and was trying to keep my temper in check.

"I don't know, Daddy. It was there, by the door."

She hiccupped a little and I took a deep breath. I could see she was getting upset.

"Okay, how about we find another pair? What about those pretty pink ones?"

"No, Mommy loved those, I don't want to wear them."

Taylor had taken to not wanting to wear anything she believed her mother loved. The fact was; her mother bought pretty much everything in the wardrobe and all the shoes in the closet. I guessed she didn't want the reminder.

"Mommy hated these ones, I think Grandpa bought these."

I held up a pair of black sneakers, knowing full well where they'd come from. I was hoping the thought that her beloved grandpa had bought them would tempt her to wear them. I was in luck; a broad smile broke over her face. She reached out for them.

Hand in hand, we walked the short distance to the local school. It was a bright sunny day and Taylor skipped alongside me. Some days it was as if nothing had happened, she was internalizing so the therapist told me. Other days, it would all crash down on her and my heart would shatter at her cries and screams. That day looked to be a good day.

"Who's that lady?" she asked, looking up at me.

“What lady?”

I followed her gaze across the street. There was no one there.

“There was a lady, I’ve seen her before. She came to our house once and Mommy was upset.”

We had arrived at the school gate and I crouched down to Taylor’s level.

“When, baby girl?”

“Yesterday.”

It was always ‘yesterday.’ Taylor was too young to really understand the concept of time, and since her mother’s murder, she was more confused than ever.

“Was it day time?” I asked.

She nodded her head. “Before or after school?”

“After, I think, I was drawing and she knocked on the door.”

“Okay, can you remember what she looked like?”

Taylor shook her head at first. “She had the same color hair as you.”

So a brown-haired woman had come to my house yesterday. I gave my daughter a hug and told her to be good. I stood and watched her run into the playground, her backpack jiggled and swayed, clearly too large for her little body. Her teacher, the new one, waved from the door as she ushered the children in. I raised a hand back and then turned to make the short walk home.

“Gabriel, how are you?” I heard.

Across the road I saw my oldest friend. We shook hands once he’d reached me.

“Doing okay, I guess. Don’t suppose there’s any news?” I asked.

Thomas shook his head. He was a member of the useless local police force. “You know the case is cold. I still have it, though. I made a promise to you that I wouldn't give up and I won't. I just don't have any leads. I'm sorry."

We had the same conversation every time we met. I was thankful, I guessed, that Thomas had kept the files. He'd even shared details with me, details that could have cost him his job.

"Got time for a coffee?" he asked.

"Sure."

We made our way to the diner, where the owner, Mary, greeted us. We'd grown up together in that town, a town where everyone knew everyone. Although, I'd left for a few years, only to return with a pregnant Sierra. She had no family; I thought it best to be around mine. It would be support for her when Taylor made her appearance. She was immediately welcomed with open arms, but then, there was nothing not to love about Sierra.

"Coffee?"

Mary stood on one side of the counter, and as we sat on the stools, she poured two cups, not waiting for an answer.

"Taylor told me a brown-haired woman visited and Sierra got upset," I said, as I took a sip of the rich black coffee.

"Does she know when?"

"No, yesterday she says. I don't recall Sierra mentioning anything. But what was strange was Taylor thought she saw the woman today, outside the school. I looked, there was no one there."

"Could it be someone in her imagination?" Thomas asked.

I shrugged my shoulders. "She's still in therapy, obviously. And to be honest, I think we might have to move out of the house. Her nightmares are getting worse, I'm not being fair staying there. I'll speak to my folks later today about it."

Thomas was one of Taylor's godparents and, like the rest of the town, had been devastated by what had happened. He'd often stop by for a beer after his shift, or to read a bedtime story to Taylor. He always bought her candy and she had a great relationship with him.

"You heard from your brother?" he asked.

"No, not for a while. I guess he's busy saving souls and all that shit," I replied with a chuckle.

My brother was a man of the church; he had been the local parish priest for a while. But he'd risen up the ranks. I wasn't remotely religious so had no real understanding of what his position was. All I knew was Mom and Dad were proud of him, and he was a pompous ass. Even as kids we'd never been friends.

"I guess I ought to be getting to work," I said, as I drained my coffee cup.

"Yeah, same here. Crimes to solve and all that... Shit, man, I'm sorry," Thomas said when he saw my raised eyebrows.

"It's fine, don't worry. Go solve some crimes. I'll catch you later."

Other than the odd traffic violation, or to break up a party after a neighbor complained, our local police department, which consisted of Sheriff Thomas and a couple of deputies, weren't that busy. But they kept the townsfolk in order when necessary and were highly regarded. They'd called in reinforcements, the part-timers, when Sierra had been murdered but not the ones I'd wanted. Thomas had spent many a night consoling me, and telling me the FBI was not interested in a small town murder. It didn't offer me any comfort at all.

We parted company on the street corner and I made my way into work. I owned a small garage, fixing up cars. It wasn't what I'd planned, but it was what I loved.

Fixing up things had been a hobby; the satisfaction I got when something was broken and then repaired was wonderful. It was just a shame I couldn't fix my daughter. It was a shame I couldn't fix myself.

"Morning, Boss," Jake said, as I walked through to my office.

"Hey, buddy. How's Trina?"

Trina was due with her third child and Jake was in a panic about it. He'd worked with me for the past five years and was someone I viewed as a friend.

"Moaning about getting fat. She sent in a pie, I left it in your office," he said.

Trina had taken it upon herself to feed me. She also supplied all the pies to the diner. Her pies had made her a local celebrity and, like Sierra, she was someone the townsfolk loved.

"Smells good, maybe we'll have a slice with a coffee," I said.

The smell of cherry pie had managed to wipe out the scent of oil that hung permanently around the garage. It made a nice change.

"So, what do we have today?" I asked.

"Old Mrs. Forrester wants this beast back on the road, I told her even the scrap yard won't want this heap of shit."

Mrs. Forrester owned a Cadillac about as old as she was, ancient. It was a classic and one we'd kept on the road for her, only by the grace of God, for many years.

"What's wrong with the beast now?"

"Carburetor, I think."

"And don't tell me, she wants authentic parts?"

"She sure does. Not sure we're gonna be able to find many more for this baby."

I sat at my desk and left Jake to tinker. I had a stack of paperwork to deal with that I had been putting to one side for days. I had no enthusiasm for that side of my business. I missed getting my hands dirty, I missed being the one to hear the purr of an engine that had been brought back to life.

"Jake, Taylor said she saw a brown-haired woman this morning, somewhere near the school. You haven't noticed any strangers around town, have you?" I called out.

"No, Boss. Not recently."

"Okay, just thought I'd ask."

Jake and Trina were the oracles for the town. If anyone wanted to know anything, they were the couple to ask. The town was home to just a few hundred people, so a stranger in our midst was often news. Calling it a town was probably an overstatement.

The brown-haired woman was soon pushed from my thoughts as I started my day. Before I knew it, a very pregnant woman bustled into my office with a basket over one arm.

"Lunch, my lovelies," Trina said, as she perched her ass on the corner of my desk.

"You don't need to do this," I said, as I peered into her basket.

"I know, but I need my man to eat so you might as well, too."

I liked Trina, we had been school friends and she had become a best friend to Sierra. She was godmother to Taylor and, like Thomas, very active in her life.

She dished up a round of sandwiches and some chips, and we sat while she regaled us with the town gossip.

Chapter Two

The week carried on with no more mention of the brown-haired woman. Taylor only had one more nightmare, and I was thankful for that. I managed to get four nights of uninterrupted sleep.

At the weekend, we headed out to my folks. They had a ranch on the edge of town, and each weekend Taylor would spend two days with her grandparents, rounding up cattle and horses, and getting dirty. She loved it.

“Hey, you guys,” I heard, as we pulled to a halt on the dusty driveway.

My mother had left the porch to greet us. Before I’d climbed from the car, Taylor was out of the door and running toward her. Mom scooped her up into a hug and swung her around. I smiled at the sound of laughter.

“Gabe, beers are cooling,” my father said as he rounded the house.

‘Now that sounds like a plan,” I replied.

My father gave me a hug, he had always been an affectionate man, not afraid to hug and kiss his children. Unlike many of the older generation locally, whose only attention to their children had been when they’d beat them.

I enjoyed my dad’s company. He’d been a veteran in his day, fighting wars he didn’t believe in but wanted to ‘do his duty for his country.’ He was an honest man, a hardworking man, who loved his wife with such openness it was often embarrassing.

"So, what's been happening in the world of cattle?" I said with a smile.

"Ah, you know, the usual. Shot a couple of mountain lions the other day," he replied.

"Grandpa, you didn't?" Taylor squealed.

"No, honey, I'm just teasing. Those pussy cats are no match for my cattle," he said, taking Taylor from the arms of my mother.

Mom and I watched as they wandered off, Dad was regaling Taylor with stories of the two mountain lions that he'd fought off. I wasn't sure any of it was true but it kept her entertained.

"How has she been?" Mom asked.

"Okay, sort of, this week. She only had a couple of nightmares. I think I did wrong staying in the house. I'm wondering if it's time to pack up and move."

"Where will you go? Are you thinking of leaving town?" I detected a slight panic in her voice.

"No, she's settled here. I just don't know if I want to stay in the house anymore. Maybe we should come here for a couple of weeks over school break, see how we feel after."

"You are always welcome, Gabe. I can have another room spruced up in no time."

I placed an arm around my mother's shoulder and we walked back into the house.

I spent the weekend fixing fences and barns, generally helping around the ranch. I loved being back home. I loved being outdoors, getting tanned and working out. I'd always been fit but not into gyms, I preferred to keep toned by doing something more useful than a run on a treadmill.

Dad and I decided on a break, it was midday and the sun beat down on us. My body was covered in a sheen of sweat. We'd been moving hay bales, bringing them into the barn.

"Daddy, what is that?" Taylor said.

We sat on a picnic blanket having lunch.

"A heart, baby girl."

In the center of my chest I had a tattoo of a heart, an anatomically correct heart. I'd had it done when I'd first met Sierra. I wanted her to see that my heart beat only for her.

"Why is it there?"

"So you can see it, and you know I love you with all my heart," I said.

She'd seen my tattoo many times, and she always asked the same question because she wanted to hear that stock answer. She laughed as she placed her hand over it.

"I can feel it beating, Daddy," she said.

"It's telling you how much I love you," I said, as I scooped her up into my lap.

She placed an ear to the tattoo and listened.

"I want one when I grow up," she said.

"I think that's something you might want to reconsider," Dad said as he chuckled at the thought.

"You can do whatever you want, when you grow up," I said.

"When will I grow up?"

"Not for many years yet. Now, finish your lunch, we have work to do."

She scuttled off my lap and set about to sweep up the barn. All she managed to do was to brush dust and hay over our lunch.

Taylor didn't experience any nightmares when she was at my parents', another reason I felt so selfish in keeping her at home. I had settled her in bed, read a story, and stroked her hair until her eyes closed and her breathing deepened. When I was sure she had dropped off to sleep, I crept from the room, being careful of the old floorboards creaking as I did.

"She asleep?" Mom asked as I made my way out onto the porch.

"Sure is, today has worn her out."

I took the cold bottle of beer my dad was holding out and sat on the swing seat next to him.

"She said something strange the other day."

I told my parents about the brown-haired woman Taylor believed had called at the house, and about the fact she thought Sierra had been upset.

"And you've no idea who that was?" Mom asked.

"No, she thought she saw the woman outside the school, too. I've asked around, no one seems to have noticed a stranger in town."

"Mmm, maybe she's just remembering something from a long time ago," Mom said.

"Maybe. It just seemed odd, that's all."

I took a sip of my beer and welcomed the cold fizz as it traveled down my throat.

"If it's okay with you, she's on school break soon. I thought it might do her good to stay here a whole week instead of just a couple of days."

My parents often offered to have Taylor stay over. She was their only grandchild, and as it was, there wasn't the possibility of any more.

"We'd love that, wouldn't we?" Mom said, looking over at my dad.

"Sure would," he replied.

"I can get the realtor to come on over and look at the house, see what they think it's worth. I don't want to do that with Taylor around."

My daughter became very anxious when someone she didn't really know came to the house. I'd never pushed her to tell me what she saw that day, that was for the therapist to slowly work from her. In the beginning, I'd itched to question her but she hadn't spoken for weeks after the event. She was too traumatized. All we had were snippets of information that didn't make sense.

Taylor had told the therapist that a man dressed in black pants and a black shirt had come to the house, he'd made her mommy cry. That was as much information as we'd been able to get. She had been locked in the bathroom when I'd arrived home from work. I'd found her curled up in a ball, trying to wedge herself between the toilet and bath, with her hands over her ears. Her whole body had been shaking, and her mouth opened and closed, but she didn't make a sound.

I shuddered at the memory. We didn't think she had witnessed the murder but she would have been aware of the screams. That's one of the things that baffled me. Why did no one hear something? Why did no one see anything?

"Gabe?"

My mother's voice brought me out of my thoughts.

"Sorry, miles away there. What did you say?"

"I said, was there any more news?"

I shook my head. "Nothing. I saw Thomas recently. They have no leads, nothing to go on. I can't believe not one person heard her, saw something. It was the fucking middle of the afternoon."

My parents were as frustrated as I was. “We could hire a private investigator,” Dad said.

“I can’t afford that. And to be honest, I don’t want whoever did this to be handed over to the police.”

“I can and they don’t have to be.”

“Martin, we’ll not be having that kind of talk. Gabe, I can’t have you acting out some form of revenge. You have a daughter to care for, you need to remember that,” Mom said.

I’d stayed out of jail in my early years by the skin of my teeth. I fought a lot, I had anger issues or perhaps it was just boredom. I got paid to fight in car lots and I earned well. I traveled around for a while, doing the underground circuit, much to my parents disgust. It was at a fight that I’d met Sierra. I closed my eyes and rested my head back on the swing seat as I thought of her.

A mutual friend had brought her to a fight. She was totally out of place and huddled in a corner, looking scared. When the police had arrived to break it up, she didn’t run. She had no idea of what to do. I remembered grabbing her arm and dragging her toward my car. She hadn’t said a word as we drove away until eventually she’d started to cry. I’d taken her to a diner, where she’d questioned me, and my choices. Her fiery blue eyes challenged me and I fell in love.

“I think I might head on up,” I said as I sighed.

“Okay, Son. We’ll see you in the morning,” Dad said, as I rose from the swing seat.

I kissed my mom on top of her head as I passed and crept up to the room my daughter was sleeping in. I stripped off my jeans and t-shirt and stretched out on the second single bed beside hers. I watched her. She was the spitting image of her mother. They had the same blonde hair, the same deep blue eyes that would darken with anger. Both had just the one dimple on the left cheek when they smiled. Some days it was painful to look at my daughter and see her mother. Other days it was the most comforting thing in the world.

It was Sierra's face I had in my mind as I closed my eyes and drifted off to sleep.

Chapter Three

We had been back home no more than a few days when Taylor's nightmares started again. They'd start as her whimpering, and I'd sit beside her trying to soothe her. I was reluctant to wake her initially, in case she settled quickly. They would then escalate to full-scale screams and incoherent words. At that point, I'd pick her up from the bed, wake her, and try to talk her down. Usually it took an hour or so before her sobbing would subside, and I was able to put her down again.

I rarely got enough sleep. I'd sit in the leather armchair in the corner of the room and doze until sunlight. She never remembered her nightmares; there were times when she hadn't remembered waking at all. But every cry from her little body would be like a thousand needles piercing my soul. It bled for her. It made my resolve to avenge her mother stronger with every tear she shed.

"Mom, I'm going to take Taylor out of school, there's only a few days until summer break. Can I bring her over later?"

I had to do something and being at my parents' was the only place Taylor seemed to gain any comfort. It had become noticeable at school, she was tired and the previous day had fallen asleep in class.

"Of course, you bring her as soon as you can. I'll get onto sorting those rooms out."

"No need for me at the moment. I have to stay here for a couple of days."

It had been during the early hours of the morning that I thought back on the supposed burglary. They, or he, were after something that was in my house. I wanted to know what it was. I would tear the place apart, brick by brick, if I had to.

Taylor was a little distressed at not going to school; she thought she might be in trouble if we skipped.

"Pack your teddy, baby girl," I said as I folded clothes into a suitcase.

"Are we coming home?"

"Of course we're coming home. I thought you might like to spend some time with Grandma and Grandpa."

Taylor took her time to collect her bears, her books, and some toys. She stuffed them in her backpack. We then made the half-hour drive out of town.

I left her with my parents, and a promise to call after dinner, before heading to the garage. Jake had fixed Mrs. Forrester's car and was handing over the keys and a large invoice. I always felt guilty charging the old woman, but many hours and expensive parts were put into keeping her car on the road.

"Jake, we're closing early today and tomorrow. I've got things I need to do, so I'll see you back here Monday, okay?"

"Sure, you okay, Boss?"

"I dropped Taylor off at the folks', she's not sleeping, and neither am I. I just can't keep her at home right now."

"If there's anything you need me to help out with, you just call," he said.

I locked up the garage, left a sign on the door, and headed home. I'd gone through the house after the burglary, maybe not as thoroughly as I should have. Of course, the police had done a search, again, not as thoroughly as they should have, in my opinion. Nothing had been taken and nothing had been found.

I started in the bedroom, a room I hadn't slept in since that fateful day. I stood at the end of the bed and stared. No matter how hard I tried, I could not stop her image from flooding my mind. She was spread-eagled on the patchwork comforter she had proudly made. She was clothed, but her skirt was ruffled up around her waist. She had a large bruise to her temple, a punch probably. Her hands were grazed, she'd fought and fought hard by the broken nails and skin underneath: skin that didn't seem to belong to any body on a database.

But it was the stab wounds my internal vision centered on. Five, one fatal, marked her body. The police thought it was coincidence that three went down her body starting at the sternum, her stomach, and then her navel and two either side of the middle one. I'd seen the pictures, I'd insisted on that. It looked to me to be the sign of the cross. I'd voiced that, but it had been brushed aside.

"Talk to me, baby," I whispered.

I tried to conjure up her voice in my head. She had a New York accent, although diluted after many years of being away. She wasn't talking that day. I upended the bed, shifted the mattress from the base, and checked underneath. I pulled the frame away from the wall and checked for anything hidden behind. I dragged the rug from the floor, the wardrobe away from the wall, and the sideboard from under the window, until they were piled in the center of the room. I checked every crack and crevice for something that would give me a clue.

I went through every item of her clothing, checking pockets, shoes, and handbags. I found receipts, wrappers, gum, tampons, and the usual debris women carried around with them, but nothing that I thought was significant.

After two hours, I slid down the wall and cradled my head in my hands. I wept.

The room looked like a tornado had blown through it. Bedclothes were in a tangled heap, pillows were scattered around the room, and I was no closer to finding out why. I started the arduous task of righting the room. All the time, I kept one thing running through my mind—If I wanted to hide something, where would I hide it?

As I put each piece of furniture back in place, I checked the floorboards it would cover for scratch marks or loose planks. At one point, I was on my hands and knees testing each individual one to see if there was a hiding place underneath. I found nothing.

When the room was back to normal, or as normal as it was ever going to be, I quietly shut the door behind me and stood on the landing. I decided on the smallest room, the bathroom, next. I opened every pot and jar, emptying contents into the sink or swiping my finger around inside. I checked the toilet tank. I took off the bath panel and the skirting around the shower. I pulled out every towel from the cupboard and shook them out. Still nothing.

I was beginning to get frustrated. I wouldn't entertain the idea that whoever had done this had already found what they were looking for. I couldn't. If I did, then I'd have to give up. Instead, I focused on the rooms they had overlooked.

The only other room upstairs was Taylor's. It was a small room, at the back of the house, with a window that overlooked the yard. I stood in the middle but a pang of guilt hit my stomach. I felt like I was about to violate her space. I flicked on the light switch as the sun had started to lower, leaving a gloom over the room.

I was more careful, methodical. I took out each drawer of her dresser and gently lifted clothes, leaving them neatly folded in a pile beside me. I checked the drawer, inside and out. I repeated the process until I could rule out the unit. I slid it from the wall and checked behind. That small room took twice as long because I was more careful with my daughter's belongings. The last thing to check was her toy box.

I propped open the lid of the pine chest and removed the contents. I opened the lids of board games, even checking under the playing board. Eventually, I picked up a battered doll in a flowing dress. It looked old and wasn't something that I recognized as belonging to Taylor. I held it up and studied it. As I did I heard a rustle. It was the sound paper made when screwed into a ball. I lifted the doll's skirt and saw a zipper. I then understood what the doll was. It was supposed to house her pajamas and sit on the bed.

I slowly lowered the zipper and retrieved a single sheet of paper. All that piece of paper contained was a name and a telephone number. I held it up to the light, in case I could see anything imprinted, perhaps another word that had been erased. I placed the paper in my jean pocket and replaced all the toys.

When I got back downstairs, I sat at the kitchen table, which once had been the place of fun and joy, a table that had been the place of anguish and tears. Every decision had been made around that table. It had been used to eat at, draw and paint, it had been used to plan futures, and just sit and hold hands across. I laid out the piece of paper and used my hand to smooth it flat.

Sister Anna

Underneath was a cell phone number.

"Sister Anna," I said aloud.

I fished my cell from my pocket and dialed. The phone rang until a generic voicemail kicked in.

"Hi, my name is Gabriel. I, err, I found your number, and this is going to sound strange, but I think you may have known my wife, Sierra Malone. Can you call me back?" I rattled off my cell number.

I replaced the cell on the table next to the piece of paper. It may have meant nothing, but I wasn't passing the opportunity to find out. I could have called Thomas, but then what would I have said? I found this old doll, it doesn't belong to Taylor and it has a number in it.

I could already imagine the list of responses. The piece of paper may contain the details for the original owner of the doll; it may have been a thrift shop find; it may have been brought home from school; or it may be a clue to who slaughtered my wife.

I must have sat for over an hour, willing the phone to ring. It didn't. My stomach grumbled, reminding me that I hadn't eaten dinner. I raided the fridge that was stocked thanks to Trina. I ate some cold pie and washed each mouthful down with a beer.

I sat in the lounge and studied the piece of paper. "Who the fuck are you, Sister Anna?" I said.

Before I'd finished the sentence a thought ran through my mind. Sierra had been brought up in the system; she'd never really spoken about her family. She obviously had a mother, and I wracked my brain for any mention of her. Maybe this Sister Anna was someone involved in her care? I grabbed my laptop.

Googling Sister Anna threw up millions of responses, from saints to bands and movie stars. A jolt of something shot through me. I leapt from the sofa, narrowly missing dropping the laptop on the floor, and grabbed a pad and pen. I then Googled convents in New York. That provoked a response a little more manageable. I made notes. Could Sierra have been brought up in a convent?

I should have done the research months back, but then I wouldn't have been in the right frame of mind. I'd wanted to break down, to sob night after night, but I couldn't. I'd vowed that once I found the murderer, only then I would grieve.

Maybe it was time to contact Zachary. My older brother had left home when I was young; he was fifteen years older than me and supposed to be the only child. Mom and Dad didn't think they'd have another child, I was the surprise my middle-aged parents had been praying for. Zachary and I had never been close. I guessed the age gap was just too large and we were poles apart in personality.

I tried to think of the last time I'd spoken to him, I mean, properly spoken to him. He'd officiated at Sierra's funeral, of course, I think Mom had insisted, but prior to that it must have been a few years, and I hadn't spoken to him since. I picked up my phone and then placed it back down on the sofa beside me. Maybe I'd wait until I knew who Sister Anna was.

Chapter Four

I woke the following morning with a stiff neck from falling asleep on the sofa. I stretched out my limbs and tried to rub some life back into them. I noticed a missed call and then cursed. It had been from my mom, in all my investigating; I hadn't called Taylor to wish her a good night.

"Hey, Mom. I'm sorry I crashed out early. Is everything okay?" I asked, once she'd answered my call.

"Of course, Taylor is outside with your dad. A mare gave birth during the night, so she's out there with the foal."

"Cool. I'll be over later, I have some things to do today," I said.

"No rush, just come whenever you can. Let me know if you want dinner, I'll make extra."

"Mom, you always have enough food for the whole town, just in case someone visits."

She chuckled as she disconnected the call. It was nice to hear her snicker, none of us had laughed in a long time, especially her.

There was no other missed call, nor a missed text, and a little bit of disappointment washed over me. I deliberated on sending another message but didn't want to scare off Sister Anna, whoever she was. I decided to continue my search just in case there was something else hidden.

After I'd turned over the kitchen and living room, I took a break. I'd found nothing more that gave me any clues. I decided it was time to visit Taylor. I headed out and locked up the front door behind me. It was as I was about to climb into my truck that I saw her. A brown-haired, older woman stood on the opposite sidewalk staring at me. I hesitated, not sure at first what to do. I closed the car door and faced her. She looked nervous, checking up and down the road before she strode across. It didn't appear to me that she was checking for traffic.

"Gabriel?" she asked in a gentle voice.

"Yes, what can I do for you?" I deliberately kept my voice soft.

"I have something for you, but I can't stay here long. Can we arrange to meet?"

"Who are you?"

"I knew Sierra. She asked me to give you something."

"How did you know who I was?"

"She said to look out for a hulk of a man, who lived at this address, I take it you're the only man who lives here?"

"How do you know my wife?" I kept Sierra in the present tense, unsure what to expect from this stranger.

"I can't explain that here. Can we meet?" Her voice had risen a little. She was clearly uncomfortable. She continually looked up and down the street.

"Sure, where and when?"

"You know the gas station, out on Route 50? Meet me there in an hour."

She started to walk away. "Hold on, what gas station and who are you?"

"You'll find it. Desolate, a perfect place to meet."

I wanted to reach out and stop her leaving, but she pulled a cardigan around her shoulders and hurried off. Was she Sister Anna? Was she the woman who had visited my house and upset my wife? I watched her walk along the sidewalk until she reached the corner; she looked back, just the once, before scanning around and then disappearing.

I walked back into the house and pulled the phone from my pocket. I sent another text.

Was that you? Are you Sister Anna?

Within a minute I received a reply. **Gas station, one hour.**

I paced the living room, unsure of what to do. Of course, I would be there in an hour, but should I call Thomas? She said she had something for me and I kicked myself for not pressing for further information. It could be a set up; I could be walking into a trap of some kind. I headed upstairs and to my bedroom. Beside the closet was my gun cabinet. I unlocked it and took out a revolver. I loaded the chamber with bullets before locking it up and heading out to my truck.

It wouldn't take an hour to reach the gas station; I guessed by her description of 'desolate' she meant Mr. Townsend's. He was the only gas station owner I knew. For the poor souls who found themselves on the worst road possible, his gas station was a welcome sight and the first, or last, stop before town.

I wanted to get there ahead of her, I wanted the advantage of seeing her, or whoever, coming. I reversed out of the drive and started the half-hour journey. I wedged my gun in the side pocket of the door; I had easy access to it there. I could handle myself if whoever came were unarmed, but I wasn't taking any chances. In the footwell was a tire iron. As I pulled onto the parking lot, I reached for it, pulled it closer so it was on hand should I need it. And I waited.

A half-hour passed with no sign of another car. I rolled down my window and rested my arm on the door. The gas station was closed up that day and my truck stood out, I was an easy target. The police often cruised past and I didn't want to have to explain why I was sitting there. I checked my watch repeatedly. Another half-hour passed, that made her a half-hour late.

I was about to send her a text when a beat up old Ford pulled in at the opposite end of the gas station to me. I waited for a couple of moments to see if the occupant would exit the car. The sun was blinding me, making it difficult to see who was behind the wheel.

After a couple of minutes, I saw the driver's door open and the brown-haired woman climbed out. She stood by it, looking around. I opened mine slowly and stepped down from the truck. She made no attempt to walk to me, and I could have kicked myself for not putting my gun in the waistband of my jeans. I'd never be able to retrieve it without being seen, and I didn't want to spook her.

I started to walk toward her. She kept the door between us as a shield, I guessed.

"Sister Anna?" I said as I approached.

"I have something for you. She asked me to give this to you if something should ever happen to her."

"Who killed my wife?"

"It's all in here."

She held in her hand an envelope, the padded type.

"Who killed my wife?" I asked again, perhaps a little too aggressive. My heart was hammering in my chest.

I watched her swallow hard. "More people could get killed for this," she said, waving the envelope in the air.

I reached for it but she pulled back slightly.

"What are you afraid of?" I asked.

"Dying, Gabriel."

"Are you in danger?"

"We're all in danger. You want to know who killed your wife?"

I nodded my head as she reached out with her arm.

"Religion killed your wife. Good luck, Gabriel."

She dropped the envelope on the ground and quickly got back into her car. By the time I'd reached down for it, she was backing away. Her tires kicked up dust as she expertly spun the car around and roared off.

Chapter Five

My hand shook as I held the envelope. I was paralyzed to the spot. What the fuck did she mean by Religion killed my wife? Sierra wasn't remotely religious, as far as I was aware. Taylor had only been christened to give her godparents, not because we wanted her brought up within any religion.

"Fuck," I said.

"Fuck, fuck."

I pulled my phone from my pocket and dialed Thomas.

"Tom, I need to see you, right now," I said when he answered.

"Okay, what's wrong?"

"I have information on Sierra."

"What the fuck do you mean, information?"

I strode back to my truck as I spoke.

"I'm on my way, meet me at the house."

"I'll be there in five."

I disconnected the call and with the wheels spinning, kicking up more dust and stones, I pulled a U-turn and headed for home.

I'd wedged the envelope between my knees, too frightened to even leave it on the passenger seat for fear of losing it. It was an irrational thought, I was sure, but I clamped my knees together, thanking that the truck was automatic and not a stick shift.

Thomas' patrol car was sitting on my drive when I returned. I pulled in behind him, blocking part of the sidewalk. As I exited from the truck, he did the same from his car.

"Gabe, what's the problem?" he asked. I gestured toward the house.

Maybe I'd picked up on Sister Anna's paranoia, but I looked both up and down the street before I inserted the key in the lock.

"I knew that it wasn't just a burglary. They were looking for something, Tom. I tore the house apart last night and found a doll at the bottom of Taylor's toy box, an old doll I didn't recognize. You know, one of those you stuff your pajamas in? Anyway, inside was a name and a number. I called it."

"Wait. You did what?"

"I called it."

We had made our way to the kitchen, and I placed the envelope in the center of the table. I opened the fridge and pulled out two beers. My hands shook as I snapped off the caps and handed one to Thomas. Despite being in uniform, and on duty, he took it from me as he sat. His radio crackled and he fiddled with it to silence it.

"I called the number, left a message asking if they knew Sierra. I didn't get a reply. Taylor said she saw a brown-haired woman a couple of weeks ago; the same woman she believes came to the house one time. Sierra had been upset at the visit."

"Back up, I need to write all this down."

Thomas took a small notepad and pencil from his jacket pocket.

"Start at the beginning," he said.

I repeated, slowly, what I'd already said.

"So this Sister Anna replied to your text?"

"No, earlier I was in the yard and I saw a brown-haired woman across the street. She stared at me for a while then walked over." I then told him what had happened from that point.

When I finished, and he'd written up his notes, we both stared at the envelope. It was dirty, old, and not quite sealed.

"I need to take this in, Gabe."

"No way, I have to see what's inside. You have to understand that."

"There could be fingerprints all over that. I have to call this in."

"Wait here." I jumped from my seat and ran back to the truck.

I returned seconds later with two pairs of latex gloves. I threw a pair at Thomas as I snapped on the other.

He stared at me while holding the gloves. "We use them at the garage, obviously," I said.

Once he had donned his gloves, Thomas picked up the envelope. He studied it first, took some pictures using his phone before placing his thumb under the flap and prying it open. He shook out the contents on the table.

There were several pieces of paper and an old photograph. Using just the tip of one finger, he separated them out until the photograph was isolated. We looked at it. It was a group of children, miserable looking children. Behind them were a couple of nuns and a priest. I couldn't determine if any of them was Sierra, and I didn't recognize the grey stone building they were standing in front of. There was no sign, nothing to identify what the building was.

I unfolded a piece of paper; it looked like it had been torn from a diary. Written in a childish scrawl was an entry.

"Fucking hell," I said as I read.

My stomach lurched as I slid the page over to Thomas. I swallowed the bile that had risen to my throat.

"Jesus," he said.

“Do you think…?” I struggled to say the words.

“Don’t go there, not yet. We don’t know what any of this means.”

The diary entry was a child detailing sexual abuse. It was very explicit, but what had turned my stomach was the accusation that her, or his, abuser had been the priest.

I placed my elbows on the table and let my head fall into my hands. I needed to quell the nausea. I’d closed my eyes and took in deep breaths.

“Gabe, we don’t know that this has anything to do with Sierra just yet.”

“Think about it. Taylor said a man in black pants and a black shirt came to the house. That’s a fucking priest, Tom.” My voice rose in anger.

“We don’t know that. We can’t go rushing to assumptions. I need to get this back to the station so I can investigate.”

“I want copies of these, I want to know exactly what you're doing, when, and how. You’re not blowing me off on this one.”

“I wasn’t blowing you off the last time.” Thomas had become defensive.

“I know, I’m sorry, but this a breakthrough, right?”

“Possibly, yes. But we need to know this woman isn’t stringing you along, that she really did know Sierra. We also need to determine that these documents belonged to your wife and what they mean. And I need the doll.”

“You can fingerprint them, can’t you?”

“I can, I need to copy them all first and then send them off. If this is what we think it is, Gabe, this is some serious shit.”

“Serious enough to kill over?”

We fell silent as we stared once more at the pieces of paper on the table.

Chapter Six

I followed Thomas back to the station, I wasn't about to let him take those papers away and not know what was happening with them. He'd reluctantly agreed that I could watch as he copied each one, using what looked like tweezers to tease the pages open. Each one looked like a diary entry. Although the writing changed, became more mature I guessed, it seemed to me to have been written by the same individual. Was that Sierra's handwriting?

Thomas was on the phone as I read the copies. He was requesting a trace on the cell number for Sister Anna. He was organizing for the documents to be sent out of state for fingerprinting, he didn't have the resources for that.

"So what do we actually have here?" I asked, when he'd gotten off the phone.

"Diary entries, mainly. Some detail abuse. And then we have the photograph, of course. I don't suppose you recognise Sierra?"

"I can read what they say. And no, although how old do you think these kids are? I'd say they look about the same age as Taylor. The pieces of paper are identical," I said.

"Maybe they were torn from one of those multi-year diaries. We don't have years but some of them are the same day."

Three of the pieces of paper had January thirty-first printed in the top right corner.

"This is sick, listen to this…"

He pulled down my panties. I didn't want him to. He said I'd been bad and God wanted me spanked. I had to lie down on the altar and he spanked me. I cried when he rubbed the soreness away, when he pushed his thing inside me. I hate him. I hate it here. Someone, help me.

The style of writing for that piece was slightly different to the others, a little more legible, suggesting a slightly older child wrote it.

"Who was doing this to them?" I said to no one in particular.

"This one says, Father, and I don't suspect that refers to their dad," Thomas replied.

"Fucking sick bastard. We need to find out what this all means, who this child was, and how it relates to Sierra."

"I want you to contact Sister Anna again. Arrange a meet if you can."

"She's pretty skittish. But I'll try."

I picked up the note that had her number on and called. Like before, it went to voice mail.

"This is Gabriel, we need to meet, urgently. Please call me back."

"Somehow you need to encourage her to come in and be interviewed," Thomas said. "It may have nothing to do with Sierra, but this is a case to be investigated."

"Sierra came from New York. I Googled Sister Anna, I didn't get any direct hits, but there are just over two hundred convents in New York City. Is there a way we can find out if the sister is at one of those?"

"I don't know my nun history, but I don't think Anna will be her real name. I think they're given a name. I'm going to try but it's a long shot, for sure. I suspect there are a shit ton of Sister Annas."

"Yeah, but not a shit ton of Sister Annas that have gone missing."

"Fair point. We're a long way from New York; she didn't come here on a day visit. Right, give me as much detail as you can about her."

I sat down at his desk and described as much as I could. The trouble was, there was nothing remarkable about her. No scars or any other identifiable marks.

"She was way shorter than I was, maybe a foot shorter, so I pegged her at five foot. She had average brown hair, shoulder length and a little wavy, sort of unkempt, if you know what I mean. As if she'd cut it herself. And brown eyes."

"How did she speak, any accent?"

"You know, she wasn't from here, but I didn't detect a New York accent either."

I sighed with exasperation. Sister Anna was just a normal-looking woman with an accent I couldn't place.

"Age?" Thomas asked.

"Older than us, for sure. Maybe in her fifties."

"Go back to the hair. What do you mean, as if she'd cut it herself?"

"It just didn't look, I don't know, neat maybe?"

"That could tell us one of two things, I guess. Either she's frugal, can't afford a hair salon, or she cut her hair to disguise herself. Think about her hairline, did you see any coloring?"

"Huh?"

"Her hairline, was there any dye? Haven't you noticed? When Trina dyes her hair, she gets that shit all over herself."

I shook my head. "No, I don't think so. Wait, her hand. When she held out the envelope, her hand was stained. Not brown like her hair but a sort of reddish tint."

Thomas picked up his phone and made a call.

"Trina, when you dye your hair, what color is it?" he said.

"No, not the frigging hair, the product. What color are your hands when you're done."

He listened for a while.

"Okay. Thank you."

"Well?"

"The font of all that is beauty says, if she gets that shit on her skin, and bearing in mind she tries to covers her grey with brown hair dye, it's a reddish color."

"So she could have any hair color," I said, slumping in my chair.

"No, she has brown eyes. Think about it. We can rule out a red head, how many of those have you seen with brown eyes. Black isn't that common, unless she's got some Native American, but then would she be a Catholic? So I wonder if she's actually brown or blonde."

I was impressed with his logic. I wracked my brain to think of all the brown-eyed women I'd been with over the years. I'd fucked a lot of women in my days doing the fight circuit, but to be honest, I hadn't taken too much notice of what color hair or eyes they had. I was more interested in getting drunk and getting pussy.

"If she was on the run, would she be bothered to color her hair just to cover grey? So I'm going for someone who's trying to disguise herself," he said.

"What do we do now?"

"We have to wait, I'm afraid. I need fingerprint analysis and a trace on that cell. There's nothing in those documents that identifies where that took place or even if Sierra was involved. There's some connection with the doll, for sure, but what it is, we need to work out."

"She said religion killed Sierra, she knows more, I'm sure. She also said that Sierra asked her to give me that envelope should anything happen to her. So why now? Why not immediately after?"

I had more questions running through my mind than answers. The envelope contained nothing directly linking Sierra's murder to whomever the diary entries were about. I scrubbed my hand over my face.

"It had to be a priest. Think about it, the black pants and shirt, the stab wounds in the form of a cross. It has to be, Tom." My voice started to rise in agitation.

All the while I spoke Thomas was making notes. Perhaps he wasn't as inefficient as I'd believed. Maybe there had been no leads until then. He'd often told me that cases go cold and then a chance meeting or conversation will give them clues they can work with.

"I'll send someone round to the church, see if we had any visiting clergymen at that time," he said as he reached for his cell.

"Shouldn't you do that?" I asked.

"My deputies are well versed in the law, Gabe. They know what to ask and sometimes people speak a little more freely to them, rather than me. I know you thought we didn't do everything we could back then, but we did. I turned over every fucking stone, Gabe. I just didn't find any clues. It frustrates me as well."

I'd repeatedly checked my phone for a reply from Sister Anna, and as the hours ticked on, the urge to call again got greater.

"You can't spook her. She knows you know that number belongs to her; we need to take this slow and careful. Like I said, if what we're reading is true, this is a shitstorm we're about to hit."

Chapter Seven

I left Thomas and headed over to my parents'. I hadn't wanted to but I was no help, and my presence was stalling him getting on with investigating the contents of that envelope. At least I'd witnessed the collection of the original documents and knew they were on the way to wherever to be fingerprinted. That gave me some comfort, and the fact that he'd given me a copy.

"Daddy!" I heard as I stepped down from the truck. "There's a foal, come and look."

Taylor was excited as she pulled on my arm. "Okay, show me where."

She led me to the barn and climbed on top of a hay bale that had been placed outside the door so she could look over.

"Isn't she pretty? Can I have her, please, Daddy?"

"She sure is. I don't know about having her, baby girl. Looking after a foal is a lot of hard work."

"I can do it, I promise. Grandpa said I could name her. I'm going to call her Lily."

"Lily?"

"Yeah, Mommy had a friend named Lily."

I tried not to react immediately. I took a deep breath. "Did she? How do you know that?"

"She came to the school, loads of times. Mommy always hugged her."

"And you know her name was Lily?"

"I think so. So, can I have her, please, Daddy?"

"We can call her Lily, for now, and then we need to see how good a girl you are. Naughty girls don't get horses."

She laughed as she jumped off the hay bale and smiled up at me. It was the first time I'd seen her so happy. She could have the damn foal if it kept that sparkle in her eyes.

"Let's go find Grandma," I said as I took her little hand in mine.

Taylor skipped alongside me as we made our way to the house. Inside my guts were in knots. Sister Anna, Lily—who were these people, and why did I not know them?

I handed over a grubby Taylor to my mother, who ushered her upstairs for a bath before dinner. I sat on the porch with my dad.

"I found out some information today, Dad. I'm not sure I want Mom to know just yet, but I have to talk to someone about it," I said.

He leaned forward slightly. "About Sierra?"

"Yes." I then told him all that I knew from Sister Anna and Taylor mentioning Lily.

"Shit, Son. What does Thomas make of it all?"

"He's keeping an open mind, and I get that, but I can't help thinking this has something to do with Sierra's childhood, a childhood I know nothing about."

"What about calling Zach?"

"No, if this has something to do with the church or a convent, I don't know that I want him involved. It might put him in a compromised position. To be honest, Dad, they're worse than the fucking Masons. They'd cover it up."

"Do you think…?" He didn't finish his sentence, but I knew what he was implying.

"I don't know, Dad. I really don't know."

"Think back, Son. What do you know about Sierra?"

"Not much, now I think about it. She was an only child, lost her mother when she was young, never knew her dad, and was brought up in the system. It was one of those things that she didn't like to talk about, and I respected that."

"And this Sister Anna said that envelope belonged to Sierra, do you know that for fact?"

"No, I took her word for it. I don't recognise the handwriting, but then it looks to have been written by a child. And I don't recognize anyone in the photograph."

"So what happens now?"

"We have to wait and see if she replies, which is another thing I wanted to talk about. I think it best for me to stay at home for a while. If she responds, I'll need to leave there and then, and I can't do that with Taylor. If this is what I'm suspecting, I want Taylor as far away as possible."

"I can understand that. You leave Taylor here with us. I just don't know what to make of it all. Sheesh, the Church?" Dad rested back on his seat and raised his beer to his lips.

"I've never asked this before, but can we keep this from Mom, for a while? I don't want her concerned."

Mom hadn't been herself for a while. She was often agitated and refused to talk about it. I'd been concerned about some form of dementia, but I hadn't voiced that concern to my dad.

Dad waved his hand. "Sure, but I do wonder if Zach might be of help."

"Not yet, let's wait until we know a little more."

The patter of feet across the hallway halted any further conversation. Taylor climbed onto my lap. Her hair was wet and smelled of strawberries, she had on her nightgown and furry slippers.

"Hey, you smell nice," I said as I wrapped my arms around her.

“It's my own shampoo, Grandma bought it for me,” she said.

“So, how about you tell me who Lily is?” I gently said.

“Lily the foal?”

“No, Lily the person you named the foal after. I thought it would be nice for us to know the real Lily, if Grandpa is going to give you this foal.”

“You’re gonna give me the foal?” she squealed.

“Maybe,” Dad said.

“Lily comes to the school. She’s nice. She looks like Mommy.”

“Did Mommy introduce you?” I asked.

“No, I…I snuck round the corner and saw her. Am I in trouble?”

Her voice trailed off to a whisper. I was always cautious of bringing up Sierra. I didn’t want Taylor to forget her but wondered if it was still too soon for her to talk about her. I hugged her tight to me.

“No. I bet she’s a pretty lady then, just like your momma,” Dad said.

Taylor didn’t say anymore but I glanced over her head to my dad.

“I think, little lady, that it’s dinnertime, then bed,” he said as he rose.

I carried Taylor into the house and to the kitchen. Mom had laid out a feast, as usual, and we sat and tucked into ham and mashed potatoes. Once we had eaten, I took Taylor up to her bedroom. We sat side by side and she picked up my hand. She twisted my wedding band, counting to three as she did. Her action brought a lump to my throat.

“Mommy said if we were sad to turn that three times.”

“When did Mommy say that?”

“Just before…”

I cut off her sentence; I didn't want that on her mind just before bedtime. "I understand, but we're not sad, are we? You are getting a foal! How cool is that?"

The mention of the foal perked her up. She chatted about how she was going to care for it, groom it, and learn to ride properly. She'd sat on many horses, I'd sit her on front of the saddle with me on occasion, and it actually pained me to think we hadn't done that for a while.

"We'll go riding on the weekend," I said. "Now, if you want to be up early to feed Lily, you better get some sleep." I kissed her forehead as she settled down.

"I love you, Daddy," she said as I left the room.

"Love you too, baby girl."

I closed her door part way, leaving the landing light on. Although she had never had a nightmare while at the ranch, I wasn't taking any chances on someone not hearing her. I paused halfway down the stairs to listen before I was satisfied she was okay and continuing on. Dad was in his usual seat on the porch, a cigar in one hand and a beer in the other.

"So, this foal. How much do you want for her?" I said, as I pulled a beer from the cooler beside him.

"As if I'm going to charge you for her! Although that's a pretty damn fine mare she's come from," he said, adding a chuckle.

"I'll buy her. Although I don't how Taylor will manage."

"We'll sort it. Be good for the girl to have a pony."

"She said another interesting thing just now."

I told him about twisting my wedding band three times, something Sierra always did. "I'm getting a nasty feeling Sierra knew she was about to die."

"Son, we need to get Thomas to bring in the big guns. Or at least we need to do some investigating ourselves."

"I know. I have a fucking bad feeling about all this. I'm not even sure I like leaving you guys here on your own."

"We're not. Sam is staying over for a few days and of course I have Bertha."

Sam was a ranch hand who came to help out, and Bertha was a shotgun that was originally owned by my grandfather. Bertha sat propped against the wall of the house, just behind Dad.

"Why do you think she knew she was about to die?" Dad asked.

"I don't know, but think about it. She tells Taylor if she's sad to twist my wedding band, why would she say that? Leaves documents that make no sense to me with a stranger, only to be given to me should something happen to her. Nothing is making sense, but you know what? These past few days have made me realize, I didn't know my wife."

We fell silent for a moment, as I truly digested what I'd just said. I didn't know Sister Anna, I didn't know about her visit to my house. I didn't know about Lily. What secrets had my wife kept from me? I'd known her a little over five years. She got pregnant pretty quickly and we married, not that I wouldn't have married her regardless.

"And why now? Why months after she died are we finding out this stuff?" I said.

"Maybe this sister was waiting for the right time to catch you alone. Perhaps she's from out of town, and as for Taylor, maybe it's only now that she can talk about things."

It made sense but why wait so long?

Chapter Eight

I said goodbye to my parents and headed off home. If I heard nothing from Sister Anna by the morning, I'd send another message. As I turned onto my street, I saw a patrol car sitting on my drive. I pulled up alongside.

"What's up?" I asked as I climbed from my truck.

"Looks like you've had a break-in," Thomas replied.

"Oh, fuck. Who called it in?"

"No one, I'd just arrived, saw the side window smashed. Was it smashed before you left? I've called it in though. Waiting on my guys."

"No."

I walked back to my truck and took the revolver from the side pocket of the driver's door.

"You're not going in, Gabe. I am."

"Like fuck, this is my house."

"It's a potential crime scene and I don't need you traipsing all over it."

"I'll wait here, you go in, and if there's no one in there, I'm following."

It sounded like we were two dumbasses arguing by the front door. I placed the key in the lock and quietly opened the front door. Thomas had his gun raised as he crept in. I didn't wait for him to give the all clear; I gave him a minute before following him in. He sighed when he saw me.

We walked from room to room; nothing had been disturbed. We crept upstairs, taking care to avoid the treads that creaked, again, nothing looked to have been disturbed. We lowered our guns as we made our way back down. At that point there were blue flashing lights coming from outside, backup had arrived.

Thomas went to talk to his deputy while I walked around the house to check the smashed window. I froze at the sound of glass as it crunched under my boot.

"This has been smashed from inside," I said as Thomas joined me.

"I can see that."

It was a small window to the pantry, just off the kitchen. We headed in to take a look. It was nothing more than a large cupboard really, and certainly not big enough for the two of us to fit into.

"Don't touch the handle with your bare hands," Thomas said, as he pulled some gloves from his pocket.

He opened the door, other than a few old cans on a shelf, there was nothing more in there. I couldn't recall the last time we'd used the pantry and I doubted, after years of not being used and layers of paint, that window actually opened. The lock had rusted so much I couldn't open it.

"Did you alarm the house before you left?" he said, looking at a keypad on the wall as we walked back into the kitchen.

I raised my eyebrows at him. "Of course not."

"Of course not? Why the fuck not?"

"How many break-ins have we had in the past five years? And don't say mine because you and I know that was not a burglary."

He didn't answer. "None," I said.

I'd gotten the alarm on the insistence of my parents and for the safety of Taylor. She hadn't been there and I wasn't in the habit of setting it. It was a basic alarm system, just a high pitched shrill to frighten off any intruders if tripped. I'd scoffed at it, my wife had been murdered in the middle of the day, and not one of the neighbors on the sleepy little street I lived, had noticed. I fucking doubted a wailing alarm would rouse them either.

“Change the locks, Gabe,” Thomas said as he holstered his gun.

Within a half-hour I had Thomas and his two deputies doing their thing. They took notes, photographs, dusted for prints, and measured the hole in the window. It was a small hole, as if someone had thrown something through it or maybe punched it out. But there was not a shred of clothing caught on the shards of glass still left in the frame and no blood to indicate they might have hurt themselves trying.

“I don’t know what to make of it,” Thomas said.

“It can’t have been to pass something out, you’d use the fucking door, or open another window at least.”

“A warning?” he said.

“About what? And we still come back to that window was blown out from inside. The glass wouldn’t have been in the yard otherwise.”

“Let’s get it boarded up until tomorrow and can that door be locked?” He looked toward the pantry door.

“I can fix something on it.”

We made our way to the carport to see if I had any wood and found a piece that would be suitable. Once it was nailed into position, I then fixed a couple of bolts to the inside of the door. Not that it would stop anyone opening it from inside the house, of course.

“I’ll be back in the morning, but I think you should go to the ranch,” Thomas said.

“No way. Whoever did this can come back anytime they want. I have questions they might be able to answer. Don’t suppose you have news?”

“Nothing yet, it will take a couple of days.”

"Shit, I nearly forgot. Taylor mentioned another new name tonight."

I told Thomas about Lily.

"Could just be a teacher's assistant, but I'll head on over tomorrow and ask the principal."

"I can do that in the morning. I need to speak to her about Taylor out of school anyway."

"I'd rather you stayed out of any investigation, Gabe."

"You know that won't happen. It was my wife that was killed, Tom. I'm finding out things now that I never knew before. Sierra knew she was in trouble; I'm convinced of it. She told Taylor to twist my wedding band three times if she was sad, that's something she used to do."

Thomas and I sat on the porch once his deputies had left.

"I don't know what to do. What the fuck was Sierra up to, and why was I kept in the dark? It's like I didn't know her and that's a punch to the gut."

"I don't know, but I think you're right. I think whatever it was she knew, she also knew was going to land her in some serious shit. Maybe that's why she didn't tell you, maybe she was trying to protect you and Taylor."

"From what, though?"

"That's what we have find out."

I didn't sleep easy that night. I'd kept my gun lodged under the pillow, and every creak and rattle had me jumping from the bed. I lay awake thinking. I had a fair bit of information rattling around my brain but none of it made sense. Nothing tied together. In the early hours of the morning, I decided that I had to start right back at the beginning, Sierra's beginning.

With a large mug of black coffee in hand, I sat at the kitchen table and stared at a blank pad. I twiddled the pen between my fingers. I knew her maiden name, so that's where I'd have to start. But how? She had to have had a birth certificate somewhere, I was sure we would have needed that when we got married. Although it was a civil ceremony with just my family, there must have been some documentation. Trouble was, Sierra and my mom organized it all. I didn't even know where our marriage license was.

I started to make a list.

Marriage License

Birth Certificate

Mother's name – details of death?

Mother – where buried?

Sister Anna – who is she?

Lily – who is she?

Then I drew a blank again. Maybe I should take up my dad's offer of a private investigator. I had a laptop but I wasn't particularly computer literate. Still, I rose from the chair and retrieved it. I made a list of the convents. I had no idea how the foster care system worked, I doubted I could just call and ask if they knew my wife.

When the sun started to rise, I stood and stretched out my back. I was no closer to having answers than I was months ago. I picked up my phone and sent another message to Sister Anna.

I need to see you. Please, message me or call. Gabriel

I took my phone with me to the bathroom. I needed to shower, and then as soon as I could, I was heading to the school. I wanted to find out who Lily was, if only to rule her out. Something niggled me; something Taylor had said and I wracked my brain to remember. I should have added, speak to therapist, to my list.

“Mrs. Thompson, can I have a word?” I said as I crossed the schoolyard.

Mrs. Thompson was the principal at Taylor’s school and a formidable character. Fuck knows what the kids thought of her; she scared the shit out of me.

“Mr. Malone, it’s good to see you. Come on in,” she said.

I let out a sigh of relief that she was in a good mood.

“Taylor is at my parents’. She’s not sleeping and I understand she fell asleep in class. I thought it a good idea to get her out of the house for a while. She’ll spend some of the summer break there. But I have a question to ask. Taylor mentioned someone called Lily. This Lily came to the school, I don’t know when, but I think on more than one occasion. Can you shed some light on who she is?”

We walked into Mrs. Thompson’s office, and I was yet to be offered a seat. I watched her walk to her side of the desk and sit, eventually she gestured toward a seat. The chair I sat in was very possibly made for a child; Mrs. Thompson towered over me.

“Lily?”

“Yes, she said she met with my wife a couple of times. I need to know who this Lily is.”

“Are our wonderfully efficient police force any further on with their investigation?” she asked.

“We have some new leads, Lily may be one of them.”

“So why is Thomas not sitting in my office?”

“Because I need to do something, Mrs. Thompson. I can’t sit around any more, waiting.”

She sighed. “A tragedy, a real damn tragedy.”

“So?”

"We don't have a Lily working here, that's for sure. I know some of the teachers have visitors. I'll check the log, Mr. Malone. If this Lily did visit, and it was an official visit, she would have had to sign in."

"I'd appreciate that."

"Now, as for taking Taylor out of school without notifying us, that's a big black mark against you. However, I understand and will waive any penalty."

Her generosity knew no bounds. I stood and thanked her, inwardly calling out the bitch. She was a good principal, the school children feared her, heck, most of the staff and parents feared her. All the kids that went through her classrooms came out with good grades, and more importantly, good manners.

"Gabe, I told you I'd deal with this," I heard as I crossed the yard.

Thomas exited his car and was surrounded by excited children wanting to know why he was at their school.

"Coffee?"

He nodded, unhooked a couple of boys from his waist and followed me across the street to the diner.

"So?"

"Nothing. No Lily working at the school, so that's a good thing. And she'll check the log to see if there was an official visit."

"When will she get back to you?"

"She didn't say and since I was sitting in a chair big enough for a fucking ten-year-old and staring up at the bitch, I didn't question her on that either."

He chuckled as Mary poured us two coffees. "I have news on the cell that you're not going to like. It's a prepaid but we can trace it. However, before you get all excited, she's not a suspect, so I don't think I'm going to get the go ahead."

"Shit..."

"But I have a friend who might be able to help. Strictly off the record of course," he said, interrupting me.

"You have a strictly off the record friend?" I resisted the urge to use air quotes.

"Sometimes we have to bend the rules a little, Gabe."

Thomas surprised me. Even in school, everything was by the book with him. Whereas, I'd quite happily copy my neighbor's exam paper, he would sit with his arm protecting his answers.

"So, when do we speak to your friend?"

"We don't, I do. And I already have. Even with a prepaid, she would have had to give ID when she bought the phone. Whether that ID is real or not is another matter. We know her as Sister Anna; on paper she could be anyone. If she has the phone on, I'll be able to get a location."

"She hasn't answered my text messages. I'll try calling her."

"Okay." He drained his coffee and stood. "I'll be in touch, Gabe."

He collected his hat from the counter, left a few dollars and headed for the door.

"Refill?" Mary said as she scooped up his money.

"Sure, why not."

"How are you doing, Gabe?" she asked as she poured me a fresh mug.

"Struggling, Mary, to be honest. Taylor has nightmares, I'm not sleeping, and we may have some new information on Sierra."

"That girl will be fine, she's a great kid. You leave her with your momma for a few days and get some rest. I can see the dark circles under your eyes. You'll be no good to her if you're burnt out."

Whether it was because she'd suggested I get some rest or not, but a wave of exhaustion flowed over me. I was lonely, I was worried about my daughter, and I was missing my wife.

Emotion welled up inside me. I placed my half-drunk mug on the counter and left.

The cemetery was empty when I arrived. I parked the truck and climbed out. I took a deep breath before making my way over to where my wife lay. I crouched down at her headstone and ran my fingers over her name.

"What happened, baby? I so fucking wish I could work it out for you."

Tears formed in my eyes as I sat on the grass beside her grave. I missed her, I missed hearing her voice and feeling her arms wrap around me. I missed her smile, the smile that lit up a room and made her eyes sparkle. I missed the look on her face every night when she stared down at our daughter sleeping. That was a look of pure love.

Not a day went past that I didn't feel the physical pain at her absence.

"I'm going to find out who did this, you believe me, right? I won't rest until I know what happened to you."

Sitting by her grave gave me some comfort. Taylor and I visited often and laid fresh flowers. We talked to, and about, her. I only wished she could hear us.

I pulled out the list I had stuffed in my jean pocket and stared at it. The more I ran through that list in my mind, the more I knew I'd need Zachary's help. If those diary entries had anything to do with abuse by a priest, he'd need to know. What he could do with the information, I was unsure about, but I hoped he'd also be able to help me locate where that had happened.

"You've been looking for me?" I heard. The female voice startled me.

I looked over my shoulder and my breath caught in my throat. My heart missed several beats, and for a moment, I thought I had died. I gasped in a lungful of air as I stared at the owner of the voice, as I stared at my dead wife.

Chapter Nine

"What the fuck?" I said.

"I'm sorry to scare you, Gabriel."

"Who the fuck are you?"

She stood in the shadow of the trees, but I could clearly see her long blonde hair, her blue eyes.

"My name is Lily. Lily Preston."

"Pres…"

"Sierra was my sister."

"No way. No, no. Is this some fucking sick joke?"

I stood, but as I took a step toward her, she shrank back into the shadows of the trees.

"Wait, don't run, please. You need to talk to me," I said.

"I can't stay for long. She should never have given you that diary. She put us all in danger."

"Who shouldn't have given me the diary? In danger from who? Talk to me, please. I can help."

"You couldn't help your wife."

"I didn't fucking know she needed me to help her with anything." I struggled to keep the anger from my voice.

I watched as she looked around, like Sister Anna, she was skittish, scared.

"Let's take a drive, you have to help me, Lily."

"No police, okay? I will not go to the police," she said.

I nodded. "No police, just you and me. Please help me, help my daughter."

At the mention of my daughter, her face softened a little, and I saw the tear that ran down her cheek. I was in turmoil, my stomach knotted at the sight of her. Maybe she was a little younger than Sierra, but they shared so many similar features it was starting to freak me out.

She took a step toward me and I motioned with my head to my truck. While I walked across the grass, she kept to the tree line. I had the passenger door open before she got there. She threw in a large backpack and then scuttled in, keeping low in the seat.

I rushed to the driver's side and climbed in. I started up the truck and we drove. For a while we didn't speak.

"How do I know you are her sister?" I asked. It was a dumb question bearing in mind looking at her was like looking at a slightly younger version of my wife.

"You don't, you only have my word for it, I guess."

"Give me something here, Lily. Have you any idea what my family has been going through these past few months?"

"Have you, Gabriel, any idea what my sister had been going through for the past twenty-five years?"

"No, I didn't, and that's the fucking point. I don't know anything. Just a few days ago, I found out about Sister Anna and was given an envelope. I don't know what it means, who wrote the diary, who the kids in the picture are, nothing. I know fuck all and it's driving me mad. Someone broke into, or out of, my house last night, know anything about that?"

"You can get as pissed as you like, but it won't help. I can get out of this truck and you'll never see me again."

I pulled over. "You can get out, you'll be exposed on this highway with a fucking long walk to either end."

We fell silent. I watched as she turned her head to look out the window. Her side profile was as I remembered my wife's to be. I wanted to reach out and run my fingers down her cheek, I wanted to feel if her skin was as soft as Sierra's had been. I wanted to pull her into my arms and see if she smelled the same.

"I'm sorry. Seeing you, it…It's hard," I said.

"I can imagine. We've always looked alike. We're not twins, I'm two years younger. I don't remember a lot, Gabriel. I only have snippets, or flashbacks, I guess. For years I'd even forgotten I had a sister. She got in contact with me just before...Those kids in the photograph? Most are dead. All murdered to ensure their silence, so Sierra told me. It's why she got in contact, to warn me, and I've been running ever since."

"Start at the beginning, please, Lily. Tell me something."

She took a deep breath. "I don't remember a lot, maybe I've blocked it out. Our mother died, Sierra was five and I was three. Sierra and I were taken into a convent that cared for kids. I remember being forced to pray constantly. And I remember watching girls, and boys, being taken from their beds. Some returned, bleeding and weeping, some never returned."

"Where was this?"

"You know, I'm not sure. Sierra told me New York, but I think she meant state, not city."

"Who are the surviving kids?" I knew the answer before she even told me. She had to be one of them.

"One of them is me, of course. Sierra never disclosed the identity of the other ones."

She finally turned to look at me and the fear on her face was evident. I wanted to reach out to her, I wanted to hold her hand and tell her everything would be okay, but I was troubled. My brain was scrambled, my stomach churning with want, I felt like I was sitting with my wife. I wanted to drag her from the seat and hold her, kiss her. Not her, not Lily, but Sierra. I shook my head, hoping the confusion would give way to some form of clarity.

"I'm tired of running, and I don't know how to hide from these people," she whispered.

"Who, Lily? Who is chasing you?"

"The Catholic Church, Gabriel. The whole fucking organization wants to make sure we don't speak out. Sierra set the wheels in motion a year or so ago. She decided to talk. She got in contact with as many people as she could, got statements. And one by one, those people have died."

"How can the whole Catholic Church be involved in this? I don't understand. So, the priest in the picture, he abused the children?"

"Not just him, there was a group of them. From what Sierra said, they shared the children around. They took them from drugged up mothers and drunken fathers, promising care and education. Instead those children got passed around like fucking playthings. I don't suppose all the men were of the church, I just don't remember. I wish I did, but I'm glad I don't."

"Where are all these statements?"

"Now that's the million dollar question, isn't it? Those diary entries, they are Sierra's, she wrote those. After I had left I think."

"Left, where?"

"I was fostered, I think I was four at the time, Sierra said that Sister Anna was instrumental in that. I didn't see Sierra again, I forgot about her, Gabriel. It was only when she made contact that memories of her came flooding back. Why didn't she make contact before? Why did she wait so long?"

"I don't know, Lily. I don't know anything about her anymore. I'm as confused as you are."

In the distance I could see a car approaching. I watched her tense and sink down into her seat. I started the truck and made a U-turn before the approaching vehicle got close.

"My house was ransacked when they killed Sierra. Maybe whatever documents she had were taken. Was Sierra the last one killed?"

We were getting closer to town and with it, Lily became more anxious.

"I doubt it. I wish I could help more, I really do. I was too young, Gabriel. I wish whoever it was that killed her, knew that I don't know anything."

Lily started to cry, her shoulders slumped and she looked beaten and tired.

"Where have you been these past few months?" I asked gently.

"Here, there. I just keep on traveling."

"What about your foster parents? Do they know where you are?"

"I left their care when I was sixteen. I've been alone ever since. I don't have anyone."

"Let me take you somewhere safe, for now. There's so much we need to work out."

She didn't reply and I picked up my phone to call my parents.

"Hey, Dad. I need a favor. I need you to keep Taylor out of the way for a couple of hours. I'll explain more when I get there."

"I'm sure your mom can take her into town, buy her a pretty dress or something."

"I'm bringing someone over with me. I just don't want Taylor to see her yet."

"Are you okay, Son?"

"I don't know to be honest. I'm a little blown away right now. I have Sierra's sister, Lily, with me."

"Fuck, really?"

"Yeah, really. Be there in a half-hour."

We said our goodbyes and I shut off the phone. "You need to be careful using that," she said.

"Why?"

"It's easily tracked, someone could be listening in to your conversations."

"You watch too much TV," I said.

"I'm serious. You think the church is good and holy, don't you?"

"I'm not religious, I don't care for the church."

"They are about as evil as the devil himself."

She fell quiet and continued to look out the window as if the barren countryside held her attention.

Chapter Ten

Dad was in his usual spot on the porch when we arrived. Mom and Taylor were nowhere to be seen. Dad stood from his chair holding 'Bertha' across his chest. I jumped down from the truck and walked around to meet him halfway across the drive.

"So, is she Sierra's sister?" Was his first question.

"I'll let you decide, she sure looks like her. I believe she is. She doesn't know much though. She's scared and on the run. I need somewhere safe for her."

Lily opened the passenger door and cut our conversation short. She gently slid from the passenger seat and stood by the open door. It was clear she felt very uncomfortable.

"Lily, come here, girl," Dad said.

She took a couple of steps forward, not making eye contact. Dad placed his gun on the ground and met her midway. He did what I wanted to do but couldn't, he wrapped his arms around her. She collapsed into his chest and sobbed.

"I'm sorry," she said as she broke away, obviously embarrassed by her outburst.

"You cry as much as you want, Lily. You've had a traumatic time. Now, come on in, let's get you sorted."

We walked into the house and straight to the hub, the kitchen. Dad placed his hand on her back and guided her to a chair. He placed three mugs in the center of the table and poured coffee. She wrapped her hands around her mug as if to use it to ward off a chill.

"So," Dad said when he sat.

"Lily doesn't know too much, no more than we already know, other than most of the children in the photograph are dead. Sierra told her that. Oh, and there is a bunch of statements that Sierra had been collecting for some time from the abused kids somewhere."

"Want to tell me what you know?" Dad asked her.

Lily told him what she'd told me in the car. She added that since Sierra had made contact, she had, indeed, visited her at the school a few times. I tried my hardest to keep any emotion from showing on my face. Dad wasn't so subtle.

"Sierra wanted us to meet, Gabriel. She told me all about you, how you saved her. She told me how much she loved you."

"Then why are we only meeting now?" I said.

"I don't know. Maybe she thought by not introducing us immediately, she was protecting you. But if that were the case, I wouldn't have met her at the school, somewhere so public, I guess. I hope it was so we could get to know each other again, on our own."

"So where do we go from here?" Dad asked.

"It would be great if we could find those statements. Thomas has the diary pages and the photograph, although I have a copy in the truck." I turned to Lily. "Thomas is our local sheriff and also an old friend of mine."

"I won't speak to the police, I told you that."

"I'm not going to ask you to. I just want to keep you safe. Is there anything you can tell me about your mother?"

She sighed and shook her head gently. "I know her name was Lily, I was named after her, but I don't remember her. I couldn't tell you what she looked like even. Sierra said she was brought up in the convent herself. She was very religious."

"Do you know where she lived? Maybe we could find records for her?" Dad asked.

"As I said to Gabriel, New York, somewhere."

"When you spoke to Sierra, how did she seem? Was she scared?"

"No, which surprised me. She wanted to go public about what had happened, she wanted them to pay for their sins, she said. I don't know but, and this is going to sound totally weird, it was as if it was her duty and anything that happened in the process was just fate."

That made no sense to me at all. Dad's phone beeped to indicate he had received a text. He fumbled around with it, huffing as he tried to open the message.

"You're mom is on her way back. Lily, we have a little loft over the barn. You'll be safe there. Gabe can show you on up, and as soon as mom returns, I'll send her over with food and bedding."

I stood and waited for Lily, she seemed a little unsure. "Do you have any clothes or toiletries?" I said.

"I have what I need for a few days in my backpack. I won't stay long, but thank you. A decent bed would be welcomed right now."

"You'll stay as long as you want, young lady," Dad said.

Lily followed me to the truck, where she collected the backpack that had been sitting in the footwell, before we made our way over to the barn. We then headed up the wooden staircase to the small loft above the stalls.

"Mom would have kept this clean, but I think a couple of the ranch hands might have used it," I said as we got to the door.

The loft consisted of two rooms. There was a small bathroom and in the main living space: a small kitchenette to one side, a sofa and a couple of armchairs, in the corner, a double bed. I'd often stayed up there during my late teens, before I decided to do the fight circuit. It was a comfortable room and, thankfully, clean and tidy.

"It's lovely," Lily said as she stood and looked around.

"Sierra and I stayed here often, before Taylor was born. She loved it."

"I can imagine that she did."

"How about I let you freshen up? I'll speak to Mom and Taylor, explain we have a guest if Dad hasn't already, and then give you a call to join us for dinner. I need to let Thomas know about all this, but don't worry. I'll make sure he knows you're not willing to talk to him."

"Sierra spoke about Thomas before, she trusted him, I think."

"Well, if you feel you can talk to him, informally, it would help us."

"I'll think about it."

I nodded, and for a moment, there was an awkward silence as I stared at her. She gave me a small smile.

"I'll be back shortly, okay?" I said as I opened the door to leave.

"Gabriel?" I heard. I hesitated with my back to her. "Thank you," she said.

"Well," Dad said as I crossed the barn.

We walked out into the yard and out of earshot.

"I don't know that she'll talk to Thomas, but I do think she knows more than she's saying. She's scared though."

"I've told your mom, she's a little cross that we didn't fill her in before now, but it's only right that she knows since we have a guest."

"Fair enough. I'll go and see her now, then I need to head back into town, see if I can catch Thomas."

Mom was in the kitchen and Taylor was sitting at the table drawing. Taylor ran and jumped into my arms when she saw me.

"Hey, baby girl. You've been shopping I hear," I said.

"We have. Grandma bought me a new dress, do you want to see it?"

"Of course I want to see it."

I lowered Taylor to the floor and she ran back to the table to retrieve her dress. She held it to her and twirled for me.

"That is so pretty," I said. "I need to have a word with your grandma, okay?"

Mom and I walked out on the porch.

"I'm sorry to keep you in the dark, I just wasn't sure about what I'm finding out right now," I said.

"I don't like to be kept in the dark, Gabriel, and I don't especially like you asking your dad to keep a secret from me."

"It wasn't that it was a secret, I just needed to get things straight in my own head first."

"So, tell me about Lily."

I filled her in on what we already knew, which wasn't much at all. The more I retold what I'd learned, the more confused I became. I knew so much more than I had before, but none of it helped.

"Taylor is worn out today, why don't I give her a meal now and then an early night. We can have dinner after. It gives us all an opportunity to talk."

"Sounds like a good idea."

I spent an hour with Taylor checking out the horses, trying on the new dress, and I even fixed her hair before sitting with her while she ate. I felt guilty that I wasn't spending as much time with her as I should have been. I'd closed up the garage but we had work stacking up. I'd have to go back soon, meaning I'd have even less time for my daughter.

I sat with her while she snuggled up in bed and read her a story. When I'd come to the end of the book I noticed she had already fallen asleep.

"Sleep well, baby girl," I whispered as I kissed her forehead.

I knocked on the door of the loft and waited. I heard the shuffle of feet as Lily came to the other side. She didn't open the door immediately.

"Mom has dinner ready, if you're hungry," I said.

The sound of multiple bolts being released echoed around the barn.

"Your dad came over and put some security on the door for me," she said, by way of explanation for the delay.

"That's good. Are you hungry?"

"Starving, I haven't eaten since yesterday."

"Why the fuck didn't you say? I could have brought something over for you."

She shrugged her shoulders as she slipped on her sneakers. When I studied her face, it was clear she had been crying.

"Do I have time just to wash my face and brush my hair?"

"Of course, I'll wait here for you."

She smiled and made her way to the bathroom. I stood on the landing outside the door. I didn't want to walk into the loft without invitation. Thankfully my wait was short.

"Lily, come on in," Mom said as we reached the house. She had been ushering Dad from his usual spot on the porch.

We followed to the kitchen. The table was laid with a feast of chicken, sweet potatoes, corn, and vegetables grown in the garden.

“I hope you’re hungry,” Mom said. “Now, take a seat and let me fetch some drinks.”

Mom handed Dad and me a beer and filled a glass for Lily with iced tea.

“Maybe Lily would like a beer,” I said with a smile.

“Iced tea is fine by me, Mrs. Malone,” Lily replied.

“Tsk, enough with the Mrs. Malone, that was my mother-in-law’s name, and she wasn’t a nice person. It’s Rebecca,” Mom replied.

Dad chuckled as he loaded up his plate.

We kept the conversation light while eating. Lily and Mom spoke about the ranch, the garden, her vegetable plot, and Taylor, anything other than the situation that had brought her to be sitting at our table. It was a little forced, but as the evening wore on, Lily became more relaxed. It was when she laughed at something Mom said that I had to excuse myself.

I was sat on the porch, smoking a cigarette, when Dad joined me.

“Difficult for you, huh?”

“Yeah. When she talks, laughs, she reminds me of Sierra.”

“I can imagine. Are you up to a discussion? I think your mom has plans for a family meeting right now, over coffee.”

I ground the cigarette in the ashtray Dad kept beside his chair and stood. He placed his hand on my back and gave me a smile.

“You’re doing good, Son.”

“I’m trying, Dad. I’m trying very hard to keep it all together right now.”

Mom and Lily were in the process of clearing the table, a pot of coffee and mugs were placed in the middle, and we took our seats again.

"So, we need to make a plan. Lily, you are welcome to stay here for as long as you need to. We have people around to keep you safe, but in return, you need to help us. If you can do that, this nightmare ends, for all of us," Mom said, taking me by surprise.

Lily stared at her mug for a few seconds before answering.

"I always knew there was something missing in my life. I had good foster parents; they weren't loving but they cared for me. They told me about my mother, and I'm pretty sure they must have told me I had a sister. I just knew I wasn't the only one, does that make sense?"

"It does, I guess sometimes we can feel inside that we have kin. Maybe there was something in your distant memory that kept her alive a little," Mom replied.

"Well, I got on with life. I had various jobs straight from school, but then found one I liked and I stayed until Sierra got in contact."

"Can you tell us about that?" Mom said.

"I'd just finished for the day. I was packing up my desk, and I know this might sound strange, but I'd had an odd feeling all day. Something like a sense of foreboding, I guess. I left the office and was halfway across the street when I saw her. She was waiting for me. I can't say I recognized her as my sister, at first. But, as you can see, we are very alike. From where I was, initially, I thought she was my mom. I know I stumbled, a car honked because I just stood in the middle of the road. Anyway, she walked over to me, took my hand, and without a word led me to the sidewalk. We didn't speak for a while; we just looked at each other.

"I didn't know what to say, to be honest. And then we cried. I think at that point I realized who she was; I saw flashbacks of us as children in my mind. The first thing I asked her was why had she left me."

"What was her answer, Lily?" I said.

Lily turned in her chair to face me.

"She had no choice, of course. A family had come to the convent wanting to adopt initially. Sierra said she brushed my hair and made me wear the prettiest dress she could find. She held my hand and led me to the 'line up'."

"The line up?" I asked.

"Yes, it was like a cattle auction. Adults would come and we would be paraded in front of them, sold off to the highest bidder. I don't know if that's true or just a distorted memory. I remember talking to my foster parents and then it was a few days later, it could have been longer I guess, I left. That was it, I never saw her again."

"Tell us about that first meeting," Dad asked.

It was clear Lily was getting distressed having to recall those memories. She fidgeted on her chair and poured a second cup of coffee before she continued.

"We went for a coffee, she held my hand the whole time. She...She told me about her time there, at the convent. She'd run away as soon as she was old enough."

"Did you know about the diary? That was Sierra's wasn't it?" I asked. Bile had risen to my throat.

Lily nodded and kept her gaze back on her mug. I failed to stop the sob that left my mouth. I failed to stop the tears that ran down my cheeks.

"Fuckers. Fucking..." I didn't have the words to truly express the hatred, the anger, and the sickness that flooded my body all at once.

"We were bred to be abused," I heard.

Chapter Eleven

Lily had spoken so quietly I wasn't sure I heard correctly.

"Say that again," I said, my earlier tears had frozen on my face from the coldness that coursed over my body at her words.

"We were bred to be abused."

No one spoke, not a breath could be heard taken. My heart hammered in my chest and the hand holding my mug, shook. I slowly lowered it to the table and watched the rings of liquid spread outwards, as if a pebble had been thrown into the center. Fuck.

The 'pebble' Lily had just thrown us was a boulder, and the ripples were tsunamis about to destroy all the good I thought religion had to offer.

"Oh my God," Mom whispered.

"So now you know, Gabriel. Your wife was their toy, for years. She was one of the lucky ones though; she was prized. It had something to do with my mother. They thought her divine, angelic, I think. She was impregnated. Whether that was against her wishes, I have no idea. And then, according to Sierra, when she wasn't useful anymore, they killed her."

Finally she looked up at me. There was an air of defiance about her. Her earlier tears had dried up, her features hardened.

"I will say this one thing, Gabriel. Trust no one, and I mean, no one. The church is so much more powerful that you imagine."

With that she stood. "I'm sorry, Rebecca, I'm really tired now. I very much appreciate your meal and the coffee, but I need to sleep."

Mom rose from her chair and I noticed her stumble very slightly. As if the shock of what we had learned had been too much for her. She waved away my hand of support.

"I'll walk with you, Lily. I want to make sure you settle okay."

Dad and I were back on the porch waiting on Mom. We hadn't spoken a word since Lily had left the table, still digesting her words.

My hands shook as I lit my cigarette. I didn't generally smoke in front of my parents, especially Mom, who hated it.

"Do you believe that?" he quietly asked.

"Sierra obviously did," I replied.

"I don't know what to say."

"Neither do I, Dad, neither do I."

I watched Mom walk back from the barn entrance. Her face was ashen, and in that moment, she looked ten years older.

"How is she?" I asked.

"Distraught right now. I think with all the talking earlier, the dam has burst for her. She needs some time alone to digest all those suppressed memories that are flooding back. You did the right thing, Gabe, bringing her here."

"I still have so many questions though," I said.

"All in good time. She's opening up, slowly. It has to be hard for her. Her world has been turned upside down as well."

Mom sat beside me on the swing seat. "Hand me one of those beers," she said.

Mom never drank alcohol; maybe the occasional wine at Thanksgiving, Christmas, or birthday parties. I figured we all needed something to help deal with the information we had gained.

"So what do we do now?" Dad asked.

"I need to let Thomas know everything we do, I guess," I replied.

"I think we also need to ask Zachary for advice," Mom said.

"I'm not sure about that. He's part of the church, Mom. That puts him in an awkward position and will she talk to him?"

"This has all gotten so complicated, I just don't know what to think right now. I didn't know that," she said.

"None of us did, Mom."

I placed my arm around her shoulders, feeling how bony she'd become of late. I hadn't noticed how thin she was. Mom wasn't a frail woman, she was as strong as an ox and kept fit helping around the ranch and in her garden. I guessed I just hadn't thought about how old she really was.

In all the drama of the day, I had forgotten about my messages to Sister Anna. After listening to Lily, I was unsure whether to send another. I wanted Sister Anna to know Lily was with us but didn't want to do that over the phone. I didn't know who, if anyone, was monitoring our calls, our text messages. Or even if those people had the capability of doing so. Then I remembered what Thomas had said; his shady friend could, so I guessed it wasn't beyond the realm of possibility for someone in the church to do so.

I'd been around criminals, there were plenty of them in the underground fight community, but I was way out of my depth with this. I fought to earn money and because I was good at it, not because I got a thrill being involved in the criminality of it all.

I pulled my phone from my pocket and dialed Thomas, I needed to share the information, sooner rather than later. I'd hate to forget something that could be important.

I stood from the porch and walked to my truck, waiting on him to answer. When he did, it sounded like he was eating dinner.

"Hey, sorry, am I interrupting dinner?" I said.

"Yeah, but what's up?"

"I have Sierra's sister, Lily."

"What?"

"I have Lily, Sierra's sister, holed up in the loft above the barn at Mom's."

"That's what I thought you said. Shit, Gabe, I'm on my way."

I heard a muffled conversation, as if he'd covered the speaker with his hand.

"Wait up, I don't think you should come here. I'll meet you at mine," I said.

I had two concerns about Thomas visiting Mom and Dad. First, turning up in a cop car would freak out Lily and second, maybe I was being a little paranoid, but I didn't want him to lead anyone there either. It was time to start being careful.

"Okay," he said before cutting off the phone.

"I need to go and meet Thomas, I didn't think it a good idea to let him come here. I'm sorry to leave her and Taylor with you," I said as I walked back to my parents.

"You go and no apologizing. We're a family, Gabe, we do this together," Dad replied.

I kissed my mom on her cheek and Dad walked me back to the truck.

"You have a gun, Son?" he asked.

"In the door pocket, loaded and ready."

"Okay, take care," he said, as I climbed into the truck and backed from the yard.

As I drove, a thought hit me. How safe were my parents and Taylor? Once I'd spoken to Thomas I'd think about moving Lily someplace else. As much as I sympathized with her situation, I didn't want the rest of my family at risk.

"Gabe," Thomas said as I climbed from the truck.

"Let's get inside, quick."

"No, hello? How are you?" he said with a smirk.

"Hello, how are you? Now, let's get inside."

He followed me into the house; I disarmed the alarm and made a point not to look at him as I did. I didn't want to see a further smirk.

"Beer?" I asked.

"Am I going to need it?"

"Yep, maybe two or three."

I grabbed two bottles from the fridge and set them down on the table. I slumped into a chair and sighed. The scrape of the chair legs against the tiled floor grated on me as Thomas sat.

"I don't know where to fucking start," I said, as I scrubbed my hand over my two-day-old stubble.

"What's happened?"

I told him everything I'd learned that day. I watched his eyes widen and his jaw fall open with every word. He patted his chest as if looking for his pad and pencil, since he wasn't in uniform, they weren't at hand. I leaned back on the chair and reached over to the counter where I'd left mine. I handed them to him and he started frantically scribbling.

I fell silent while he wrote, letting him catch up.

"So, she really is Sierra's sister?" he asked.

"Yes. Well, I guess so. She's the fucking image of her. And that's something I'm finding hard to deal with right now."

"I can imagine. But are you sure, Gabe?"

"Yes, I'm sure. There's no way she could look the way she does and not be related. And her story stacks up."

"Trouble is, we don't have Sierra's or Sister Anna's account, for that matter. I need you to be real careful here. And I need you to get her out of your parent's house."

"I thought that on the way over. It was a dumb move, taking her home."

"Anything from Sister Anna?"

"No, and to be honest, I'm not sure I want to use my phone to contact her. What if someone is checking?"

"I'll chase up the guys tomorrow to see if they have any information on the owner of the phone. I also think it might be time to call in the state police. If that happens, I might be shoved to one side, though."

"How do we keep Lily from them?"

"We can't, Gabe. She has information on a serious fucking crime here. She needs to come in and give a proper, recorded statement. I need to verify what's she saying. For example, how did Sierra find her?"

I hadn't thought about that. "I don't know, I didn't ask."

"This is beyond us solving it, you know that, don't you? I'm just a small town sheriff; I don't have the resources to deal with this. I made a mistake, Gabe; I'll admit that now. We should have called in help in the beginning."

"And what would have been the outcome? No different to what was initially thought. There was no break-in, no evidence left at the scene, the case would have gone the exact same way, except I'd know even less because nothing would have been shared with me."

I had mixed feelings on what Thomas had said. At the time, I'd screamed from the hilltops that I wanted the FBI, or anyone, called in. Would we have gotten any further forward then? Probably not.

"Tom, we only know what we do now because I found that cell number for Sister Anna. Let's say the state police came in, traipsed all over town, would they have come to any different conclusion to you?"

"I'd hope not, because that would make me a shit sheriff, but now? I just don't know, Gabe."

"So what do we do?"

"Without Lily coming in for a formal interview, there's nothing here I can officially work with. However…" He raised his hand to stop my immediate protest.

"However, we need Sister Anna. We need Lily to make a statement and only you can persuade her to do that. I can come to your folks' and sit down with her, gain her trust before she does that. And we need the statements Sierra gained from those victims."

"What if I bring Lily here? She's away from Taylor and my parents then."

"That might not be a bad idea."

We fell silent for a while, drinking our beers. My head was a mass of confusion, of conflicting feelings and thoughts. I wanted to shake the information out of Lily; I wanted Sister Anna to make contact. I felt powerless and that was something alien to me. I was a 'doer,' I was used to having a problem thrown at me and solving it. I was used to stripping a mechanical engine down to the smallest pieces, and analyzing each individual piece, before putting it all back together, then watching it work. I could do none of that. I couldn't break down all the information that swam around my mind, until I could put it all together and solve the one question I had.

"Why didn't I know any of this?" I whispered.

I heard Thomas sigh. "I can't answer that, Gabe. I wish I could. I wish I could give you answers, but I won't rest until we have worked this through. I'll give everything I've got to this."

"So let's go over everything we know," I said, rubbing the soreness from my eyes.

We spent another two hours listing and detailing everything we knew. We made a list of questions. Some were so obvious I could have kicked myself for not thinking of them. The list I'd made earlier was incorporated. We needed to know the where Sierra's mother had lived; that might give us a clue as to where it had all taken place.

I watched Tom's cell light up; he glanced down at it and replied to a text message.

"Mom," he said by way of an explanation.

In the past few days I hadn't thought once about his elderly mother, although in a nursing home, he visited every evening.

"Shit, Tom, I'm sorry. You need to go home, it's late."

"It's okay, she understands. But I am calling it night. I want to get an early start tomorrow. How about you bring Lily here and I'll 'pop on by'?"

"Sounds good, I'll send you a message when we're here. Do you think I should try again to contact Sister Anna?"

"No, wait until I have some details on that cell number. You try too hard, you might spook her."

I walked him out to his car. He'd swapped his neat Mustang for a sensible Ford when he'd been promoted to sheriff. "You'll be in slippers with a pipe soon," I said.

"Some of us were born sensible and some of us…" he looked at me with a smile.

"I'll see you tomorrow," I said as I walked back into the house.

I sat for ages, drinking coffee to keep me alert, and read through the notes I'd copied from Thomas. So much information but not a lot of it leading anywhere.

"Break it down," I said to myself.

Sister Anna had helped foster out Lily, maybe she'd done that to some of the other kids, but why not Sierra? Was she considered too valuable? The more I knew, the more questions I had.

Chapter Twelve

I woke to the ringing of my cell. I had fallen asleep at the table. A cold cup of coffee sat to one side, and the papers I'd been writing on were strewn across the table. I reached for my phone and looked at the caller display.

"Hey, Mom," I said as I answered.

"She's gone. I went to see if she wanted breakfast and she wasn't there."

"Who's gone?" My brain wasn't quite alert.

"Lily. The bed is made, in fact, I'm not sure she slept in it at all."

"Shit. Okay, give me a half-hour to shower and change and then I'll be over."

"Oh, and one of your dad's trucks is gone, too."

"What the fuck? She stole a truck?"

"Seems that way. You know your father, he always leaves the keys in the ignition."

Once I'd finished the call, I headed upstairs with the cell to my ear, calling Thomas.

"Lily ran, took one of Dad's trucks," I said before he'd managed a 'hello.'

"I'll put an APB out, see if we can locate the truck. What's the license plate number?"

“I don’t know, I’ll have to call you back. I’m having a shower, then heading over there.”

“Okay, I’ll call your dad myself. I’ll meet you there, I have an idea.”

Without a goodbye we disconnected the call. I threw the cell on the bed and stripped as I walked to the en-suite shower.

“Fucking woman,” I mumbled, as I stepped under the warm jets of water.

I was pulling my t-shirt over my head when I heard the cell ringing. Thomas was calling me back.

“Hey, any news?” I asked.

“She’s back. She got up early to go fetch her things, so she told your dad. She’s upset at causing a drama, she didn’t think anyone would mind nor notice.”

“Seriously? She takes his truck and she didn’t think anyone would notice?”

“Exactly what I said, anyway, I’m heading over there, but I think it might be better if I arrive after you. So get your ass in gear.”

“I’m out the door soon as I grab a cup of coffee.”

The fact that she went to retrieve her things gave me comfort yet unsettled me slightly. It meant she was planning on hanging around, but why not ask for a ride? Why sneak off during the night, possibly, without asking to borrow the truck?

As I sat at the kitchen table, I remembered the broken window. Shit, I’d forgotten to call someone out to fix it. The temporary covering would do for another couple of days, but Thomas and I still hadn’t figured out who had broken it. I looked at the bolts on the pantry door. I decided, as soon as I could, I’d get a locksmith in and add a proper lock and key.

I sipped on my coffee, wincing as the hot liquid burnt my lip. I should have really added a splash of cold water to it. Sierra used to laugh every time I burnt my lip; then she’d straddle my lap and kiss it better. My stomach tightened at the thought of her. No matter how hard I tried not to, the image of Sierra naked as she rode me, as she lay beneath me, caused a myriad of sensations. I was both aroused and repulsed. The knowledge I'd gained had tarnished a memory of something so beautiful.

Dad's missing truck was in the driveway when I arrived. I pulled up alongside it. Through my open window I heard laughter, Taylor's laughter. The sound of Lily talking followed it. I wasn't sure I'd wanted them to meet. I followed the sounds to the barn and to the stable the foal was housed in.

"See, Lily, I'm grooming her," I heard Taylor say as I approached.

"You're doing a wonderful job," Lily replied.

"Daddy!" Taylor said, dropping the brush when she spotted me.

"Hey, baby girl, what are you doing in there without your grandpa?" I asked.

Taylor wasn't old, or confident enough, to be around the foal and her dam without her grandpa. I wasn't happy about it, not that I'd let Taylor know that.

"Lily was showing me what to do, look, Daddy, watch me," she said.

"I think we should leave the foal with her mom for a while. Grandpa can teach you all you need to know when the foal is a little older."

"Aw, Daddy. We were having fun," she said.

"I'm sorry, Gabriel, I didn't realize I was doing wrong," Lily said. She looked nervous.

"It's okay, but that foal is just a few days old. Taylor needs to learn how to be around her. I don't want either of you to get hurt," I said.

"Lily won't hurt me, she loves me," Taylor said.

I was unsure which Lily she meant at first. Human Lily smiled over at her, foal Lily was oblivious as she suckled on her mother.

"Come on out now," I said.

Lily rose from the crouched position she had been in. I noticed she wore clean clothes, a white shirt and jeans. Something knotted in my stomach as I watched Taylor take hold of Lily's hand and smile up at her. It was an image I'd seen many times before but with a different person. I held open the stable door, bolting it closed once they'd walked through.

"Baby, Daddy needs to speak to Lily, you run on in and help your grandma, okay?" I said.

Her face displayed the sulk that was coming and she reluctantly let go of Lily's hand. She stomped off, leaving me smiling at her retreating back. She had spirit, my daughter did.

"I'm so sorry, Gabriel. I've been around horses; Taylor was perfectly safe. But I'll check with you before I do anything with her again," Lily said.

"Your foster parents had horses then?" I asked, as we slowly walked toward the house.

"No, I worked on a farm for a while, a few years back."

"I think it would be safer for you to come to my house. If someone is after you, I don't want that here, not with my daughter around," I said, filing away her mention of working on a farm for a later date.

"I understand. I'll move on, Gabe, I feel like I'm intruding. I'm a burden here. I don't want to cause any trouble."

I wasn't sure I liked her shortening my name, it felt a little too intimate, then inwardly cursed myself for being grumpy.

"You're not intruding, I brought you here, remember? I just think you'll be safer at my house, that's all. Whoever is looking for you is expecting you to be in hiding, so why not hide in plain sight?" I offered her a smile.

"I can't believe how kind you are, Sierra was a very lucky woman to have had you," she said, her face colored slightly as if embarrassed by her words.

"I'm the lucky one," I replied, not sure I liked what she said.

We walked toward the house in silence. Was I being overly cautious? I guessed it was the way she looked, how closely she resembled Sierra that still had me freaked. Their voices was similar, the laugh I'd heard earlier, could have been from my wife. I held open the front door for her and she walked in. As her arm, accidently I imagined, brushed against my stomach, my skin tingled.

Mom had set out a tray of pancakes; Taylor had already loaded her plate when Lily and I took a seat. I caught the glance from my father when Taylor asked Lily to help her cut her food, when she asked Lily to pass her the syrup, when she asked her to retie her hair. It was at that moment, I believed having Lily in Taylor's life, for however short it was likely to be, wasn't healthy for her. She was treating her as if she were her mom.

I wasn't hungry but accepted the cup of coffee Mom held out for me. She was another one stilted in her movements, tense. I guessed the morning's activities had disturbed her as well.

"Can I smell Mrs. M's famous pancakes?" I heard.

Thomas, out of uniform, strode into the kitchen.

"Thomas! This is Lily, she's my..." Taylor said when she saw him; she then turned to Lily. "What are you?" she asked.

"Aunty," Lily replied, her voice was slightly quieter than normal.

"This is my Aunty Lily, Thomas," Taylor said, waving her fork around as she spoke.

"Young lady, sit still while you're eating. You'll have someone's eye out with that fork," Dad said, reprimanding her.

I caught the look that went between Taylor and Lily; I also saw the slight conspiratorial smile, I didn't like it.

"Hi there, Lily. It's a pleasure to meet you," Thomas said.

He showed no outward signs of awkwardness or hesitation. He was a good actor when he needed to be. Only I saw the slight twitch to the side of one eye that was often his display of anxiety. He'd never been a good poker player; that twitch, although so subtle, always gave him away.

Lily hadn't responded to Thomas, however she did give him a smile. She turned back to the table to resume her breakfast and Taylor filled the room with her chatter.

"I'll be outside with Thomas," I said, as I rose from the table.

"Fuck, Gabe. No wonder you're all over the place. It's like seeing a ghost," Tom said, once we'd taken a seat on the porch.

"I know. I've got to tell you though, there's something in my gut making me cautious. I don't know if it's because of how she looks or something else. I think I made a big mistake bringing her here. Mom is on edge around her. I want her at my house as soon as they're done with breakfast. I have this urge to keep her away from Taylor."

I explained what had happened that morning.

"Go with your gut until you know different. I was hoping she'd still be out in the truck; we could have pulled her in on an automobile theft charge. That way we'd have her safe and hopefully be able to interview her."

"She said she needed to get her things. I'm not sure how long she was gone, so I have no idea where her things were."

"There's a lot she needs to answer but she's a flight risk. We need to take this slow, Gabe."

We finished our coffee and headed back to the kitchen. Lily was clearing the table and Taylor was attempting to help. Dad stood from the table and beckoned to Taylor.

"You and I, little lady, are going horseback riding this morning, how does that sound?"

"Can Lily come too?"

"No, your daddy needs to take Lily home for a while," he replied.

A look of disappointment crossed Taylor's face. Lily kept her head bowed and didn't respond.

Once Dad and Taylor had left the room, Lily quietly spoke, "I guess I'll go grab my things." She left the kitchen and headed for the barn.

"Mom, I need a favor. Go through that loft; see if you can find anything Sierra may have hidden in there. We should have done that before putting Lily there, but we need to find those statements. I doubt Sierra would have hidden them there but you never know," I said.

"Of course. I'm glad you're taking her away. I don't like that relationship building between her and Taylor, not yet anyway. I didn't realize Taylor had snuck out to see the foal, that's when she bumped into Lily. I wouldn't have allowed it, had I known."

"What's your gut feeling, Mrs. M?" Thomas asked.

"I'm not sure about her, Thomas, if you want the truth. She's not that forthcoming with information, and I would have thought she'd be spilling her guts by now."

"Maybe she doesn't know anything other than what Sierra told her," I said.

"It's more than that, Gabe. I asked her about her foster parents, she was very vague," Mom said.

I nodded my head and pulled her into a hug. "I'll call later, okay?" I said.

Thomas and I walked to the yard; Lily exited the barn at the same time. She had her backpack but nothing more. I looked to Thomas, who was staring at me; he very gently nodded his head in understanding. Wouldn't she have had more if she'd been to collect her things?

"Here, let me get that," I said, reaching for her backpack.

"It's okay, I've got it," she replied with a smile.

"I'll meet you at home," I said to Thomas, as I closed her door and walked around to my own.

Lily didn't speak at first; we left the ranch and were driving along the short stretch of highway before branching off for town.

"I'm causing problems, aren't I, with your mom?" she said. She hadn't looked at me but kept her head turned toward the window.

"I guess shooting off in the middle of the night, in my father's truck, was a cause for alarm. Why didn't you just wait? I could have driven you wherever you needed to go."

"I wasn't thinking. I couldn't sleep, to be honest. And I didn't want to be driving around in the day. I didn't want to be seen. I thought I was doing the right thing, but it seems no matter what, I keep getting it wrong. I don't know how to do this, Gabriel."

Her voice hitched halfway through her sentence, and I started to feel like a shit for doubting her. It was a plausible enough explanation.

"I saw the look on your face, too, when you found Taylor and me in the stable. She's all I have left of a family I only just got to know. She's kin, Gabe, as are you. Maybe I was a little over enthusiastic about making friends with her. It won't happen again, I'll check with you before I say or do anything. I'll speak with your friend, and then it's probably best that I be on my way. Don't worry, I'm not going to run, I'll stick around for a couple of days, tell you all I know."

I took a deep breath. "I'm sorry. I don't want you to just stick around for a couple of days. It's hard for me, Lily. You look so much like her. I don't want Taylor to think of you as a replacement. Not until this is all over and we can get on with a normal life," I said.

She turned toward me and smiled sadly before nodding her head. Her eyes were filled with unshed tears. I reached over and squeezed her hand.

"It will be okay, Lily. We sit down with Thomas, tell him all you know, and then we can decide the best way forward. I'm grateful to you, I can't rest, I can't move on with my life until I know who and why. Do you understand that?"

"I do, and I wish I had more answers for you, I really do."

I smiled at her. "You ready for this?" I said as we pulled onto the drive.

"Yes."

I pulled onto the drive, leaving Thomas' car to straddle the sidewalk that time.

"Put that on and pull the hood up. I don't think my elderly neighbors need to see the ghost of my wife walking around," I said. I added a forced chuckle as I handed her a sweatshirt I'd found on the back seat.

When I thought she was suitably camouflaged, I opened her door and ushered her to the front of house. I opened the front door, disarmed the alarm, making sure to keep my back to her before she walked in behind me.

"Kitchen's through there," I said, pointing down the hallway.

Without a word, she walked on through. She clutched the backpack to her chest like her life depended on it.

"Ready?" Thomas asked as he joined me.

"As I'll ever be."

I didn't want to hear about my wife being abused by the people who were supposed to care for her, but I had no choice.

Lily was sitting at the kitchen table. She'd set the coffee machine to percolate. "I thought we might need it," she said, noticing my glance toward it.

"Okay, let's get started. Gabriel tells me that you won't speak officially to the police, so I'm here as a friend, Lily. I will say this though. I'm obliged, off duty or not, to report a crime. It would help us keep you safe and find who killed your sister if you'd make this official."

I noticed his use of 'keep you safe' and 'sister.' He was personalizing the conversation.

"I'm scared, Thomas. I led a quiet life before Sierra got in touch, and now I don't know where I am or what to do."

"I understand that, but unofficially, there is only so much Gabriel and I can do for you. I need you to start at the beginning. Tell me as much as you can remember from your days at the convent, and more importantly, was it a convent?"

"That's the thing, I was three or four; I don't remember much. I remember nuns and the father; I remember visiting priests, so I guess we can assume it was a convent. It wasn't in New York City because it was rural."

"Sierra had a faint New York accent, as in a city accent," I said.

"Maybe that's where she ended up, maybe she took on that accent as she grew up. I can't help you there."

While I poured coffee, Lily went through what she had already told me. I listened intently to see if anything was added. She was mechanical with her delivery and that niggle returned. It was too rehearsed for my liking. Something wasn't adding up with her.

Thomas would interrupt occasionally to ask her to expand on what she'd said or ask a question.

"Did Sierra tell you how she found you?" he asked.

"Sister Anna. From what I know; she was involved in all the fostering and adoptions. She followed the children. It was Sister Anna that got in touch with Sierra, I believe it was to check she was okay when the murders started."

I tried my hardest not to show anything, such as confusion, on my face. That was a departure from what we already knew. Previously Lily had said, or implied, the murders had started once Sierra had begun to collect statements. That tick started in the corner of Thomas' eye, and it comforted me to know he'd likely picked up on that as well.

"So how old is Sister Anna?"

"I don't know, fifties maybe," Lily said.

"You've met her then?"

"Only once, with Sierra. We met here."

"When was that?" I asked.

"About a month before... Sierra gave Sister Anna the envelope then, the one containing the diary entries and the photograph."

Taylor hadn't mentioned Lily coming to the house, only Sister Anna. I wondered if, under pressure, Lily's story was coming apart?

"Why not the statements?" Thomas asked.

Lily shrugged her shoulders. "I don't know if they even exist on paper. I use the word statements because that what Sierra said. Perhaps she talked, they told her stories, I really don't know. Have you checked the house?" She turned to me as she spoke.

"Of course. This house had been checked thoroughly by Thomas, and his deputies, and by me. You said you met her here, was that in this house?" I said.

She looked at me before answering.

"Here, as in town. If there are written statements, they have to be somewhere, and I think the priority should be to find them. They hold the key to all this," she said.

She seemed more concerned with finding the statements than her sister's killer to me.

"Can I say one thing, Thomas? I can only tell you what Sierra told me and I'm confused. So much has happened over the past months and the fear, the constant moving from place to place, some of what I remember might not be accurate."

There again she blew my theory out the window. It was another plausible reason for her story differing. I wondered if she'd realized she'd made a mistake earlier and tried to correct it.

"That's okay, and we understand. You're under a lot of pressure, you've had a traumatic few days, you're bound to make mistakes," Thomas said, offering her a smile.

"Where did you live, Lily? When Sierra came to see you?" I asked.

There was the slightest but noticeable pause before she answered. "Out in Richford, about a two hour drive from here."

"And what time of day did Sierra visit?" Thomas asked.

"I'd just finished work, earlier than usual, I think. I'd say, about three o'clock."

Thomas scribbled on the pad he brought in with him.

"It might have been a little earlier, or a little later," she added.

"You're doing great, Lily, this is all really helpful," he said, again smiling at her.

I watched her place her mug to her lips, then realize it was empty. She looked over to the coffee machine; we had already drained it.

"I'll make some more, shall I?" she said. I nodded.

Lily rose from her chair and walked to the exact cupboard that housed the coffee beans. She reached up to her left to pull down the grinder from a shelf. She moved around my kitchen as if she belonged there, as if she'd been there before, and not just for a fleeting visit with Sierra and Sister Anna. I glanced at Thomas. Once she'd set it to on, she sat back down again.

"I'm going to have a smoke while we wait for that coffee," I said.

"May I join you?" Lily asked. I stood and nodded at her.

We sat in the backyard and I offered her a cigarette. As I struck a match, and cupped it to keep the flame from blowing out, I leaned forward so she could light her cigarette. Her hand rested around mine. I glanced through the kitchen window to see Thomas on his cell.

"Am I helping?" she asked, as she leaned back and exhaled the smoke.

"You are, thank you. You've been amazing so far," I smiled, as I brought my cigarette to my lips.

"I want to help, I want all this to end and for us to get on with our lives," she said. She rested her head back and closed her eyes.

There were times when she looked frail, demure, and there were times, like then, when she looked hardened. It was very hard to put my finger on it, but the way she smoked her cigarette, how expertly she inhaled, blew out smoke rings, there was something masculine about it, which contradicted how she had behaved previously. Or maybe I was tired, it was all getting to be too much, and I was reading some strange shit into how the woman smoked.

"Do you know where Sister Anna is?" I asked.

"No, she sort of flitted in and out, all mysterious like," she replied.

Another contradiction.

"Coffee's done," Thomas said, as he stood by the kitchen door.

I stubbed my cigarette out in a flowerpot beside the chairs we sat on. Lily did the same. We took our places around the table again.

"What can you remember about the convent?" Thomas asked. I got that he was taking her back and forth in time.

"Not much, there were dormitories. My bed was next to Sierra's. I remember it was cold, and we'd sleep in our clothes some nights. We had chores, or the older ones did. We went to church and had schooling," she said.

It all sounded very Annie to me. My level of suspicion went up a notch.

"Sierra told me children were beaten, abused. I think I was one of the lucky ones, as was Sierra, in that it seemed we were treated differently," she said.

"How?" I asked.

"The father and the priests fussed over us more than the others. Sierra seemed to be able to get us extra food if we were hungry. She'd leave me for a while then come back with snacks."

"Did she share those with the other kids?" Thomas asked.

"No, she'd sneak them under our bedcovers, and we'd wait until lights out to eat."

"How many children were there?" he asked.

"I don't remember, about ten, I think."

"If I show you the photograph, can you point yourself out? Can you remember the names of any of the kids?" He slid the photograph toward her.

Lily took her time staring at a copy of the photograph. She sighed before placing a finger on one girl. "That's me, I think."

The child she had pointed out was blonde but bore no resemblance to the Lily sitting in my kitchen. I couldn't dispute whether it was her or not, children change as they grow. Taylor had a completely different hair color to when she was a baby.

"Where is Sierra?" I asked.

"She's not in the picture. I think that might have been Sister Anna."

The youngest nun, standing slightly to one side, was the woman she'd pointed out as Sister Anna. I looked at her. It seemed a lifetime ago I'd met her in the gas station, but it was only a matter of days.

"Do you know, which ones are the other children still alive?" Thomas asked.

Lily took her time, "I think that one but I don't know a name." She pointed out a small boy.

Thomas circled the boy and Lily with his pencil.

"I need to rest, I'm sorry. I have a terrible headache. Can we take a break?" Lily asked.

"Of course. I'll write all this up, and we'll see if any of it makes sense with what we already know," Thomas said.

"How about I show you to a bedroom, where you can rest," I said, standing as I did.

Lily stood while reaching for the backpack she'd left between her feet. I walked up the stairs and showed to my bedroom.

"There's a bathroom just through that door. Come back down when you're ready," I said.

"Gabriel? I'm not sure you believe what I'm saying when I tell you I don't know much."

"It's not that I don't believe you, Lily. Like you, I'm trying to get my head around it all. One minute I had a wonderful marriage to a beautiful woman and the next, that was all ripped away from me."

“I can understand that. I’ll help as much as I can. Have you had word from the sister?” she asked.

“No, and that worries me. I’ll see you downstairs when you’ve had a nap.”

I closed the bedroom door, halting any further conversation.

Chapter Thirteen

Thomas was in the backyard on his cell again. I sat and lit another cigarette while I waited for him to finish. He referred to his notes as he spoke. He stared at his phone for a little while, once he'd finished his call, then looked over to me. He glanced up to the windows above us.

"She's in the front bedroom," I said, but kept my voice low.

"She's lying."

"I know. She contradicted herself a couple of times. But what gave her away for you?"

"It was all too precise. She repeated nearly word for word what she'd told you earlier, no one does that unless it's been practiced. She's been in this house more than once; she knew where the coffee was stored. First she said she'd only met Sister Anna the once, then it was, what did she say?" He consulted his notes.

"Flitted in and out, it was," I said.

"I'm worried about her being in your house, Gabe," Thomas said.

"I'm not, keep your enemies close and all that. Who knows, she might slip up big time. Do you think she really knows something or just wants some attention?"

"That's something I can't determine. If she was three, or four, it's likely she can't remember much. I get that. I'm just not convinced she's telling us the whole truth."

“So what do we do?” I’d lost count the amount of times I’d asked that question.

“Befriend her, keep her talking, see if she says more or slips up,” he said.

“Is there anything she said that you can use?”

“Not officially, well, I say not officially. Whatever she says can be used to help our investigation, but if she made a formal statement, when it comes to arrests it would sure help some.”

“I’ll keep on at her about that. Did you get the impression she seemed, at one point, more interested in the statements Sierra supposedly took than finding her killer?”

“Yeah, it crossed my mind. What also niggles me is, she wouldn’t have given a statement to Sierra, and she was too young to remember any abuse. So I’d like to know why Sierra needed to contact her at all.”

“Anything on the Sister Anna cell?”

“No, not yet. I had Pete chase it up today.”

Pete was one of the deputies who had called at the house with the broken window incident. He was a young guy but very keen.

“I think it’s strange that she hasn’t replied,” I said.

“So do I. To be honest, Gabe, I wonder if someone has gotten to her. I also asked Pete to check any Jane Does within a thirty-mile radius of us; I’ll expand that if we don’t get a hit. Now, where’s your laptop?”

We headed back into the kitchen and I grabbed my laptop from the counter. Thomas sat at the kitchen table and flipped open the lid.

“What are you looking for?” I asked, again keeping my voice low.

“Richford.”

“I’ve never heard of it,” I said.

"Which is why, my friend, we are Googling it."

There was a town called Richford, population two thousand, three hundred and seventy, and it was a two-hour drive away. It always amazed me that population figures tend to be rounded.

"That reminds me, she said Sierra visited her late afternoon, she wouldn't have got back for the school run. Even if she'd had the day off work, which is possible, I don't recall having to pick up Taylor because Sierra was out for the day in the last few months she was alive," I said.

"What time would you normally get in from work?"

"Six, normally. It's possible someone else collected Taylor, or she stayed behind in after-school club. I wouldn't know, I guess."

"Still didn't leave a great deal of talking time, bear in mind they hadn't seen each other for years, I can't imagine it was quick meeting," Thomas said.

I stared at the pictures on the screen of a town, not dissimilar to our own. It had a small central area with stores, a park for the kids, a supermarket just on the outskirts that had caused a fuss, according to the Internet. The locals hadn't wanted it.

Thomas picked up his phone and sent a text message. He read aloud as he typed.

"Lily Preston, Richford. Check Social Security, housing departments, run through database. Find me everything you can."

"I guess Pete will be busy tonight," I said.

"He doesn't have anyone to go home to, and I'm sure he'll appreciate the overtime."

"Talking about anyone at home, who were you having dinner with the other night?"

Thomas smiled at me. "Remember Heather Scott from school? She just got back into town. We hooked up for a drink, I cooked her dinner."

"You cooked her dinner? Fuck me."

"Well, I'd rather be fucking her than you, but yeah, I cooked. I can, you know."

Thomas' comment caused my chest to constrict. I missed my wife. I missed the intimacy of a relationship, the normalcy of cooking a meal. I missed the laughter and the occasional arguments. I just fucking missed her.

The feeling of losing a loved one was like nothing I could explain. I tried to rationalize the pangs of loneliness, the bursts of anger. There had been times I'd wanted to smash the house to pieces. I'd wanted to use my hands and dig at the earth covering her body. I'd wanted to scream at the injustice, just stand in the middle of the street and shout as many expletives as I knew skyward.

So when I heard of others having a lovely time with their partners, whether that was a new relationship like Thomas, or waiting on a birth like Jake, it hurt.

"I'm going to head back to the station, type this lot up and see if Pete's made any progress. I still think we need to call in the state," Thomas said.

"Can we wait just another day?"

"Every day we don't have help, is another day further from the truth, just keep that in mind."

"I will."

I walked Thomas to his car and watched him drive away. I'd wanted him to call in support initially, but now? Now I wanted to know why I was being lied to.

The sun had begun to set by the time Lily made her appearance. Her wet hair was piled on top of her head and the waft of vanilla, a familiar scent, preceded her as she came to stand at the kitchen door. I'd been concentrating on some long overdue paperwork for the garage.

"Come on in, don't just stand there," I said, offering a smile.

"I'm sorry. I didn't want to intrude."

"You're not, it's just accounts, it can wait."

"Maybe I can help, I did a little accounting at my last job." She took the seat beside me.

"It's okay, like I said, it can wait. It's not exactly keeping my attention. Are you hungry?"

"I am, starving actually."

"I'm not the best cook but let's see what we have."

"I can cook, you can carry on for a little while," she said.

I stood and walked to the fridge, ignoring her offer. "We have pie, we'd have to cook it to see what kind. Could be savoury or sweet. We have some steaks I can grill."

"Steak sounds good. Please, let me help."

"I guess you can chop some salad," I replied.

I placed the ingredients on the counter and watched as she went straight to the correct drawer for a chopping knife. She paused slightly; looking for a board before finding what she wanted resting against the wall at one end. I took the steaks and a pan, opting to place them under the broiler. I could have put on them on the outdoor grill, but I didn't want to leave her alone in my kitchen.

I wasn't comfortable having her move around my home as if she belonged. I wasn't happy listening to her hum a tune, but I'd dug a hole I wasn't sure I was able to climb out of.

"Would you like a beer?" she asked, as if I was the guest.

Maybe she realized how tense I'd become. She quietly continued to prepare the salad. I needed to relax, or at least pretend to. I sighed as I opened the fridge and took out the two beers. I snapped off the caps and handed her one.

"Lily, I haven't had a woman in my house since Sierra. So this feels strange for me. Please, don't take offence, okay?"

"I'll try not to. I did say I could move on if this is too awkward."

"I know, and I appreciate that offer, but for now, your safety is important."

While we waiting for the steaks to broil we sat. "Tell me about this farm you worked on?"

"Farm?"

"At my folks, you said you worked with horses for a while."

"Oh yeah. It was for a real short time, just a weekend job really. Maybe I made it sound more than it was. I used to go and help out, care for the horses and cattle. I really enjoyed it," she said.

I likened her to a duck. Above water she was calm but underneath she was swimming like fuck. She'd made a mistake and realized it. I pretended not to notice.

"I loved living at the ranch. Being outdoors is where I feel the most comfortable."

"How did you meet Sierra?" she asked. It was the first time she questioned me.

"At a fight." I didn't think there would be any harm in telling her the truth. "I used to fight for money, Lily. Sierra came along with a friend, the cops arrived to break it up, and we had to run. Somehow she ended up in my car and I took her for breakfast. The rest, as they say, is history."

"Sounds romantic," she said with a laugh.

"Well, if fifty sweaty guys baying for blood and waving dollars around is romantic, then yeah, I guess it was."

“Why did you do that?” she asked, as I stood to check on the steaks.

“Easy money, I guess. I wanted to travel a little, get out of Dodge, so to speak. I picked up a couple of fights and then got invited on the circuit.”

“Did you win?”

“Undefeated. I quit not long after I met Sierra and came home.”

“Why?”

“Because she was expecting Taylor. I wanted a home for them and for her to be around my family since…” I didn’t finish the sentence.

“Since she didn’t have any, you were going to say.”

“I was. Sorry.”

“It’s okay. I guess I was lucky, I got fostered out, and like I said, they weren’t bad parents.”

“What were their names?” I asked, pretending to be distracted by plating up our meal.

“Anna-Marie and Lou. Regular churchgoers, pillars of the community, those types.”

“Did they know what went on at the convent?” I asked, as I placed the plates on the table.

Lily rose to gather cutlery, again heading straight for the correct drawer.

“I doubt it. Nothing untoward happened, certainly to me. They had three foster kids, including me. I’m not sure where the others came from.”

I filed that information away.

“This looks great,” she said as she tucked in.

“Let me get another beer.”

“Trying to get me drunk?” she said then laughed.

'No, I can pour you a soda if you'd prefer."

Not drunk, Lily, just loose lipped, I thought.

"One more will be fine," she said.

As I watched her at my table, eating, drinking her beer, it was yet another version of Lily I was seeing. This one seemed a little more natural, yet still a far cry from the shy, modest one she portrayed herself to be at my folks.

"Will you tell me a little about Sierra?" she asked.

"She was the kindest person I knew. She didn't have a mean bone in her body, never a cross word about anyone. She had more compassion in her little finger than I have in my whole being. Everyone loved her."

"She must have had some flaws," Lily said.

My fork, laden with food, paused just outside my lips at her comment. I detected bitterness in her voice.

"I'm sorry, that was really inappropriate. I'd just like to know her, know how alike we are," she said.

I continued to eat. "Of course she had flaws, everyone does. She was too kind, too compassionate sometimes. She was a rose-tinted glasses person."

"Is that a flaw, though?" I shrugged my shoulders. "You seem a little...jaded, although I'm not sure that's the right word," she said.

"Jaded? For sure. My wife was murdered, Lily. I guess that would do some strange things to a man." My voice held a level of aggression.

Lily kept her head bowed and her eyes focused on her meal, but I noticed she had stopped eating. She blinked a few times and then I saw a tear roll down her cheek. I laid down my cutlery and reached over. I placed my hand on her arm and watched her stare at it.

"I'm sorry, I guess that was inappropriate of me," I said.

“We’ll figure it out, Gabe. Between us, we’ll catch who did this,” she whispered.

I rested back on my chair, my appetite gone. “Will we? The police didn’t do a good job of that initially.”

She turned to face me; it was her turn to lay her hand on mine.

“I believe in hope and faith, Gabriel. If we don’t have that, we have nothing.”

“Faith is not in my vocabulary, sadly,” I said with a chuckle. I wanted her hand off mine so used the pretense of picking up my fork to continue to eat.

“I guess I’ve never left the religion. Faith and hope are my go-tos.”

“Even now, knowing what you do?”

“Even now. What happened to those children was dreadful, disgusting, but it can’t be representative of the whole religion. If I don’t have faith, Gabe, I don’t have anything.”

Yet she was running scared from the Catholic Church, I thought.

“I guess if religion is a comfort for you, then it’s the right thing to have,” I said, not for one minute believing a word I just said.

“Well, that was lovely, thank you,” she said, pushing her cleared plate away. “Shall I make coffee?”

I nodded, “Sure, why not.” I didn’t usually drink coffee so late, not that I needed a stimulant to keep me awake. It was just something Sierra never did so neither did I.

She collected the plates and stacked them on the countertop before preparing the coffee. I made a point of not watching her, for fear of seeing my wife puttering about her kitchen.

“I think I’ll go outside for a cigarette,” I said, anything to distract me.

“Okay, I’ll bring it out when it’s ready,” she said, smiling at me.

I sat outside and the evening was balmy. The sound of crickets echoed around, their chirping had annoyed the hell out of me for many years when I was younger. It symbolized everything I'd disliked about the small town, Hickville life. I chuckled as I recalled a conversation where I'd used the word 'Hickville' and received a clip to the back of my head from my dad. There was nothing hickville about where I lived. It was a pleasant town, people were generally friendly, and it had been the perfect location for Sierra, and to bring Taylor up in. But once the investigation was done? Once I'd found who killed my wife? I wasn't sure I wanted to stay around.

"You look lost in thought," I heard. Lily stood at the back door staring at me.

"Listening to the sounds of the night," I said.

She took a step out, holding two mugs of black strong coffee, and sat at the small metal table. She slid one across to me.

"May I?" she said, picking up the pack of cigarettes.

"Help yourself. How does this town compare to, what was it called, Richford?"

"Yeah, Richford. It's pretty similar actually. Although, here is a little smaller, a little more quaint. I like it here."

As the evening went on, she relaxed a little, her body became less tense. We chatted about small town life, about my job, anything other than Sierra. On occasion, she'd bring the conversation around to Taylor, and although I answered, I kept what information I gave her brief. She wanted to know about my friends, about Sierra's friends, again I measured any answers against knowingly giving her information I didn't think she needed.

As much as I didn't want to, I began to enjoy the conversation. Having company, sitting out in the yard, and just chatting was probably the thing I missed the most. In the beginning, after Sierra had been killed, the house was always full of visitors. Trina still popped over once a week and loaded the freezer, and of course, Thomas came by for a beer, but most nights, after putting Taylor to bed, I sat on my own in silence. I hated TV; I didn't really listen to music, so all I had were the conversations that went on in my head.

"I think I'll head on up to bed," Lily said, and then stood.

I was glad, I needed a shower and an early night myself, but I hadn't wanted to leave her alone. I didn't want to think of her snooping around the house.

"Good idea. I'll lock up and then head to bed myself. If you want to take a drink up with you, I can alarm the downstairs then."

"Where will you sleep?"

"I don't sleep, but I'll take Taylor's bed."

"I can sleep in her room, if you want your bed back," she said.

"It's fine. I often sleep in there with her."

"You're a great dad," she said.

"I try to be. It's not easy sometimes, what with working and juggling school holidays."

"Good night then."

She paused before she finally walked through the kitchen, took a glass and filled it water then headed for the stairs. I heard her moving around and the sound of water running as I locked up. I'd lied to her about the alarm system, it wasn't sophisticated enough to arm part of the house. Maybe that was something I'd need to address. I just wanted her to think she was restricted to the upstairs.

I gathered up all the paperwork, relating to our conversations and the investigation, and carried them upstairs with me.

I tucked the documents under the mattress, stripped off my t-shirt and kicked off my sneakers and socks. I then left the room and was halfway across the hall to the bathroom when my bedroom door opened.

"I…err. I'm looking for fresh towels," Lily said.

I was standing in just my jeans and her gaze was focused on my chest. She was staring at my tattoo I imagined. I saw her eyes widen and her tongue run slowly over her bottom lip.

"There's a linen cupboard in the en-suite, beside the shower," I said.

"Oh, I didn't want to poke around. Thank you." Her cheeks colored.

So she didn't want to poke around in the obvious place for a fresh towel, but was happy to walk around the house looking for one?

"Goodnight, Lily," I said, holding my position in the hallway.

"Yes, sorry. Goodnight." She backed through the bedroom door and gently closed it.

I stood in the bathroom, resting my hands on the sink and looking at my reflection in the mirror. I looked tired and in need of a haircut. My brown hair had flecks of blond, bleached from the sun I guessed, or maybe it was grey. I ran my hand over the scruff on my chin; I quite liked it. It was the excuse I gave myself for not shaving. In truth, I just couldn't be bothered. I slid my jeans over my hips and climbed in the shower. When I was done, I wrapped a towel around my waist, grabbed my jeans from the floor, but hesitated before opening the bathroom door. It was enough to be standing topless with Lily in close proximity, let alone naked with just a towel.

I couldn't hear anything, so opened the door and quietly walked to Taylor's bedroom.

I lay for what felt like ages, just staring at the ceiling and thinking. Thoughts rushed through my brain, adding to the confusion and list of questions.

It must been the early hours of the morning when I heard a tap on the bedroom door. I bolted up and reached under the pillow for my gun.

“Gabriel?” I heard.

“It’s open.”

The door slowly opened and Lily stood there dressed only in a white shirt. I could see the outline of her breasts and the white panties she wore as the light from the hallway illuminated her.

“I think there’s someone outside,” she said, her voice just a little over a whisper.

“Okay, stay in here.”

I swung my legs over the side of the bed, and then realized I was totally naked. I’d kept the sheet over my lap but I guessed she would have known. She turned her back. I climbed from the bed and grabbed the jeans I had worn the previous day. I quickly pulled them on and grabbed my gun from under my pillow.

“I’m scared,” she whispered.

“It’s okay, stay here, do not leave this room, you hear me?” I rested my hand on her shoulder as I passed.

I crept to the doorway and paused, listening for any sounds from downstairs.

“Where did you hear the noise?” I asked, again, keeping my voice low.

“The side of the house, I heard a crunch, like footsteps. The bedroom window is open, I was too hot.”

I kept my back to the wall as I gently walked down the stairs. I held the gun in my hand, down by my side. If there was an intruder, I didn’t want them to immediately see I was armed, people got shot that way simply through panic.

I stopped at the bottom of the stairs to listen. I didn’t hear any sounds. When I looked back up, Lily was standing on the landing. I waved my arm, gesturing for her to return to the room. There was a fucking large window just behind her. If there was an intruder, they'd see her standing there. I crept through the house, checking each room until I ended up in the kitchen. I stood for a minute, waiting for my eyes to adjust to the darkness. I crouched down and made my way to the back door. As I passed, I grabbed my phone from the counter, annoyed with myself that I had left it there and not taken it to be bed with me.

I reached the back door and angled myself so I could see out the window. I listened. I still couldn't hear anything, and although dark, I didn't see any movement or shadows in the yard. While I watched, I sent a text to Thomas, not expecting him to see it but hoping that he might.

"Is there anyone there?" I heard; the voice startled me.

"For fuck's sake, Lily, you just scared the living shit out of me," I replied.

"I'm sorry, I'm too scared to stay upstairs on my own."

I shook my head and muttered under my breath. "Get down low," I said.

She scuttled across the floor until she was beside me, under the back door window.

"If I tell you to stay put, I mean it, okay? I know you're scared, but no one is going up those stairs without me knowing about it."

I watched her bite down on her lower lip. She was either a fucking amazing actress or genuinely scared. Tears formed in her eyes and her hands visibly shook.

"Get behind me," I said.

I reached up to unlock the door. The sound of the lock disengaging seemed so much louder than perhaps it was. I waited a minute more before reaching for the handle and slowly opening the door. As it did, I stood and raised my gun.

I wasn't law enforcement, I wasn't trained in how to apprehend an intruder, and I'd probably have gotten myself shot the way I stepped out through the door. But thankfully, there was no one there. Keeping my back to the wall, I followed it to the corner of the house and peered around. I looked down the side of the house that had the broken window and toward the front yard. It was empty.

I walked around the house, being careful to keep to the sides of the pathway in case I disturbed footprints. I inspected all the windows: each was firmly shut. By the time I'd made my way back to the rear of the house, I saw the blue flashing lights of a police car.

"Anything?" Thomas asked as he climbed from his car.

"Nothing. Turn those fucking lights off, you'll have the whole street awake."

"So glad I responded so quickly," he said with a smirk.

"I wasn't expecting you to, thought you'd be asleep," I replied.

"I wasn't asleep. Now let me get a flashlight so I can check. Where's Lily?"

"In the kitchen, wouldn't stay in the fucking bedroom when I asked her to."

Thomas raised his eyebrows at me. "She's sleeping in my room, I'm in Taylor's," I said.

We circumnavigated the house a second time, slower. Thomas scanned his Maglite from left to right over the grassy area, until it came to rest on a shoeprint not far from the boarded up window. He crouched down to inspect it.

"Whose is that?" I asked.

"It's too large for mine and right now, you're barefooted. I can't say it isn't from the other day though. In the trunk of my car is a plastic box, like a tool box, can you grab it?"

When I walked to his car, I noticed Lily at the front door. She stood there, still in just the shirt for the entire street to see.

"Go inside, Lily. I told you before, I don't want the neighbors to see, and a blue flashing police light draws them like a moth to a damn flame."

"I just wanted to check you were okay," she said.

I walked to the front door, causing her to take some steps back.

"There's no one there. I texted Thomas before I went out the back, he's just having a check himself."

"Okay, are you sure there's no one out there?"

"I'm sure, now wait in the kitchen."

She turned to walk away. I swallowed hard and closed my eyes at the sight of her. A knot formed in my stomach when I realized she was wearing Sierra's shirt. I'd address that issue once Thomas had left. I closed the front door and made my way back to the car.

I retrieved the box from the trunk of his car and joined him. He was inspecting the boarding over the broken window.

"Anything?" I asked.

"Doesn't look like it, but I need to come back in the daylight. Hand me that box."

He laid it on the ground and took out a tape measure. He measured the footprint and took some photographs.

"Don't you need to make a mold or something?" I asked.

"You watch too many crime movies," he muttered as he did his thing.

"I don't watch any TV, let alone crime movies. I've had enough of that in real life," I said.

He paused. "I'm sorry, I didn't think. And no, I can't take a cast of this. It's not deep enough and it's on grass."

Eventually, he stood and packed up his box of tricks. He measured, photographed, and sketched. He'd taken photographs of the boarded up window, although it didn't look like it had been disturbed.

"I need to be back here in the morning, Gabe. We'll talk some more to Lily, and we need to get that window sorted."

I said goodbye and watched him leave. A curtain in the house opposite twitched as I stood on the front step. I made a note to call on the occupants and see if they'd seen anything.

"Anything?" Lily asked when I walked back to the kitchen.

"No, nothing. Maybe it was an animal," I lied.

"I'm sorry if I've caused a fuss. I swear I heard something, well, I think I did anyway."

"It's okay. Thomas will be back in the morning and take a second look, perhaps you'll be up for another chat."

She stood from her chair and gently nodded.

"Lily, is that my wife's shirt?" I asked, quietly.

"I'm not sure. It was in the closet. I don't have any clean clothes to sleep in. Have I done wrong?"

"I'll show you where the laundry room is in the morning," I said, not answering her question.

Chapter Fourteen

I didn't head straight back to bed; I sat at the kitchen table and drank a cup of coffee. I prepared the coffee maker for later that morning. Eventually I climbed the stairs. As I passed my bedroom door, I heard a noise. It was more of a muffled sound. I paused and listened. It sounded like a cry that had been stifled. I tapped gently.

"Lily, are you okay?"

At first she didn't answer, and I wondered if the noise she had made had been in her sleep. I was about to walk away when she answered.

"No," came her reply.

I opened the door. She was sitting on the bed; her legs were brought to her chest. She had her arms wrapped around them and her chin resting on her knees.

"I know this isn't right but…can you stay with me?" One tear leaked from her left eye and rolled down her cheek.

I hesitated. The only furniture in that room was a bed, a chest of drawers, a couple of wardrobes and two bedside tables.

"Get under the cover," I said, as I walked into the room, closing the door behind me.

She stretched out her legs and pulled the sheet over her. I sat on the other side of the bed, on top of the covers with my back resting against the headboard.

"I'm scared, Gabriel. I know they are coming for me, and I have no way of stopping that, of telling them that I don't know anything."

"Shush, it's okay. Try to get some sleep now."

"I don't think I've ever felt so alone," she whispered.

I didn't answer; I knew that feeling only too well.

I woke to sunlight filtering in through the muslin drapes. I hadn't intended to fall asleep. I must have slipped down the bed as I was lying on my back, and Lily had her arm across my chest. I tensed at her touch. She was asleep but had kicked the sheet off during the night. The shirt she wore was skewed and a button had come undone. One pert tit was exposed, the nipple slightly puckered as if she was aroused. She stirred slightly and her hand clawed on my chest. Her nails scraped against my skin and sent a shiver over me. The sight of her, the feel of her, caused my cock to harden against the confines of my jeans. I didn't want that, my body was betraying me with feelings that weren't welcome.

I gently lifted her hand from my chest and placed it on the pillow beside her head, then slid from the bed. I should never have agreed to stay in the room with her. In fact, I needed her out of my house.

I was dressed and downstairs when I heard the shower run. Her footsteps across the bedroom caused the floorboards to creak, and although not directly above my head, I could hear her move around the room. I listened as the door opened and she made her way downstairs.

"Hi," she said as she padded barefoot, in jeans and a tank that seemed familiar, into the kitchen.

"Coffee's brewed if you want one," I replied.

She poured a cup and brought over the jug to refresh mine. "Another coffee?"

"Sure."

For someone who had been up half the night, terrified, she sure seemed bright and breezy. I wouldn't crawl out of my grump until at least my second cup of highly charged caffeine. But then, she had the luxury of afternoon naps, I guessed.

"Thank you for staying with me last night, I really appreciated that," she said.

I ran my hand over my face before answering.

"That's okay. You were scared."

"You look exhausted."

"I'm fine. I just need a couple of cups of this stuff to get me going in the mornings."

My cell alerted me to the fact I had a text message. I picked it up and looked. Jake had sent a message. He'd opened up the garage and wanted to know if I was going to be in. I replied, letting him know he was on his own for the next couple of days. I trusted Jake; he'd often been left alone and was more than capable. I felt a little guilty keeping him in the dark and told him that I'd catch up with him as soon as I could.

"There are pastries on the counter if you're hungry," I said. "Or I can fry some bacon."

"Pastries are good, thank you." She helped herself before sitting beside me.

I wanted to ask if she was always so polite. I didn't think I'd ever heard so many 'thank yous' and 'I'm sorrys' before.

"Thomas will be over shortly, don't forget. Are you up to talking again?" I asked.

She didn't speak but gently nodded her head. "I appreciate your kindness, Gabriel. But I kind of feel like I'm going stir crazy here."

“I can understand that, but what’s the alternative?”

“I’ve done okay up to now.”

“And last night? You can take your chances on your own, I won’t stop you leaving, but be sure that’s what you want to do,” I said.

I didn’t want her in my house; I didn’t want her to leave. Not because I wanted her company, but she was a key player in what had happened to Sierra, I was sure of it. I still believed she knew more than she was letting on.

“Can we at least sit outside? It’s too nice to be cooped up indoors.”

I stood from my chair, picking up my coffee as I did. “Sure, let’s sit outside.”

My pack of cigarettes was sitting on the metal table and I shook it. I’d need to head to the store to replenish them at some point. Or I could ask Thomas of course. I sent him a text.

While we sat, I called my parents and spoke to Taylor. She was missing me but excited that she was getting a riding lesson that morning. I was thankful that she had the prospect of owning her own pony to keep her occupied. I spoke to Dad but was unable to say too much in front of Lily. I think he got that I wasn’t able to speak freely when he’d told me to call him back when I was alone.

“You have a great relationship with your parents, I feel a little jealous that Sierra got that experience. Is that so terribly wrong?” Lily said.

I shrugged my shoulders. “I’m not sure how to answer that. They are great parents.”

“What about your brother, do you see him often?”

I was about to answer when something pulled me up short. I couldn’t recall speaking to her about my brother. I played it safe.

"He's a busy man, we don't get to see him as often as we'd like."

"He's a priest, isn't he?"

"I think he's a little further up the chain than that. As I said, I'm not religious, I have no understanding of the hierarchy."

"You shouldn't trust anyone in the Catholic religion," she said.

"Why, Lily? Why do you say, 'anyone'?"

"Because they cover it all up, they protect their own, close ranks. How many priests have been accused of abuse lately? Tons. How many have faced charges? Not many." There was a bitter tone to her voice and I couldn't blame her for that.

"I wouldn't know to be honest. I don't follow the news."

We were interrupted from further conversation by the arrival of Thomas. He walked around the side of the house to join us in the yard. Although he didn't say anything, I suspect that was so he could inspect the footprint and window again.

"Good morning, all. Can I smell coffee?" he said, planting a large smile on his face.

"Let me get that for you," Lily replied before I'd even had a chance to.

She left her chair and made her way into the kitchen.

"You look tired," Thomas said.

"I am."

"She sure made herself at home."

"Mmm, and that top, I think it's Sierra's. She was wearing her shirt last night, said she didn't have anything clean to sleep in."

"Really? That's not good."

"I know. There are times when I think she's genuine and then others… I don't know, Tom. I feel like I'm falling apart right now."

"You need some sleep. Why not take a nap?"

"Because I don't want to leave her alone in my house," I said.

Our whispered conversation was halted when Lily came back, carrying fresh mugs and the pot of coffee.

"I'm sorry that you got called out last night, Thomas. I guess I heard an animal and overreacted. It was nice to have Gabe sleep with me though," she said as she poured.

"I'd prefer if you didn't quite say it that way, Lily," I said, irritated at what she'd said.

"Oh, I'm sure Tom knows what I mean," she said with a smile.

There again was the shortening of our names, as if she was integrating herself into our friendship, becoming over familiar.

Thomas laid his pad and pencil on the table while he sipped on his coffee. He glanced over the rim of his mug at me.

"I've got some questions, are you up to answering them?" he said.

Lily nodded.

"When you first saw Gabriel, you told him you knew he was looking for you. How did you know?"

"Sister Anna had said she'd given him the envelope, so I guess I kind of assumed."

Thomas glanced at me, that twitch had returned. I kept quiet. Lily wasn't mentioned in those diary entries. There was no way Sister Anna giving me them could have led her to believe I was looking for her.

"You said you'd visited Sierra at the school, obviously that was after she'd made contact. Was there a time when you, Sierra, and Sister Anna were together?"

Thomas' comment reminded me to send a message to the principal; she didn't need to check her log.

"Yes. I didn't remember Sister Anna; it was Sierra who told me who she was. I was thankful that she'd gotten me out of the convent."

"What did you talk about?"

"How to expose the church, mainly. Sierra wanted to go to the press; Sister Anna wanted to take it up the chain first. We persuaded her not to. As I said before, they would close ranks, deny, and protect. They'd place the blame elsewhere. Maybe a rogue priest."

"Is there such a thing?"

She shrugged her shoulders. "I don't know, I just know that going to the church would have been a bad thing. Sierra said so."

"Did you believe everything Sierra told you? Was there anything that you felt might be remotely exaggerated or untrue?"

"No! She was my sister, why would I not believe her?"

"So, she told you she was gathering evidence then going to the press. Where I'm a little confused is when did Sister Anna make an appearance? Who contacted who first? Can you help me with that?"

"As far as I know, Sister Anna approached Sierra. She told her that she'd kept track of everyone from the home, all those that had been fostered or adopted. She kept records, addresses, and change of names, that type of thing. I guess that's how Sierra knew where I was."

"And I imagine that information would be very useful to whoever is chasing you. But what confuses me is this, how did Sister Anna know where Sierra was?"

"I don't know, she didn't say. I'm not sure I know where you're going with this," Lily said.

"What if Sister Anna isn't who she says she is? What if Sister Anna was the one who killed those people and is the one after you?"

"No way. She couldn't have."

"Why? You didn't know her. None of us know her."

Lily didn't answer. Maybe she didn't have an answer or was stuck in where to take the conversation.

"Why do you say, 'she couldn't have'?" I asked gently.

"I just don't believe it, she's a nun. I have to believe someone was good in that fucking place."

She was getting agitated. She continually shifted in her seat, her brow furrowed, and she kept her gaze on her empty cup.

"Did Sierra give you any indication when she was going to blow this all open?" Thomas asked.

"Soon, it was going to be soon. She had all the information. If we can find the statements, it will prove what I'm saying is true."

"I don't disbelieve you, Lily. I just need to get as many facts as possible."

"You need to find the statements, and you need to find Sister Anna."

"I wasn't aware Sister Anna was missing," I said.

"Have you spoken to her?"

"I have, and I'm due to meet her soon," I replied.

Her eyes widened. I noticed a very slight shake to her hand as she lifted her coffee cup. Although I imagined it to be cold, she took a sip anyway.

"Can we take a break? Maybe I'll make some fresh coffee. My nerves are jangling from last night still," she said. She planted a smile back on her face.

"You know what, that would be great. And you're doing well, Lily. This is such a help for us," I said.

"While you're doing that, I've got some traps for you, just in case that animal makes a return. Want to help me lay them?" Thomas said, looking at me.

"Sure, why not."

We left Lily in the kitchen and walked around the side of the house.

"She's cracking. She's desperate for those statements and now worried that I'm speaking to Sister Anna. She seemed adamant that Sister Anna couldn't have killed those people. Makes me think she knows who did," I said.

"I agree. Although, playing devil's advocate here, that doesn't mean she was involved, just that she's on the run from someone she knows. Gabe, I know we said we'd wait another day, but I've passed over all that I know to the state police. I've flagged Lily as a flight risk and spoken to someone I know well. They're going to take a look at the file today and then advise.

"And I have a name for the cell Sister Anna used. Surprise, surprise, it's not registered to Sister Anna but, and you're not going to like this, it's registered to Sierra Malone."

"What the fuck?"

He raised his eyebrows at me. "She didn't have a cell. I used to moan at her for not having one."

"Perhaps she got it just to have contact with the sister. And knowing how naïve she was, she wouldn't have thought to use a fake name."

"If you traced it, then so could anyone," I said.

He nodded. "It could be how they came to know your address, Gabe."

"Or Sister Anna is involved."

He sighed. "This is why I called in the state, this is getting beyond my capabilities to investigate."

I pulled my phone from my pocket. "I know what I'm going to do. I'm going to send a text and tell Sister Anna, or whoever the fuck we're dealing with, that I have Lily here. If they are after her, they'll come for her. If not, we know Lily is part of the problem for sure."

"Gabe, think about that. These people have killed. Without being caught."

"Done." I showed him the text.

Sister Anna, please, it's real important you get back to me. I have Lily here, at my house, I need to know if what she's telling me is true. We think we know where the statements are.

"Fuck, Gabe." Thomas pinched the top of his nose and screwed his eyes shut. "You might have just brought the devil to your door."

Lily was back in the yard when we returned. It was time to escalate things.

"I think I might know where Sierra hid those statements," I said.

She turned toward me. "Where?"

"I'm going to check first, I might be wrong."

"Gabe, we need those statements, then we can go to the police, or the press," she said.

"I know. That's what I intend to do. I'm going do what my wife wanted and blow this whole thing wide open."

"I'll get the feds involved soon as you have them," Thomas said, playing along.

He picked up his pad and pencil, not that he'd written a word; hopefully he'd committed it to memory.

"I'll head off to the station and check in later, okay?" he said, and made his way back to his car.

A couple of minutes after he'd left, I received a text. Lily tensed when she saw my phone vibrate on the table. I picked it up.

Round the clock surveillance, don't fucking shoot anyone unless you know it isn't me.

I deleted it and chuckled.

"What's funny?" Lily said.

"Thomas reminding me not to walk down the alley, he set some traps."

"I'm worried," she said.

"Why? Exposing these people is what Sierra wanted. It's the right thing to do and once that's happened, you will be safe."

"Will I?"

"You can't spend your life running, Lily."

"I'm just not sure you understand who you are dealing with," she said, her voice fell to a whisper.

"Then tell me." I leaned forward and took one of her hands in mine.

At that moment she looked vulnerable. She looked scared, and again my mind was in turmoil. Had I got it all wrong? I was confused. One minute I disliked her, the next I felt sorry for her. One minute I felt she was lying to me, the next she just wasn't sure of the truth herself. I had to get a grip. I'd set wheels in motion that could end up terrifying or satisfying.

Chapter Fifteen

Lily and I spent the day either in the house or the yard. She was getting bored; I could see that. I sat at the kitchen table and carried on with some accounting, she sat and read. I took a couple of calls from Mom, enquiring after Lily, and spoke at length to Taylor about her riding lesson. She told me all about the foal, how she'd watched it feed, and her and Dad had led them both to a small paddock for the first time. The enthusiasm in her voice as she described the foal's first gallop around the paddock had me smiling.

"You become animated when you talk to her," Lily said. She'd walked into the kitchen to refresh her drink.

"She's my life."

"I can see that. May I?" She indicated to a chair at the table.

I piled my paperwork to one side and smiled.

"I wish I had that. Sometimes, I'm jealous of Sierra and the life she had, and then I remember her start was so much worse than mine. I'd love a family of my own."

"You don't need a partner to have a child," I said.

She chuckled bitterly. "I can't see anyone wanting to settle down with me."

I wasn't going to answer, I wasn't prepared to offer sympathy or pander to her self-doubt if she was just playing me.

"You want to go out for a drive?" I said. As much as she was going stir crazy, so was I.

"Oh, yes, that would be great. Maybe we can go and see your folks, Taylor?"

I checked my watch. "They'll be having dinner, I imagine. We'll visit them tomorrow."

"I'll grab my sneakers," she said and rushed upstairs.

While she did, I sent a text to Thomas.

Going out for an hour, house will be empty.

He replied. **Sure you should? I got Syd in a car outside your house.**

Syd was one of the part-timers Thomas relied on. He was a fully-fledged, sworn in deputy but not required full time. He wasn't someone any of us really knew, kept himself to himself mainly.

I'll keep in touch. I replied.

I heard Lily bound back down the stairs. She was sat on the lower step, tying her laces, when I got to the front door. I grabbed my truck keys from a sideboard and set the alarm. Without asking, Lily slipped on my hoodie and covered her head.

We drove out of town with nowhere really in mind until I remembered a spot I'd visited when I was a teen. I found the dirt track and headed up toward a ridge that overlooked the town. At night it was a pretty place to park and watch the stars. There was a small parking lot for hikers, who wanted to head off in the woodland that snaked around one side of the town.

"This is a pretty spot when the sun goes down," I said as I parked the truck.

"I bet. It's just good to get some fresh air." Lily opened her door once I'd come to a stop and climbed out.

I wasn't concerned about her running, she'd have a long fucking jog back to town, and the opposite direction was just miles of forest. I watched her pull the hoodie off and then stretch. The tank rose showing a toned midriff.

"I need this, thank you," she said.

I opened the back of the truck bed and sat with my legs dangling. "Climb up," I said.

I held out a hand to help her. She laughed as she sat beside me. She placed her hands slightly behind her and leaned back, closing her eyes, and raising her face to the sun.

"Did you have a good childhood?" I asked.

Without opening her eyes, she answered. "I guess so. They were very religious, probably why they went to a convent to get me. We didn't do holidays or fun days out, but they were kind enough. I was homeschooled for most of the time, as were the boys."

"Do you keep in contact with any of them?"

"Not really. I'm not saying they were in it for the money, but I always felt, they didn't want children but felt they had to. Does that make sense?"

"Sure. I guess, considering they were Catholic they probably felt duty bound, or whatever."

"Oh, they weren't Catholic, they were Divinus Pueri, close though."

"Never heard of it," I said as I casually shook loose a cigarette. I lit it and handed it to her.

"Tell me something about you," she said as she sat upright again.

"What do you want to know?"

"How old where you when you skipped town?"

"Twenty, I think. My parents weren't pleased, as you can imagine. I'd gotten involved in a couple of fights, not paid ones. Tore up the diner," I said with a laugh.

"So you were a bad boy then," she said.

"Bored, more likely."

The conversation was easy, or so I wanted her to believe. I was filing away anything she said worthy of reporting back. But somewhere deep inside, I was, for the first time in a while, enjoying myself. If I closed my eyes and didn't look at her, if I took myself out of the past few days to another time, maybe in the future when my life wasn't such hell, I'd be having fun.

"What is that tattoo you have?"

She'd remembered the tattoo from seeing me heading to the bathroom, I guessed.

"A heart, an anatomically correct heart."

"That's a strange tattoo to have."

I shrugged my shoulders. "I tell Taylor it's there for her, it beats only for her. If she puts her hand over it she feels my real heart." I omitted the real reason.

Lily slid from the truck then turned to face me. She didn't speak as she took the one step needed to be close enough. She reached forward and placed her hand on my chest. My body stiffened at her touch, and I felt her lift her hand away just slightly.

"I'm sorry, I just wanted to feel," she whispered.

I tried to relax as I felt the pressure increase when she placed her hand back. She stared straight at me. I saw her eyes darken as she took another step forward until she was between my knees.

We didn't speak, and I slowed my breathing, so she wouldn't feel my heart beginning to race at her touch. In my mind, as much as I tried not to, I saw Sierra, I felt Sierra.

Lily closed the gap between us, her face was just inches from mine. I could feel her breath against my skin and her fingers curled in my t-shirt, bunching it in her fist. Just as her lips ghosted mine, I spoke.

"We need to get back," I said.

Her hand slid down my chest, and she only pulled it away when she reached the top of my jeans. She took a step back.

"I'm so sorry, I don't know what came over me. I..."

Again, tears formed in her eyes, and as she walked to the passenger door, I saw her angrily brush them away. I took a deep breath as I slid from the truck and bolted the tailgate closed. I took an even deeper breath as I placed my hand on the door handle, opened it, and climbed in.

She didn't look at me all the drive back; she didn't speak. I was grateful, she would hear the huskiness in my voice that arousal created. I pulled onto the drive and she didn't wait to put the hoodie on. That made me pissed. I slammed the car door shut as she made her way to the front door. I covered her with my body as I leaned over to place the key in the lock. I felt her shrink away. She stumbled into the house as I pushed the door open.

"I said I was sorry," she said.

"I know."

"Then why are you mad at me?" Her voice hitched as she held back a sob.

"Because you just got out the truck, not fucking caring if anyone saw you. How many times have I asked you to protect yourself? Anyone could have seen you. Forget the fucking neighbors, I'm talking anyone after you. Sometimes, I get the impression you want to be seen."

She ran her tongue over her lower lip before sucking it into her mouth. It was a childish gesture but one that made my cock twitch. She wouldn't look at me, opting to keep her gaze lowered to the floor.

"I won't do it again. I didn't think, I was embarrassed, okay?"

"Until this is fucking solved, I have to keep you safe, Lily. Do you understand?"

Finally she looked up at me. Tears rolled down her cheeks.

"Why, Gabe? Why? No one else has ever wanted to, bothered to. I lied to you. I didn't have an okay childhood; it was hell on earth. I just made up a childhood, so it was a little more bearable. Somewhere along the line, I started to believe it myself."

That was my undoing. Whether what I did was born of anger, lust, frustration, or just sheer fucking desire for my wife, I wasn't sure. I pushed her against the wall. I cupped her chin with my hand and forced her head up to mine. I pressed my body against hers until her breath hitched in her throat and her eyes darkened again. My mouth crashed down on hers, I forced my tongue between her lips. I kissed her like a man starved of water taking his fist sips.

Her hands slid up my sides, dragging my t-shirt with them. I pulled back long enough for her to raise it over my head. I threaded one hand in her hair, behind her head, and held her still as I devoured her mouth again. She moaned as she wrapped her arms around my shoulders.

I reached down and grabbed her thigh, wrapping her leg around my waist as I ground into her. She raised her other, and it was my body weight pinning her against the wall that held her there.

My cock was painfully hard, straining against the tightness of my jeans. I wanted to bury myself in her; I wanted to fuck her so hard she cried out. I lowered my hands to cup her ass, supporting her as I took a step back and carried her up the stairs. She broke our kiss, her tongue trailed over my chin, across my jawbone as I stumbled up and to my bedroom. I kicked open the door and lowered her to the bed.

I watched as she ripped the tank over her head, undid her bra and slid it from her arms. I unbuttoned my jeans and let them fall. She'd only just managed to wriggle from her own before I climbed on the bed and covered her body with mine. I held myself above her as she hooked her fingers under her panties and lowered them. Not one word had been spoken and I was glad. I didn't want conversation, I wanted her body and my pent up release.

Without any foreplay, I positioned my cock at her entrance, feeling how wet she was. She raised her arms, gripping the headboard as I sunk insider her. I fucked her hard. The headboard banged against the wall, the legs of the bed slid on the wooden floor and her moans grew louder.

Sweat dripped from my brow landing on her lips. I watched as her tongue slid across them and tasted it. The eyes that stared back at me were hard, challenging.

"Harder," she whispered.

I pulled out of her and flipped her body over. I pulled at her hips until she was on her knees then pushed into her again. Her body jolted up the bed with every angry thrust. Her moans had become screams of pleasure as she came. I wrapped my hand in her hair and pulled hard, forcing her head up. Between her gasps I heard her chuckle.

"So you like it rough, huh?" I said through gritted teeth.

She didn't answer but I felt her nod her head.

I wasn't sure what had come over me. The person that reached under with his fingers to tease her clitoris, to coat them with her juices, the person that used that to lubricate her ass and insert one finger, then two, wasn't me. Or was it? I felt like I'd left my body, I was on the outside watching.

The screaming of the word, 'stop' in my head was drowned out by the desire to fuck her ass, which I then did. From her reaction, that wasn't something new for her. Without lubrication, she should have been crying out in pain, instead she was slamming it toward me every time I withdrew and plunged back in.

The tightness of her and the willingness to accept my cock so deep inside, scrambled my brain. I could no longer think rationally. A sheen of sweat coated her skin as I withdrew one last time. My cum spurted over her back, hot milky liquid gently slid down her side and dripped to the bedding. I watched as she reached for it before rolling to her back. Her fingers were sticky as she placed them in her mouth and sucked my cum from them.

She placed one hand between her thighs, teasing herself. She arched her back off the bed, and I sat back on my heels and watched. Her pussy glistened as she inserted two fingers and worked out another orgasm. My mouth watered as her scent hit my nostrils. Instead of doing what I wanted, which was to sink my tongue inside and taste her, I slid from the bed. I grabbed her wrist as I did and dragged her to the bathroom with me.

My heart was pounding in my chest and my hands shook. I caught sight of myself in the mirror. I looked wild, deranged. I punched the fucking mirror, and it was with pleasure that I saw the glass shatter and blood spurt from my knuckles. Lily squealed in shock. I stepped into the shower, pulling her with me and turned the dial to the hottest I could stand. I stood with my hands on the wall, my head bowed, watching the water run red as it washed the blood from my hands, trapping her inside my arms. Her skin had turned a bright shade of red from the heat of the water.

I soaped my cock, cleaning it before grabbing her shoulders and forcing her to her knees. She reached up and took hold of my hips. I ran my thumb over her lips, she parted them slightly and her tongue darted out to lick over the pad. I pressed down, prying open her jaw, while my other hand massaged my cock until the soapsuds had disappeared and I was hard again. I then fucked her mouth. Her fingers dug into my skin and she hummed as she sucked. The vibrations caused my cock to twitch and my stomach to tighten, as the desire to come quickly took over. I held her head, not letting her release me as I did. I watched my cum spill from her lips and run down her chin as I pulled my cock free.

Without allowing the water to clean me of her yet again, I opened the shower door, and holding her wrist, walked back into the bedroom and to the bed. I let her go and she fell, curling into a ball. She attempted to pull the sheet tight around her wet body. I pulled it from her.

"I'm not done with you yet," I said.

Like a cat, she unfurled, slowly, provocatively, until she lay on her back and that challenge was back on her face. There was no emotion other than pure lust in her eyes. I wanted to slap the look from her face. At that moment, I hated her but I was going to fuck her again.

I was having an internal fight as I pulled her legs apart and, for a second time without foreplay, pushed into her. My brain was telling me to stop; my body wouldn't let me. I felt like I had lost control. Images of Sierra flooded my mind. I was punishing the body beneath me for the murder of my wife, for the loss and anger I had harbored for nearly a year, and for the fact that I wanted to fuck. I selfishly wanted my release. It wouldn't have mattered who that was with.

I lost track of time, my heart raced with exertion and my arms shook as I held myself above her. Sweat ran from my brow and I was thankful of that. I was thankful, because as I came so hard that my stomach ached, the sweat camouflaged the tears rolling down my cheeks.

I pushed myself from the bed and on unsteady legs grabbed my jeans and pulled them on.

"Gabriel?" she said, as she pushed herself to her elbows.

"Gabe."

I didn't reply. I buttoned up my jeans and walked from the room, leaving behind the sound of her sobs.

I inhaled the smoke from my cigarette as I sat in the garden. It had been a couple of hours ago that I'd left Lily crying in the bedroom. I'd heard the shower run, but there had been no sign of her. I wasn't concerned; but the guilt that wracked my body was overwhelming. Rationally, I knew I hadn't betrayed my wife, but I sure felt like shit. And something else that I didn't like: I felt relief. How fucking shallow was I? My wife had only been gone a few months, and all I felt was relief that I'd fucked, that I'd let out some of that sexual frustration that had been building.

I'd never fucked my wife; I had way too much respect for her to do that. We made love, sometimes it was gentle and loving, and sometimes fast and furious, but it was always with respect. I hadn't given a shit about the person lying underneath me earlier. I hadn't given a shit about her feelings, the fact she came wasn't my intent. I wanted one thing only, my release.

I leaned back in my chair and raised my face to the sun, warming my body. I closed my eyes. When I opened them, Lily was standing in the doorway. She had dressed in jeans and another t-shirt that looked familiar.

"Do you want a beer?" she asked with a forced cheerfulness.

"Sure, why not," I said, a little confused.

I expected tears or anger, I didn't expect her to play wife again.

She handed me a beer and stood, as if waiting to be invited to join me. I gestured toward the chair.

"May I?" she said, as she reached for my pack of cigarettes.

"Stop it, Lily, just fucking stop it."

She startled, making the chair scrape against the brick patio. I sighed, feeling even more of a shit.

"I'm sorry, okay? Sure, have a cigarette, you don't need to ask."

I took a sip of my beer.

"What happened earlier, it can't happen again," I said.

She interrupted me, "Don't tell me you regret it, please? Don't make me feel that."

“I didn’t regret one minute. But it’s not right for me at this time, okay?” I stumbled through my words.

It wasn’t strictly true but not a lie either. Her hands shook as she lifted her bottle to her lips. Her body said one thing, her eyes another. They held a slight sparkle. Was she fucking with my head? I began to wonder. There were just too many ‘Lilys’ for me to know which one was real anymore.

Chapter Sixteen

It was another sleepless night for me. I tossed and turned in the child-sized bed with my feet hanging over the edge. Lily and I had eaten a cold dinner of ham and salad, washed down with forced conversation and fake laughter. My nerves were jangling, and it wasn't from the large black coffee I'd consumed before bed. I didn't feel I was the same person I'd been just a week prior. Nothing felt real, yet I knew it was. I missed a call to my daughter, something I'd never done before. I'd silenced the ringing from Thomas, something I'd never done before. I did text him and tell him all was okay, but that was only from fear of him turning up and seeing the mess I'd become.

In just half a day, I'd gone from being in control to feeling like I was losing my mind.

Lily had done that. She had set the bomb off inside me. Had she done it deliberately? That was something I needed to figure out.

It must have been in the early hours of the morning that I finally drifted off to sleep, to be woken just a couple of hours later by the scrape of the door opening. I didn't sit bolt upright that time, my body was just too exhausted for that level of activity.

"There is definitely someone outside. I swear this time. I saw them," Lily said. She stood in the doorway in just her panties, her nipples erect and I doubted that was from a chill.

"Was it…?" I cut short the sentence, not wanting her to know there should be someone patrolling the house—the police.

I didn't care that I climbed from the bed naked, or that her eyes trailed down my body. She took a few steps into the room and closed the door behind her.

Maybe it was my imagination, but every step she took, when she bent at the waist raising her ass in the air to pick up my jeans and hand them to me, felt seductive. I pulled them on, not making eye contact. I followed her back to my bedroom.

"Look," she said as she walked to the window.

I walked until I was close behind her. I placed my hands on her hips with the intent of moving her; I heard her sharp intake of breath. That girl was definitely fucking with me. I shoved her to one side, too tired for her games.

"Where did you see them?" I asked, as I peered through the muslin drapes covering the window.

"Out front to start with, then they walked to the side of the house."

"What did they look like?"

"A man, tall, dark clothing."

"You sure it was a man?" I asked, as I scanned the road looking for one of Thomas' deputies.

"I think so, he was fairly well built."

"Stay here, I fucking mean it this time. And put some fucking clothes on."

I walked back to Taylor's bedroom and it irritated me that Lily had followed. I reached under my pillow for the gun I had taken to bed with me and knew at that point I'd made a mistake. Lily had seen me retrieve it. I'd need to find another hiding place.

I crept back to the hallway, listening for any sounds of an intruder. Like before, I kept my back close to the wall as I descended the stairs. I paused halfway when I heard the gentle rattle of the back door. Lily had been right, there was someone on the property. I heard my heart beat frantically in my chest, and a wave of adrenalin flooded over me, washing away my earlier tiredness.

I took in a couple of deep breaths to steady my nerves as I continued down the stairs. It was only when I was at the bottom that I'd realized I'd left my phone beside the bed. I was too far down to call up to Lily, not that I wanted her to find my phone and prayed that she wouldn't be able to work out the password if she did.

I knew the minute I rounded the bottom of the stairs, I'd be exposed if someone were looking through the back door window. I held still and continued to listen. When I thought enough time had passed, I slowly rounded the corner with my gun raised and moved as quickly, and as quietly, as I could toward the kitchen. I couldn't see anyone; there was no noise, but I thought I saw a shadow cross the window.

I decided it was time to brazen it out. I stood tall and walked to the back door, making as much noise as I could opening it. I stepped out in the yard, holding my gun in front of me. Nothing, no one.

I walked to the front of the house and checked both ways up the street. There were cars parked, and in one I saw the subtle flash of a flame as a lighter was lit and then killed. That was Syd's signal, asking me if all was okay. I covered my mouth as if to stifle a cough, cheesy, but effective communication. As much as Thomas accused me of watching too many crime shows, I'm sure he did the same. I meant to ask him where he'd come up with that.

I took two tours of the outside of the house; there was no evidence anyone had been there. Yet I'd heard that rattle, I'd seen that shadow. Or had I? Could it have been the wind, I didn't actually see the handle move. Could it have been the shadow of a tree as the branches swayed in the breeze? Paranoia was setting in.

I began to doubt what I saw, heard. I closed my eyes and sighed.

"Anything?" I heard as I walked back into the kitchen.

"I thought I told you…never mind. No. Now, tell me exactly what you saw and where," I said.

I switched the coffee machine on, thinking I wasn't going to get any more sleep that night. I slumped into a chair and placed the gun on the table. I scrubbed my hands over my face, dragging them down my cheeks then raising my face to look at her as she sat.

"Exactly, what did you see?" I repeated.

"I saw a man, Gabriel. I know I did."

"Hair color?"

"It was dark, I think. It certainly wasn't blond. I think I would have been able to tell if it was blond."

"What was he doing?"

"He just crossed the front yard. He didn't look up at any of the windows, then walked around the side of the house."

"As if he knew where he was going?"

"Yes."

"What were you doing at the window, Lily?"

"The wind had picked up, I was shutting it. I'd left the sash open just a fraction for some fresh air, but it was blowing the drapes."

It was always plausible. Everything she said could be fucking true, or a shit load of lies. I didn't know anymore. I wasn't sure about anything. Was she a good enough actress to produce the fear on her face, the tears that rolled down her cheeks?

"You don't believe me, do you?" she said, quietly.

"I'm tired, Lily. For months, I've been lucky to get just a few hours sleep a night. I'm not sure what I believe anymore."

She sucked in her lower lip and lowered her gaze before nodding slowly. She stood from her chair and looked around the room.

“I need to leave. I’m so sorry I brought all this to you.”

“Sit down, you’re not going anywhere,” I said and sighed.

She didn’t. Instead she walked toward the hallway. I rose to follow.

“Lily, stop right there.” I wasn’t up for games anymore.

Her shoulders were slumped and she wrapped her arms around herself. It was clear from her body movement that she was crying.

“I can’t do this anymore, Gabriel. I’m scared; I’m also tired. For every hour you’re wake, do you think I’m not? I lay there, night after night, wondering if it’s my last. Do you have any idea what that feels like? To know you’re next on the list to be murdered. I think about how they’ll do it. Will they stab me like they did Sierra? How much will it hurt? How much will I beg for my life, knowing those words will mean nothing? You want to know why I lied about my childhood? Because I’m sure you’re busting to know. I spent ten years being fucked by men who believed they were servants of God. They fucked every part of my body, including my mind. You want to know why? Like Sierra, I’m a Divine Child.”

She laughed, bitterly, and I was rooted to the spot.

“Ask me, Gabriel. Ask me what a Divine Child is.”

At first I couldn’t find the words. “What is a Divine Child?” My voice was hoarse.

“I’m the daughter of an angel, can you believe that shit?” Again that bitter laugh echoed around the hallway.

“I don’t believe in angels,” I said.

“Neither do I. And I doubt the pedophiles that abused me, abused Sierra, really believe that. Let me tell you about the Cult I grew up in. You see, they are some fucked up individuals. They thought my mother was angelic, as I said before, the purest mated with her. Those poor men went through hell to prove themselves worthy of her, of her body. Shall I tell you what they do? What their initiation is before they're deemed worthy of my body? Blood has to be spilled, that blood has to drip over my body, coat my skin, claim it…"

"I don't want to hear…" I said. My stomach recoiled at the thought.

"But you have to, Gabriel. You have to know. Only the bravest will slit their wrists in the sign of the cross, only the toughest get to mate with me. Only the worthy. And the worst part? The women, children, writhed with pleasure when that hot blood sizzled on their skin. We were conditioned to, programmed to be aroused by its metallic smell and taste."

"Enough…" I wanted to heave. She kept talking.

"But they didn't want sex; they didn't want to fuck a child. No, they wanted to keep my bloodline going. I was supposed to give birth to daughters. Except it didn't quite work out that way."

I took a step closer to her until just an inch or so separated us. For a moment neither of us spoke.

"Why didn't you tell me this?"

"Yeah, that would have made for great conversation, wouldn't it? You knew about the abuse, you knew about Sierra. I didn't need to tell you my story. I didn't want to relive that life, a life I had pushed so deep in my memory that, for a while, I believed it to be fantasy. It didn't really happen. I shut off, created a new life. And then my sister got in contact and hell returned." She spat the word 'sister.'

"So these people think angels exist and you're the child of one?" I asked.

"What part of what I've just said wasn't clear?"

"That's about the most fucking ridiculous thing I've ever heard."

"So now you don't believe that? What version would you like to believe? Tell me, what works in your perfect little world, with your perfect wife, your prefect child, and your perfect house? Tell me, and maybe I'll spin a tale that suits your fragile mind."

I grabbed hold of her and spun her around to face me. My fingers dug into her arms.

"Don't you fucking dare bring my family into this. I've done all I can to help you. I want one thing, Lily, I want to find out who killed my wife. Who came into my home with my daughter inside and stabbed her five times?"

I hadn't realized I'd been shaking her all the time I spoke.

"You can't hurt me, Gabriel. I'm beyond that. You want the truth? I hope those fuckers hurry up and find me. I hope they put me out of my misery, sooner rather than later. You know what I'll do? I'll walk into the police station, I'll tell them everything they need to know to arrest the people that fostered me, to hopefully track down that convent and bring those men of God to justice. But it won't bring Sierra back. It won't answer your question. Sierra's murder will be lumped into that investigation, solved, buried, filed away, forgotten."

I was broken, beat. My arms fell to my sides, my chin dipped to my chest and I closed my eyes. When I raised my head and looked at her, her face mirrored mine, I imagined. Her eyes were red, her lips puffy. Her tears rolled down her cheeks. I reached up and using my thumb, wiped under one eye. She closed the gap between us, and I wrapped my arms around her while she sobbed into my chest. I nuzzled into her neck, breathing her in, trying to absorb some of her pain.

We stood that way for a while until a wave of exhaustion rolled over me.

"We need to sleep," I said, my words were slightly muffled by her hair.

Without another word we walked upstairs to my bedroom. I climbed on the bed; she did the same. At first we lay side by side, until I reached my hand under her neck and pulled her close. She snuggled into my side.

I wasn't sure if what I was doing was to comfort her, or to find some comfort myself.

"Can you keep me alive?" she whispered.

“I’m going to try.”

Lily placed her hand on my stomach, my skin goose bumped at her touch. She ran it down to the top my open jeans. I placed my hand over hers, intending to lift it from me.

“Please, I need just one last night of thinking I have the perfect life. That’s all I ever wanted, just a taste of what Sierra had. She talked about you, about Taylor, and I fell in love with her life,” she whispered.

Was it sleep depravation? Was it lust, confusion, the need for a woman’s touch to soothe my bleeding soul? Whatever it was, I lifted my hand and let hers slip under the waistband of my jeans. My cock hardened at her touch. I placed my hands above my head and closed my eyes. I raised my hips so she could lower my jeans and my cock sprang free. I kicked the jeans off.

She wrapped her hand around it, sliding gently up and down. A moan left my lips as my arousal rose. My stomach tightened as she increased the pressure, the speed. I wanted to come so badly but did my utmost to delay that. As much as Lily wanted one night of perfect, so did I. I didn’t want to think, just feel. I wanted someone to make me feel good, to ease the constant pain in my heart and my head. I wanted to lie back and be pleasured, let someone else take charge just for a few minutes.

I felt her shuffle on the bed. When I opened my eyes, she had removed her panties and straddled me. She held my cock at her entrance and smiled before she slowly lowered. My fingers dug into her hips as she rode me. She moved so slow at first. She placed her hands on my chest, as her desire grew and her need to come increased, she clawed down my stomach. I welcomed the sting as her nails drew blood. It was a different pain to the dull ache of the previous months. For the first time in a while, I felt alive.

She rode me hard; I raised my hips to meet her downward movement, thrusting into her. The sounds of our bodies colliding, the moans of pleasure, filled the room. Sweat beaded on her upper lip, her hair stuck to her forehead. The room was hot, sticky, and humid, it smelled of her arousal. I spiralled out of control; my mind was lost in a myriad of sensations. Blood pumped so fast around my body I could hear it rush past my ears to feed my brain. My heart hammered in my chest. I heard her cry out as she reached her orgasm; at that point I let go as well. My balls tightened, my stomach knotted as I pumped my cum into her. It felt never-ending.

I rolled her to her back and with my cum coating her pussy, I pushed two fingers inside her. It wasn't Lily I saw, it wasn't Lily I smelled or felt; it was Sierra. It was Sierra's pussy that clenched around my fingers as I stroked. It was Sierra's voice I heard call out my name, moan with pleasure. It was Sierra's hands that gripped my hair as I lowered my head and took a nipple into my mouth.

It was my wife's body I explored and reclaimed. I mumbled Sierra's name, over and over. I might have even told her I loved her. I was lost; my mind was totally fucked. I'd willingly thrown myself over that abyss and into darkness. I was surrounded by sound, by hot flesh, by intoxicating scent. My eyes wouldn't focus. When I looked up at her, she smiled, she knew she had lost me to my wife and she didn't care.

She grabbed my face and pulled me toward her. She bit down on my lip then ran her tongue over it, licking away the blood she'd drawn. She moaned as she tasted me.

My head swam as I positioned myself over her, white noise drowned out any further sound as I pushed into her. She scraped her nails up my back, breaking my skin as I fucked her until her hands came to rest on my head. She gripped my hair, pulling hard as I bit down on her shoulder.

"Sierra!" I cried out when I came and tears coursed down my cheeks.

"I'm here, baby, I'm here."

I wasn't sure if I was dreaming, still intoxicated from her scent, or simply fucked up when I heard a voice.

"What the fuck?"

I couldn't open my eyes at first, my eyelids felt heavy and stuck together.

"Gabe, for fuck's sake, man. Open your eyes," I heard.

Zachary. It was my brother's voice I heard. But then I heard another.

"Jesus! Is he okay?"

I moaned. My head pounded and my body ached.

"Gabe, come on, man. Open your eyes."

The sunlight hurt my eyes as I dragged my body into a sitting position. I looked around the room.

"Where is she?" I said, my voice was croaky. "What the fuck happened?"

"She's gone. Fuck, Gabe. Taylor is missing."

I blinked; it took a few seconds for that information to sink in. I threw back the bed sheet and winced as I climbed from the bed, pausing to sit on the edge as a wave of nausea rolled over me.

"Gabe, what happened last night?"

My vision came into focus. Zachary had been sitting beside me on the bed. Thomas was running around collecting clothes and throwing them beside me.

"We've been trying to call you. I've been at your folks'. Taylor is missing, Gabe," Thomas said.

"Fuck. Why didn't someone come and get me?" I stood, ignoring the pounding in my head.

“Because I’ve been at your folks’,” he said again.

I pulled a t-shirt over my head, hopped from one foot to the other trying to get my jeans on and shoved my bare feet in my sneakers. I grabbed the phone from my nightstand. I swallowed down the panic and bile that rose to my throat.

“Tell me what happened?” I said as we rushed down the stairs. I paused at the bottom causing Thomas to collide into me.

“My gun,” I said.

I ran to the kitchen, remembering that was the last place I had it. It was gone.

“Fuck!” I screamed the word out loud.

Sitting on the table though, where the gun should have been was a key. No fob, just a single silver-colored door key. I grabbed it; somehow knowing the exact lock it would open.

Thomas watched as I inserted it in the lock and twisted, it was a key to my front door. Lily had swapped a key for my gun.

“Shit,” he said.

“Get in the car, Gabe,” Zach said. There was no time to worry about the key.

Outside stood three police cars, their lights were blazing. Neighbors stood on their lawns, watching as if the fucking Easter parade was in town. I slammed the door behind me and raced for the first car. Thomas climbed behind the wheel and Zachary threw himself in the back just as Thomas sped off.

“I got a call, a half-hour ago. Your dad had been trying to call you. Taylor is missing from her bed. I’ve organized a search party to check the ranch. She could have just got up early and gone for a walk.”

“My daughter, my five-year-old daughter, wouldn’t get up and go for a fucking walk!”

“Where’s Lily?” Zach asked.

"I don't know, she was in bed."

Thomas looked over to me. "Please, tell me you didn't…"

"Just fucking drive, okay? Zach, what do you know?"

"You cannot believe one word that woman told you, Gabe. She is evil. Oh, Lord. If I'd known she was here, I would have got here faster. Why on earth did you not tell me?"

"How do you know now?"

"Sister Anna is dead, Gabe. I'm sorry. Her body was found a couple of days ago. I saw your text message. I had no idea they'd got to you so fast."

I turned in my seat. "Who? What the fuck is going on?"

Thomas cornered so fast I lost my balance and had to reach out for the dash to steady myself.

"Who killed her?" Acid burned my throat and again I had to swallow down the bile.

"Lily, her friends, I don't know yet."

"It can't have been Lily, she was with me."

"You called in state police yet?" I asked Thomas. He nodded.

"And the feds are involved. This is all out of my hands now. I expect we'll be hauled over the coals at some point," he said.

"The FBI has been investigating this from the beginning, Gabriel. I have been assisting them," Zach said.

"That's bullshit. She's been at my house, she hasn't been in hiding."

"She's been hiding very well. Lily isn't her name."

I felt like a bow had shot a fucking large arrow straight through me. "Come again?"

"I'm not sure she's even Sierra's full sister. Sure they look alike, all those kids do because they share some of the same parents. They were brought up in a cult, Gabe. It's the cult that the FBI is investigating. They all look the same because of inbreeding. Incest, child abuse, you name it, it's going on."

"Pull over, quick," I said.

Thomas swerved to the side of the road; I'd just managed to get my door open before heaving my guts all over the pavement. I retched until there was nothing left but acid that burned my throat and coated my mouth. Sweat dripped from my brow.

"Here," I heard, as a bottle of water was placed in my hand.

I took a mouthful, swished it around before spitting it out.

"Go," I said. I drained the bottle in just a few gulps. The thirst I felt wasn't satisfied with just the one bottle though.

I clung onto the door handle as we bounced, at high speed, up the unpaved drive toward the ranch. I could see police cars, neighbors' trucks and a group of people ahead of me. Before we'd come to a halt, I was out and sprinting across to the house. I barged through the door, calling out Taylor's name.

Mom was sitting at the kitchen table, sobbing. Dad was standing to her side, with one arm around her shoulder, his other hand holding a phone to his ear.

"He's here. I'll call you back," he said.

"Where is she?" I said.

"We don't know. Oh God, Gabriel. I went to get her up, thinking she'd overslept and she was gone. I didn't want for that to happen," Mom replied.

"Where's Lily?" I said.

"Lily?"

"Lily is missing as well, Mrs. M," Thomas said.

"You don't think…"

"We don't know what to think, right now," he said.

For a moment the only sound was the crackle of Thomas' radio.

“I don’t know what’s happening,” I said.

“Sit,” Zachary said, placing his hand on my shoulder.

“I’ll sit when I’ve found my daughter.”

“There are close on fifty people searching right now, Gabe. They’ve had a half-hour head start on you. There are dogs, if she’s on this ranch, they’ll find her,” Thomas said.

“And you think me sitting here is going to happen?”

“You sitting here and telling us all you know certainly will,” a voice said.

None of us had noticed the two men walk into the house.

“FBI,” one said.

I’d expected the FBI to be wearing black suits, dark glasses, and shiny shoes. I hadn’t expected two guys, one in jeans and a shirt, the other in cream-colored pants and a t-shirt. They both did, however, have dark glasses pushed up on their heads.

“Agents Midley and Romney,” Zachary said by way of an introduction.

“When my daughter is found, I’ll sit and talk,” I said.

“If your daughter was taken by the Divinus Pueri, your information will help us locate her, sooner rather than later.”

“Divinus what?” Dad said.

“It’s a cult, Dad. It’s where Lily, although that isn’t her name, came from,” Zach said.

“Holy Fuck,” I said. “Fuck! Fuck!”

“What?” Thomas asked.

“They think she’s one of them, don’t they?” I said.

“Who? Who’s one of them?” Mom asked.

“Taylor,” I said.

My mom paled, her body shook as she slumped into a chair. “What have we done?” she said. I looked at her, not understanding.

“Possibly, in which case she’s safe.” I wasn’t sure whether that was Midley or Romney that answered.

“Safe! My daughter is with those fucking nut jobs and you think she’s safe?” I shouted. “She took my gun,” I said, lowering my voice.

“Lily?” Midley or Romney asked.

“Yes, fucking Lily. What is her fucking name, anyway? And which one are you?”

“Midley. Her name is Rachiel, with an I,” he said.

Why the fuck did we need to know the spelling of her name?

“Someone better tell me what the fuck is going on here,” Dad said, surprising me with his cuss word. He never swore in front of Mom normally.

The kitchen was filled with too many people, all talking without making sense. Mom was crying, Zachary sat beside her and wrapped her in his arms. Thomas was talking on his cell, Dad was pacing, and the feds were as cool as ice. I was a mess; my head thumped as if I’d woken with a hangover, but knew I hadn’t. My body ached as if I’d woken from a deep sleep.

“Gabe?” Somewhere, and it felt like in the distance, I heard my name being called.

I felt arms lift me from the floor. Had I fainted? Do guys faint? My head was swimming.

“We need a medic,” I heard.

I shook my head. “Drink, I’m thirsty,” I said.

I was helped to a chair, where I kept my eyes closed and my head resting on my folded arms. A wave of nausea rushed over me. When that nausea settled, I looked up; a glass of water had been placed in front of me. I drained it in one.

"I think we need to get you to the hospital," Thomas said.

"No way. I'm fine."

"Do you think she drugged you?" he asked.

"No. Just give me a minute."

I didn't get that minute. The rush of footsteps across the porch had us all standing to our feet.

"They found her," a man I didn't recognize said. He was breathless as if he'd run some distance.

"Where?" I asked.

"In the woods. She's okay, I think," he said.

I pushed past him and ran. I stopped at the edge of the woodland that surrounded the ranch, not sure where to go.

"This way," he said as he ran past me, followed by Thomas.

My lungs burned at the exertion, yet they shouldn't have. I was more than fit enough to sprint the distance I'd already covered. I could hear voices and dogs barking. As the trees thinned slightly, I saw a crowd. I pushed through them to see my daughter looking scared.

"Baby," I said as I scooped her up.

"I'm sorry, Daddy," she said as she started to cry.

"It's okay, it's okay." I held her in my arms as I ran back to the house.

I pushed past the crowd that had formed on the porch and headed straight to the living room, kicking the door shut behind me. It was a cool room, calm. I placed her on the sofa and knelt in front of her.

"What happened, baby girl?" I said gently.

Before she could answer the door creaked. I looked over to see Thomas. I nodded, signaling that he could come in. He knelt beside me.

"She wanted to see the foal, that's all. We went to play, and when I turned around, she was gone. I got lost, I'm sorry, Daddy."

"Who wanted to see the foal?"

"Lily."

"Start at the beginning. Grandma said she went to get you up but you were gone."

"I dressed myself, I thought I was being good." She hiccupped through her sentence.

"You were, baby, you were. Now, tell me, when did you see Lily?"

"I came downstairs, I didn't see Grandma but I wanted to check on the foal. She was near the paddock. We played for a while. I showed her the foal. We were just playing."

Taylor started to cry. "Hey, it's okay. So you played in the woods and she left you?" Thomas asked.

Taylor nodded. "She said it was okay, you were coming to play with us, as well. But when I turned around she was gone. Am I in trouble?" she asked, her voice had lowered to a whisper.

"No, you sure scared us though. You know you can't run off, ever, without Grandma or Grandpa knowing," I said.

"I miss Mommy, I want to go home," she whispered.

I pulled her into my arms and rocked her as she cried. "I know you do, baby girl, I know you do."

A half-hour later the living room door opened again and Mom walked in. I guessed the waiting crowd was anxious for news.

"She was playing with Lily, but then Lily ran off, and Taylor got lost in the woods," I said. I watched Mom's brow furrow.

"Lily?" she said. I shook my head gently, hoping she'd understand to not push.

"I'm sorry, Grandma. I just wanted to see the foal."

"You know what I have baking? Cherry pie," Mom said.

"Can I have some?" Taylor asked, her earlier tears having dried up once she believed she wasn't in trouble.

"You sure can, want to get some now?" Mom held out her hand.

I stood, allowing Taylor to take her hand. "I'm sure Daddy needs to speak to his friends." I understood then what she was doing.

When she was out of the room, I punched the sofa. "Fucking bitch," I said.

"You need to tell me what happened yesterday and last night," Thomas said.

"I fucked her, three, four times. I don't know. We went for a drive, she told me a shit ton of stuff. And then when we got home, I fucked her."

My voice broke and finally I cried. I'd suppressed those tears for so long, but everything came crashing down around me. The guilt wrapped itself around me so tight I felt like I couldn't breathe.

"She got to my daughter. That was her telling me how fucking easy it had been," I said.

"We don't know that," he said.

"I fucking fell for her bullshit last night. I felt sorry for her; I started to believe her. Oh, she's fucking good, all right. She had me, hook, line, and fucking sinker."

I don't think I'd cussed as much as I had the past few hours. "I need a smoke."

I brushed the tears from my cheeks and stood.

Taylor was sitting at the kitchen table eating cherry pie, as if nothing had happened. She was chatting to Midley, I guessed he'd gotten what he needed from her but I was pissed. No one questioned my daughter without me around. He glanced up when he saw me.

“Can I have a word?” I said.

He followed me, as did Thomas, Zachary, and Romney to the front porch. I spun around so quick it took him by surprise, and he instinctively reached for the gun he had holstered at his waist.

“Don’t you fucking question my daughter without me being there. She’s five-years-old,” I said.

He raised his palm to calm me. “I didn’t, Gabriel. I was sitting there when your mother brought her in. We talked about pie and horses, nothing more. I’m more than aware of what I can and can’t do. And believe me, this investigation is way too important for me to fuck it up by interviewing a minor. Besides, she isn’t a credible witness, so we wouldn’t interview her anyway.”

I slumped into Dad’s chair. “Someone better tell me what the fuck is going on. Lily was here earlier. She took Taylor into the woods, to play!”

Chairs were pulled up, a circle formed and everyone sat. Dad joined us.

“I should be with Taylor,” I said, looking up at him.

“You should be right here, she’s okay. Still a little shaken but your momma’s taking good care of her.”

I didn’t give the response that sprang to my mind. Taylor should never have been able to leave the house unnoticed.

“We have a full report from the sheriff. I guess I don’t need to tell you how you could have hampered our investigation, do I?” Romney said.

“You guys weren’t interested when my wife was killed, so don’t start that shit with me,” I said.

“There was no connection between your wife and the cult we are investigating, initially,” he replied.

“You sure got that wrong then, didn’t you?”

"You guys can argue all you want, but that won't get us anywhere. How about we settle it down and talk?" Zachary said, he'd been mostly quiet the whole time we'd been there.

All eyes were focused on me.

"We took a drive, she was going stir crazy being cooped up indoors. She told me a little about her foster parents, she said they were part of a religion called Divinus something. I guess that's not important because you know who they are anyway; she said they were close to the Catholic Church.

"She got a little, familiar shall we say, I stopped that and we drove home. I was pissed. My head has been all over the place, I don't know who to trust or believe right now. At first I thought she was lying to us, things didn't stack up. But then she told me the truth. She told me how she'd made up an okay childhood because she'd been subjected to years of abuse. She claimed to be a Divine Child. Apparently those assholes believe she is a child of an angel, as was Sierra, and therefore they need to mate with them to reproduce, keep the bloodline going, or some shit like that."

"Did you have sexual intercourse with her?" Midley asked.

I didn't answer immediately, and I figured my hesitation was an affirmative answer in itself. I nodded my head.

"Once, twice?" he asked, a little aggressively I thought.

"Does that matter? Three, four times, I don't know. I felt sorry for her, I felt sorry for myself. I haven't fucking slept for more than two or three hours a night and for some reason, yesterday, last night, whenever it was, I escaped for a little while. I escaped from the madness and the pain, okay?" My voice had risen in anger.

"Could you have impregnated her?" he asked.

I looked at him; shock must have registered on my face. "What?"

"It was just a question."

"A fucking stupid one."

Zachary placed his hand on my arm, I closed my eyes tight as he gently squeezed.

Shit, could I have gotten her pregnant? It only takes one time, I thought.

"The sheriff tells us that you've had an attempted break-in and since then a possible intruder," Midley said.

"Yeah, each night she woke me after hearing a noise. The first night we found a footprint, the second she said she saw someone. I thought I heard the backdoor rattle, maybe a shadow cross the glass, I'm not sure now."

"She was manipulating you, Gabriel. Causing sleep deprivation so you'd be confused, I imagine," he said.

"Was anything she told me the truth? She's terrified, on the run, frightened for her life. There were times she cried, visibly shook. Can someone act that well?"

"Most of what she told you was a version of the truth. She was on the run, from us. The cult members, who believe her to a Divine Child, want her back. We're unsure of why she tried to leave the cult initially."

"Other than, sort of, confirming she's telling the truth, you're not actually telling me anything I don't already know," I said.

"And I can't, I'm sure you can appreciate that. You know what we're dealing with here."

"Why can't you go in and get those children out, at least."

"Because after a previous siege involving a cult, we have very different practices now. The children over age of consent, we can't remove. They are so brainwashed, like Lily, it's not as simple as removing them and placing them in care elsewhere."

"She scoffed at the thought she was a Divine Child, as in a child of an angel," I said.

"Maybe she did, maybe she doesn't believe that, but she's still doing their work for them. She's the one chasing down those statements, she's the one we're looking for in relation to at least three murders."

"She said something that's only just hit me. She wanted what Sierra had, a perfect life, perfect child, etc. Are you sure she's just not searching for that?"

Why I was defending her, I wasn't sure.

"Possibly, and it's our belief that she feels if she completes this task for them, she'll be released."

"What's your role in all this?" I asked Zach.

He looked to Midley before answering, and only did so once he received a nod.

"The founding father, for want of a better word, was a priest. He is the one in that photograph you saw. He was under investigation for child abuse. What Sierra experienced in that convent, although I'll use the word convent loosely, is true. Most of those children suffered some form of abuse, whether that was physical or sexual. They were also passed on."

"Passed on to be further abused?"

Zachary nodded his head.

"And the Catholic Church has been open about this? I'm pretty sure I haven't seen it in the press. Who was investigating this?"

"Most investigations are done internally, initially," he answered.

"That's fucking handy. You mean covered up, don't you?"

"Gabe, I'm not defending this or any level of abuse. There are some serious problems and flawed individuals within all religions. And yes, I'm sure, in the past, this kind of thing had been covered up. But not now. If you bothered to read the papers or watch the news, you'd see, sadly, it's quite topical."

"What happened to Sister Anna?"

“A body was found a few days ago that Zachary has been able to identify as Sister Anna. I’m not at liberty to tell you how she died, but she was discovered not too far away,” Romney said.

“It was your messages on her phone, well, I say her phone, we know it wasn’t, that alerted me to your involvement,” Zachary said.

“Lily said Sister Anna tracked all the children from the photograph, it’s how she managed to get in touch with Sierra,” I said.

“We believe so, yes. She was instrumental in the fostering and adoption program at the convent, although I’d like to believe she knew nothing about the abuse.”

“So, this convent was a Catholic one then?”

“Yes.”

“And the kids don’t go through the state adoption services, I take it. It’s all ‘in house’ so to speak?” I asked.

“There are rules, Gabriel. We don’t force single mothers to hand over their children and then farm them out anymore.” Zachary’s voice had taken on a defensive tone.

I raised my eyebrows. “Really? Anyway, I left my cigarettes at home, anyone have a smoke?”

I was shocked to see Zachary reach inside his jacket pocket and pull out a pack. He slid them, with a lighter, across the small table separating us.

“How are you feeling?” Thomas asked.

“Better, still a little nauseous, but I’ll live. I guess it’s all the stress and anxiety that’s caught up with me.”

I took some time to light the cigarette and inhaled deeply, letting the smoke gently waft from my nostrils.

“So, what did Lily, or whatever her name is, want from me?” I asked.

"The statements, I guess. It's what everyone seems to be after. They may contain some damning evidence," Zachary said.

Thomas' eye twitched.

"And no one knows where they are," I said.

"We may need to check your house, Gabriel. Organize a thorough search," Midley said.

"Feel free. I've checked, Thomas and his deputies have checked, there's nothing there."

I stood and stretched. "I need to walk about a bit," I said.

"I think we're done here, for the moment, anyway. Gabriel, I take it you'll be staying here for a few days? We'd like to talk again, obviously. And I guess I don't need to say this, but if Lily, sorry, Rachiel, get's in contact, we need to know as soon as possible," Midley said, placing a card with just his name and cell number on the table.

Agents Midley and Romney stood, in perfect sync, and bade a farewell to my dad and Thomas. Zachary accompanied them to their car.

I watched Thomas pick up his phone and text something.

"Well, that was sure interesting," Dad said, he hadn't contributed at all during the conversation.

"In what way?"

"Those guys are not feds," he said.

"Why do you say that?" I asked.

"Because that wasn't a Glock holstered at his waist."

I stared at my dad. "Feds are issued with Glocks, Gabe. Everyone knows that."

Obviously I didn't. It wasn't that I doubted my father's knowledge, but I still picked up my phone to Google, cursing at the lack of signal.

"And, I never mentioned the statements in any report I've sent over to state police," Thomas added. "I kept that out until we knew it was a fact."

"We need to get you all out of here," I said.

"And Zachary?" Thomas asked.

"Maybe he believes they are genuine," Dad said. "Besides, I'm not going anywhere."

"Dad…"

He held up his hand, cutting off my sentence. "Son, I've lived in this house for over forty years. I've survived three tours of Vietnam and horrors you couldn't imagine. No cult or fake feds are going to run me from my own home."

Our conversation was halted by the return of Zachary.

"So, how did you get involved with the feds then?" I asked, as I lifted the lid from dad's cooler and pulled out some beers.

"They contacted me, actually. Well, I say me, my office. We knew about the priest, I can't divulge his name, and the abuse."

"How recent was this?" Dad asked.

"Just over a year ago. I wasn't aware, Gabriel, that Sierra had anything to do with this." He sighed and closed his eyes. His mouth moved in a silent prayer.

"How could you not be aware Sierra was involved, if she was at the convent?"

"There is no child registered by the name of Sierra, on record at that home, Gabe."

I stared at him. "I don't understand."

"We're not sure Sierra was ever at the home, or that's not her real name."

"We got married, Zach, she would have had a birth certificate." My mind was instantly transported back to the original list I'd made. I tried to recall what else was on it.

"I can only say what we found. There was no child of her age by that name."

Until then, it hadn't crossed my mind that Sierra might not be her real name. "But her mother died? She was a child; someone would have taken care of her. Sister Anna said she knew my wife, she was the one who handed me the diary entries."

"She said she knew your wife, but that doesn't mean Sierra was a child of that convent."

I sat back down; my earlier need to stretch my legs completely forgotten.

"How do you know she was at the convent?" Zach added.

"Lily said…" I sighed. "No, Sister Anna said, 'religion killed my wife' when I met her."

"The cult, perhaps?"

"What the fuck is going on? What part of all this fucked up shit is real? Is there a convent that Sister Anna worked at, or whatever you call it?"

"Yes, it exists."

"They fostered out kids to this cult thing, yes?"

"Yes, although she wasn't aware of that."

"The priest liked fucking children, yes?"

Zachary winced at my choice of words before answering. "Yes."

"So, we have a cult on one hand that, according to your friends, is involved in incest, abuse, and whatever. And a convent that supplied them with the kids because one man ran both the cult and the convent. A fucking Catholic priest!"

"That about sums it up from where I'm sitting," Dad said.

"Where does this Divine Child come in, and where was Sierra's mother, the convent or the cult?" I asked.

Zachary stared at me; I could see his jaw work from side to side. "Tell me, Zach, because I think you know," I said.

"There was a child, thirty years ago, her name was Lily. She either came into the convent at fourteen as pregnant, or became pregnant shortly after. Obviously the records are a little sketchy."

"She can't be Sierra's mother. Sierra wasn't thirty years old," I said.

"As far as you know, of course. I know that this woman produced a daughter, blonde hair, blue eyes, and fair skin, perfect in every way, an exact replica of her mother. We have made the assumption the child is the daughter of the priest, and for some reason he believed he had created an angel or something divine."

"Do you believe in angels? Do you believe in all that…stuff?" I asked.

"I believe in the Lord, Gabriel. I believe his son was sent to earth to teach us, and he died for our sins. I believe in the Bible, I believe in hope and faith, if I don't have that, I have nothing. I don't believe anything divine can be created from human flesh, bone, and blood. We are too flawed for that. So, no, I don't believe the child of a priest and woman can be anything more than just a child."

I believe in hope and faith, Gabriel. If I don't have that, I have nothing. Lily's words flooded back to me.

"I need to get back inside with my daughter," I said, standing once again.

Taylor didn't appear to be overly fazed by her expedition, and I put that down to only being five-years-old, with the attention span of a goldfish. She was busy making pies with Mom.

"Hey, baby girl, what are you doing?" I asked.

I'd wrapped my arms around her waist and lifted her up. She was covered in flour. She placed those floury hands either side of my cheeks.

"I like this fluff but it scratches my face," she said, rubbing her hands over my stubble.

"I'll shave it all off, just for you."

"Well, I think we have enough pies to last until Thanksgiving," Mom said.

I looked at the counter top, there must have been at least ten pies waiting to be baked.

"Which one did you make, baby?"

Taylor twisted in my arms, she thought for a moment then pointed to a random one in the middle. I leaned over.

"This one?" I said, pointing. She nodded.

I poked my finger in the middle making a hole. "So we know which one is yours," I said.

"I think it's time to get cleaned up," Mom said.

"How about I stay here, with you, tonight?" I said to Taylor.

Her smile was all the answer I needed. "Go wash up, and then we'll go check on the foal. I'm sure Grandpa has some jobs for us."

Taylor rushed to the bathroom. "Mom, we need to talk. I need to find my marriage license, I'm hoping Sierra's birth certificate is with it."

"Oh?"

"I need to find out her real name and her date of birth."

"I don't understand," Mom said.

"I just need to. Can you remember what happened to them? I don't have them at home, I just wondered if they were here somewhere."

"I'll make sure to look. I have some things from your wedding; I stored them all in a keepsake box. I'll check for you," she said.

She dried her hands on a dishtowel before gesturing with her hand to sit at the table.

"What can you tell me?"

"Lily was here this morning." I then told her an abbreviated version of what we already knew.

I omitted any fears I had about the feds; I didn't want to scare her. I was at a loss as to what to do. I couldn't return home. I believed in safety in numbers, so perhaps us all staying at the ranch was the best thing to do. We could call in some reinforcements.

Dad and Thomas walked into the kitchen. "Where's Zachary?" I asked.

"He had to pop into town. He said he'll be back for dinner though," Dad replied.

"That's great, we haven't sat and eaten as a family since…" Mom trailed off.

"It's okay, since Sierra." I said.

"So, I guess you called Zach this morning, Mom?" I asked, as I poured some iced tea. That thirst hadn't been completely quenched.

"No, he arrived with his friends, just after I called Thomas and tried to call you. I left a message on your voicemail," she said.

I made a point to look for Thomas' twitch.

"I'm sorry, Mom, I had my phone silenced. I'd had a rough night."

She placed her hand on my cheek, "No harm done though, so it's all good. And tonight, my boys will be here, my granddaughter, too."

Mom seemed pleased to have the whole family together, I wasn't so sure it was a good idea.

Taylor returned from washing her hands and face, not that she'd done a great job of it. I should have helped her really. I took hold of her still wet hand and we headed out. She skipped alongside me and chatted the whole way to the paddock.

"When you saw Lily, where did she come from?" I asked.

"The house, no, the barn, I think," she said.

"Okay, so, tell me what you know about looking after a pony?"

She rattled off what she'd already been taught. She knew how to groom the hair the way it lay, how to pick up a hoof, although she had to wait until she was nine-years-old to be able to do that alone. Where the nine came from, I had no idea. She knew to make sure there was fresh water every day, and hay in the winter. While she talked, I sent a text to Thomas.

Lily came from the barn this morning, might be worth checking it. I vaguely remember a conversation about whether Sierra hid statements there.

There wasn't a reply, but I did see him leave the house and walk toward the barn.

All the while we leaned on the paddock fence; I scanned the area. I watched for any movement in the woodland beyond. She was here somewhere, I was sure of that. Taylor chatted and I should have listened. I should have paid more attention to my daughter, but my mind kept wandering. I didn't know who to believe, Lily, the fake feds and Zachary, or my instinct. I chuckled; I couldn't trust my instinct as far as I could throw it right then. I'd made so many bad calls over the past few days.

"So, anyway, Lily said…"

"Whoa, back up. What did you say, baby girl?"

She huffed, aware I hadn't been listening to her and placed her hands on her hips.

"Were you listening to me?" she asked before pouting.

"You talk so much, it's hard to listen to it all," I teased. "Now, what did you just say?"

"Lily said did I know the difference between a truth and a lie."

"And do you?"

"Yes. She said I had to ask you if you did. So, do you?"

"Yes, I know the difference. What else did she say?"

"She said she always tells the truth, and it's important that I tell you the truth always, too. So if you ask me any questions, I have to make sure I tell it as it."

"Tell it as it is?" It was a strange choice of words from a five-year-old.

"Yeah, that's what Lily says. I must tell it as it is. What does that mean?"

"It means tell me everything, exactly as it happened. She told you that this morning?" I asked, wanting to be sure.

"Yep. She always tells the truth and so should I, and you, Daddy."

"I will, baby girl. What else did you talk about?"

"I miss her, I like Lily. She misses me too, she told me. She wanted to give me a big hug, that's all. She's gone on vacation now."

"Don't suppose she told you where, did she?" I knew I was probably clutching at straws.

"No, far away though. She said she'd be back to see us both."

"Both?"

"Yep, she said me and Daddy."

I wondered how accurate Taylor's memory of that conversation actually was. But it hit me then that maybe Lily had used Taylor to send me a message. She wanted me to know she was telling the truth. But was she? Or was she the master manipulator fake feds suggested she was?

Lily had certainly played me; I had no doubt about that. Had she drugged me the previous night? That I doubted. My earlier sickness was most probably fear. I thought back to our conversation in the hallway. She had seemed so sincere, but then she'd told lies, she'd slipped up on many occasions. The headache I'd had that morning started to make another appearance, a result of my confusion, perhaps.

I took hold of Taylor's hand and we walked back to the house. She had wanted to run ahead, but I was letting her no more than a foot away from me. She showed her displeasure by kicking up dirt and scraping her sneakers along the ground, something she knew she'd normally get scolded for. I ignored it.

"Hey, little lady," Thomas said as he left the barn.

I let go of Taylor then and she ran to him. He lifted her up and placed her on his hip. She liked to play with the badge on his uniform. He'd given her a badge for her fifth birthday and sworn her in as his deputy. She'd been so serious, so proud. She wore that badge for weeks, even to school.

I needed to talk to Thomas, and was thankful to see my dad and a ranch hand in the barn.

"How about you go help Grandpa?" I said.

The prospect of getting dirty always attracted Taylor.

"Taylor said that Lily had told her she always speaks the truth and that she would be back to see her, and me. I think that was a message to me."

"Or she's fucking with you again. And I don't mean literally. You know how dumb that was, don't you? She cries rape and your DNA is all over her, or in her."

"I know, but just for that moment, Tom, it felt good. All the shit, the pain, disappeared. I felt like a man again."

As much as we had been friends from childhood, we didn't do 'emotion.' There was an awkward pause.

"Did Zach leave his smokes?" I asked as we sat on the front porch.

"I want the pack and lighter for fingerprinting. Which means, I need your fingerprints for elimination."

"You think he's involved?"

"I'm not ruling anyone out. Not now."

"Fuck! That would destroy my parents."

"I ran a check on fake feds plate, it's unlicensed," he said.

"What does that mean?"

"It means it could be an official vehicle, or a fake plate."

"Do you think those feds were fake?"

"I'm not sure. I have to be honest; I haven't had a great deal to do with the feds. I have asked a friend over at the state to see if their names are familiar. I'm going keep Syd at your house tonight. But I don't have the manpower if this get's nasty."

"I thought you passed this over to the state police?"

"Yeah, and the minute they got wind that the FBI was involved, they backed off. They'll assist if required, but I don't have that call."

"I need to stay here tonight, but I also need to get some clothes. You reported my gun missing, didn't you?"

"I did. How about I drive you home real quick? You can come back in your truck."

"I don't want to leave Taylor. I just don't know what to fucking do for the best right now."

"Want me to get some clothes for you?"

"It's fine, you can drive me. I'm sure Dad can keep Taylor safe and it's mid-afternoon, I can't imagine anything happening now."

I walked to the barn and told Dad of my plans. I watched him pat his lower leg and knew he was armed. I was glad he'd concealed though. I didn't want Taylor around guns.

It was as I opened my front door that I remembered the key.

"Lily had this key, she had to have," I said as I picked it up.

"It was on the table, wasn't it? Where you'd left your gun, you know that loaded weapon that should have been locked away?" His level of sarcasm often amused me, but not then.

"It would explain how she knew her way around my kitchen. Maybe she's been coming and going for a while. Again, it could explain why she just so happened to be in town."

"You called the locksmith, right? To change the locks?" Thomas said.

I stared at him.

"Fuck's sake, Gabe. Call the fucking locksmith, now. And while we're at it, let's do something more secure with that window."

"But if she left the key…"

"She left one key, who knows how many others she has, and who knows if she's the only one who had a key."

There was one locksmith in town, well; he owned the general store and Thomas believed he should have had a career as a housebreaker. The guy could walk around and point out every vulnerable place in any house.

"You got his number?"

Thomas sighed and scrolled through his phone. He would have the number, if they needed access to a property it needed to be made secure after. He made the call and left a message on his voicemail.

"He'll be here quicker if he thinks it's anything to do with the police, nosy fucker that he is," Thomas said, once he'd disconnected and we walked through to the kitchen.

It felt like hours ago that I'd last been there. Half-drunk coffee cups littered the counter in the kitchen. Thomas took a seat while I headed upstairs.

The bed sheets were a tangled mess and pillows were scattered on the floor. The drapes were still drawn and the room smelled of sex. There was no time to tidy up. I opened a wardrobe door and grabbed a couple of pairs of jeans from a shelf. Next were some t-shirts and underwear. I searched around for a suitcase, finding one at the bottom. I leaned in to grab it and as I pulled it out, something caught my eye.

"Thomas, up here," I called out.

I heard his footsteps as he rushed up the stairs.

"What?"

"Look, what do you see?"

"A wardrobe."

"Look closer, in the corner."

He frowned as his eyes focused on the same thing that had caught my attention. A large, new, bright, shiny screw head stood out against the dark wood of the wardrobe floor.

"You checked in here though, didn't you?"

"Yeah, I opened the door, removed all the clothes and looked on shelves. I didn't think to check for a false floor."

I watched as he pulled a utility knife from his pocket. He inserted the tip into the screw head and turned. The screw released easily enough and he swiped his arm to remove the piles of shoes and sneakers in the opposite corner. We didn't find another shiny new screw and he took out the old ones. When all four, from each corner were removed, he used the knife to pry the plank up. It came away too easily for an old piece of furniture.

Sitting in one corner was an envelope, not the large padded one we'd been given by Sister Anna, just a standard, letter-sized, once white envelope. I reached for it but Thomas grabbed my arm.

"Don't touch it." He used the knife to flick it over. Written in black ink on the front was my name.

He fished again in his jacket pocket and pulled out one latex glove. He slipped it on and lifted the envelope from its hiding place.

"Screw that floor back down," he said.

"Why?"

"Because if someone comes looking here tonight and see's that, they'll know you've found something."

He handed me the knife and I screwed the board back in place, we refilled it with the shoes and sneakers.

"I need to take this back to the station," he said.

"Open it now, Thomas. I need to see what that says. That is Sierra's handwriting. I'm not allowing you to take it. It's my property."

I was desperate. It was the first piece of communication I'd had from my wife. I reached out for it and Thomas let go. I held it in my hands for what seemed like an age, too afraid to see what was inside. I sat on the edge of the bed, and eventually slid the knife under the flap and pried out a plain piece of paper.

Gabriel,

I pray that you will find this, and if you have, I'm not with you anymore—how clichéd is that?

Know one thing. I love you, from the moment you dragged me from that fight, I loved you. You, and my baby girl, are my world. Whatever time we have would never be long enough. But I need to tell you the truth.

I know someone is after me, I know I won't survive this, and that breaks my heart. I could run, but I can't leave you behind. And I can't tell you, to protect you, you and Taylor. The less you know, Gabriel, the better it is.

You're going to hear a lot of lies and hopefully some truths. I wish I could have been honest with you from the beginning. I also pray that you'll forgive me.

I was brought up, initially, in a convent. My mother had been murdered by my father, Gabriel. The beast that ran the convent is a man named Father Samuel. I know you'll be told that a father would not 'run' a convent, but he isn't a conventional man, and he did.

A woman, Sister Anna, will contact you. She contacted me and asked for my help. She will give you evidence of what happened to me and a photograph. The diary was mine; I'd forgotten about it. I must have left it behind when I ran. All of those children were given to families, members of the same cult, it was taken the day those children left. They went on to suffer immeasurable pain and abuse. Like me, they grew up. Those that were not so indoctrinated, left, or rather, escaped.

The cult has a name, Divinus Pueri. Let me tell you what that means. Divine Children. Father Samuel believed my mother to be divine, angelic if you will. He raped her, and then he raped her daughters. His belief is that if he can 'breed' divine children that will be his pass to God. It's madness, he is mad. There is no such thing as a divine child or angels. And, he is my biological father.

I managed to escape in my early teens, but I did a terrible thing, something I will pay for, for the rest of my life. You see, Taylor wasn't my first child. I aborted a baby girl; I had no choice. I could not allow a child of mine, of my father's, to live and be subjected to the horrors I was. I never believed I'd be able to have another child, so can you see now, why I treasure our daughter so much?

Hopefully you understand now. My greatest fear is that he will come for Taylor. She is of my blood, and he will believe, no matter diluted by your genes, she is still divine. I beg you, Gabriel, keep her safe.

Trust no one, I believe there are people very close to you that mean me harm. The Catholic Church knew of his abuse, they covered it up. They stripped him of his title and threw him out, but they did nothing to protect the children that should have been in their care.

I spent time with Sister Anna, tracking down those 'children,' talking to them. We were going to make it public, tell the world that the greatest religion on earth covered up years of abuse. We were going to expose them all. But one by one they were silenced.

Is it Father Samuel, or his friends, after me? Or is it someone within the Roman Catholic Church? I truly don't know yet.

I'm sorry, Gabriel, I wish, in a way, I had never gotten involved. I wish I'd had the strength to walk away when Sister Anna asked for my help. But I couldn't. And I never believed the depth men of God would go to, to protect themselves.

I say this again; I love you, with my heart and soul. Forgive me.

Sierra

My hands shook, tears coursed down my cheeks, and I lowered the letter to my lap.

"Gabe?" I heard.

Wordlessly, I handed it to him. I was numb; ice ran through my veins. I clenched my jaw shut so tight, to stop the scream from leaving my mouth, my cheeks hurt.

"Oh, God," Thomas said. "Oh my God."

I stood, mechanically and without thinking. I threw some clothes in the suitcase, picked it up, and walked from the room. I heard footsteps behind me; I knew Thomas was following. I alarmed the house and locked the front door behind us.

"Gabriel, talk to me," he said.

I turned to him.

"I promise you one thing. I will kill the man who did this, you can take that as my confession."

Chapter Seventeen

I drove on autopilot. Maybe I shouldn't have, perhaps I should have asked Thomas to drive me back to my folks'. But I needed time alone. I didn't need a copy of that letter; every fucking word was imprinted on my brain, never to be forgotten.

I noticed Thomas' car in my rearview mirror; he followed slowly behind. I wondered if he thought I'd act on my promise immediately. My only concern at that moment was to get to my daughter.

Words swam around my mind, images of my wife, of Lily. They all had it wrong, there were no statements written down, and they'd killed so many innocents over it.

I tried to clear my mind, I tried to concentrate on just driving and getting to my family. I needed to be around them, to hold my daughter and breathe in her scent. I needed to feel her arms around my neck as I held her to reinforce that something good had come out of Sierra's tragic life. Then I needed to find a way to keep her safe.

Somehow, I managed to make it back without crashing or leaving the highway. I pulled onto the drive in time to see my mom walk from the house with Taylor by her side.

"Daddy!" she shouted as she ran toward me.

I climbed down and caught her as she leapt into my arms.

"You, baby girl, are getting too big to keep doing that," I said.

She giggled as she nestled her head on my shoulder. I watched Thomas pull up alongside the truck.

"I was just telling her that it's time for a bath," Mom said.

"I think your grandma is right, you stink," I said.

"You stink, Daddy," Taylor replied.

"You stink more. How about I take you for a bath?"

"It's okay, Daddy, Grandma can do that, it's called girl time," she said.

I lowered her to the ground and she took Mom's hand to be led back into the house.

"We need to talk, Gabe. It's important," Thomas said.

"I don't know that I can right now."

"Please, just give me a few minutes, and then I need to head back to the station."

I nodded as we walked to the porch and sat. I grabbed a beer and drank it straight down before reaching for another.

"Fuck, smokes," I said.

Thomas threw over a fresh pack and I wondered where he'd managed to get them.

"Always have them in car, just in case," he said.

Thomas had quit smoking some years back, and I guessed the cigarettes were as old. I didn't care, stale or not, I needed the nicotine rush.

"She's not the only one," he said quietly.

I looked at him, not understanding. "She said, 'daughters,' Gabe, plural," he said.

"Lily?"

"Maybe. Maybe everything she told you was true."

"There are no written statements, Thomas."

"We don't know that, she says she talked to them, that doesn't mean at some point those 'talks' weren't written down. I've got a list of things to check out today, I'm not going to be around but I want a couple of deputies here."

I nodded my head. "Who do you trust?"

"Only my guys, Gabe. Until I know more."

Thomas left and I sat for a moment trying to process. My family were just, for the most part, law abiding small town people. I had no idea how to deal with all the deceit.

I walked into the house and followed the sound of my daughter singing. She was in the bath; her hair was spiked on her head and surrounded with a halo of bubbles. I laughed when I saw her. Mom was on her knees, attempting to mop up some of the water that had been splashed over the side.

I wanted to commit the image to memory. It was a snapshot of normalcy that I wasn't sure I'd ever be able to get back. Whatever the outcome, unless Father Samuel was dead, my daughter would spend her life at risk.

Zachary returned in time for dinner, he looked a little harassed. As Taylor was a constant by my side, it was difficult to talk. We sat and ate, we sat on the porch with coffee, and finally I was able to take her up to bed. I read to her, the same book I think I'd read a thousand times. I knew it word by word and was surprised that it still made her chuckle as if hearing the words for the very first time.

As I watched her fall asleep, her long dark eyelashes fluttered as her eyelids closed.

"You're wrong, Sierra. There are angels, not in the biblical sense, but we made a perfect one," I whispered.

I sat beside Taylor, just looking at her; I knew every freckle. I remembered how she'd walked into the corner of the kitchen table and obtained that small scar just above her left eyebrow, and how both Sierra and I had gone into a blind panic and rushed her to the hospital. I wished that she would stay that age, that she'd never have to grow up in world filled with horror and pain, filled with Father Samuels. But that wasn't possible. All I could vow was that I'd prepare my daughter for any eventuality. I chuckled as I stood; I was beginning to sound like some of the loony Doomsday Preppers.

I checked the windows before I left her, satisfied with the extra locks to keep her secure, then made my way downstairs.

"Been a rough day, huh?" Zachary said as I took a seat on the porch.

"Been a rough few months," I replied.

"What can I do to help? I won't offer to pray for you," he said, adding a chuckle.

"Tell me what you know about this cult?"

"There are thousands of cults, all around the world, Gabe. The founder of this one was a priest, for sure. He was suspended as soon as his actions were brought to light. But we don't know how far back his 'activities' go."

"Suspension? Why not thrown out, or whatever you call it."

"Laicization is the correct term, or defrocking, I think the press says. Think of the church as a business, we suspend, investigate, and then make a decision. If the priest had repented, then his suspension would have been lifted."

"Can you repent and be forgiven for an act so disgusting?" My voice had risen to a challenge.

"All sinners can repent in the eyes of the Lord, Gabriel."

"And that's why I don't do religion."

"You don't believe in second chances, do you?" he said.

"No, not for a crime so heinous as that. What is it your God teaches? All life should be treasured and children are a gift, but when that is abused, a simple sorry cures all?"

"It's not as simple as that. But I understand your anger, this is very personal for you and I want to help, Gabe, I really do."

I shook a cigarette then offered him the pack. "Are you allowed to smoke? Isn't it a sin or something?"

He chuckled as he lit his and reached down to pull a couple of beers from the magic refillable cooler.

"If we say we have no sin, we deceive ourselves, and the truth is not within us." He gave me a wink as he snapped off the caps and handed me a bottle.

"So, this convent. I thought that was a bunch of nuns. How did this priest 'run' it?"

"Technically you're correct. The mother superior is in charge, but there are convents that are more of a community, shall we say. And it's not uncommon for a priest to be involved. There were boys at that facility, a man amongst the ranks would have given some balance to their upbringing."

"Is the mother superior involved?"

"I can't answer that, Gabe. I can't answer a lot because I either don't know or I'm not allowed to."

"Who says you're not allowed to? Your FBI friends or the church?"

He didn't answer me. Instead opting to take a sip from his bottle of beer and then a puff on his cigarette.

"Look, mistakes were made. Many mistakes. For sure, this whole thing was covered up; I'm not going to deny that. A lot of what went on was before my time, of course. I'm a bishop, Gabriel. The convent isn't in my diocese. I was only called in to advise on the cult because I've had some dealings with it. Some years ago, I helped a family retrieve their child from them. A child that had been kidnapped and then so brainwashed to believe they were divine. The parents of that child wanted me to re-educate the child on what divinity was. The FBI has a deprogramming...program." He shook his head at his choice of words.

"And you're involved in that?"

"Only when required."

"You said there was no record of Sierra at that convent, what if that wasn't her real name?"

"I very much suspect that wasn't her real name. It's possible she changed it in later life, or they changed it."

"Midley and Romney, have you worked with them before?" I asked.

"No, this is the first time. There's a team at the FBI, from what I understand, a fairly large dedicated team, whose purpose is to deal with cults."

For a moment I stared at my brother, the brother that I hadn't really grown up with, the brother that I didn't really know. Did he have the capability to deceive me? Was he one of the good or bad guys? It saddened me to realize I didn't know him well enough to make that call.

"Are there secret organizations with the Catholic Church?" I asked.

"There are no secret organizations that the church officially recognizes."

"That was a very diplomatic answer, you should run for president."

"Have you any idea how vast the Catholic religion is? Millions and millions of people believe. There are hundreds of thousands of, let's say, officials, who work in the religion. I'm not a stupid man, I'm sure there are sections I'm not privy to."

"What about that, oh, what are they called? That guy wrote a book about them?"

He laughed. "Opus Dei?"

"That's them."

"Well, they are hardly a secret if someone wrote a book, and you know about them, are they?"

"Fair point."

The sun had long set, but the glare from every light in the house switched on, illuminated the yard.

"It's been a long day, I'm calling it a night," I said.

I said goodnight to my parents and climbed the stairs. Mom had prepared a room for me but I opted to sleep near my daughter. I lay on the spare bed and dozed.

At some point during the night I remembered the message I'd sent to Thomas asking him to check out the loft. I quietly rose from the chair and deliberated. I had no idea if Dad was a light sleeper, if I left to check the loft, would he hear if someone came into the house?

I crossed the room and opened the door. The hallway light was on and the house quiet. A floorboard creaked as I made my way to the top of the stairs. I crept down and to the front door.

It was a hot night; the air was dry and dusty. I stood for a while on the porch deciding what to do. The prudent thing would have been to wait until the morning, but being prudent, or sensible, didn't seem to work so well with me. I crossed the yard and slid open the barn door.

I heard horses shuffle around, and a snort of surprise when one had been woken from his doze. As I peered into the gloomy barn, a prickly nose gently brushed against my arm, startling me. One of the horses had decided to investigate.

I spun around at the sound of a scraping noise. "Shit, Dad, you nearly gave me a heart attack."

"Good. You come out here, with all the shit going on, unarmed?"

He walked toward me and slapped a revolver against my chest. "Now, what are you doing?" he said.

"I just want to check the loft, something came to me earlier. I'd had a conversation with Lily about it being Sierra's favorite place. I don't know; I just wanted to check she wasn't up there."

"Well, she sure won't be with you noisily creeping about."

"Yeah, well, this is all new to me, Dad. I didn't get army training, nor am I a CIA operative."

He chuckled. "Thankfully, there's no way out of that loft that doesn't result in broken bones or coming down those stairs."

"I shouldn't have left Taylor," I said.

"I put her in with your mom. That woman could scream loud enough for the town to hear. Now, are we going up or not?"

We climbed the stairs to the loft door. It was unlocked, as expected, and I pushed it open. Of course it was empty, and it surprised me to feel a little disappointed that Lily wasn't sitting on the bed.

"Someone's been up here," Dad said. He raised a cup that he'd found on the counter. "Still got a little coffee in it."

"Ranch hand?"

"Doubt it. I'll ask your mom when she cleaned it last, but I think it was after Lily left. Can't imagine she'd have left a dirty cup on the counter."

"If I could just find something, anything…" I stopped mid sentence. "Dad."

I'd walked into the bathroom. Written in red, possibly lipstick, across the mirror were words.

It's all lies, trust no one.

My eyes flicked between the words and my reflection. Sierra had said the same thing. I rested my hands on the sink and let my chin fall to my chest. I wanted to scream, to cry, I wanted to punch something to release the building frustration. If the intent was to fuck with my head, it was working.

"She's here," I said.

"Lily?" Dad said.

"Thomas checked, earlier, he would have seen this. I know one thing; I'm fucking tired of it all. All I wanted was the truth so I can put Sierra to rest, in here.” I tapped my chest as I spoke.

Dad placed his hand on my back, and that small gesture caused the tears that I was so desperately fighting to hold back spill down my cheeks.

“I can’t say I know how you’re feeling, because I don’t. I can see, in your face, how much you’re hurting and that pains me. What is the one thing that needs to be done to stop all this?”

I raised my head and looked at his reflection. There was knowing in his eyes.

“My daughter will only be safe when Father Samuel is dead,” I said.

His face didn’t display shock; it was something else. Resignation.

“I found a letter from Sierra, I didn’t tell you because, like that says, I can’t trust anyone, and I haven’t been able to talk to you alone. Father Samuel is Taylor’s grandfather, Sierra believes he’ll try and come for her.”

“Then we need to make sure that never happens,” he said quietly.

Without another word, we left the loft.

* * *

There seemed to be more people than usual around the ranch the following morning. Most I knew; some Dad introduced me to. All were big ranch hands or friends of my parents. Some had dogs. All had guns.

I was sitting on the porch when Thomas pulled up. “Fuck me, it looks like a scene out of Deliverance,” he said when he joined me.

“Just a little extra security. I thought of sending Mom and Taylor away, but I think they’re safer here,” Dad said as he left the house.

"I can't let Taylor out of my sight, Dad, not yet, anyway."

Taylor had been upset earlier that she couldn't go riding, that she couldn't walk over to the paddock on her own even. I wasn't sure how long it was fair to keep her confined to the house. But the thought of her and Mom being so far away was just out of the question.

"Zachary around?" Thomas asked.

"No, a meeting or something, he left early," I replied.

"Good. Okay, I have news. First, my man over at the state ran some checks; spoke to whomever. Midley and Romney, unless they are very secret, don't show up as FBI agents. It's a federal offence to masquerade as an FBI agent, but I call that in, we have a lot of questions to answer. Somehow, I think that's likely to happen at some point anyway."

"So who were they?" I asked.

"That is something I'm trying to find out. License plate wasn't registered but a vehicle, same make and model, was stolen from a rental company in Richford."

"Richford?" Dad asked.

"Richford is where Lily said she came from. Do you think that's where the cult is?"

"I do. Anna-Marie and Lou, remember those names? Well, there is a couple registered as living in Richford." He pulled out his pad and consulted his notes. "Anna-Marie and Louis Marsh, both deceased."

"Dead?"

"From old age and a little over five years ago."

"So, not the foster parents then?"

"Not officially, for sure. Also, no females, mid-forties to mid-fifties, brown hair, five feet tall, have been found dead in the past month."

"But Zachary told us he'd identified Sister Anna's body," I said.

Thomas shrugged his shoulders. “There was a female, right age, blonde, death by carbon monoxide poisoning, suicide it was recorded as. She left a note.”

“And your man over at the state police told you this?” Dad asked.

“Yes.”

“So where does this leave us now?” I asked.

“Lily lied, there’s no doubt about that. Her motive for lying might not be what we initially assumed though. I’ve been thinking about this. She, and the fake feds, drop those statements into a conversation way too regular for me not to assume that’s all they’re after. But I think for different reasons. The fake feds want them to ensure there is no evidence. I’m not sure who they are working for just yet. But Lily…I can’t make my mind up why she’d want them.”

“So it’s a race then. Lily wants them, fake feds want them, Zachary, even, wants them, but they don’t exist. Believe me, if they did, I’d be fucking handing them over to stop this nightmare.”

“Those statements, Gabriel, are only part of this sorry mess. Taylor is the other. I think we need to draw them out. Bring them to us, let them think you’ve found the statements,” Dad said.

“And have them all turning up here? No way, this isn’t the O.K. Corral and he’s no Wyatt Earp.” I pointed to Thomas.

“I think we should grab some of the food Mrs. M’s set out and think on this,” Thomas said, I was pleased he seemed to be in agreement with me.

We headed into the kitchen, and I pulled Taylor off her chair, she laughed as I sat and placed her on my lap. She broke off pieces of bacon and fed me. We tried to chat about mundane things, but the strain was started to show on everyone’s faces. Mom looked tired and I noticed her hands shook a little more than normal when she lifted her mug. I was barely holding it together; the pretense was the hardest thing. Not letting my daughter see anything was wrong was tiring. Measuring every response, checking every word before it was spoken, was exhausting.

One of the ranch hands walked into the kitchen, they generally had free rein of the house, and Mom spent most of her day making sure they were fed.

"All done," he said to Dad, who smiled and nodded. "Thanks, Jim, appreciate that."

"What's all done?" I asked when Jim had grabbed a plate of bacon and left.

"Traps, gotta big bad bear out in those woods. We don't want it near the foal do we now, little lady," Dad lied, tickling Taylor.

"We going to catch a bear?" she said, turning in my lap to look at me.

"Yep, and that's why you need to promise me you will not go for a walk on your own. Don't want you caught in the trap now, do we?" Dad said.

Thomas' phone started to vibrate on the table; he looked at it and rose. He answered his call as he walked back outside.

"Shit! Are you sure?" I heard him say.

I placed Taylor in my dad's arms and rose. I followed Thomas back out.

"I'm on my way. No, keep it all there," he said into his phone.

He disconnected the call and turned to me.

"A package arrived at the station, Gabe, from Sister Anna," he said.

"I'm coming with you," I said before rushing back to the kitchen.

"Baby girl, I need to go with Thomas, I'll be back shortly, okay? You do what Grandpa tells you now, you hear?" I gave her a kiss and left.

Thomas had the car started when I climbed into the passenger seat.

"What's in it?" I asked.

"I don't know, Pete opened it, it wasn't addressed to anyone in particular until he pulled out an envelope that had your name on the top. He didn't read any further."

We made the half-hour journey in half the time.

The station was no more than a room with a front desk and one cell at the back next to the kitchen and bathroom. Pete had the counter raised as we came in the front door.

"On your desk," he said.

Thomas sat in his chair and I sat opposite. He donned a pair of gloves and lifted the small envelope that had been left on top of a brown padded one, the same type that she'd given me just over a week ago. He opened it.

Thomas was silent as he read through; he then laid it on the desk and slid it toward me. "Don't touch it," he said.

"Pete, I need that fingerprint analysis back, pronto."

I read.

Gabriel

I was unsure of your address, although I have visited your house, once. But I do know you are friends with the sheriff. I've added this note to an envelope I was supposed to deliver.

I am so sorry that I agreed to be a part of something that has resulted in so much heartache. I need you to know, I had no idea what was going on, not at first. I had no idea about the abuse. My heart bleeds for those poor children.

We've all been duped; we've all been made to believe so many lies over such a long time. I can't live with myself, knowing I've played a part in it. I can't live with myself, knowing what I did may have resulted in your wife's death.

I can't be involved anymore; I'm scared for my safety, so very scared. I want to tell you everything, I want to tell you who is behind this, but I can't. And you'll understand why when you find out.

I hope you can find some peace, and I hope you'll find it in your heart to forgive me.

God bless, Gabriel.

Anna

While I was reading, Thomas had emptied the envelope; he looked up at me and smiled. "Statements," he said.

There were five folded pieces of paper, each one a document that gave a name and address, the details of the abuse they suffered, not only at the convent, but then when they were moved on. I read one; my stomach and heart would not allow me to read the rest. Tears formed in my eyes as I thought of those children, of my wife, and the suffering they endured. I even felt a pang of sympathy for Lily.

"We need to find Lily," I said.

"Look at the date, Gabriel." He showed me the front of the envelope. "Sent the same day as the blonde woman committed suicide."

He shuffled through some papers on his desk and pulled out one. "She was found ten miles out of Richford."

"So she was Sister Anna?" I asked.

"Possibly."

Thomas copied all the documents including the letter. He then made some calls.

I tried to listen to him, but it was at that moment the strength I had no idea I'd managed to contain, left me. It was coming to an end, finally. The realization that my beautiful wife had been subjected to those horrors yet had gone on to be a caring and loving individual hit me. She was a true survivor. She hadn't let her past destroy her. She hadn't let the knowledge that she held inside affect her ability to love.

I stood from the chair and without a word walked from the station. I heard Thomas calling me, but my wife was calling me more.

I walked to the cemetery. I sat at her grave and I wept one last time. I let out the anguish and despair I felt. I lay down next to her, not caring to acknowledge the glances of passing mourners, which, thankfully, were few.

A shadow fell over me and I looked up to see my brother. He sat beside me and placed his hand on my head. He mumbled a prayer.

"I saw you come in, I was praying," he said before I'd even asked how he knew I was there. I didn't believe him.

"I know it all, Zachary. I know every sordid detail now."

He nodded his head and I noticed the tears that formed in his eyes.

"And what will you do with that knowledge, Gabriel?" he asked.

"What my wife wanted. What should have been done in the very beginning. Those children need a voice, Zachary. They need their story to be told and they need justice."

"Those children are dead, how will this help them now? So many people are going to be devastated."

I blinked a few times, holding in my initial response.

"It will help stop this ever happening again. They didn't die in vain. So, what are the words, Zachary? Forgive me, Father, for I'm about to sin…"

I rose and without another word left him sitting on the grass on that bright summer's day. His prayer of absolution followed me. His words floated through the air but they hit the brick wall I had erected around myself. A wall that would take forever to dismantle.

Thomas was outside his office, I saw him look first one way, then the other, along the street. I guessed he was looking for me.

"Gabe, I'll take you back to the ranch now. We're going to have visitors over the next few hours. The whole case has been reopened, and I'd really like to sit down with Taylor. She was the only witness that day. I need to know if there is anything else she can remember."

I nodded. It wasn't what I wanted, I didn't want my child to relive that day, but it was important. I only hoped I'd be able to help her through it relatively unscathed, and if anyone had to talk to her, it had to be Thomas. Someone she loved.

I didn't tell Thomas of my plan, not that I had a detailed one, of course. I wouldn't put him in that position. He was a lawman through and through; it's all he ever wanted to be. He'd 'policed' the schoolyard, he studied for one purpose only, to be the local sheriff. I'd have thought he might leave for the state police, but he wanted nothing more than to look after the people where he'd grown up, he'd often told me.

He dropped me off at the entrance to the ranch with a promise to return later.

Mom had erected an inflatable pool in the front yard. Taylor and a couple of dogs were busy splashing about. I chuckled slightly and mentally corrected myself, hounds. They were bloodhounds, and I wondered if their owners were happy they were cooling off in a child's swimming pool.

"I'm learning to swim, Daddy," she said when she saw me.

"So you are, baby girl. Mommy would be so proud." I checked the level of water, pleased to see it just a few inches high.

I wanted to reintroduce Sierra into the conversation. It wasn't that I refused to talk about her to Taylor, I'd been cautious of provoking a nightmare.

Taylor splashed, the dogs leapt about, bringing mud and grass into the pool, and I sat beside my mom and watched her.

"Thomas wants to talk to her," I said.

"Is that wise?"

"Yes, we have more information, the case has been reopened, although I was led to believe it hadn't actually closed."

I sighed and rubbed my hand over my chin. The scratch of stubble reminded me that I needed to shave.

"When?"

"Later today, I guess."

Mom sighed and took a deep breath. I looked at her. Something about her had changed; there was a sense of resignation about her. Her body had relaxed a little, she wasn't held so stiff and tight. Like me, she could sense the end was close, I guessed.

"Gabriel, I'm worried about you. You've lost weight; you've got dark shadows under your eyes. You…You've changed, hardened. And before you say anything, you have good reason to. But you need to start taking care of yourself; otherwise you'll be no good for your daughter. She needs you, when all this is done; she's going to need you more. When she grows up and people start to talk, and she understands what they're saying, you need to be here for her. She's going to hear things that will upset her greatly."

"I'm not going anywhere," I said.

"Not physically, but mentally?"

I didn't answer immediately. I leaned forward and placed my elbows on my knees, my head in my hands.

"If I'd have known; if Sierra had been honest from day one, if her killer had been caught…"

"That's a lot of 'ifs,' none of which you can do anything about," she said.

"When this is all over, I might take Taylor on a road trip, go see a little of the coast."

She smiled at me, but I noticed that it didn't quite reach her eyes. She patted my thigh and stood.

"Taylor, how about we get you out of that mud pit and you can help me in the garden? I think I'll have you stand under the garden hose," she said.

Taylor stood and the bottom half of her was covered in mud. I laughed, there was no making my baby girl in to a lady, no matter how much anyone tried, and I loved her more for that.

I sat for a moment and looked out to the woods, I could see men wandering in and out of the trees, hear the occasional howl as a dog picked up the scent of something. I was thankful to those people but wondered just how long we'd be doing that. How much longer would we be confined to the house?

My phone vibrated in my pocket, I pulled it out to see I'd received a text message. I swiped the screen to see one word, 'Loft' from an unknown number.

"Loft?" I repeated.

I stood and stepped down from the porch, I hesitated. I returned to the house and took the stairs two at a time to the bedroom I'd been sharing with Taylor. I reached under the cushion of the chair and pulled out the revolver Dad had given me. Without alerting Mom or Taylor, I made my way to the loft. I sent a text to Dad not for one minute believing he'd receive it. He was fixing fences, and I doubted he'd thought to keep his phone on him. I copied the text to Thomas.

Do not, I repeat, do not go there. On my way. Was Thomas' reply.

Too late I typed.

I wasn't waiting. I hoped I knew who had sent that text. I wanted to get to her before she ran again.

I was halfway up the stairs in the barn when Dad appeared. I placed my fingers to my lips and indicated with my hand he should stay where he was. I pointed to the gun tucked in the waistband of my jeans, at my back, and covered with my t-shirt.

The loft door was ajar. It hadn't been the last time we'd visited. My heart started to pound in my chest. I stood to one side and gently pushed it open. After a minute of hearing nothing, I stepped into the room. It was empty; it was as we'd left it. I looked around, not sure what I was searching for.

And then I heard a ringing. I followed the sound to the bed, lifted the mattress and saw a black cell. I shouldn't have, but I picked it up. There was a missed call from an unknown number and a text message.

I need to see you. Flashed on the screen when I'd opened the text.

Lily? I replied.

I waited, hearing the footsteps of my father on the stairs, who clearly didn't have the level of patience I'd hoped for. He strode across the room and I showed him the phone. For some reason, despite knowing she wasn't in the loft, we didn't speak but communicated with hand gestures. The phone beeped.

Yes

Come to me. I know it all now. I can help you. I have the statements. I typed.

I showed it to Dad, who nodded, and then I pressed send. We stood in silence for a few minutes; there was no reply.

"Well, I guess we've put the wheels in motion, now to prepare. Come with me, Son," Dad said.

I followed him from the apartment, instead of heading to the house; he walked further into the barn. Toward the back were a couple of rooms, one used to house cattle feed, farm machinery, and the other was an office, neither had been used in years. It was the office door that Dad pushed open. A layer of dust covered every surface, and I stifled a cough as it was disturbed by our presence.

Dad walked to a cupboard, built in between the corner of the room. He opened the door and then crouched. I heard the scrape as he dragged a chest into the middle of the room.

From the level of dust covering the lid, it was clear that chest had not been opened in a long time; he wiped his arm across the top before reaching into his pocket and pulling out a bunch of keys. He unlocked it and before opening the lid, he looked up at me. There was something in his face that I hadn't seen in many years. Excitement. His eyes held a sparkle, his lips curled into a smile but one of mischief, not happiness. He slowly opened the lid.

"What the fuck!" I said. "Are you kidding me?"

He chuckled gently as he lifted one of the smaller items.

"That is a fucking grenade!" I said.

"Your powers of observation astound me sometimes, Son," he said.

"Why, what…?"

The chest resembled an army munitions store.

"So I fell for it, that millennium thing; thought I'd prepare."

"You're shitting me, right?"

"No, it was plausible. Computers go down, the world falls into chaos."

"Jesus, Dad. How fucking stable is that lot? They look old."

"They've sat here quite happily for sixteen years."

I shook my head. "Put it down, Dad, you'll fucking blow yourself up."

"I spent three years fighting a war, Gabriel, I think I know how to handle these."

“Dad, I don’t think we’re going to need to start shooting off bombs at people, okay?”

“You reckon? Son, sit down a minute.” He closed the lid of the chest and I sat beside him on the dusty floor.

“What do you think’s going to happen?” he asked.

“I’ll tell Lily I don’t have the statements, the police do. And if she goes to them, tells them what she knows, they’ll have to offer her some protection. Sister Anna says she can’t get further involved, maybe it’s all blown up beyond her expectations, but she’s fucked off. Thomas has the state and, I think, the FBI involved. Whatever I want, whatever justice I wanted to dish out, isn’t going to happen now. And let’s be fair, an abuser of children in prison is probably a far worse punishment than a bullet in the head.”

“Maybe he will go to prison, maybe not. Maybe at some point overnight they’ll come here. I want to be prepared.”

“Why is it always overnight?” I said with a chuckle, not that I found anything funny.

He raised his eyebrows at me. I stood, brushing the dust from my jeans. “You do what you’ve got to do, Dad. I appreciate your support,” I said, patting him on the shoulder.

I’d lied to my father. I’m sure I’d probably lied many times as a teenager. I had no doubt, like back then, he hadn’t believed me. Father Samuel would never make it to prison, I’d make sure of that.

Chapter Eighteen

Thomas arrived and looked about as good as I did.

“Beer?” I asked.

“No, official duty here. Tell me about the text,” he replied.

“Never stopped you before.”

“Never been in this position before. I’m not in control any more; I’m a mere servant of the Fuck-It-Up Bureau of Investigations. I don’t even have office space left.”

“So you called them in then?”

“I had to, this is beyond my capabilities and beyond the state’s. We have just too many factors to consider about who is actually involved in what. On one hand, we have the church, and on the other, we have the cult. They’re linked, for sure, but who killed Sierra, who killed those children, adults rather, I just don’t know anymore. But I have control over one thing. I persuaded them that I’d interview Taylor, and it had to be done here, in a place of comfort.”

“I wouldn’t have it any other way.”

“As I said, she’s not classed as a credible witness but she’s a little older, she may have forgotten what she originally said, or she might be able to tell us more.”

I nodded. “One thing, if she gets overly upset, no more, okay?”

I’d deliberated over whether to subject my daughter to questioning, no matter how gently that would be from Thomas. I’d thought of calling in the therapist to sit with her at the same time. But I’d pushed that thought from my mind because I didn't want to make it formal in any way. I didn't want for her to feel pressured to speak at all. Maybe I was about to do wrong, only time would tell.

"Now, stop delaying, what was that text about?" he asked.

I told him what I'd found and the messages that had been received and sent.

"Fuck's sake, Gabe. I told you to wait for me. I need that phone."

"Let's deal with Taylor first," I said. I then called for her.

I picked her up and sat her on my lap. "Baby girl, we need to talk about some things that might make you sad. We need to talk about Mommy. Do you think you can do that with Thomas?"

She nodded her head. Thomas laid his phone on the small table.

"You remember that you told me the brown-haired woman had visited Mommy and made her upset?" he asked. She nodded again.

"Did they shout, is that why Mommy was upset?" he asked.

"No, I don't think so."

"Did they hug?"

"Yes."

"When the man came to the house, can you remember what color his clothes were?"

She shrugged her shoulders at first. "Were they like Daddy's jeans?" I asked.

"No."

"Were they like Daddy's t-shirt?" Thomas asked. She looked at me, and then shook her head.

Thomas glanced at me. I wore a black t-shirt.

"Like your pants," she whispered.

Thomas was wearing blue, a dark blue uniform.

“Are you sure, baby girl?” I asked. She nodded her head.

“Did he have a blue shirt on, Princess? One like mine?” Thomas asked.

At her nickname, the one Thomas used often; she smiled. She nodded again.

“Did he have one of these?” he asked. At that point my heart started to hammer in my chest. He’d pointed to his badge, pinned to his chest.

She reached out and ran her fingers over it. “Not on his heart, but he had one,” she said.

I looked over her head at Thomas.

“What color was his hair?” Thomas asked.

Again, she shrugged her shoulders. “Can we see Lily today?” she asked, looking at me.

“Lily?”

“The foal, can we see the foal today?” Despite the question and the slight bounce of excitement on my lap, her eyes had begun to fill with tears.

“Absolutely. How about you grab something to eat with Grandma, and when you’re done, we’ll take a walk,” I said. She climbed from my lap.

“Fuck!” I said once she was out of earshot. “All this time I thought it was a priest, because of the clothing.”

He picked up his phone and fiddled with it. “I recorded what she said, I take it I have your permission for that?”

I nodded. “It answers why he was able to just walk into my house. Sierra would never have a doubt about inviting a cop in.”

“I feel like we’re back to the beginning, which I guess isn’t a bad idea. But I’m totally out of my depth here,” he said.

“We all are, Thomas, we all are.”

“So, the phone,” he held out his hand. “I have to take it in.”

I stared at him. “Unless you tell me there is no phone, of course, and it was all a mistake.”

“It was all a mistake,” I said.

“Fair enough. I have to get back in town, but I’ll be back later, okay?”

He stood and with just a sigh and nod of his head, he made his way over to his car and left. I watched his tires kick up dust and stones as he drove down the drive.

I sat and Dad joined me. We just waited, without having any idea how they’d come, who would come, only knowing that someone would.

Chapter Nineteen

The rest of the day passed uneventfully. Taylor and I took a walk; the warm steel of the revolver against my skin gave a little comfort. My nerves were jangling; waiting wasn't something I was particularly good at. Taylor chatted, but it was clear she was on edge. I hoped my anxiety wasn't transferring to her.

It was hard to concentrate on her chatter while constantly scanning for movement. Dad's friends had set up a rotation to patrol the perimeter, but I wasn't sure how long they'd be willing to do that. It was taking them away from their daily lives, their families, and jobs.

I started to become frustrated. When all you can do is wait, time ticks by slower than ever.

Taylor and I arrived back at the house, as we walked in I could hear the sound of a hammer, then a drill. I followed the noise upstairs, while Taylor grumbled to Mom about being bored.

Dad was fixing some locks to the inside of Taylor's bedroom door.

"Thought we'd make a safe room," he said.

"Shouldn't that be lined with concrete, blast and bullet proof, with an iron door?"

"Stop with your attitude, it's the best we can do in a wooden house. Of course, it won't stop anyone getting in, if they really wanted to, but it will sure delay them."

"I'm sorry, I'm on fucking edge here. I don't know how much longer I'm going to be able to hang on."

"I know, Son, I know. Now, get to work. I want that window boarded up."

Taylor had two windows in her bedroom. Leaning against the wall under one was an iron plate. Six holes were drilled along the sides; they matched six holes in the window frame. Dad had been busy.

I fixed it to the inside of her window and chuckled.

"I can't believe you're one of those Doomsday Preppers."

He huffed as he continued to add additional bolts to the inside of her door.

"I've told your mom, if anything happens, she has to get in here and bolt this door."

"Is she scared?"

"Yep, and that's a good thing. Keeps us all on our toes if we're scared."

"Why are we blocking just one window?"

"Don't need to let everyone know there's something in this room being protected, now, do we?"

"How the fuck do you know all this shit?"

He laid down his drill and hammer, and it was only when he closed the door to check the bolts, I noticed he'd reinforced the inside with more wood.

"When your ass deep in shit, mud, blood, and body parts, and scared out of your wits knowing that if you're caught, you hope your heart gives out real quick. When you know the torture you're about to endure will last for hours, you learn a lot about survival."

That was the most Dad had ever spoken about his time at war.

"What was it like?"

"I've seen, and done things, that I'll never forget and have me on a path straight to hell, Son. There's no redemption for me. I've killed, maimed, I've saved, and I lost my mind for a while."

"Is that why you packed up and moved here?"

Mom had told me once that Dad was a city man, loved the buzz and the noise.

"Yes, I needed the quiet, the peace."

"And now you've got all this," I said.

He smiled and shrugged his shoulders. For a seventy-five-year-old, he was still fit and agile. He was intelligent; always able to solve a problem, yet to look at him, in his jeans and checkered shirt, you'd think he was a simple, country man. He was a man who harbored many secrets, of that I was sure.

"You know what we did back then? We killed our own men. Injured men that we knew we couldn't get to safety, killing them was kinder than leaving them behind. That can do something to a man's mind."

"I bet," I said, not knowing what the appropriate response was.

"So, bring on the fake feds, the cult, and whoever, I got myself a little pent up aggression to release." He chuckled and resumed his renovation.

"I know how to use my fists, but I don't know if I really could kill someone," I said.

"You could, anyone could if their life depended on it. You know, I won a shit ton of money on you once."

"You what?"

"Yeah, one of your fights. You didn't know I was there, of course, best thing I ever saw."

Any further conversation was halted by the sound of a drill as he fixed the last bolt.

Thomas hadn't returned by the time Mom, Dad, Taylor, and I sat for dinner. Neither had Zachary.

"Where's Zach?" I asked.

"Working, saving souls," Dad said, earning him a slap to the arm from Mom.

"I guess he'll have to return home soon," I said.

"Maybe, he's doing his rounds," Mom answered.

"Rounds?"

"He has to visit the parish in his care," she said.

"Bit late to be doing that, isn't it?"

She shrugged her shoulders as she plated some food for Taylor. Mom's earlier demeanor had changed, again. Tension flowed from her. Her movements, her voice even, seemed forced, stilted. We kept up the pretense that everything was okay throughout dinner.

I picked Taylor up and despite her protests, carried her up to her bedroom. She sulked as I pulled her t-shirt over her head. She kicked her shorts across the room. I sensed a tantrum on its way.

"Teeth," I said as she reached for her PJ's. She stomped to the bathroom.

I would have chuckled had I not been stressed out. I followed her and leaned against the bathroom door. Normally she would try to hum a song or chat, but she kept her back to me, throwing her toothbrush in the sink when she was done.

"Rinse that, then put it in the mug," I said, sternly.

Tears brimmed in her eyes but she jutted her chin out in defiance. When she'd walked back in to the bedroom, I tried to help her climb into her PJ's, but she was in a mood. She slapped my hands away and grunted her displeasure.

"Taylor, stop it. Tell me what's bugging you," I said.

"I want to go home."

"We can't just yet. Grandpa and Grandma will be upset, you don't want to upset them do you?" I hated to result to blackmail but I was too tired for tantrums.

Taylor climbed onto the bed, angrily pulling the covers over her and turning her back to me.

"Baby girl, tell me what's wrong. Why do you want to go home?"

"Because I do."

I sighed. "Tomorrow, okay?" Hoping that when 'tomorrow' came she'd have forgotten. "Do you want me to read to you?"

"No."

"No story?" She'd never gone to bed without either a conversation or a story.

She shook her head.

"Are you sad?" I asked.

She nodded.

"Want to tell me what you're sad about?"

"I miss Mommy."

In the beginning, she had begged for her mommy constantly, and as time had gone on it seemed to be something she said when upset.

"So do I, baby girl. Want a hug?" I sat on the bed beside her.

"No. I don't want you, I want Mommy."

I'd had the, 'I hate you.' I'd smiled at the, 'I don't like you,' but those words cut through me. They wouldn't have normally and I tried not to react.

"Okay, how about I just sit over here for a while." I sat on the edge of the second bed.

I turned off the main light, leaving just the subtle glow of a wall light and sat. Taylor didn't speak but I could hear her sigh every now and again. I'd learned over the past months, sometimes she needed some space, time out. Usually five minutes and she'd be climbing in my lap and putting her arms around my neck. Ten minutes passed and still she lay in silence. It took an hour before she finally fell asleep.

I could hear the call of a dog every now and again, I could imagine the men patrolling when a thought hit me. How would Lily get to me if we were under such guard?

That thought niggled me so much that I rose and quietly crept from Taylor's room. I stood on the porch and lit a cigarette. A light glowed above me; I was putting myself on show. All I hoped was, it was to Lily and not some nutcase with a gun. But then, I reasoned, I wasn't so good to them dead, they'd never know where the statements were. The thought gave me a little comfort, and I settled into a chair beside the front door.

Sam walked past and nodded. I couldn't recall a time the man had ever spoken, maybe he was incapable of it. From what little I knew of him, he'd served alongside my dad, got fucked up, and became a drunk until Dad had rescued him. He'd been a ranch hand for as long as I could remember. Mom had offered him the loft but he'd chosen to sleep in the barn, among the horses. Even in the depths of winter, he'd be found huddled in the hay. During times when he wasn't really required, he'd disappear, only to reappear without a word as if he'd been called upon telepathically.

The night air was humid; my t-shirt was stuck to my back. I pulled it over my head and hung it across the railing of the porch. We were back to waiting.

A hand gently placed on my arm sent a cold shiver over my body. I jolted awake, not realizing I had fallen asleep on the porch.

"Gabriel," I heard.

I blinked a few times before her face came into focus; she had crouched down beside me.

"Lily, where the fuck have you been?"

"Here, there."

She leaned back on her heels. When I looked at her, she looked broken. Her hair was a tangled mess; dark circles framed her eyes, they displayed such sadness. Her cheeks were blotchy, as if they'd absorbed so many tears, and her lips slightly chapped.

"Here?"

"Plain sight, remember?" she said. Her voice broke as she caught a sob in her throat.

"I don't understand."

"I told you, Gabriel, I've been on the run for long time. I know how to hide."

"I know it all," I said.

She gave me a small smile. "That I doubt, but hopefully you know enough."

"Why did you run?"

"Because I didn't want to get close to you, and I was. I've lied, I've deceived you, and I've told you the truth."

"That makes fuck all sense."

"Nothing makes sense in my life. It never has."

"Enough with the cryptic shit, okay? I'm done with that. I'm tired and I just want this all over."

She sighed. "It will never be over, Gabriel."

"It will, if there is no more Father Samuel."

"There will just be another, then another. You can't rid the world of them all."

"So what's the answer, huh? Live like you do? Lie, cheat, steal."

She winced at my words. “I haven’t stolen anything.”

“My gun. Give it back.”

“I didn’t take your gun.” She looked around, nervously.

“Brought them with you, have you?”

“Who?”

“The fake feds, your cult friends maybe.”

She blinked a few times, shook her head slightly as if not understanding.

“I don’t know what you mean.”

“Sure you do, everything about you is so fucked up. You tell me you’re telling the truth, and then admit to lies. Like my wife, I have no fucking idea who you are.”

She closed her eyes and lowered her head.

“Her name was Savannah, and what you know of her, the time you got with her, that was real. You’re the only person who got the real, the perfect.”

“And it’s all tarnished, Lily. Thanks to you and Sister Anna, it’s all tarnished.”

Maybe it was tiredness, maybe it was all the waiting for something to happen, for someone to come, but a bubble of anguish rose up in me so fast, I couldn’t stop it. A tear rolled down my cheek. She reached forward and brushed it away and I let her. I let her touch me. I let that knot in my stomach form, and I let my cock twitch in my pants. Why I was so fucking desperate, I had no idea. I disliked her; I wanted her.

I stood and grabbed her wrist, not dragging her to her feet but making it clear she was to follow me without argument. I led her to the barn; the only place I knew was empty of the patrols.

The moon filtered through the clear plastic panels in the roof, illuminating the walkway between stables and pens. I kept on walking until I came to the furthest end, to where the neatly stacked bales of hay were, to where the unlocked door of my dad's office was, and to where I knew I could access a weapon if I had to.

"I'm not a bad person, Gabriel," she whispered.

"But you came here to lie, to deceive me."

"Yes, and for good reason."

"You want the statements, maybe you want to bargain with them. Why, what are you hiding?"

I might as well have just shot her; such was her reaction. She clutched herself and folded slightly at the waist. A sob left her lips, yet she tried so hard to contain the emotion. She bit down on her lip, while tears flowed down her cheeks.

"What lengths would you go to, to protect your child?" she whispered. I froze at her words.

"I'd kill, man or woman, Lily, I'd kill." I took a step toward her.

"I want the statements, Gabriel, so I can do exactly what you've just said, bargain with them. If there's no evidence, then there's no need to continue. We can all go back to normal. I have a child, like you, that needs protecting."

"You have a child?"

"Yes, a beautiful boy, his name is Benedict."

"And where is this Benedict?"

"Not far, it's why I took your dad's truck, I needed to see him."

"Who is his father?"

She didn't answer me at first. "Father Samuel is an old man, Gabriel, not capable of fathering a child now. But he has sons, many sons, who continue with his quest."

Then it hit me. I recalled the words that had taken me by surprise.

Could you have impregnated her?

Impregnated. It was such a strange word to use; yet I hadn't thought that at the time. It was also a word Lily had used. It was clinical, as if describing a laboratory experiment.

"Midley," I said.

Her reaction told me all I needed to know. She screwed her eyes shut as if she was disgusted.

"Richard Midley. Father of my child, child of my father," she whispered.

I reached out, I wasn't conscious of where I was placing my hand, but it tightened around her throat. She made no attempt to stop me.

Words flowed through my head. Inbreeding; incest; abuse.

"When I'm dead, will you promise me one thing? Make sure my child doesn't end up with him."

When, not if, when. Her eyes were emotionless; she might as well already be dead. I guess, inside, she already was.

She placed one hand on the tattoo on my chest and for a moment we were silent.

"I fucking hate you," I said, just before my mouth crashed down on hers.

I hated her for making me want her; I hated her for making me hate her. I hated her for making me feel so sorry for her that my heart ached.

Our teeth clashed, she bit my lip before allowing my tongue access. She moaned, louder as my hand tightened a little around her throat.

"You love that, don't you," I mumbled, breaking away.

"Pain is all I can feel," she said.

I walked her backwards, skirting the hay bales until we were in the shadows and she was against the wall. I held her there as I fumbled with her jeans, popping the button, and lowering the zipper.

She used her free hand to help me lower them. I tore the skimpy panties from her body as she stepped out of her jeans. I slapped her hand away when she went to raise her t-shirt. I didn't give a shit about her being naked; I wanted one part of her body only.

"I fucking hate you for being alive and my wife isn't," I mumbled into her neck, as my tongue trailed a path to her ear.

"I fucking hate you for looking and sounding like her," I said, as I bit down on her earlobe and was rewarded with a moan of pleasure.

I undid my jeans, letting them fall, then cupped my hand under her ass and lifted her. She wrapped her legs around my waist, tilted her hips to give me access, and with just a little guidance, I pushed into her. Her pussy was wet, warm, and her scent had me spiraling. I fucked her hard. Whatever spell she weaved, I was caught, again.

She threw her head back, hitting the wooden wall behind her. I sunk my teeth into her shoulder to stifle a growl that rumbled from my chest. I wasn't sure where the intensity came from; where the adrenalin that flooded my body had come from. All I knew was I needed to be buried deep inside her, and I wanted to hear her call out my name as she came.

My legs began to shake; my stomach knotted as the desire to come intensified. I released my grip on her neck and slid my hand up her cheek, into her hair. I gripped and she drew in a sharp breath. Her legs tightened around my waist, letting me know she was close. My name echoed around the dusty barn as her body shook and she came. I gave in to my release.

I was panting hard, trying to drag enough air into my lungs to quell the nausea born of guilt that bubbled in my stomach. I shouldn't want her; I didn't even like her. I took a step back and she lowered her legs. Without a word I pulled up my jeans. I reached down to where hers were, picked them up, and handed them to her.

"Get dressed," I said.

She went to speak and I held up my hand, I didn't want to hear her voice. Was I being fair? No. But then nothing that had happened the past months had been fair.

"If you don't have the statements, Lily, what's the next best thing?"

"I…I don't understand."

"Yes, you do. Ultimately, what, or who, does Father Samuel want?"

I watched her swallow hard before running her tongue over her lower lip and biting down.

"He won't be caught, he'd kill himself before then. He's mad, Gabriel. He believes he has his seat next to God; no man can take that away from him. But it isn't him we're all running from." She chuckled bitterly.

I strode toward her so fast that she stumbled backwards. "Then who? Who the fuck are you running from?"

"His sons, all of them." She stared me down.

"I give them the statements and my child has a chance to live," she added.

"Where's your child?" I asked.

"Safe, for now. Hidden, but I don't know for how long."

"So all this was just to get the statements."

"Tell me what to do, Gabriel. What choice do I have? That might have been my intent in the beginning, but not now."

"What changed?"

"I met you. I had a taste of normal. Even if it was all in my head, all one-sided. For once in my life I had family. I could pretend you cared. Don't tell me you don't feel anything for me, you couldn't make love to me if you didn't."

I took a step closer to her. "I didn't make love to you, I fucked you, that's all. And that was for my pleasure only. Don't think for one moment there was anything more in that."

Tears rolled down her cheeks. "Now look me in the eye and say that," she said.

I couldn't.

"Where's your child, Lily? How safe is he?"

"I bring you back to your words, if you want to hide, hide in plain sight."

"The person who has him, are they part of your fucking cult?"

"No, someone I met after, when I worked on the farm. A wonderful woman who I'd trust with my life, who I trust with my son."

"Tsk, Tsk," I heard. I spun on my heels at the same time as Lily gasped.

A figure stood just outside the glow of the moonlight. A hooded figure.

I glanced at Lily. No matter how many lies she'd told me, the fear on her face and the wet patch that spread down her jeans, between her thighs, could not mask the level of fear she felt.

"Here, child," he said.

I extended my arm as she took a step forward and held her back.

I couldn't make out his face. I tried to place the voice; there was something very familiar about it.

"You did as you were asked, you will be rewarded," he said.

"What did she do?" I asked.

"She gave me access to your house, Gabriel. She took your wife's key and I made a copy."

"So who smashed my window?"

"She did, I guess she enjoyed being in your house, wanted a way to get in and out as she pleased."

I turned to Lily, "Why…"

I hadn't finished my sentence before I saw another enter the barn, a hooded man carrying my child. I ran toward him, I was brought to an abrupt halt at the sight of a gun raised from the man immediately in front of me, my gun.

Fear caused my heart to race as I looked at the second man, holding a sleeping Taylor in his arms, and who had stepped into the light so I could clearly see him.

"What have you done?" I whispered.

"I'm sorry, Gabriel, but this is the only way," my brother replied.

Lily fell to her knees, her sobs echoed around the barn. She whispered words I couldn't decipher. Was she crying from relief or fear?

"No, Zach, please, no. Not my daughter," I said.

"I will give you one chance. Come to me," the man said.

I didn't try to protect her that time, I let her stand and slowly make her way forward. I heard her kneel at his feet, but all the while I kept my eyes on my brother as he walked toward us.

"What have you done to her? Why is she still asleep?" I asked.

"She was given something to keep her calm," the man said.

I shook my head. "What can I give you? I have the statements, take them but leave me my daughter."

He laughed. "Do you think we care about those statements?"

"My wife was killed for them. So I think you do care about them."

"There are far more important things than five pieces of paper, five pieces of fake paper, full of lies."

"I know what you want. Please let Taylor go." I heard. Lily had spoken.

He swiped his hand, catching the side of her face and rocking her sideways.

"You're diseased now. You let him touch you! You're not pure; we have no need for you now. It's just about protecting the faith, Rachiel. You know that." He had used her real name.

Things happened so fast it took my brain a moment to register. I heard a noise, the bang of a door being opened so fast it bashed against a wall. I heard the rush of feet and then a scream. Lily jumped to her feet and threw herself forward and then I heard a gunshot.

I ran forward, lowered my shoulder and dove into the man. We fell backwards and rolled across the dusty ground. He smashed the gun into my face and I felt my nose break, hot blood ran down and covered my lips. I aimed as many punches to any part of his body as I could. Eventually he lay still. I scrambled to my feet to see Sam standing, holding a baseball bat, having already swung it into the back of my brother's legs. Zachary was on his knees, still holding Taylor to his chest.

The scrape of a body against the ground alerted me to the fact the hooded man was still conscious. I turned on my knees and punched and punched, until his face was a bloodied mess, until he was still again. I didn't let up until I felt someone grab my shoulders. I could hear talking and I could smell blood. Horses whinnied, stomped, scared by the activities.

"Gabe," Sam said. Somewhere in my brain it registered that was the first word he'd ever said.

I paused my assault; my breathing was ragged as I tried to drag air into my lungs. I fell back onto my heels as Sam stepped forward. I watched him pick up the gun where it had fallen, and as if in slow motion, he aimed it at the man's forehead and pulled the trigger. The sound echoed and horses panicked, their hooves kicked the wood of their stalls.

"Taylor," I said.

I scrambled on all fours to where she lay, Zachary had fallen forward and his body partially covered hers. I dragged her from him. His mouth opened and closed as if he was trying to speak but was unable to. His eyes were wide with shock as he refused to give in to the pain, or fear at what he'd witnessed.

"Taylor," I said, louder that time, I shook her gently.

She murmured and it was only then that I let the tears fall.

I heard a gentle cough and turned my head, following the sound. Lily lay face down but had extended an arm, her fingers curled as if clawing the ground. Still holding Taylor I crawled toward her. With one hand I turned her over.

"Oh, God." I said.

She was covered in blood, she held one hand over her chest but it flowed from between her fingers. Sam pulled Taylor from my arms and I let him. I trusted him.

I held my hand over Lily's, pushing down hard on the wound. I couldn't stop the blood; I couldn't stop her bleeding out. I should have been running out of there, with my daughter in my arms, and left Sam to deal with her, but I was fucked. I couldn't think straight, and I wasn't sure that I could leave her.

She looked at me, tears rolled down her cheeks.

"Hold on, okay, just fucking hold on," I said.

"Call the paramedics!" I shouted. It was at that point that I saw my dad run into the barn.

Dad stopped beside me and he knelt. "Call someone," I said.

"They're on their way, Gabe."

"Hang on, Lily, hang on," I whispered over and over.

She opened her mouth; I leaned down closer to hear.

"I just...wanted...perfect," she managed to say.

"I know, baby, I know."

Dad took the gun from Sam. I watched as he wiped it clean on his shirt, then wrapped his hand around the grip, and placed his finger on the trigger. He nodded to Sam, who handed him Taylor; Sam simply nodded back before leaving the barn.

Zachary was mumbling; tears ran down his cheeks as he slid to the ground.

The barn was soon full of people. Lights were turned on and it was only then that I saw the hooded man. I looked at him. Although his face was bloodied, it oozed from the bullet wound, it had smeared from the broken nose and the split lips, I recognised Syd immediately.

Things fell into place. He had been tasked with protecting me, sitting outside my house, yet we'd had intruders.

"Gabriel," my brother called out my name.

He'd crawled forward, using his hands to drag himself, but I refused to look over at him. Instead, I watched Lily try to take a breath. Blood foamed at her mouth, and as she coughed, it splattered over my face. I raised her body to mine and cradled her. I felt the last amount of her hot blood run down my chest, and then she died in my arms.

"I'm sorry, I'm so sorry," I whispered before lowering her to the ground.

"Get Taylor out of here," I said to my dad as I rose.

"Gabe, don't..." He didn't finish his sentence; he simply nodded.

I took the steps required toward Zachary, the brother that had betrayed me. I grabbed a fistful of his hair and raised his head. I dragged him to his knees. While I held him, while he raised his hands to defend himself and tried to speak, I punched him. His nose broke, his blood splattered over my hands, hands covered with Lily's blood. I punched again and again. The crunch as his cheekbone shattered was a satisfying sound, as were his screams of pain.

Blue flashing lights lit up the outside; cars screeched to a halt, the noise of feet running and voices shouting didn't distract me from wanting to kill my own flesh and blood.

"Gabriel!" It was my mother's scream that stopped me tightening my hold on his throat.

I looked up at her and the anguish on her face froze me. I looked down at Zachary, who had long since stopped trying to defend himself. I let go of his hair and he slumped forward, rolling to his back with a groan.

Thomas ran into the barn, nearly knocking my mother sideways. He skidded to a halt at the sight in front of him.

"Fucking hell," he said when he saw Syd, and then he saw Lily.

"Fucking hell," he said again, when he looked at me.

I was covered in blood; it ran down my chest and coated my arms. It dripped from my hands. I had no idea whose it was: Lily's, Syd's, or my brother's. I fell to my knees as exhaustion took over and I closed my eyes.

I heard noises, I heard sobbing. I was incapable of moving. I had failed and I knew it. I hadn't kept Lily safe, I hadn't rid the world of Father Samuel, more importantly, I hadn't been able to keep my daughter safe.

"Gabe," I heard and opened my eyes to see Thomas crouch in front of me.

Behind him, Mom had Taylor in her arms; my father has his arm around them both. I ached to hold her in mine, but I wouldn't tarnish her with the blood I was coated in.

"I failed her," I whispered.

"Who?"

"Sierra, I failed her."

Chapter Twenty

The following day I sat beside Taylor in the hospital. She griped and moaned, wanting to go home. She had been mildly sedated, and in one way, I was thankful of that. The thought that she could have witnessed the carnage haunted me. The doctors wanted her kept until they were completely sure her little body was drug free, she hated it.

"You're going home in an hour or so," I said after the eighth time of being asked what time we were leaving. "We just need some paperwork."

"Are we going home or going to Grandma's?" she asked.

"Home, baby girl. I think Grandma has had enough excitement for the moment."

The truth of the matter was, I couldn't face her. I'd disfigured her son. I'd wanted to cut off his air supply, smiled as he struggled for breath, and it angered me that it had been her presence that had stopped me. Not that that was her fault. It was irrational, I knew, and I held no malice toward my mom, I just couldn't face her. She had been distraught, so Dad had told me; she had been confined to her bed and had the doctor visiting her regularly. But she hadn't been to see Taylor, she hadn't enquired after me, and that hurt.

"Grandpa!" Taylor shouted as she saw a figure through the window in her door.

It opened and he stepped in. "Hello there, little lady. Are you ready to go home?"

She jumped from the bed and ran to him.

"We're waiting on paperwork," I said.

"Have it here," he waved a small envelope.

It was as I saw Thomas standing at the open door that I realized my dad was a little on edge. He picked Taylor up in his arms.

"Little lady, your dad has to speak to some people, about why you got sick, okay? So you're coming home with me, just for a little while."

"Whoa, no she isn't." My daughter was not being taken away from me under any circumstances.

"Gabriel, the FBI is here," Thomas said as he stepped into the room.

"Then they can follow me to my house and they can talk to me there."

I tried to keep my voice calm but it had angered me that both Thomas and my dad hadn't forewarned me, they'd brought it to my daughter's hospital room.

"They don't work that way," Thomas said. He looked apologetic and I guessed it was out of his control.

"You're not taking her to the ranch. You take her home, okay?"

"Of course, we'll see you later," he said.

"Baby girl, I will see you in a couple of hours. Don't be wearing your grandpa out, you be good, okay?"

Although she nodded, there was uncertainty in her eyes. I kissed her forehead as they walked away.

"I'm sorry, I kept them away from you for as long as possible, but you know the drill, they need to interview you."

I picked up the bag of Taylor's clothes Dad hadn't taken and followed him from the room. I thanked the nurses at the station as I passed, then climbed into his car, parked out front.

"There are some things you need to know. Your dad confessed to shooting Syd," Thomas said. "I'm not sure I believe him, but I'm not asking any questions right now."

I nodded as I remembered seeing my dad take the gun from Sam's hand.

"How is my mom?" I asked.

"She's a broken woman right now. I guess she can't come to terms with what happened. The other thing you need to know. Zachary is protesting his innocence."

"How the fuck can he do that? He walked in to that barn holding Taylor."

"He says he got to Taylor after she'd been sedated. He says, if he had her, they couldn't get to her."

"That's fucking bullshit. Who sedated her then? And where was Mom?"

He shrugged his shoulders. "That's what we are trying to determine."

"Tell me you don't believe him?"

He sighed before he answered. "It doesn't matter if I believe him or not, if they do, he's a free man."

"Fuck! I know what I saw, Thomas."

"You saw him walk in with Taylor, Gabe, nothing more," he answered quietly.

Flashbacks, snippets of conversations flooded my mind but they were jumbled. I knew I needed to remember something, but I just couldn't bring whatever it was that niggled me to the front of my mind.

We fell silent as we continued our journey. Had I got it wrong, again? I saw Zachary walk in that barn with Taylor in his arms, that can't be disputed. I heard him say something and I struggled to remember it. The problem I had, the only people there at that moment were either dead or, as was the case of Sam, missing.

We pulled up at the station and sat for a moment. I wasn't ready to be interviewed. I couldn't piece it all in order and I worried for my daughter. I trusted my dad to keep her safe, but I didn't like the fact she wasn't with me.

"Am I going to be charged with something?" I asked.

"Unless Zachary presses charges, then no, I don't think so."

"You don't think so?"

"Gabe, this is all one big fucking mess that I have little control over. I've done all I can to give you some breathing time, but you're a key witness. We have two dead people, one a deputy, a fucking cult member, a beaten up bishop, and a whole load of statements that appear to be fake."

"Fake?"

"Well, maybe not all of them. One of the victims died in a car crash."

"That doesn't mean he wasn't killed."

"No, but it's just a load of circumstantial evidence."

I opened the car door and walked into the station. Pete stood behind the counter, and instead of his usual top button undone, his normal high five greeting, and offer of a coffee, he was in full uniform and stiff as a board. He didn't immediately raise the counter end so I could enter. Instead he turned to a suited man and spoke quietly.

Suited man came forward with a smile. "Gabriel, we've been expecting you, thank you for coming in voluntarily."

I was shown to the back of the room and offered a coffee and to sit.

"It's not ideal, unfortunately, but it's the only place we have to work," he said, gesturing with his hand.

"And you are?" I was on edge, bearing in mind my last experience with the FBI.

He chuckled, as he did a second suit walked in with Thomas. He scowled over to me. I wanted to laugh. So, bad cop, good cop, did they really teach that at the academy?

“My name’s Special Agent Curtis, but you can call me Mich. There’s no need for formalities. This isn’t a formal interview, yet.”

“And you have proof you are who you say you are?”

He fumbled in his jacket and pulled out a black leather wallet, he opened it and laid it on the table, sliding it across to me. It held his credentials and I inwardly cursed at falling for a business card from fake fed. However, I pulled my phone from my pocket and angled the camera at it, I looked at him before I clicked.

“Go ahead, always prudent to check, Gabriel,” he said.

I ignored the dig and took a photograph. I wanted something I could use to verify if I needed to.

While I took a sip of the coffee Pete had placed in front of me, he undid his suit button and slid off his jacket.

“Another thing, can I see that gun?”

He frowned slightly. “Humor me,” I said.

Mich retrieved it from the holster at his side; he released the clip before laying it on the table. I didn’t touch it but leaned forward to look. On the barrel was a small word, Glock. Satisfied, I leaned back in my chair.

“Care to tell me what that was all about?” he asked as he holstered it.

“My dad spotted the fake feds, he said the gun he had wasn’t a Glock and a Glock is standard issue.”

“Clever man, your dad,” he said with a smile. “So, let’s get down to business, huh?”

He opened a folder and whether it was a normal tactic or not, he spread the photographs of Lily and Syd over the desk. He shuffled his papers, taking his time before he settled into his interview. I guessed that was so I focused on the dead.

“Tell me what happened?” he asked without looking up.

“Since my wife was killed? Or that night?”

“Just that night, Gabriel,” he answered.

Despite my past days on the fight circuit, despite my odd run-ins with the police, I’d never been interviewed before. I was cautious as I recounted that evening’s events. I omitted fucking Lily of course.

I stumbled as I tried to put it all in order, as I tried to recall the exact words spoken by everyone.

“Everything happened so fast, and when Zachary came in, my focus was on Taylor. He held her in his arms,” I said, hoping that would explain some of my confusion.

“Let’s get to Zachary.” He consulted his notes. “Broken nose, fractures to the right cheek and eye socket. Severe bruising to the back of the knees, most likely hit from behind…” He paused and looked at me, clearly letting me know that he knew there was someone else in that barn. “That’s some punch you have there.”

“He’s involved, I know it. Why would he have my daughter?”

“He said that he was looking for you, he had information. He heard a commotion and thought it safer to keep hold of your daughter.”

“No way, absolutely no way. My mom knew what to do; the barn isn’t close enough to the house for him to hear a conversation because that’s all that was going on when he walked in. He has to be involved.”

“He is involved, just not in the way you believe him to be.”

“What the fuck does that mean?” I was getting annoyed, both with myself, and Mich.

“I’m not at liberty to say at the moment, as I said, this isn’t a formal interview.”

"Don't bullshit me, my head is fucked up enough." The minute the words left my mouth I knew I'd made a mistake.

"And therein lies the problem, Gabriel," he said, quietly.

"That's not what I meant. My wife was killed by Syd, you believe that, right?"

He stared at me. "Your wife was killed by an unknown assailant. There is nothing to place Syd at your house that day. Your daughter is too young to be a credible witness and one who has changed what she remembers."

"But we had intruders, Thomas can verify that, and Syd was sitting outside, in a patrol car."

"Awake? Asleep? It's odd, I grant you that, but it's not evidence enough."

He sighed and leaned forward to gather the photographs and papers, which he placed back in his folder. He reached into his jacket pocket to retrieve a pack of cigarettes, shaking one loose before offering me the pack.

"Look, Gabriel, it doesn't take a fucking genius to figure things out, but what will hold up in court is a whole different ball game to what we have here. Was Syd your wife's murderer? Probably. And at the end of the day, we have two witnesses that saw him kill the woman. Your father confesses to wrestling the gun from him…" He paused and raised his eyebrows at me.

"Then shooting him. I'm not even going to go down the, 'shooting an unarmed man straight between the eyes is not a shot made from fear or defense,' right now."

"Lucky shot?"

"Damn fine lucky shot."

"Sydney Cooper, not his real name, came to this town just a few months before your wife was killed. Your sheriff will most likely lose his position for not doing enough thorough checks. And before you ask, no, he didn't come from Richford, but from a small town in New York State, near Auburn."

"So he has to be involved, he has to be a member of that cult, that's got to be where the convent is, isn't it?"

"Being a member of a cult isn't against the law. And yes, it is where the convent was. It was closed down many years ago."

I ran my hands over my face. "So what's real? Of all the stuff I know, what the fuck is real?"

"That's what we are trying to determine. Gabriel, there was no Sister Anna registered at that convent. There was no one with the name Sierra..."

I cut him off. "Savannah, Lily said her name was Savannah."

"There was no child with the surname, Preston. But, before you say it, that doesn't mean she didn't exist there. The convent burned down, maybe that was a convenient way to get rid of records. Who knows? This is the problem; we know what went on, we've been investigating the connection between Father Samuel and the convent. We know he was defrocked, we know of the abuse at the cult."

"Then you have to believe what I've told you," I said. Desperation crept into my voice.

"I do, honestly, I do. I'm on your side here, but without any hard evidence, our hands are tied. Getting those involved to talk is proving a problem."

"Why can't you just arrest him?"

"Because without testimony, or a confession, I don't stand a chance in hell of bringing it to court."

I physically deflated. I felt my body sag, the breath leave my lungs, the tension I'd held for so long leave, and not because it was over, because I was beaten, we all were.

"So where does that leave me, leave Taylor?"

"Assuming Zachary doesn't press charges, which I doubt he will, my advice to you would be to leave town. You're not a suspect in the shooting, but we know someone else was there that night. I could charge you for withholding evidence, but I think we have greater things to worry about right now."

"You'd just let me leave?"

"I'd ask you to stay in contact, and I have no doubt you'd want to know how this investigation progresses."

"Where do I go?"

He shrugged his shoulders. "Gabriel, I personally believe there is a threat to you and your daughter, but not enough to put you in any kind of program, because you're not a witness to a crime that warrants that. If you choose to stay, I have no doubt you'd be able to 'defend' yourself, and I'll make sure the sheriff can make arrangements. Until I have something to go on, my hands are tied."

"But they want my daughter."

"So you say, and until there is an attempt to kidnap her, no crime has been committed. I can't even decide on the level of risk until I have more facts."

"So, I'm fucked then, really. My daughter is fucked. You want me to help you, but I get nothing in return?"

"Go talk to your dad, Gabriel. I will tell you this one thing; his records are classified. Ask him why. You might find you have all the protection you need."

"And my brother was not involved?" I asked.

"Not in the way you believe. He is helping us with our continued investigations, I think is the official line."

"What are you going to do about the fake feds? They're cult members." For some reason, I didn't want to tell them Midley was not only Lily's half brother, but also the father of her child. She'd had enough abuse throughout her life, what good would it do now to disclose that?

"It's an offence to masquerade as a federal agent, for sure. Is it one we'd spend money and time investigating? Like I keep saying, Gabriel, as much as you have a whole load of useless knowledge, so do we. If we can arrest them for something that will result in a decent prison sentence, then we will."

"And yet you said you've been investigating this cult for a while." I shook my head as I spoke.

I didn't know what to do, what more I could say to convince them my daughter was in danger. They had Sierra's letter, they had the statements Sister Anna sent, but it didn't seem to be enough.

"Can I get my gun back?" I asked.

"No, it's part of the investigation. I need to determine how Sydney came to have it."

"Lily didn't take it," I said.

"Then who did?"

"Syd."

"How?"

I shrugged my shoulders and rose. "He had a key, he must have taken it. I don't know what more I can tell you, to convince you. I just need to be with my daughter right now."

He stood and walked with me to the entrance of the police station. We stepped outside to see Thomas leaning against his car; he looked as dejected as I felt.

"Be safe, Gabriel," he said and then nodded at Thomas.

I pulled my phone from my pocket and called my dad. I needed to know he had gone to my house and not his own. I wanted some peace and quiet. I wanted to sit in the dark and not think. I wanted to sleep.

Once I'd received the confirmation I needed, I patted Thomas on the chest and without a word, walked home. The sun shone, a neighbor waved, life went on as if nothing had happened: as if I hadn't witnessed a murder, been covered in blood, and beaten my brother to a pulp.

I found Dad changing the locks to the front door, he handed me a new key as I took the steps up to join him. In all the drama, I'd completely forgotten about telling anyone we had a locksmith coming.

"Window's fixed, all new locks, and I'm about to do something with that back door," he said.

"We need to talk," I replied, as I walked into the cool hallway.

"Daddy! You're home," Taylor squealed. She seemed none the worse for her brief stay in hospital.

I picked her up and hugged her tight. I'd made many mistakes over the past few days, few months even. I'd let rage get the better of me in that barn, instead of leaving with my daughter; I'd beaten the shit out of someone who could be innocent.

I carried her through to the yard, Dad followed. I placed her to the ground and she skipped off. I sat at the small metal garden table. I reached forward to the pack of cigarettes that had been left there,

"I haven't a clue what's going on anymore. I don't know who's lying and who's telling the truth," I said. My voice hitched as sadness and tiredness washed over me.

"We need to sit down and evaluate what we know, Gabe. What we know for fact. Why don't you get a couple of hours sleep, I'll watch her."

"I can't. I close my eyes and I see it all. I see the blood, the tears, and the fear. I smell it. I can't get rid of the fucking smell from my body, from my mind."

"What happened at the station?"

"Not much, I told them what happened, they gave me some snippets in return. I don't know what they believe right now, other than they don't have enough to charge anyone who isn't already dead. And talking of that…Sam?"

"How about a coffee first?" Dad said.

Was that a delay tactic? I didn't really care, I guessed. How much more information could I absorb before it all finally tipped me over the edge?

I made my way to the kitchen and turned on the coffee machine. I rested my back against the counter and looked around. Sierra had loved this room. It was bright and airy, the walls were painted a soft yellow and one housed pictures and paintings Taylor had done. It was meant to be homely, bright, and cheerful. The total opposite to how it felt then.

I knew at that moment I would sell the house quickly. I'd take the first offer. There were just too many memories, too many incidents, for me to ever feel happy again. When the coffee was brewed, I poured two mugs and took them out to where Dad still sat.

"Is Mom okay?" I asked.

"Sort of, she just needs a little time to process."

"She blame me for beating Zach?"

His silence was all I needed as an answer.

"She's overwhelmed, Gabe, give her a little time."

"She's overwhelmed!"

"She's torn. She's nursing Zachary and she's terrified for you, I'm sure. She's never seen you fight, Son, she's never been around that level of violence. Just give her time."

"Back to Sam," I said.

Dad leaned back in his chair and studied me. "Sam was in Vietnam with me. We weren't delisted as soon as we returned home, Gabe. We still had to serve our time. The army did some pretty bad stuff back then, experimental shit that left a lot of our boys fucked up. Sam..." he sighed. "Sam doesn't exist, Gabriel. He died on the battlefield."

"Come again?"

I could see he was trying to come up with the right words, he glanced over my head, pursed his lips before he spoke again.

"Sam was part of a program, a military program. It affected him greatly."

"Let me guess, he's Jason Bourne?" Although I hadn't wanted to make a joke of what I was being told, it all seemed too unreal for me.

"Watch your smart mouth, Son. You have no idea what most of those soldiers went through, what shit the government did to them to make them the fighting machines they needed."

Even at nearing thirty-years-old, my father's rebuke stung a little.

"I'm sorry, I'm just…"

"I know, but you asked the question, let me answer. So, Sam was supposed to be an ultimate fighting machine, drugged up and full of aggression. We were losing that war long before we actually lost it. When it was all over, when we were finally able to leave, he disappeared. He turned up on my doorstep a couple of years later. I don't know where he'd been, I never asked. But he needed my help and I gave it. Obviously, Gabriel, he can't risk being interviewed by anyone, let alone the FBI. As I said, he doesn't exist."

"And you? Do you exist? Your war records are classified." I wasn't sure I wanted the answer.

"No, don't answer that. Sierra, or Savannah, Lily, Sister Anna, no one exists in the way I believed them to. I can't take knowing that's the same for you," I added.

My world had been turned on its head. My wife wasn't who I thought she was, or was she? Did it matter that she had changed her name? I tried to focus on the woman I'd spent just over five years with. It wasn't long enough, no amount of time would have been long enough, but I had to get back to that. I had to focus on the good times, the times she loved me, the times she gave herself to me; the times she sang our daughter to sleep, and the times she'd cried or we fought. I needed to find a way to erase the past months.

I sat and watched my daughter play, she was making something, a daisy chain perhaps. She gently sang to herself as she threaded small flowers through stalks. I wanted to capture and hold on to those precious few seconds of watching her. I wanted to believe that life was normal. A tear leaked from one eye.

"I'll get back to those window locks," Dad said, giving me some space, I imagined. I simply nodded.

It was a half-hour or so later that the first friendly face I'd seen in days walked around the corner of the house.

Trina stepped up to me; she cupped my face in her hands and kissed my cheek.

"Hey, how are you doing?" she asked.

"Not good."

Trina had called me a couple of times, as had Jake. In fact half the townsfolk had enquired after Taylor's illness.

"If you want to tell me, I'm here for you."

"I can't Trina, not right now. Something's going on, and I don't want to involve anyone just yet." I was too frightened to involve anyone knowing what the consequence of that could be.

She nodded her head. "Want me to take her a while? You look like you could do with some sleep."

I shook my head. "Well, at least go and lay down for an hour. I'll sit with her. Your dad's here, I'm sure we'll be just fine," she said.

"Let me just sit here for a minute and doze. I can't go to sleep and relive it all in my dreams."

She patted my shoulder and left to sit with Taylor. I closed my eyes and slid down in my chair and placed my feet on the table.

Chapter Twenty-One

"We got some storms rolling in," Thomas said, as I opened the front door to him.

We hadn't spoken since I'd left the station three days ago. We'd barely spoken during the time Taylor was hospitalized. It had been three days of hell. Three days of not knowing what was going on, of quiet, and the quiet had me worried.

"Shift over?" I said as I let him in. He was out of uniform.

"For a while, suspended."

"Aw, fuck, I'm sorry," I said.

He shrugged his shoulders. "How is she?" he asked.

"Asleep, for now. Her nightmares have returned."

I grabbed two beers from the fridge and we sat at the kitchen table.

"So, what happened then?" I asked.

"Some bullshit about not doing checks. Which I did, I can only dig so far and when I'm given fake fucking ID, there's not much else I can do but take it on face value," he said.

"Syd?"

"Yeah, Syd. A dead deputy who may, or may not, be a member of a cult was an embarrassment to the force, so I was told."

"Or may not be?"

"I'm as in the dark as you, Gabe. All I know is they don't have enough evidence to blow the cult open and the deaths of the children can be easily explained."

"How?"

"One was a vehicle accident, another an industrial accident. There is only one that's questionable and he was found in an alley frequented by prostitutes and drug dealers."

"Anything on the fake feds? At least we still have them, and Father Samuel, of course."

He shook his head. "Not a thing, they've disappeared."

"So we're back to waiting then," I said.

"Or it's over."

"No, it's not over, Tom. Not by a long shot."

"Heard anything from your brother?" he asked.

"No, he left the hospital and Mom is taking care of him. She hasn't spoken to me since it happened, won't return my calls either."

"I don't understand that. What ever capacity he's involved, you can't be blamed for what you did, for making a mistake."

"Do you think I made a mistake?"

"I just don't know, Gabe."

It seemed I was losing the support of those that I trusted, of those closest to me. It was an isolating feeling and made me feel lonelier than I had before.

"I asked Taylor if she remembered anything, she doesn't. How did they drug her, if it wasn't Zachary? The hospital said it was likely to be something she had ingested, a drink maybe. I put her to bed, she didn't have a drink with her then."

"I wish I knew, Gabe. There's going to be so much of this that I don't think we'll ever know the answers to."

"Will the police register Sierra's killer as Syd?" I asked.

"If they do, it's only to close the case. I believe he killed her, but like Mich said, there's no evidence."

"So I'm just expected to move on, carry on and go about my day as usual?"

"No, you're expected to get over the self-pity and work with me to fucking solve this."

"How? I'm beat, Tom."

"We start right at the beginning. Where's that pad?" he asked, looking toward the counter.

I stood and opened a drawer, grabbed it and a couple of pencils.

"What do we know?" he asked, pencil poised.

"I have something I've held back. I think Lily was telling us the truth and I know why." I then told him about the conversation from the barn, her child, and his father.

"Fucking hell. Jesus. I…I don't know what to say. Oh, man. The poor woman. Did you tell this to Mich?"

"No. Right or wrong, Tom, she needed me. She just wanted a normal life, and I wanted to protect her child by withholding that. I wanted to just give her that one thing."

"Okay, I get that. How about we focus on what we know?" He smiled at me, understanding what I'd said.

"We believe Sierra and Lily are sisters, same father, same mother. Sister Anna has disappeared and doesn't want to help further, now that's something I find very strange, so is she the blonde woman who gassed herself because of guilt? I think so. The statements are supposed to be fake, and bearing in mind we have nothing to compare Sister's Anna's handwriting with, her letter might even be fake. Let's go with Syd as Sierra's killer for the minute," he added.

We spoke, recapped, and wrote.

"There's one thing I just thought of. Why wait all this time to take Taylor, when they could have done that when Sierra was killed," he said.

"Because the cult doesn't want Taylor. It's the church. Go back to the beginning, Tom. What did Sierra say, they wanted to blow open the Catholic Church for allowing it to happen."

"Hold up, Gabe, slow down. Syd, Lily, they're not part of the church."

"No, but what better way to kill off a cult than to have someone else do your dirty work. Doesn't pay to have a bunch of priests running around town shooting it up, does it?"

"Why would they kill off the cult?"

"Because, ultimately, they were responsible for it. What was it Mich said? The convent burned down, maybe to erase records. Would a cult do that? Is this cult that powerful, or are we all being manipulated by the church?"

"We need all the files."

"Then go get them."

"I'm suspended, Gabe, I can't walk in there and pick up files."

I picked up my phone and called my dad.

"Dad, I need some help. I need to break in somewhere."

"Where?" he asked, as if it was the most natural request in the world.

"The police station."

"Fuck me," he said with a chuckle. "Son, I'll be over in half-hour."

"You're not doing that, I can't let you. I'd have to…" Thomas said.

"What? Arrest me?"

"Fuck's sake, Gabe. Do you know often I've broken the fucking law for you?"

"No."

"That fucking F150 you have sitting on the drive? For some reason it's doesn't appreciate the speed limit!"

"We need that file, Tom. Or we need to remember, word for word, what those letters say, can you?"

"Sierra said she feared they would come for Taylor."

"And who put that fear into her head? Sister Anna: the sister from the convent. The same sister that said, religion killed my wife, but not what religion."

"Do you really think the Catholic Church is capable of running around killing people?"

"Not the Catholic Church, but what's to say there's not an organization within it that is? Think about it, the feds, the real ones, said that Zachary was involved but just not in the way we believe. He turns up here at a very opportune time with the fake ones. I don't think Lily recognized him, so he isn't part of her cult, but what if he's part of an organization within the church that wants it all silenced?"

"It's a little far fetched, but...It's all we have."

For the first time, in a while, excitement bubbled within me. Maybe, just maybe, we were finally getting somewhere. It seemed unbelievable that the greatest religion on earth could be involved in something so heinous, but it wasn't outside the realm of possibility.

I stood and paced, running over events in my mind. Who said what? What were we made to assume? There was no doubt Father Samuel was evil, there was no doubt such horrific abuse had happened at his hands. But would the Catholic Church go to such lengths to cover it up? I was beginning to think so.

It was less than a half-hour when I heard a car pull up outside. Since we had new locks, and I was the only key holder, I had to let dad in.

"Sit, and you, Tom. Now tell me what the fuck is going on," Dad said.

"I don't think the cult has anything to do with this. I think someone in the church is manipulating us all to do their dirty work for them," I said.

"Which is?"

"Kill off the members of the cult."

"Why?"

"To silence them? I haven't gotten that far yet."

"And you think breaking into a police station is going to give you the answers?"

"I think breaking into a police station is going to get me the file so I can check, word for word, what Sierra's and Sister Anna's letters said. From memory, they don't mention the cult; they mention religion. Would they classify the cult as religious?"

"And you're up for this?" he asked Thomas.

"Hell, no. I'm fucking suspended right now. That will be it for me, career over if I got caught."

"Then I guess you got yourself a babysitter, Son."

Thomas closed his eyes and let his head fall to the arms he had crossed on the table. Dad checked his watch.

"I take it the station is alarmed?" he asked.

"Of course it's alarmed, it's a police station," Thomas mumbled.

"Care to tell us…"

"No! Anyway, I would have thought the code would have been changed the minute they shoved me out the door."

"So for now, let's see what you've written down," Dad said, eyeing the papers on the table.

We went through all that we could remember of the past few days. I was conscious of the fact I'd named Zach and I'd listed questions. Dad didn't make mention of that as he read through.

I repeated what I'd remembered Syd saying.

"Lily didn't react to Zachary," I said quietly.

"Because she knew him?" Thomas asked.

"I don't think so, she…She wasn't scared by him, if you know what I mean. Only that he had Taylor."

"So we have two things going on here, side by side. The abuse and then the silencing," Dad said when we'd finished talking.

"I think so," I said.

We fell silent, digesting the magnitude of what we'd been discussing, of what we were coming to believe.

"Let's go," Dad said and stood.

"Where?" Thomas asked.

"The station, of course."

"You're not going to break in now? It's still fucking daylight out."

"No, we need to do a recon," he said. "And we need daylight for that."

Thomas groaned but said nothing as Dad and I left the house and climbed in his truck, although the station was a walkable distance.

"I'm going to ask you this, Gabriel, if you know all the answers, if you solve this, and I have no idea how this is going to end, will you be satisfied?"

I looked at him, my brow furrowed.

"Satisfied?"

"Will it enable you to move on with your life?"

"Yes," I answered without hesitation. "I need to know who killed my wife."

"Sometimes the truth is uglier than you imagine, you prepared for that? You prepared to learn things that will alter you? Destroy people?"

"Dad, you're not making sense. I want to know who killed my wife, why is that so wrong?"

"It's not wrong, if it doesn't open a can of worms, and I have a feeling this will."

"My daughter deserves to know, one day, that I did all I could. What kind of a father would it make me if I didn't try?"

"Then you need to know, I found this, in the house."

He handed me a small black cell, an older style one. I stared at it.

"Turn it on, check the text messages," he said.

I did. What I saw were the conversations I'd had with Sister Anna.

"How…?"

"I don't know, okay. I just don't know."

"There's only one person, Dad, that connects this all, who happens to be staying in your house."

He didn't respond. We fell silent as we pulled around to the rear of the station, to the compound that housed Thomas' car. We stepped out of the truck. The gates were locked, of course.

"Can you see any cameras?" Dad asked. I scanned the building.

"No, that's unusual, isn't it?"

"Small town, small budget. See that window? The frosted one? I bet that's into a bathroom. No cameras in a bathroom."

"Or a cell?"

Dad looked at me and shook his head. "Do you think there would be a window in a cell?"

I wanted to laugh at my error but the situation was too serious.

"You don't need to do this, you know that, don't you?" I said.

"I don't need to do a lot of things, Son, but this is important to you."

"What if we get caught?"

"If you believe you're going to get caught, then we need to turn around and go home right now, and put this out of your head completely." He was pacing alongside the metal fence.

"Okay, we're done," he added.

"Done?"

"Yep."

We climbed back in the truck, and at first, I was unsure what he meant. Before he pulled away, he took out his phone and sent a text.

"You'll stay at home, Gabriel. Leave this one to me."

"You won't know what you're looking for."

"I'll find the file."

Thomas was pacing the kitchen when we returned. He had a steaming cup of coffee in one hand and held his phone in the other.

"Well?"

Dad patted his shoulder as he passed to help himself to coffee.

"Well?" Thomas asked again.

"Well, what?" Dad said.

"What did you do? I was half expecting a call to say the station had been broken into."

"I told you, we went for a recon."

"And how do you plan to get in?"

"You want me to answer that? Really?" Dad said.

"You need to see this," I said, handing him the cell.

He read the text messages and then looked up at me.

"Sister Anna's phone, correction, Sierra's phone. Where did you find this?"

"I found it in a drawer, and since I didn't recognize it, I turned it on and saw the text messages from Gabe," Dad said.

"So we're back to Zachary?" Thomas said. "I need to hand this in, suspended or not."

Dad stood, a little shaky. "I think I'll head home, I have chores to do," he said.

Thomas and I watched him leave. I didn't think he had chores to do, the news that his son may be involved far more than we realized, seemed to have knocked the wind out of him.

"I'll go and hand this in. I'm going to say you found it, okay. So come up with a story," Thomas said. I nodded, neither of us wanted to involve Dad in implicating Zachary.

"I'm going to check on Taylor," I said, as I walked with Thomas to the front door.

Her door was ajar and I pushed it open slowly. She didn't stir as I crept to the side of her bed and sat. I ran my hand over her head, pushing her hair from her forehead. She'd need a haircut soon, before school started.

School. I had no idea if she would ever return to her small school, to a place she loved. When this was done, I doubted we'd stick around. I'd promised her once I'd take her to see the sea; maybe that's what I'd do. I'd pack up the truck and we'd just drive.

I looked around her room, what would she miss? I should have given the quest for revenge up; I should have been a better father. But something inside me kept propelling me forward. Something kept that niggle going, burning inside like a cancer. I had to know, I just had to.

The following day passed without incident or visitors. Taylor was bugging to go out, to visit her grandma. I decided to distract her by going through her things.

“Baby girl, let’s sort out all these old toys, the ones you don’t play with,” I said.

We sat on her bedroom floor as I emptied the toy box and she refilled it. Even a broken crayon made it’s way back in, it was needed, I was told.

“Clothes next. We want to give the clothes that don’t fit you to the other kids, the ones who can’t afford pretty dresses,” I said.

We had a little more success with that. By the end of an hour or so, we had a pile of clothes that she loved and fit, and a pile to discard. I bagged up the old ones.

“Want to help me do the same?” I said.

She laughed as we threw clothes all over the bed; she rolled around in them, attempting to put on my t-shirts. What was left was enough to fill a suitcase and plenty for me. When, if, we left, I wanted to travel light.

While Taylor decided to reinvestigate her toy box, I made a call to the local realtor. I wanted the house up for sale. I had no idea of it’s worth, I had a small mortgage but the balance would keep us going for a while. I also needed to decide what to do with the garage. It earned me enough to pay Jake, the bills, and some left over to live on. But was it worth anything as a business? I wasn’t sure. I owned the premises, maybe that needed to be sold as well.

Chapter Twenty-Two

I missed being at my parents'; I missed being able to sit on the porch with a beer and chat. For two days I hadn't left the house, for two days the only conversation I'd had was with a five-year-old. As much as I loved spending time with my daughter, we were both going stir crazy. The yard was small and only held her attention for so long. We weeded and mowed the lawn; we planted seeds and made up stories about fairies living in an old tree trunk.

I missed company the most those hours after I'd put Taylor to bed and before the sun rose again.

I thought about Sierra, I didn't care what her name was. I thought about Lily. I swallowed down the guilt I felt whenever she came into my mind. I remembered some of my last words to her, telling her how much I hated her, but I hadn't. I was hurting her to ease my own guilt. Guilt that I was fucking her and enjoying it.

I sat in the yard with a cigarette after putting Taylor to bed and tried not to think. I just needed an hour's peace.

"Gabe?" I heard a man's voice float through the air. It startled me enough to have me nearly fall from my chair.

Sam walked around the corner; it was only the kitchen light illuminating his face that helped me recognize him. He wore dark clothing, a cap, and gloves. Without another word, he laid a large envelope on the garden table, and then left as silently as he had arrived. I stared at his retreating back.

I reached out for the envelope; my fingers gently traced the brown paper. I wanted to call Thomas, but I hadn't heard from him for a couple of days. I imagined the strain must have gotten to him. Maybe he needed to distance himself a little; maybe I needed to push him away.

I picked up the envelope and walked inside. I slid my thumb under the flap and opened it, letting the contents spill onto the table.

All the pages, neatly clipped together, were photocopies, and I wondered how long it had taken Sam to do that. The letters were there, the statements, notes, copies of photographs, and official looking documents. There didn't seem to be any order, so I unclipped them and started to read.

The first thing I saw was the photograph of the children, some had red pen circling their heads, and some had blue. I found the diary entries, written on them were questions—'Who wrote this?' 'When were these written?'

The questions surprised me, Thomas knew who and when, Sierra had told us. But then, maybe it wasn't Thomas wanting to know.

I found a document tracing Sister Anna's phone back to Sierra; we already knew that. There was a transcript of what I'd said in my informal interview, it was pretty accurate. I wondered if that was normal to have a transcript. Since it was pretty accurate, someone must have recorded me speaking. I didn't recall Mich taking notes. Written in the margin, near where I'd detailed Syd's death, were two letters SC.

Each of the statements had how the narrator had died, I sighed as I realized, Thomas, Mich even, had been right. Their deaths could have been accidents, could have been something else. The red circles, I found out, were explained deaths, unquestioned. The blue circles, of which there were three, were questioned. Lily had a blue circle around her head.

So far, I'd found nothing that I didn't already know. My heart started to sink. There had to be another file, what I had couldn't be it all. It was as I started to flick through the remainder that I found what I was looking for.

I held up a piece of paper with details on Father Samuel. There were dates he had been questioned by the church and references made to statements that had been taken from him.

It was an inventory, I guessed. At the very bottom it was signed, Zachary Malone. I was about to put it down when I saw the date. That document had been written, by his hand, nearly twenty years ago.

“Twenty fucking years ago!” I said.

I calculated that Sierra would have been five, Lily three. My brother was aware of Father Samuel’s activities when my wife had been in his care. I tried to think, Zach wouldn’t have been a bishop at that point, so what would he have been, a priest? Did priests investigate others? I doubted it.

Something came to mind; I scanned back through the documents and couldn’t find the name of the convent. I grabbed my laptop and Googled. How many convents burned to the ground in the past twenty years? It couldn’t be that many. I got a hit.

Sisters of Mary Convent burned to the ground a little over ten years ago. I read as much information as I could, short of having the fire department’s report; it seemed to be a mystery. Although not officially recorded, arson was eluded to. I continued to read, hoping I might come across a list of nuns or photographs even. There was very little detail until I came to one eyewitness account. A Stephen Connor, residing in Auburn, had told reporters he’d been walking his dog when he saw flames through a broken window, he was the one to call the fire department.

Where had I heard the word, ‘Auburn’ before? I closed my eyes to think, scrolling through all the information in my head.

“Auburn, Auburn…SC!” I said. Syd had to be Stephen Connor.

Syd, or whatever his name was, had come from Auburn, I was sure that Mich had told me that. But did that connect Syd to the convent or the cult? Or both?

“Fuck! Syd and Zachary knew each other.”

Why hadn’t I connected that? Syd hadn’t turned around to see who had walked up behind him; he didn’t react to hearing Zachary because he was expecting him. Syd had arrived in town a little before Sierra had been killed. Was that so he could keep an eye on her? Was he the one that was tracking down the children and silencing them? In which case, unless I had done a full circle, he wasn't part of the cult, but the church.

I bashed my fist against the side of my head. He couldn't be, Lily knew him.

I wanted to scream as I went round and round in circles. I was close; I could taste it, feel it in my gut, but not close enough.

I knew I would have no choice but to speak to Zachary. I didn't want to, until I was sure of his involvement, but I wanted to watch him lie to me. I wanted to be able to justify the beating. I wanted to be able to prove I wasn't wrong, that he wasn't innocent. But I had to know, what did Mich mean when he'd said he was involved in the cult, just not in the way I thought.

I wanted to punch something, to let my frustration out in a satisfying way, to feel skin and bone connect on someone, or something. I slammed my fist down on the table. The pieces of paper jumped a little as if terrified.

I grabbed a cup of coffee.

"Think, Gabe, think," I said.

I tore a fresh piece of paper from the pad. Zachary and Syd knew each other. Zachary had interviewed, or at least documented interviews from Father Samuel twenty years ago. A thought ran through my head and I slid the laptop toward me again. I Googled my brother, not for one minute expecting to find anything. I was wrong.

My brother's biography, including date of birth, education, and his progression through the church was listed. I cursed at not having a printer so I copied everything. My hand faltered over a date.

I didn't seem to be able to focus on anything else. My eyes were sore as I rubbed them. I gathered the papers and carried them upstairs with me. I needed some sleep and to start again with a clearer mind.

I stepped into Taylor's room to check on her. She was sleeping soundly. I hesitated before leaving her room, and for the first time in a while, I chose to sleep in my own bed.

I stripped naked, leaving my clothes in a pile and the papers on the bedside table and took a shower. I let the cool water run over my body, washing away the stickiness of that day's heat. I tried not to think, I wanted respite from all the thoughts. I wanted a blank mind, just for a couple of hours, and I prayed Taylor stayed asleep the whole night.

When I was done, I wrapped a towel around my waist and stood in front of the broken mirror. My reflection, like the knowledge I had learned, was distorted. I watched a tear run down my cheek. Another followed, then another. I gripped the edges of the sink as my legs began to shake and as the grief I'd been trying to desperately hold in threatened to overwhelm me.

I knew I was on the edge; I was losing it. I took a large breath in, held it before slowly exhaling. I couldn't do that; I needed to be strong, just for a little while longer. I could fall apart when it was all done. I could give in when the pieces of the puzzle in my brain were connected.

I slipped under the cotton sheet and closed my eyes. Sleep did not come easy, regardless of how exhausted I was. My body ached with it.

I wasn't sure where the answer came from, but I sat bolt upright. I blinked a few times, unsure what it meant, whether there was a connection or not. I reached over to the bedside cabinet and grabbed the papers, flicking through until I found the one I wanted.

Zachary had been born while my dad was in Vietnam.

Zachary had been born before my parents had even married.

Chapter Twenty-Three

I sat at the kitchen table in just a pair of jeans and a held a cup of coffee. It was way too early for Taylor to be up, and I was thankful she had slept through the night.

My parents had married a year after Dad had come out of the army, and somewhere in my brain I had that as 1970, just shy of his thirtieth birthday.

The biography for Zachary had his birth year at 1966.

I knew my brother was fifteen years older than me, but for some reason I'd never thought back on his year of birth. We didn't send each other birthday cards; I could count on one hand the amount of times we'd spent any time together over the past ten years, and those meetings had been fleeting.

Zachary had been five-years-old when my parents married. Was that relevant? Or just a family skeleton I'd stumbled across? More importantly, did I broach that subject with Dad? Yet more questions were added to the list in my mind.

I decided enough days of no intruders had passed and feeling isolated by my mom and Thomas was having a negative affect on both of us. It was time to get out of the house. I loaded the car with a picnic and told Taylor we were out for the day. Of course, I took the papers with me. I turned off my phone and threw that, with the papers, in the glove box.

"Are we there yet?" Taylor asked from her car seat.

"Not yet, baby girl."

I had no idea where I was heading, I just wanted out of town for a few hours. I wanted my daughter to be able to play freely, and for me to forget everything for a little while.

We'd driven for over an hour when I saw a sign for the nature reserve; somewhere I'd visited as a child but forgotten about. I pulled off the highway and followed the directions. We parked near a visitors' center and I climbed from the truck. I stretched my back before opening the door for Taylor to join me.

We picked up a map, a booklet of what critters to look out for, and we took a walk. We held hands and we talked, just like we used to before all the shit happened. For a couple of hours we both forgot, just enjoyed the day and being out of our self-imposed confinement.

After we'd completed a circuit, we ended up back at the parking lot. I pulled a blanket and our picnic from the truck and we sat on the grass.

"Is Grandma mad at me?" Taylor asked.

"No, why would you say that?"

"Because we haven't seen her."

"No, Grandma is busy, that's all. No one is mad at you, baby girl."

Taylor sat in on a lecture about local wildlife that a ranger was giving for the children, although only three attended. I watched from the back as she continually raised her hand to ask a question.

"She's very inquisitive," I heard. Twisting in my chair, I saw a woman take the seat next to me.

"She is, drives me mad sometimes," I replied with a laugh. "How did you know she was my daughter?" My adrenalin had spiked.

"Well, those two are mine, and you're the only other adult in here." She laughed.

I relaxed, only a little. "Have you been here before?" she asked.

"When I was child, and I don't recall all this." I waved my arm around the visitors' center.

"I've just moved to the area, so first time. Are you local?"

"No, couple of hours drive away. I just woke up, it was a beautiful day, so packed up the car for a mini road trip."

"That's wonderful. It's nice to see a dad and his child spending some time alone together." There was sadness to her voice.

"Her mother died, a little while ago."

"Oh, God, I'm so sorry."

"It's okay, no need to be."

"Hard work, being a single parent, isn't it?"

I nodded. "Yeah, sometimes it is."

The lecture had finished and I stood, she stood. Taylor ran toward me, wrapping her arms around my legs and smiling up at the woman.

"It was nice to talk with you," I said, as I pulled Taylor off and took hold of her hand.

"Maybe your daughter would like to join us for ice cream?"

"Can I, please, Daddy?" Taylor said. I smiled down at her.

"Thank you, that's a kind offer but we have to be going now."

The woman smiled, nodded her head, and was then distracted by her children. Taylor and I walked from the center and back to the truck.

Was I always going to be suspicious? There was nothing in that conversation that should have had me on alert, other than the fact someone was just being nice, and all I'd wanted to do was to get away as quick as possible.

Within a half-hour of leaving the center, Taylor was asleep. She was normally so active but I smiled. Nights of nightmares must wear her out as much as it did me. I turned the radio on low and took a slow drive home. As a treat I pulled into a drive-through and ordered a couple of burgers. As much as I'd have loved for Taylor to sleep longer, she needed to eat. We sat in the parking lot, got greasy fingers, and food stained t-shirts before continuing the journey.

Taylor was asleep again by the time I pulled onto the drive. I killed the engine and just sat for a while looking at her in the rearview mirror. I'd cherish that day, that one day of near normalcy. She was grubby, her hair was tangled where it had fallen from her ponytail, but she was perfect to me.

I unclipped her from her seat and carried her straight to bed. She could bathe in the morning. As usual, I sat and watched her, only leaving the room when I was totally satisfied she wouldn't wake. I went back to the car and retrieved the papers I'd stuffed in the glove box and finally turned my cell back on.

I had two missed calls and three text messages. One text was from Jake, checking in and telling me what he'd been up to. One was from my dad enquiring if I was okay, his text made me chuckle, **U O K?**

The other text was from Thomas. He'd been trying to call, as had the realtor. I decided to call Thomas; the realtor could wait.

"Hey, how have you been?" I asked when he answered.

"Okay, you home?"

"I am, took Taylor out for the day, remember that nature reserve?"

"Vaguely, did you have fun?"

"Yeah. I needed a day away, no thinking, or other shit."

"Fancy some company?"

"Sure, pick me up a pack of cigarettes on your way though."

"They'll kill you one day," he said with a laugh.

"Hopefully, see you in five."

While I waited for Thomas, I replied to my dad's text. I should have been kinder and called; it would take him forever to figure out how to open the message. Dad was a newcomer to all things technological, every message sent was 'text speak' but not because he knew it, more because he was terrified of cell phones so opted for the quickest form of communicating.

All fine, took Taylor out for the day. Will call tomorrow, got some questions, nothing to worry about tonight.

I grabbed a beer from the fridge, snapped off the cap and took a sip as I waited.

I was at the front door as soon as I heard Thomas pull up outside.

"Here," he said as he threw the cigarettes at me.

"Beer?"

"Of course."

He followed me into the kitchen.

"How have you been?" he asked.

"Feeling a little isolated, if you want the truth. Mom doesn't seem to want to talk to me and you disappeared." I was partly teasing.

"I needed to do some things, Gabe. And some thinking."

"I'm just kidding you. Let's sit outside."

We made our way to the yard and I lit a cigarette.

"Did you get it?"

"What?"

"The file."

"I got half a file, there's a lot missing."

He nodded his head. "I didn't break in, Thomas. They were given to me by someone else," I said.

"Who?"

“I don’t know, I found them on my doorstep.” I think that was the first lie I’d ever told him.

“Want to go through it?” he asked. I smiled, thankful that he was back on board.

I grabbed the papers from the kitchen and set them down between us.

“This isn’t even half,” he said as he flicked through.

“Where would the rest be?”

“I’m guessing Mich took what he thought he needed. I don't know to be honest. What’s this?”

He held in his hand the biography for Zachary’s I’d written down.

“I don’t know if this is relevant or not, but Zachary was born before my parents even met, before they married for sure.”

“You're kidding me?”

“Nope. My dad left the army in 1970. Zach was born in 1966. My parents met and married a couple of months after meeting, which was a year after Dad got out.”

“No way! And you didn’t know this?”

“No, I mean I know how old he is, and I know the year my parents married, but I didn’t connect it. Another interesting thing, Zachary was a priest in Auburn. I found a biography.”

Thomas looked at me, not understanding.

“Syd came from Auburn,” I said,

“Fuck! So they could have known each other?”

“I think so, but not just because of that. When Zachary walked into the barn with Taylor, Syd didn’t turn around or react in any way, he was expecting him. Another thing I just thought of, Lily gasped, was that because she recognized Zach, or just because he was holding Taylor? I thought she hadn’t responded to him initially because she didn’t recognize him, but maybe she did.”

"If Lily knew Zach, then surely Sierra would have?"

"I've been thinking about that. I can't recall a time they ever met. But look at the date of that form." I handed him the inventory. "It was written twenty years ago. Twenty years ago, if we can believe it, Lily and Sierra were at the convent."

"We need to find the statements that Father Samuel gave. This is a list of them, but it would sure be interesting to see who interviewed him."

"I'm not sure that would have been Zach, I mean, he would have been a priest then. Would a priest investigate another priest?"

"Possibly not, unless he wasn't your average priest. Unless he was part of a secret organization within the church."

"That the Catholic Church says doesn't exist."

"Well, they would, wouldn't they?"

"Mich said that Zachary was involved, just not in the way we believe. Can you shed any light on that?"

"No, I've been thinking about that too. I don't have access to their files, the minute they came on board, that was it. I was out."

"I know Zachary is involved. I know he drugged my daughter, he had that cell, I just have to prove it," I said.

"Something's been bugging me. It's all quiet when Zachary is not around. Like now, he's incapacitated and there have been no intruders, nothing."

We fell silent as he continued to read through what I had. He'd made a point I hadn't thought about. But it hadn't all started with him, it started with the elusive Sister Anna.

"You know what doesn't sit well with me? Sister Anna was the one, supposedly, who started the whole thing by gathering the statements. She made a point of seeking me out to hand Sierra's diary entries to me, personally, now she can't, or won't, help further?"

"Because, maybe, Sister Anna doesn't exist," he said.

Chapter Twenty-Four

The more I thought about it, the more I wondered. I hadn't gotten verification the woman handing me the envelope that day was Sister Anna. Taylor had said a brown-haired woman came to the house; I met with a brown-haired woman. Both Lily and Sierra talked about a Sister Anna, but that didn't mean she was the one I met. It didn't mean that she was the one who turned up at my house to meet Sierra.

Those pieces of the puzzle were starting to take shape, whether they'd give me the whole picture, I wasn't sure.

"The more we know, the more confusing it is. Sierra said I'd be contacted by Sister Anna, she said they were gathering statements together. She has to exist," I said.

"I'm not saying she didn't exist, just that maybe she doesn't now. And maybe the woman you met isn't the same one Sierra met," Thomas replied.

"They'd already gotten to her?"

"Possibly. Think back, Gabe. We believed she was a woman who had dyed her hair, changed her appearance because she was scared and on the run. What if, the woman you met had dyed her hair to resemble the woman in the photograph?"

I sifted through the papers and found the photograph. I stared at the woman Lily had pointed out as Sister Anna.

"For what reason?" I asked.

"To help silence the victims. What better way to get close to someone than to pretend to be helping them? She talks to those victims, finds out what they remember, what they know, then either kills them or hands those statements back to whoever does. We have five here, look…" He pulled the statements from the pile of paper. "We have eight children."

"Five explained, accounted for and investigated by the police, deaths," he added.

"So you think we were given those specific statements because those deaths are not classed as murder?"

"I think exactly that."

"Why?"

"What have we been doing for the past few weeks, Gabriel? Running around chasing our tails and going nowhere. We've been kept busy, and out of the way."

"So we need to strip out everything we think is irrelevant then," I said.

"Who knew you were on a quest to find Sierra's killer?"

"My family, you, erm…"

No one else. It hadn't been a topic of conversation among the few friends that I had.

I stood from the chair and walked out into the yard. I needed a smoke. I needed to think. So many things pointed back to my brother—so many things didn't.

I stood looking out over the yard as the sun set. It's orange hues blazed and fought against the darkness. I heard Thomas' footsteps as he joined me.

"Did my brother kill my wife?" I whispered.

"I don't know, Gabe."

"My father said something interesting, it didn't register until now. He said, 'sometimes the truth is ugly.' I'm not sure he knows anything more than we do but he might just be right."

"He doesn't seem the kind to protect your brother if he believed he did wrong."

"Especially as he's not Zach's father."

I wanted to laugh out loud as a clap of thunder rumbled above us. Those storms Thomas had spoken about were getting closer. I could picture my dad right then, bringing in the horses for shelter. I pulled out my phone and sent him a text.

Storm's coming

I know, Son, I know came his reply.

Was that a play on words? Or was I beginning to finally lose my mind?

"I have to go there, Thomas. I have to confront Zach."

"Now?"

"Yes, now."

"You can't go alone, Gabe. And what about Taylor?"

I scrolled my finger across my phone and selected a contact.

"Trina, I know it's late, I know your about to drop that kid of yours, but I need a real big favor. Can you sit with Taylor? Possibly overnight, tonight."

"Gabe, what's happened?"

"I think I know who killed my wife."

"Give me five minutes, okay?"

I didn't reply, just disconnected the call. I didn't speak to Thomas as I ran through scenarios in my head. There were still so many 'what ifs' and 'maybes,' but I was only going to get it clearer in my head if I started to ask the questions of the one individual who connected it all.

Trina arrived and with her came the questions. Questions I still couldn't or wouldn't answer. I promised her that I'd tell her everything as soon as I could, but right then I needed to confront someone. She didn't push me as she set an overnight bag down at the bottom of the stairs.

"Be safe, Gabe," she said as I hugged her. I nodded.

"Wait for me," Thomas said.

"You don't need to come," I said.

"I want to. But we need to go someplace first."

We climbed into the truck and Thomas asked to go to the station. I pulled up outside and watched as he opened the front door. He reappeared some ten or so minutes later.

"I thought you didn't have keys," he said.

"I wasn't about to hand them over to you. I was protecting you, hoping you'd give up the idea of breaking and entering."

He hadn't finished his sentence before he handed me a revolver, it wasn't mine, but it felt comfortable in my hand.

"Untraceable," he said.

I looked at him, "Huh?"

"From the evidence lock up."

"You stole from the evidence lock up?"

He chuckled. "Time to find a new career, I guess."

"Tom, you've spent your whole life wanting to be the sheriff. I can't let you do this. Get out the truck."

"What?"

"Get out the truck. This is something I need to do alone. I can't let you throw your life to the dogs just for me."

"What to know something? It's all gone to the dogs anyway. I've been as manipulated as you have. I'm done with following the 'law' because the law doesn't give a shit. It's about statistics and numbers. You know how many times I have to lump a shitload of crimes on someone I knew didn't commit them? Just so the figures look good. No, not this time. Unless you drag me out, I'm coming."

Without another word I started the truck and we drove.

I killed the lights and let the truck drift to a halt halfway up the drive, shielded by the trees that lined it. It was quiet and I guessed Dad's friends had long since left. We climbed from the truck, and I tucked the revolver in the waistband of my jeans, concealed by my t-shirt. I doubted I'd need it, I didn't think Zachary would carry a gun.

Using the trees as cover, we made our way to the house. I could see lights on in both the house and the barn. We made our way to the barn first, hoping to catch my dad.

"That's enough now," I heard Dad say.

On hearing my dad, I stepped in. I expected to see him talking to the horses, maybe soothing one or two anxious about the claps of thunder over our heads. Instead I saw him facing me and on his knees.

A figure stood before him, dressed in black with his hood up, and his back to me.

"Zachary, this isn't the way, Son," Dad said.

"It's the only way," came the reply.

My father was kneeling at the feet of my brother. What I couldn't see was why. Did Zachary have a weapon?

If I moved any further into the barn, I'd be exposed. Stalls lined both sides, leaving a corridor down the middle. I would have one chance to rush him. I calculated the distance. It was just too far. The minute I moved, Zachary had ample time to do whatever he intended before I got there. I was fucked.

I was aware of Thomas behind me, but I was totally unsure of what to do. I felt him tap me on the arm, and I retreated as quietly as possible to where he stood outside the barn. He leaned closer to my ear.

"I think someone is in one of the stalls. I saw a shadow. We need to call this in."

I nodded and watched as he moved away; he'd have to make it back to the start of the drive before he got a signal.

I knew what I had to do. I prayed the 'someone' was Sam. I reasoned, if it was a friend of Zach's they wouldn't be hiding. I walked into the barn, not attempting to conceal my footsteps.

"Zachary," I said quietly, so as not to startle him.

"The son returns," he replied, lowering the hood of his sweatshirt.

"What are you doing?" I asked.

"What I have to, Gabriel." His voice hitched slightly.

"On whose order?"

He chuckled and shook his head. "Shall I say, The Lord? Will that get me the insanity plea?"

"Are you insane? Did you kill my wife?"

He openly laughed then. "Oh, Gabriel. Is this the part where I confess all my sins, you get all the answers you so desperately need, I die, and all is right with the world again? Is it?"

"Or the part you tell me, if I'd left well enough alone, no one else would have died," I said.

"I don't blame you for wanting to know. I'd have done the exact same thing."

"Then tell me."

"You know who killed your wife, you figured that out already. What you don't know is why."

"Because she was about to blow your game wide open."

"Game? Game! It was never my game, I am but a mere pawn on this chessboard of hell."

"You talk shit, Zach. Riddles, cryptic enough to just not give it up."

He hadn't turned toward me, and my father was still at his feet. I could see tears rolling down his cheeks and he shook his head.

"Don't, Zach, please," Dad said.

"Don't what? Don't tell me the truth?" I asked.

"Have you ever found out something so awful, it destroys your world?" Zachary said quietly.

"Yes, the day I walked in my house to see my wife dead. The day I held my sobbing daughter in my arms, after finding her locked in a bathroom. The day I laid my soul mate to rest."

"Recall that pain, Gabriel. Feel it in your whole being. Then multiply it, times it by ten, a hundred. You'll be somewhere closer to what I have."

"You think losing my wife is less than what you're going through?"

"It's less than knowing your father is a child abuser. It's less than knowing most of what you grew up believing is a lie. It's less than knowing you have to protect the devil."

I couldn't answer at first. My dad sobbed, and for some reason that sound was all that I heard. That sob overshadowed the words I'd just heard because it was a sound I'd never heard before.

"Your dad is a child abuser?"

"We are only half brothers, Gabriel. Why that was ever kept from you, I don't know. What would it have mattered? It's not like we were ever close."

"Who is your dad?" I asked, my voice quivered. Somehow I knew the answer.

"You're the super detective, are you going to tell me you don't know?"

"Father Samuel," I whispered.

"Father Samuel," he repeated.

"Did you know this?" I shouted at my dad. "Did you fucking know this? All the time you've been by my side, helping me, you knew this?"

"No, I didn't care who fathered Zachary, he's my son. I brought him up, I love him," Dad replied.

My hands began to shake. With anger, fear, sadness? I wasn't sure.

"So you killed to protect a fucking child abuser?" I said.

Zachary finally turned to face me. "No, Gabriel. I have never killed anyone."

"You knew Syd, though."

"Yes."

"You investigated your father."

"Yes."

"Please, Zachary, I'm begging you. Give me something, if there is a good bone in your body, tell me the truth."

I heard Thomas enter the barn; he walked and stood beside me, his gun raised.

"You'd be doing me a huge favor, Thomas, if you pull that trigger. But will it get you the answers you want?"

He sighed, turned his head toward my father then back to me.

"Your father is on his knees, not because I forced him to, but because I gave him the information he so desperately wanted. It has broken him. Are you ready for that?"

"I'm ready."

"Syd, or rather Stephen, killed your wife, but on the orders of another. On the orders of a very manipulative person: someone who wanted to silence the victims but not to protect the father. To protect me, to protect themselves.

"This person has spent years, Gabriel, years covering up what happened. Before you judge, you need to know her story."

"Her?"

"Sister Anna, Gabriel, you need to know about the real Sister Anna."

It hadn't been Zachary, or my father, that had spoken. The voice came from behind and caused me to spin on my heels.

I looked straight down the barrel of a gun, a gun held so steady in the hands of my mother.

Chapter Twenty-Five

"Sister Anna was an innocent child. Until that innocence was stolen from her in a brutal way. She was raped, repeatedly. She bore a child. She fought to keep that child; he's her flesh and blood and not to be blamed for how he came to be.

"But the man who raped her continued. He raped others, he fathered more children and he became madder." She chuckled as she shook her head.

"I don't get what's funny," I said.

"Oh, it's not funny, not at all. You see, all you know about Father Samuel is correct. He thinks there are divine children; he fathered your wife, her sister. But he's an old man now. He stopped his activities some time ago, when the FBI started to investigate him the first time. The trouble is, no one would speak out against him. He's not long for this world, and that's a good thing."

"Who was Sister Anna?" I asked, again, already knowing the answer.

"Me, Gabriel. I was Sister Anna. I was that innocent."

"You can't be, Sierra would have known you and the woman in the photograph? She was younger."

"Sierra was too young to remember anyone, the woman in the photograph? Who told you she was Sister Anna? Lily. And who told Lily? Sierra, and my Sister Anna."

My father sobbed loudly and I let the tears flow down my cheeks.

"Put down the gun, Mom," I said. She wasn't making any sense.

"All I wanted was to protect my son, protect myself," she said.

"How? How did you do that?" Thomas had finally spoken.

He lowered his gun slightly after I'd placed my hand on his arm.

"I will tell you, Thomas, because I won't go to jail. The Sister Anna you met, Gabe? Fake, a woman, like me, that didn't want to have to relive her past."

"But Sierra met Sister Anna, they collected the statements," I said.

"She met my Sister Anna. I wasn't even at the convent, Gabriel, when those girls were born."

"I don't believe you, the letter Sierra left…"

"Sierra met the same Sister Anna you did. She was led to believe what she wrote in that letter. Was there anything that actually told you they had been at the convent at the same time? Or was it just information on who she was? Think hard, Gabe."

I couldn't, I could not bring the words in that letter to mind.

"Why, Mom? Why all this?" I asked.

"Exposing Father Samuel exposes my son. The son who, without his knowledge, investigated his own father and covered up his crimes. Exposing Father Samuel, bringing it all out in the open, exposes me."

"So you did all this, and I'm still not sure what happened, just to protect yourself?"

"As if it was as simple as that. Zachary's position depended on…"

"You did this to save his fucking career!" I shouted, cutting off her sentence and startling her.

Pain ripped through my shoulder, a burning, searing pain. A faint hint of scorched flesh hit my nose, and I found myself spinning enough to cause me to fall. My mother had shot me.

Through the pain I looked up at her, nothing registered on her face. Not anguish, not fear, not empathy, nothing.

“Put the gun down, Mrs. M, or I will shoot,” Thomas said.

“Please, Tom, wait. I need to know,” I said through clenched jaws.

“I did this, so I didn’t have to relive it. I did this, so I didn’t have to look at your father and see pity or disgust in his eyes. I did this, hoping I’d never get to this point.” Her voice had changed, it was hard, yet heartbreaking at the same time.

“You killed people,” I said.

“I shouldn’t have been forced to!” she shouted. Her voice echoed around the barn, startling horses that stamped and whinnied.

“The FBI wanted to interview me, can you imagine how that felt? To have to publically talk about it? They wanted to track down the children. They started it all. I had to get in first, Gabriel. I knew where the children were; I had the records. Stephen retrieved them before he burned down the convent. I knew who Sierra was the minute you asked me to help organize your wedding. I needed to know what she could remember.”

“So you invented Sister Anna?”

“Yes, she visited all the children. I needed to stop them talking.” Her voice had fallen to a whisper.

“If you weren’t there at the same time, why? Why did you need to stop them talking?”

“Why don’t you understand, Gabriel? If they talked, if it all came out, there would be more investigations. Zachary would have been exposed.”

"So you killed them, made it look like accidents. Or was that Syd, or whatever his name is?" I asked.

"Stephen did what I asked him to do."

Bile rose to my throat. "You're fucking insane," I said as I climbed to my feet.

"Maybe. I wasn't until you brought it all to my doorstep, Gabriel. It wasn't until you went on a quest to solve something that should have just been left alone."

"So this is my fault?"

In the background we could hear sirens, through the open barn doors I could see blue and red lights. Still she didn't react. And that's when I knew.

I rushed her, stumbling and losing precious seconds. I watched as if in slow motion, as she raised the gun to her chin. I didn't get there quick enough, Thomas didn't get there quick enough before blood and bone erupted from the top of her head.

She crumpled to the ground. I turned and threw up.

The barn was full of noise, screams, sobs, and voices that seemed as if they were a million miles away. The echo of running feet, stomping horses, and angry words swamped me.

In my quest to find the killer of my wife, I'd started a chain of events so fucking awful, I wasn't sure I'd ever recover.

I walked out of the barn. I walked away from my mother's body, my brother, my dad, and my friend. I got as far as the front yard before I collapsed to my knees. My mind emptied of everything, of the images and the words. I closed my eyes.

The rain came down. Heavy drops hit me, washing my broken body; washing away the grime I felt so deep within my soul. It mingled with my tears, and it diluted the blood that ran from my shoulder.

I looked up to the heavens and I laughed. Manic laughter left my lips as a clap of thunder rumbled overhead. Lightning streaked across a dark sky.

"So now you're pissed, huh?" I screamed. "Well, you're too fucking late."

Chapter Twenty-Six

It was dark when I woke, in a room that smelled of antiseptic. It took me a moment to orient myself. I looked through the window, a street lamp shone; it was the only source of light into the room. My dad sat in the corner, his head was slumped to his chest, and his feet rested on the frame of the bed I was in.

I winced as I pushed myself up, into a sitting position. One arm was in a sling and when I moved, pain ripped through me. With the pain, came the reminders.

I had no idea of time or even what day it was. I searched the room for a clock, anything to help me.

"Son?" I heard.

"Dad."

"You're awake," he said.

"No. Sleep talking," I replied, earning me a chuckle.

"You need some help?" He rose from his chair and switched on the overhead light.

"I could do with sitting up a little more. I fucking ache. How long have I been here?"

"Only a couple of days, you slept for most of it. How's the shoulder?"

"Sore, very sore."

"It was a straight through shot, just a little tissue damage," he said.

"Sheesh, that's okay then, I guess. Where's Taylor?"

"At home, with Trina and Jake."

"So?"

"We're all under arrest for something, you've got a cop outside your door," Dad said.

"All?"

"Thomas for stealing evidence. You for having a concealed weapon you didn't have a license for. Me for withholding evidence."

"And Zachary?"

"Zachary is still innocent, so he says."

"Where do we go from here?" I asked.

"We start by telling the truth, I guess." Dad leaned back in his chair and took a deep breath.

"Your mom already had Zach when I met her. I didn't know and nor would she tell me who his father was. Over the years, it just wasn't something that we talked about again. I gave him my surname. We left Auburn and moved here, for two reasons. Your mom, obviously, was desperate to move away and I wanted a ranch. For years everything was okay, until you came home with Sierra…"

He held up his hand to stop me interrupting.

"I didn't know, Gabriel. I didn't know a thing. Your mom changed and I didn't know why. I can't hate her, even after what she did to you. I guess she buried her past as much as Sierra did, and then it was all brought to the surface. Zachary went into the priesthood as soon as he was able; I guess you could say it was in the blood. Your mom was distraught at first, which I did find strange but then, as the years went on, they seemed to have a closeness I was excluded from. I just assumed it was because they were blood."

"Why was it a secret?"

"It wasn't, not really. It was just something not spoken about. We're going back a lot of years, Gabe. Young girls got pregnant, and it was covered up. Young girls that were…well, you know what I mean, covered it up even more."

"So me bringing Sierra home kicked it all off?"

"As I said, your mom changed, she started to become, depressed, I guess. She started having nightmares. The doctor prescribed some sleeping tablets for her; they helped with the nightmares. When Sierra died, she seemed to, I hate to say this, perk up a little."

"Because the immediate threat was gone," I said.

"I imagine so. Did she kill anyone? I can't let myself believe that, Gabriel. If I do, my life has been a sham. Can you understand that?"

I nodded, not because I agreed but because it was what he needed to know.

"Where's Zachary?"

"At home."

"At home!"

"Zachary says he only recently found out who his father was, he didn't know. He confronted your mom, he tried to deal with it all but he was caught in the middle. He was working with the feds in bringing down the cult, and he knew once he had, your mom would be exposed. He didn't know what to do, he covered it up, I guess."

"And he told you all that? Do you believe him?"

"Yes, that was what he was confessing when you came in the barn. He's as sickened by it all as we are. More so in one way, to know he's the product of rape."

Something in my gut held me back from believing that to be true.

"Will they arrest Father Samuel?"

"Yes, Zachary is going to testify, but again, it's all still hearsay, it's just what his mother told him. According to the women at the cult, they all, your mother included, willingly slept with him."

"But the children..."

"The only children that can state he abused them are dead. There are no witnesses to that, or witnesses willing to speak out."

"So he'll walk then, won't he?"

Dad didn't need to answer the question.

"What did Mom actually do?" I asked.

"All I know is that your mom and Syd were related, cousins. She asked for his help."

"To do what?"

"Well, since he was in town, I guess to keep an eye on Sierra, get rid of witnesses."

"Yet she could have so easily kept an eye on Sierra herself."

"She knew who Sierra was the day she helped plan your wedding, Gabe, she told us that. But I don't know that we'll get all the answers. And right now, all we have is Zach telling the story she'd told him."

I sighed and closed my eyes. "You got your answer though, Gabe," he said.

"And what a fucking answer. My mom had her cousin kill my wife."

"I'm not sure that was your mom's intent..."

"Don't, Dad. Don't defend her. I can't hear that, okay?"

I looked over at him, in that moment, or maybe I just hadn't noticed, he'd aged so dramatically. Gone was the rugged, tanned face with the bright blue eyes. Instead his skin sagged, the whites of his eyes were yellowed and the blue irises dull. His shoulders had sunk; he didn't hold himself like the proud man he'd been. Everything about him looked beaten, defeated.

"I'm sorry, I just…I'm tired," I said. He simply nodded and left.

The following day I discharged myself. I was taking up a bed unnecessarily, in my opinion. I dressed and sent a text to Thomas to collect me. The cop sitting outside jumped to attention as I pulled open the door. He followed me to the nurses' station. The nurses fussed around, cursing, and organizing paperwork. When I had what I needed I left.

I raised my face to the sun and closed my eyes to absorb its warmth. Then I lit a cigarette.

"Are you going to arrest me?" I asked the cop, who'd stayed silent the whole time.

"I, err. No. I was just told to watch your room, make sure you didn't get unwanted visitors."

"So you were there for my protection? If you're going to lie, be confident about it. I'll be at my house if anyone needs me."

I climbed into Thomas' car and we headed for home. I rolled down his window and exhaled the smoke I'd been holding in.

"How's your shoulder?"

"Sore. How are you?"

"Unemployed," he chuckled.

"Did they arrest you? Dad said something about us all being under arrest."

"If I go quietly, lose my pension and all that shit, all charges are dropped."

"I'm sorry, I gave you the chance," I said.

"I know. My choice. So what do we do now?"

"I don't know. I can't think straight. Will we get to know anything?"

"I would imagine you would, Sierra was still your wife and your mom was…"

"Yeah, let's not call her that, for now."

I held in the cry of pain that wanted to force its way out of my body when Taylor jumped into my arms. My eyes watered though.

"Daddy, you're crying," she said.

"Happy tears, baby girl, I'm glad to see you."

I nuzzled into her neck, inhaling her sweet scent of innocence.

"She's been a really good girl, look what she made you," Trina said, walking up the hallway toward us.

"I drew you a picture, Daddy," Taylor said reaching out for the piece of paper.

Two stick figures held hands. I guessed the brown splotch beside them was a tree and then there was a horse.

"I think that needs to go on the wall," I said as I lowered her to the ground.

Trina placed her hand on my arm as Taylor ran off into the kitchen.

"I'm so sorry, Gabe," she said quietly.

I nodded, not sure what she knew and what she didn't.

"Beer?" I asked. She laughed as she patted her belly, her very round belly.

"Coffee then?" I asked.

"No, thank you. We'll head off now."

Taylor was chatting, asking me all about my accident. She'd been told I'd fallen from the loft, while helping her grandpa, she knew nothing about my mom. I would have to tell her, but I wanted to do that when we were alone. I had no idea of what to say, only that it wasn't going to be the truth. And then I had another decision to make.

I was angry, so bitterly angry with my mom. There would be a funeral at some point, and if I hadn't had Taylor, I wouldn't go. But was that fair to my daughter who doted on her grandparents? Should a five-year-old even go to a funeral? She hadn't attended her mother's.

Trina and Jake left, I walked them to the door and followed them to their car.

"Thank you, both. I really appreciate what you've done," I said.

"I just don't know what to say, Gabe. Do you know why your mom did it?" Jake asked. The question earned a slap from Trina.

"No, we don't. She lost her mind for a little while, I guess," I replied.

"You just concentrate on you and that little girl in there. I'll be over tomorrow to stock your freezer," Trina said.

I watched them drive away, wondering what the townsfolk knew, what assumptions had been made, and what whispers were going on behind hands.

Thomas sat at the kitchen table nursing a beer, he handed me one as I sat next to him. I looked at my daughter; she looked back. She cocked her head to one side as she stared at me.

"Baby girl, I've got something to tell you," I said, deciding not to wait any longer.

I put Taylor to bed after hours of crying and sobbing, questions and silence. She was wrung out; I was wrung out.

Her eyes were so swollen from her tears she could hardly open them. Her body was so exhausted from the outpouring of emotion that she fell asleep almost immediately.

I left her door wide open, so I could hear her and joined Thomas in the yard. He had a cigarette lit in one hand. I raised my eyebrows.

“Certain times, it’s called for,” he said.

I lit one myself and took a swig of my beer as I sat in one of the garden chairs.

“I couldn’t do it, Gabe. I couldn’t do what you do, be a dad and all that.”

“You could if you had to,” I said.

“What will you do about the funeral?”

“I don’t know, to be honest. I guess I have to go, if only for Dad’s sake. But there is one thing I have to do and soon. I have to speak to Zachary.”

I then told him what Dad had said in the hospital.

“So Zach was innocent all along?” he asked.

“I don’t know. He covered it up, to protect…her. And she tried to silence the victims to protect him, as well as herself. But something still niggles me.”

“She went about it in an extreme way.”

“I think she was starting to lose her mind. Dad had said she’d been prescribed sleeping tablets…Fuck!”

“She drugged Taylor,” Thomas said.

“Could she do that to her granddaughter?” he added

“She had no problem with shooting me. So, I guess so. Why, I don’t know, but from what I understand that would have been about the same time Zachary confronted her.”

“Do you think we’ll ever get to know the truth?” he asked.

I shook my head. “I don’t think so. Sierra died because she was going to expose the failings in the church, which would ruin Zachary. Is that motive to kill her? I don’t know.”

Chapter Twenty-Seven

Two weeks later, which was way quicker than any of us were expecting, we laid my mother to rest. I'd laughed at those words. I didn't want her to get 'rest.' Zachary, my dad, and I sat in the front row of our local church. The rest of the pews were filled with townsfolk, who had come to pay their respects. They'd loved her, there was a level of disbelief that she'd taken her own life, and I knew they were desperate to know why.

I'd decided Taylor wasn't to attend the funeral; she was too distraught. I'd do something with her, when she was ready. I'd find a way for her to say a private goodbye.

I didn't listen to the service; I didn't listen to the words of praise for a wonderful woman taken early. It was all bullshit. I couldn't look at the enlarged photograph that stood beside her casket. It would remind me of a woman that had betrayed me, that had lied. My dad gently sobbed and my heart broke for him. No matter what she'd done, he'd loved her so desperately.

I'd tried to rationalize it all over the past couple of weeks. I wanted to shed tears but I couldn't. As the service droned on, I thought back. She was a woman raped, who bore a child. I had to find that goodness in her to keep that baby, to love that baby, and not look at him and be reminded. But no matter what, my wife died because of her. She'd started it all, whether she'd lost her mind or not.

I was taken by surprise when I saw my father rise, the service was over and we were expected to follow the coffin. I accepted the pats on the back and the smiles as we walked down the aisle, out of the church into bright sunlight, and to a hole in the ground. I stood, as expected, beside my brother and father and watched her being lowered into the ground. Then I left.

I couldn't keep the pretense up anymore.

"Hey, baby," I said as I ran my fingers over my wife's name.

I sat beside her grave, not caring about the suit pants, and wrenched off the black tie. I shrugged off the jacket and loosened my collar. I wouldn't sit with my wife as if in mourning.

In hushed tones, I talked to her. I told her about Lily, what I'd done and how sorry I was for that. I told her how Taylor was doing, promising to bring her to visit soon. I cried. I wasn't sure how long I'd sat for, but the funeral party was making their way out of the churchyard. I watched my dad being supported by Sam, neighbors, and friends, weeping, wiping eyes, as they left. A shadow fell over me.

"It's time, Gabriel," Zachary said.

"I'm not coming back to the house. I can't fucking mourn her."

"No, it's time to put an end to all this."

I stood, not sure what he meant. We hadn't had a chance to sit down and speak, as much as I'd wanted to. I found it hard to be around him, to face him. No matter what he said, no matter the fact he'd face no investigation for his part in all that happened, I still didn't trust him.

"Come," he said.

I followed him to a waiting car. I hesitated by the passenger door.

"I know this is a lot for me to ask, but will you trust me, just this once?" Zach said.

"On one condition, you fucking tell me the truth," I said. He nodded his head.

I pulled open the door and got in. I was more than confident that I could overpower Zachary, if I needed to. I was more than confident that I could kill him, if I needed to. And he knew it as he watched me scan my eyes over the bruising still evident on his face.

"Twenty odd years ago I was asked to attend a meeting. I was just a priest then. That meeting was an invitation to join a committee dedicated to, let's say, cleaning up the church. I never denied that the church had spent many years covering up abuse. I was part of that. I believed I was doing the right thing. The church couldn't be compromised, the faith couldn't be questioned."

He started the car and we drove, I wasn't sure where and I didn't want to ask. I didn't want to interrupt him.

"I wasn't the one to interview him, but I was involved. I documented paperwork, that's all. In the beginning, I guess, I was no more than a clerk. I had no idea who he was, and I had limited information. But a few years ago, I was contacted by the FBI to help with their deprogramming. By then, I was a bishop and I led the clean up committee. As you can imagine, I was torn. I'd hidden crimes, Gabriel, and then I was working with law enforcement. I was trapped."

"Who were Romney and Midley?" I asked, knowing the answer but wanted to check whether he'd tell me the truth.

He sighed before he answered. "Who do you think they were?"

"Cult members."

"Yes."

"So how were you working with them?"

"I wasn't working with them. Recently I found some documents, details of the staff at the convent. I found a name, Gabe, our mother's name. I thought it coincidence at first. But dates and locations made me want to investigate further. I joined the cult, Gabriel, to find out, to help further expose what I knew I'd been covering up."

"If I had a dollar for every plausible story I've been told lately…"

"I don't expect you to believe me. What you've been through, I wouldn't wish on anyone. But I'm not the bad guy here. I found that phone, Gabriel, Sister Anna's phone. I hid it until I knew what to do with it. It was when Dad then found it I had some explaining to do."

"And Taylor, why did you walk into the barn with her?"

"I saw Mom go in there with a glass of water, I didn't think anything of it. I saw you on the porch, I saw Lily, and I saw you head to the barn. But it was when I heard Mom quietly talking to someone that I knew something was wrong. I heard her say, 'she's here.' I wasn't sure if that meant Taylor or Lily. I went to Taylor's room, I wanted to hide her: she didn't wake up. I panicked. I picked her up and carried her downstairs. I had no idea where to hide her; I walked around the yard at first. Until I saw Syd. Whether you think what I'm about to say is right or wrong, I used your daughter. I know what you thought of me, and if you saw her in my arms, I knew you'd react."

"React?"

"Yes, you'd fight."

"So you used my daughter to scare me enough to fight?"

"I used your daughter to help you find that level of aggression to save your life."

We fell silent for a while. I ran his words through my mind, over and over. I hadn't taken too much notice of where we were headed, until we pulled off the highway and onto a dirt road. We bounced along, following it through woodland. After a few minutes, the trees thinned and in front of us was a log cabin. There were many dotted around, vacation homes, hunting lodges, and a great place to hide.

“How did you know Syd?” I asked as he brought the car to a halt.

“At first, before I knew, I wondered if he was my father. He and Mom met up occasionally. Years ago, I even thought they were having an affair,” he chuckled as he spoke.

“But he is related, a cousin, I think. He was also an elder in the cult. Anna is dead, Gabe, she killed herself because she couldn’t do what Mom wanted her to do, she fixed a hose to her tailpipe and gassed herself. The statements sent to Thomas were something Mom concocted to give you something and then discredit your investigations. I had no idea; until I found the phone that Mom had Sierra involved. Everyone was manipulated; Mom fed Anna information to feed back to Sierra. Sierra delivered all that to everyone else. It became a race; get to the victims before the feds did. Mom used Sierra to do that in the hope they would speak freely as they might remember her.”

“And all that just to protect you and save her having to give testimony that she was raped,” I said, not believing a word he was telling me. “No, there’s way more to it than that.”

Zachary shrugged his shoulders. “Anyway, no more time for talk.”

He opened the car door and stood, looking at the cabin. I climbed from the car and followed him as he walked to the door, knowing I was very possibly walking into a trap. He took a key from his pocket and unlocked the door. As he did, I reached down and took the gun from the ankle holster I’d worn. I stood, making sure he was aware I held it in my hand. He opened the door and we walked in.

“The prodigal son returns,” I heard.

Sitting in the corner was an old man with thinning grey hair; bony, curled, arthritic fingers gripped the arms of the chair he sat in.

“Gabriel, meet my father.”

Zachary walked around the sparse room. He began to mumble.

“You see, Dad, you’ve caused so much pain to so many people, do you not see that?”

It seemed to me that this was a continuation of a conversation already started. I stood quietly.

“My Son, the Lord let his only son suffer. I am doing the Lord’s work.”

“You are neither the Lord nor I his son,” Zachary said.

“But you are mine, if your mother is to be believed, of course. How is she? I remember her well.”

“Dead, she blew her fucking brains out,” Zachary said, with such venom in his voice, it took me by surprise.

“Weak, you see. The women are all weak.”

I couldn’t detect one ounce of remorse or sympathy in his voice.

“So this is your brother?” he said.

Cold blue eyes looked over to me.

“Different father, thankfully,” I said.

He chuckled. “Gabriel. Such a powerful name. Do you know much about your namesake?”

Before I could answer, Zachary swung around; he held a gun in shaking hands, tears rolled down his cheeks. He took a step toward him and I watched Father Samuel smile. I stepped beside Zach and placed my hand on his arm, I gently lowered it. As I did, I noticed something that had my stomach lurch. The sleeve of his shirt had risen when he’d extended his arm, exposing his wrist. A wrist with a raised scar in the pattern of a cross.

I took another step, that time closer to Father Samuel, and I crouched down so I was face to face.

“I do know my namesake, and I bring you a message,” I said.

Slowly, Father Samuel brought his gaze away from Zachary and to me. I hid the shiver that ran up my spine and threatened to have my body involuntarily recoil. I wasn't religious, but in that moment, I saw evil, pure evil.

"You do not have a seat next to God. You do not have a place in heaven at all. You're going straight to hell."

I stood and took a step back. With his eyes still fixed on mine, and the smile still on his lips, I raised my gun.

"This is for Savannah," I said, as I pulled the trigger.

Zachary fell to his knees. He held his hands together in prayer. He didn't pray for his father, he prayed for himself, and for me. He begged forgiveness.

"Don't pray for me, Zachary."

Chapter Twenty-Eight

We drove the couple of hours home in total silence. We only spoke as we pulled up outside my house. Trina's car was sat on the drive.

"I'll give you one week, Zachary," I said.

He looked over to me.

"I'll give you one week to confess your part in covering up that abuse, and to being an active member of that cult. A high ranking member."

"But…"

"Don't give me any bullshit!" I shouted. "I saw an inventory, Zach. You documented statements taken from Father Samuel twenty fucking years ago. Twenty years ago my wife, and her sister, were in that convent. If you had done something then, they would not have led the life they had. Both would still be alive today. And I saw that scar. You went through initiation, Zachary. You cut your wrist; you bled over women and children as you fucked them. Where was your vow of celibacy then? At what point did you stop investigating the cult and embrace it? Where was your God, Zachary?"

He had the grace to lower his head and once again, I saw tears roll down his cheeks. The knowledge that he was more than an infiltrator had come to me when I'd seen the scar.

"Mom wasn't protecting your position in the church, was she? She was protecting your position in the cult because she knew you were part of it. You brought those fake feds to our house because they are your half brothers! You needed to know what Sierra had discovered, you, Zachary. It was never Mom was it? Did you tell her she would be exposed? Did you use her rape as an excuse to have her do your dirty work?" My voice rose on every word.

"She wasn't innocent, Gabriel. I told you the truth, I had no part in killing…"

I didn't let him finish his sentence.

"You manipulated Mom into killing, didn't you? You were the gun, it was your finger on the trigger, she was just the bullet."

He struggled to meet my gaze.

"You can run, you can hide, but I will find you. I will out you. I'm giving you the chance to do the right thing; I'm giving you the chance to redeem yourself. Children, God's children, suffered such terrible fucking lives, some by your hands. You've lied all the way through this. You're as guilty as Mom, maybe more so."

I couldn't look at him as he sobbed. His tears did not affect me in any way.

"I made a promise to my wife, that I would find out who and why, and I'd do something about it. I won't break that promise."

"I'll lose everything," he mumbled.

I slammed my hand on the dash so hard, he startled.

"Sierra was murdered, her daughter lost her mother, and I lost my wife. Lily was murdered, there's her child somewhere, now motherless. What about them? What about the hundreds of children who suffered? What about your mother, she took her own life, Anna, Syd even? What about their deaths that ultimately you caused?"

I opened the door and climbed out of his car. Before I closed it, I leaned down.

"One week, Zachary. And I'm only giving you that for the sake of my father, otherwise I'd have put a bullet through your fucking brain and let you rot with yours."

I walked away from him, opened my front door, and caught my daughter who had ran the length of the hallway and jumped into my arms. I buried my face in her neck to hide the tears that coursed down my cheeks. I didn't cry for Father Samuel, I didn't cry for my mother. I cried for all those children, the same age as my daughter. I cried for Lily's child and hoped that whoever had him, would care for him. I cried for my father because I knew that he would soon be burying his son.

Zachary would never turn himself in, he would never confess to what he did. Of that, I was sure. To do that, he also had to confess to all the sins both he and the Catholic Church had committed.

One week later my brother was found hanging from a beam in the barn. It had been Sam who'd found him. That was the only thing I was thankful for.

My dad was a broken man, a man not capable of leaving the house since he'd buried his wife and his son. I didn't attend Zachary's funeral. I knew a lot of the townsfolk questioned why. Thomas had told them I was caring for Taylor, she had suffered enough loss to not be subjected to another. The truth of it was, Taylor didn't know Zachary, she'd met him less than a handful of times. I hadn't even told her he had died. There was no way, not even for my father, that I could stand the hypocrisy of all the bells and whistles of a Catholic funeral for him.

I spent days and nights with Dad, Taylor was shipped from one house to another, and I told him what I knew. I documented everything and I handed it to Mich. I told them where to find Father Samuel but did not confess to killing him. I left that open and let them make the incorrect assumption that Zachary had. I felt no remorse for that.

As time went on Dad became frailer, he'd given up on life. Not even Taylor could rouse him from his rapid decline. He'd brushed away my request to see a doctor, he'd refused any help, and after a while, he shut himself in his bedroom. Taylor and I packed up our house and moved in with him.

I took him meals; I sat with him. We talked a lot. He relived his past, days in the army, the early days with Mom. He spent a long time teaching me what to do with the ranch, not that I didn't know what to do, of course. He was preparing me for when he wasn't around. He naturally assumed I'd take over from him.

Sam stuck around; he helped. He sat with Dad, sometimes for hours. I'd stand outside Dad's bedroom door and listen. I'd smile when I heard them talk, I'd smile more when there was silence. They didn't need words; they'd shared a lifetime together.

"How is the old man?" Thomas asked. He'd arrived for his twice-weekly evening visit.

"Sleeping when I checked, I'll go see if he wants anything, in a bit. How's Heather?"

"Moving in tomorrow," he said.

"That's great, Tom, I pleased for you."

"Yeah, I'll propose at some point," he said with a laugh.

"And the garage?"

"Doing good, want to see accounts?"

I'd handed the running of the garage to Thomas. He had surprised me, and Jake, with his administrative skills. What he knew about engines you could fit on a postage stamp, but he took the worry off me. I felt some responsibility for Thomas being booted out of his job and offering him mine seemed a sensible solution to both our problems. My heart wasn't in it, but it was an investment for Taylor.

"House sale going through?" he asked.

"Yeah, should be completed this week. Just a little paperwork to finish."

"And then what?" he asked.

"I want to rebuild this place, get rid of the ghosts, so to speak."

"Okay to go on up and see your dad?" he asked.

I nodded as I lit a cigarette. "Tell him I'll be up in a bit."

He'd been gone just a few minutes when he reappeared. He didn't need to tell me, I'd seen it in his face. I lowered mine to my hands and wept. I'd known it was coming; he'd given up. I just hoped I would have had a couple more months with him.

In the space of a couple of months I'd gone from having parents and a brother, to nothing but my daughter and a handful of friends.

It was those friends that kept me going through Dad's funeral. It was those friends that helped me look after Taylor and around the ranch. But it was only my daughter that kept me from joining my wife.

There were days the struggle to get out of bed was just too much of an effort, but I'd see Taylor and knew I had to. I had to put one foot in front of the other and take one step at a time, one day at a time. More so when reports started to come in.

I'd relived the past when Mich made an unexpected visit one day. He brought me up to speed on investigations. As I suspected, no charges were brought against Father Samuel, or Zachary, there was no point; they couldn't stand trial. It wasn't in the public's interest I was told. The only good thing that happened was Zachary had left a suicide letter, a long rambling, woe is me letter confessing everything. That resulted in a public announcement by the Catholic Church. They'd apologized for their failings; they'd made promises to right wrongs and to tighten their procedures. They'd assured the world they would be more transparent when it came to investigating some of the serious accusations that started to flood in. I had my doubts about that. As for cult? Well, it moved locations, was all I was told.

Chapter Twenty-Nine

"Horses are in," I heard. I'd been sitting in my dad's chair on the porch.

"Thanks, join me for a beer?"

Sam sat. He'd moved into the loft and was a permanent fixture. He didn't want pay, just lodging. I made sure that his fridge and cupboards were stocked each week. I had no idea if he had money, but he always had a fresh pack of cigarettes and gas in his truck.

"So, plans for next week?" he asked.

"We build a pavilion," I said with a smile.

"Be nice to have a party, liven this place up a little," he said.

Thomas was getting married; the ranch was the venue for the celebrations. I was looking forward to it. I was looking forward to seeing my baby girl in a pretty dress and the sneakers she was still insisting on wearing. I was looking forward to seeing my best friend settle down with Heather, the love of his life, so he kept telling me. I was looking forward to having some fun.

"It sure will, Sam. And who knows, maybe you'll find a nice woman to keep your bed warm," I said with a laugh.

"I don't need no woman, Gabe. I have all I want for now." He gave me a salute, and holding his beer, made his way back to the loft.

Once the wedding was out of the way I was going to make a start on building a new home. I'd decided that the old one had to go. It wasn't to erase memories, but Taylor and I deserved a fresh start. I was excited about it, I'd be back to doing something useful with my hands.

"Daddy?"

"What's up, baby girl?"

Taylor had been playing with a new puppy. I hadn't wanted her to have a puppy, but I couldn't seem to refuse her. She took care of her foal, so I had no doubt she'd take care of her dog.

"Is Grandpa a strange name for a puppy?"

"Erm, yes, it is. How about we think of something else?"

"I miss Grandpa," she said. It had been noticeable that she didn't mention her grandma, but I wouldn't question her on why.

"How about Gramps then?"

"Gramps is dumb," she said with a laugh.

"Gra?"

She laughed out loud. "You're silly," she said.

"You're sillier," I grabbed her sides and tickled her.

The puppy jumped up at us. The sound of her laughter soothed my soul. I didn't need anything, or anyone, but my daughter.

"I think it's time for you to go to bed, little lady."

She stopped laughing and looked up at me. I hadn't realized what I'd said until I saw her smile. Those were the words my dad used.

"Well, you're not a baby girl anymore," I said as I lifted her up.

"I'll always be your baby girl, Daddy," she replied, wrapping her legs around my waist and her arms around my neck.

I laughed as I carried her up to bed.

"Tell me about my new bedroom," she said, as I settled her under her covers.

"It's going to be all pink and pretty."

"Eww, I don't like pink. Can I have horses on the wall? Please?" she grinned at me.

"You can have whatever you want."

She snuggled down and I sat in the chair beside her. I picked up a book that we had started the night before and opened it to start a new chapter. I read. I didn't get to the end of the chapter before she'd fallen asleep. Living at the ranch had changed her. She didn't have nightmares, she slept straight through the night, and being outdoors for most of the day ensured she was tired out.

I left Taylor sleeping and made my way back to the porch. The sun was setting and I rested my feet on the railing. I'd been so keen to leave the ranch when I was younger, I guess I had to do that to appreciate just what a beautiful place it was.

"For fuck's sake, will you stop panicking? If she doesn't turn up, there's plenty of fucking bridesmaids to choose from," I said.

Thomas and I were standing at the church and he was pacing. We should have been inside but he insisted on checking where Heather was.

"She's late," he said.

"She's a couple of minutes late and isn't that what they do?"

An elderly woman rushed up the church steps. "She's here, you can't see her yet," Heather's mom said as she ushered us in.

Thomas and I stood at the altar while he beamed, waiting for his bride.

Sierra and I hadn't had a church wedding, so I wasn't aware of the service. I observed Thomas watch Heather walk down the aisle. I watched her smile broadly at him.

I listened and when prompted handed over the rings. When the ceremony was over, I posed for a couple of photographs with the bride and groom, with my daughter, who wore her sneakers, and then I snuck off to see my wife.

“Hey, baby, I missed seeing you last week, it was madness with Thomas.”

I told her all about the bachelor party, Thomas was pretty much out of it within the first hour. We’d hit a bar in town, got thrown out of the diner with a wink from Mary, and then partied at the ranch.

When I was done talking with my wife, I jumped in a car and headed for the ranch, there were preparations to check on before the married couple arrived. Taylor would follow on with Thomas’ new, already moaning, mother-in-law.

Sam had everything under control and it wasn’t long before the wedding party arrived. We’d erected a pavilion in the front yard. We had caterers in and out of the house and delivering food. Heather had forbidden the hog roast Thomas wanted.

When that was done, I had to do the most terrifying thing ever; I had to give a speech.

I stood and scanned the faces looking back at me. Most I knew, townsfolk that Thomas and I had grown up among. It was a short speech, the traditional thanking of the bridesmaids, wishing the bride and groom all the luck in the world, and a couple of funny stories from our childhood. Once I’d sat down and gathered Taylor in my lap, I relaxed; official duties were over.

Evening guests had started to arrive and I’d taken Taylor back in the house a little earlier to change. She was filthy, but happy. She’d spent most of the afternoon playing with Trina’s two children and wanting to hold the new baby.

“Don’t they look wonderful together?” I heard.

I'd been resting my back against the bar, watching the first dance.

I turned to look at a woman, one of the evening guests who had recently arrived.

"They do, I'm pleased for them."

"Do you mind if I join you? It's not the easiest being the only singleton at a wedding," she laughed.

"Sure, what can I get you to drink?"

"Whatever you're having is fine with me," she said.

I smiled as I raised my bottle of beer. "A bottle of beer will go down nice right now," she said.

Something in my stomach knotted. Her voice, with its gravelly tone, hit me right in the center of my chest.

"So, I take it you're one of Heather's friends," I asked.

"Yes, we've known each other a while, from college. I've recently moved to town. I'm taking over at the veterinary clinic. Oh, excuse my manners…"

She turned to me and held out her hand.

"My name is Victoria, Vicky for short. I'm your new vet," she said.

"Then I'm pleased to meet you, Vicky. Gabriel, and this is my ranch."

We clinked our bottles before each taking a sip.

"So, a vet," I said.

"Yes, small, large, domestic, farm, you name it, if it's sick, I'll fix it," she said.

I liked her confidence, and I liked listening to her voice.

"Daddy!" Taylor came running at me.

"Taylor, meet Vicky, she's a vet, she looks after sick animals," I said.

"No way! I want to be a vet, can I be a vet?"

Vicky crouched down and took one of Taylor's hands.

"Well then, Miss Taylor, if you ask your daddy nicely, he can bring you to the clinic one morning. We'll see how good you are as a vet's assistant."

"Cool, when, Daddy?"

"When Vicky says it's convenient, baby."

"Tomorrow? I have a foal and a puppy," Taylor said.

"Tomorrow is fine by me, but let's leave the foal and puppy at home, shall we?"

"Tomorrow, Daddy?"

"I can hear, Taylor, and sure, why not."

Vicky stood, "Maybe we'll get an ice cream after, I heard that diner is something not to be missed."

Taylor skipped off. "I'm sorry, she's a little excitable," I said.

"She's adorable. Tomorrow then, it's a date," she said before taking another sip of her beer.

Heather came over, squealed and hugged Vicky. "You made it, and you've met Gabe I see," she said, with a wink.

"Get the feeling that was supposed to happen?" I said.

"Mmm, I do. Hold that beer for me, I'll be back," she said, handing me her bottle then dragging Heather off by the arm.

"Well?" Thomas said as he sidled up beside me.

"Well, what?"

"Nice isn't she? I met her a week or so ago."

He looked at me and smiled. "What are you up to?" I asked.

"Nothing, my friend, nothing. Now, how about I go get my wife back, and you get to talk to the rather attractive Vicky? The vet, in our town, living here now, needs friends, got a son, same age as Taylor, perfect match."

I shook my head and laughed as he walked off.

The attractive Vicky, 'the vet, in our town, living there, in need of a friend, with a son, perfect match,' walked back to join me. She took the beer bottle I was still holding and smiled, shrugged one shoulder and took a sip.

"Well, this is awkward now," she said. I deflated a little.

"Oh?"

"I wasn't aware I was being set up on a blind date, feel free to go do what groomsmen do, no need to be polite."

"Vicky, I wouldn't be a good groomsmen if I didn't take care of the guests, and I'd like to take care of you right now," I said.

"Are you flirting with me, Gabriel?"

I laughed, "Honestly? I wouldn't know how."

"Me neither. So, how about we get drunk instead?"

I laughed. It was the hardest, loudest, and most honest laugh I'd experienced in a long time.

"I think, Vicky, you and I are going get along just fine."

I saw Thomas in the distance; he was giving me a thumbs up. I wouldn't be as crass as to return the gesture, so I raised my bottle of beer instead.

"How off putting would it be, since this is our first blind date, if I say I need a cigarette?"

I pretended to think about it, I screwed my eyes and furrowed my brow as if in concentration.

"I think, for a first blind date, I'd say, let's go, I'll join you."

We sat on the porch and rested our feet on the railing. We were interrupted constantly by Taylor, until eventually, she curled up on the swing seat and fell asleep. And we talked. We didn't stop talking, laughing, and drinking beers. The evening wound down, guest started to leave and eventually Vicky looked at her watch.

"Thomas said you have a son," I said, hoping to delay her leaving.

"Yes, I'm in the process of adopting him, so not biological. He's a wonderful boy."

"That sounds fantastic, how old?"

"Five, well, he'll be five in a few weeks. Maybe Taylor can come over and party. Other than Heather, I don't really know anyone here yet."

"Why did you come here?"

"The job, basically. I started off in a rural practice on a farm just a couple of hours drive from here, but the lure of the city lights enticed me. I've kind of had my fill of pampered pooches, I want to get back to what I love," she laughed as she spoke.

"So you thought you'd try your hand at the big stuff?"

"I sure did. And I wanted somewhere nicer for Benedict to grow up. He hasn't had the best start, not that he's fully aware of that, of course. Anyway, I guess I ought to be getting back," she said as she stood.

"You're not driving, are you?"

"No, I'm catching a ride." She leaned toward me. "See the miserable mother-in-law, the one stamping her feet a little because she wanted to leave an hour ago, and Thomas wouldn't let her?"

"I do."

"That's my ride."

"Shit. I don't think I'd keep her waiting any longer."

She pulled away and I missed the closeness.

"Tomorrow then?"

"Sure, we'll look forward to it," I said.

She gave me a smile and left.

"We're off," I heard. Thomas strode across the yard.

He shook my hand, "Thank you, for all this," he said.

I gave Heather a kiss to her cheek and watched them depart as well. They were heading off on their honeymoon the following morning, flying to California for a week. I'd offered to drive them to the airport but was then informed the mother-in-law was joining them! I'd stifled laughter at that.

When the yard was empty of people I surveyed the mess. It would wait.

I picked up my daughter and carried her into the house. We climbed the stairs, and I laid her on the bed. I pulled off her sneakers, pulled the second grubby dress over her head, and pulled the sheet from under her. I kissed her forehead and left her sleeping.

I stripped off my clothing and took a shower. I thought about Vicky, I thought about Sierra. She'd be happy for me, I was sure of that.

I climbed under the sheet of my bed and smiled. I had a date in the morning! I had a date with someone I thought I could really like and with the added bonus of a son, a son called Benedict.

I sat bolt upright—Where had I heard that name before?

A cold shiver ran over my body as I remembered.

I didn't get all the answers. Those went to the grave with Lily, Zachary, Mom, and Syd.

From that moment on, though, I made a pledge to myself. I'd leave the past where it was. I'd remember my wife, as I knew her, from the five wonderful years we'd spent together, and I'd forget the rest.

I owed it to Lily to protect her son. I owed it to Taylor to keep her safe.

It was time to move on, time to stop chasing answers from dead people and wait for those still alive to pick up where we hadn't quite left off.

The End

Acknowledgements

My heartfelt thanks to the best beta readers a girl could want, Karen Shenton. Alison Parkins and Rebecca Sherwin- your input is invaluable.

Thank you to Margreet Asslebergs from Rebel Edit & Design for yet another wonderful cover, this makes our ninth collaboration!

I'd also like to give a huge thank you to my editor – Karen Hrdlicka

A big hug goes to the ladies in my team. These ladies give up their time to support and promote my books. Alison 'Awesome' Parkins, Karen Shenton, Karen Atkinson-Lingham, Marina Marinova, Ann Batty, Fran Brisland, Elaine Turner, Kerry-Ann Bell and Louise White, Catherine Bibby & Ellie Aspill, – otherwise known as the Twisted Angels.

To all the wonderful bloggers that have been involved in promoting my books and joining tours, thank you and I appreciate your support. There are too many to name individually – you know who you are.

Gabriel is my first foray into the thriller/suspense genre – I normally write romantic suspense. You'll find a little sexy in here, I'm afraid I can't not write it! The photograph you see on the cover inspired this book. I have to thank Wander for introducing me to his amazing photography skills. I saw this picture and the image called out to me. I bought it without knowing what I would write. I sat and studied it for ages until Gabriel came to me.

If you wish to keep up to date with information on this series and future releases - and have the chance to enter monthly competitions, feel free to sign up for my newsletter. You can find the details on my web site:

www.TraciePodger.com

Life is not about the destination but the journey.

Cover design – Rebel Edit & Design
Model – Fin
Photographer – Wander Aguiar
http://www.wanderbookclub.com

About the Author

Tracie Podger currently lives in Kent, UK with her husband and a rather obnoxious cat called George. She's a Padi Scuba Diving Instructor with a passion for writing. Tracie has been fortunate to have dived some of the wonderful oceans of the world where she can indulge in another hobby, underwater photography. She likes getting up close and personal with sharks.

Available from Amazon, iBooks, Kobo & Nook

Fallen Angel, Part 1

Fallen Angel, Part 2

Fallen Angel, Part 3

Fallen Angel, Part 4

Evelyn - A Novella – To accompany the Fallen Angel Series

Rocco – A Novella – To accompany the Fallen Angel Series

Robert – To accompany the Fallen Angel Series

Travis – To accompany the Fallen Angel Series

A Virtual Affair – A standalone

Gabriel – A standalone

Coming soon

The Facilitator – August 2016

Jackson – November 2016

Letters to Lincoln – 2017

Rocco: The Missing Years – 2017

Harlot

Stalker Links

https://www.facebook.com/TraciePodgerAuthor/

https://twitter.com/TRACIEPODGER

Amazon Author Page – https://author.to/TraciePodger

http://www.TraciePodger.com

Book Trailers

A Virtual Affair - https://youtu.be/6UR68KtLQPc

Gabriel - https://youtu.be/VOgduZqo_io

26770082R00172

Printed in Poland
by Amazon Fulfillment
Poland Sp. z o.o., Wrocław

CR
COROMANDEL

MARCO ZANUSO IN SOUTH AFRICA

Edna Peres & Andrea Zamboni

Artifice

Foreword | Fulvio Irace

An unfair bias persists with regard to Marco Zanuso, whose extraordinary talent seems even to this day almost unbelievably confined to factory architecture and industrial design. Zanuso's image as an ingenious chronicler of constructive forms derived from prefabrication and modular construction prevails throughout his prodigious professional portfolio of over 250 projects, but for which Italian architectural history reserves a footnote or, at most, an ambiguous quote used without true appreciation for his work.

If projects such as the Olivetti factories in Argentina, Brazil and Italy, those of IBM in Santa Palomba and Segrate, the Necchi factory in Paiva or Brinel in Caselle d'Asolo were all that his legacy consisted of, they would still offer enough evidence to secure him a place as a leader within an architectural panorama where the search for thoughtful responses to reality was engrossed by the creation of "space" and "identity". His prolific work in housing remains an enigma: despite the quality of the houses, they are often overlooked as though to imply that they are insignificant "exceptions".

This accurate monograph written by Edna Peres and Andrea Zamboni records an episode that we knew about but had not investigated in detail – the home designed for Sydney Arnold Press and Victoria de Luria in the South African veld – and serves to remind us of the necessity to look at Zanuso's work beyond the frayed division that separates different genres and formats: industry, residency, design.

The meticulous analysis of the house's design, the complexity of its construction, the additional competency required to include complementary knowledge (such as botany, zoology, landscaping), the evidence from new sources (such as private archives made available for this occasion) and, above all, an anti-ideological and passionate reading that one would expect from a new generation of authors lead us to consider this book as much more than an in-depth monograph. In fact, I propose it marks the beginning of a process of reviewing historical twentieth-century literature, an advancement that anticipates future syntheses in which weights and hierarchies are redistributed more convincingly to bridge the gap between "words" and "things".

In this sense, it would be useful to continue these observations beyond the limits of this subject and include perceptive views about the relation between Zanuso's projects of this distinct genre and other protagonists who had similar and overlapping experiences. For those who embark on meticulously recording the relationship between a young Milanese architect and his distant clients, it may be useful, for example, to recall the empathetic relationship that interlaced another great Milanese, Gio Ponti, in his later years, with Venezuelan clients Anala and Armando Planchart, who travelled to his studio during the hot summer of 1953 to propose the construction of a villa on their *quinta* on the El Cerrito hillside. It opened an important chapter in the internationalisation of Italian architecture, also in part due to the pivotal role that an architectural publisher played in being the window to the world at that time: the Plancharts discovered their interest for Ponti's work in *Domus*; Mr and Mrs Press were impressed by Zanuso's work in Sardinia while paging through *Réalités*.

The "tropical paradise" that Ponti discovered in Caracas was not unlike that of the archaic South African savannah: the reaction by both architects was to resist exoticism in favour of modernity with an ancient heart. Going against the prevalent model of the American glass house, Ponti proposed a Mediterranean house that implodes its comforts internally, rather than passively opening them up to the landscape. Ten years later, immediately after exploring the site, the idea of an open "dam" became Zanuso's founding act for creating shelter in an area that required protection before passive admiration. The patio of Villa Planchart thus corresponds to the design of the long, shaded patios of Coromandel House: the origins may be Italian, but they find their logic in the management of a well-tempered environment. These are the same reasons that motivate Peres and Zamboni to define Zanuso's method, and those that the old master so appreciated through regular features in *Domus*.

On the other hand, Zanuso's archaism, far from being contradictory to his precisely designed prefabricated beams and panels, finds an unexpected parallel in Angelo Mangiarotti (also afflicted by the same fate), who, in the middle of his quest for total prefabrication, found the time (in *Domus* no. 465 of August 1963) to praise "Tradition" with a case study of 1700 Val Divedro. Furthermore, was it not the noble father of ethical rationalism, Giuseppe Pagano, who suggested that the benefits of modern architecture should aspire to the effectiveness of an anonymous architecture which he termed "rural"?

Within the limits of this brief foreword, I would finally like to highlight the work of Alberto Ponis in Sardinia, produced during the same time and in the same place as Zanuso's masterpiece: both followed an identical path of taking cues from the topography, but their response to creating a new landscape differed. Zanuso's austerity (which contrasts with the way Ponis's delicate geometry favours the ground) strengthens his creation, demonstrating that, if necessary, the pathways to authenticity are infinite and the time has arrived for you to open your eyes if you truly want to follow the path of a freer and more conscious history.

Fulvio Irace is professor emeritus at the Politecnico di Milano. An architectural historian and critic, he is a recipient of the Bruno Zevi Prize, and his invaluable research and multiple publications on the Italian response to Modernism have laid the foundation for new perspectives and insights into this pivotal period of contemporary architectural history.

●●●

Contents

Introduction | Christian Sumi

In the summer of 2021, the Icelandic artist Olafur Eliasson placed Renzo Piano's Fondation Beyeler in Basel "under water". The building's glass facades were dismantled, while newly created interior water ponds were drawn out into the exterior landscape and filled with green-coloured water. Consequently, the building, designed with four parallel walls, became interlinked with the exterior environment, rendering it comparable to Marco Zanuso's Coromandel House in South Africa: massive quarried-stone walls cut and stretch into the landscape like spatial canyons, which, along with pools at one end, anchor the 240-metre-long building into the terrain. The perception and significance of these two interventions could, however, not be more different. The artificiality of Eliasson's installation contrasts with Zanuso's Brutalist intervention – abstraction and immediacy are diametrically opposed. Zanuso's apparently simple and "natural" intervention is in fact extremely exacting, as seen in his various sectional and detail drawings – for example, cladding, an extensive concrete structure, green roof – demanding that the architect command an extensive technical knowledge.

As architects and academics, Edna Peres, from South Africa, and Andrea Zamboni, from Italy, are ideally and legitimately placed to present the various aspects of Zanuso's multifaceted project – landscape, architecture, construction, typology, and so on – within the broader context.

MARCO ZANUSO (1916–2001)

Marco Zanuso belongs to the third generation of Milanese architects who pursued a tradition of Rationalism, among them Gae Aulenti, Angelo Mangiarotti, Bruno Morassutti and Vico Magistretti. From 1945 onwards, they cultivated an approach towards Classical Modernism that was more open and relaxed, with many also working in the emerging field of industrial design, Zanuso included.

He was committed to the legacy of Modernism, not its doctrine, hence he constantly explored and reflected upon his approaches and potentials, as demonstrated by the numerous essays he published. As with Mangiarotti, technology and construction turned into the generative and formative force for the design, but always remained subordinate to the issues of space, function and location. A decisive factor in Zanuso's work was the integration of structure and infrastructure in response to a pursuit to veer away from a mechanical towards an organic conceptualisation of architecture. This applies in particular to Coromandel House. It further implies that Zanuso operates in the interface between different disciplines and is therefore a team player.

CENTRING THE VARIOUS PROJECT PARAMETERS

The authors provide a detailed overview of the social and cultural interests of Zanuso's distinguished clients: Sydney and Victoria Press. The input and requests, particularly those of Victoria Press, are decisive in the construction process. These are multilayered and extremely challenging, yet Zanuso repeatedly handles them with great skill, astuteness and patience, by focusing on the essentials, breaking them down and tying them back into the architectural concept so as to prevent the design from fragmenting into separate episodes.

INFRASTRUCTURE MACHINES AND GESAMTKUNSTWERK

The house is a linear, "five-aisled" 240-metre-long bulwark, broken up in the middle and with a portico in front.

The relationship between length and width, or rather width and the proximity of the individual layers that enclose space, resemble narrow medieval city streets, creating an enormous spatial tension and density. Quite rightly, the authors refer to Zanuso as a designer. In his Doney television set (1962), the transistor plates are packed tightly around the neck of the screen, comparable with the tightly nested niches of the shower, washbasins and toilet present within the *poché* of Coromandel House. The nesting and density are reminiscent of Le Corbusier, and Amédée Ozenfant's purist paintings of closely interconnected glasses and carafes.

STONE WALLS AS ENCLOSURES OCCUPYING THE TERRAIN

Step by step, Zanuso analysed the landscape, looking to the mines and to the archaic structures on site. The building, with its concrete-frame structure clad by six basalt-stone-walls stepped slightly one below the other and incised into the ground, is erected parallel to the topography at the threshold between the plateau and the ascending hillside. The authors discuss in detail the reference projects, in particular the two houses in Arzachena (1964) that were built with local stone. In the broadest sense, their slightly twisted positioning in relation to each other resembles Robert Venturi's Trubek and Wislocki Houses (1972), which were built using balloon-frame construction typical of that region. Both projects raise the question of regional architecture, but at Coromandel Farm it is implemented with a breathtaking directness: the quarried stone walls, or the enclosures per se, mark the primary act of taking possession, of demarcation or reinforcing the terrain. In the 1946 *Casa per Vacanza economica* project, published in *Domus* no. 211, two retaining walls staggered behind each other create the base support for the building. In House Press, Zanuso radicalises the concept: the stone walls themselves become the building.

A CONTEMPORARY RECORD

The authors compellingly refer to the importance of Coromandel House as an example of an architecture that infiltrates the South African landscape and combines the qualities of a contemporary architecture with an archaic one. The question of preserving this contemporary example of post-war Modernism is therefore central, and early efforts to safeguard it have begun. Perhaps nature will eventually take over in future. As a ruin – the most authentic state of any building – it will become part of the fragments of archaic structures in the surroundings and imbue the spirit of one of Michael Heizer's land art projects. As an accomplice to this notion, the Italian landscape architect Pietro Porcinai, "extended the vision" to produce partially realised plans for the rest of the farm with its dams, paddocks and canals. Roberto Burle Marx, too, became involved. However, it was Patrick Watson who brought the vision to fruition.

RETURNING TO THE "TRIED-AND-TESTED" AND MONUMENTALISATION

From 1969, Zanuso planned and supervised the construction of the new Edgars corporate headquarters for Sydney Press. After the planning limitations posed by an office tower design in Johannesburg city centre and the consequent relocation of the site to its outskirts, Zanuso used the opportunity to completely revise the project, by adopting an open, horizontal and expandable floor plan, like an "environmental structure" with supporting service rooms for delivery, entrances and technology. Zanuso adopted the 12 metre x 12 metre x 12 metre triangular grid that he used ten years earlier in the Olivetti factory in Brazil. The return to a proven structural system and its adaption and modification for a different use is typical of Zanuso's thinking: a rational design process underpinned by efficiency and experience. The relationship between structure and use is open, reflecting the Structuralist ideas of the time, such as those of John Habraken.

In contrast to Brazil, where the grid structure generates, or rather defines, its outer edge, in Johannesburg the cantilever makes it more autonomous, a type of "façade libre" that surrounds it and acts like a "spatial elastic band". Infrastructure takes the form of monumental columns, and the external escape stairs are integrated into every corner. Due to the inclination of the ground floor panels, the base and consequently the building complex as a whole are monumentalised.

This publication by Edna Peres and Andrea Zamboni contributes an important piece in the mosaic of ongoing archival research within the Zanuso collection at the Archivio del Moderno at the Università della Svizzera Italiana (USI).

Christian Sumi is professor emeritus at the USI, architect and university lecturer. His practice, with Marianne Burkhalter, is dedicated to an exploration of the nature of materials and construction, which includes the research interest into Zanuso's building methodology and construction systems. Their recent works are published in *Burkhalter Sumi Architects: Documenti di architettura*, Electa, 2016.

01

The pools at the eastern end of Coromandel House

02

Olafur Eliasson's "Life" installation at Fondation Beyeler, Basel, 2021

01

02

03

04

1. Origin

03

Coromandel Farm c. 1969

04

Coromandel pine plantation

The clients

The unusual design for Coromandel House was initiated by Sydney and Victoria Press, who aspired to create a home that belonged to the veld. Their interest in contemporary architecture as an expressive and innovative, functional art form can be understood from their international background and local business activity, which led them to commission four distinctive architectural projects in South Africa

05

In creating and developing a remarkable home, there are at least three essential components: a thoughtful architect, an engaged client, and a sensational setting. A large budget can also help, but does not guarantee a noteworthy result. For the house created at Coromandel Farm, South Africa, these ingredients for success were present. But to understand why a building like Coromandel House (1975)[1] exists in South Africa, we must begin with the clients as the project's progenitors: Sydney Arnold Press (1919–1997) and Victoria de Luria Press (1927–2015).

Sydney and Victoria nurtured a deep and longstanding quest for excellence. In their ambitions and insatiable curiosity for learning, they were kindred spirits, as demonstrated both by their individual successes and the impressive projects they undertook together during their marriage (1952–1984). Their interest in architecture resulted in the creation of four significant buildings in South Africa. Understanding what motivated their architectural and other accomplishments can be gleaned from their backgrounds – how they defined excellence and sought to achieve it, how they seized opportunities, and how they persevered through obstacles to attain their objectives.

The couple's respective ancestors hailed from the Kovno province of Imperial Russia, now part of Lithuania. Institutional prejudice and persecutions there, as well as consequent social and economic instability, led many Jews to emigrate to the New World – the United States in pursuit of the American Dream – but also to South Africa following the discovery of gold in the Witwatersrand in 1884. While Victoria's family relocated to the former in the early 1900s, Sydney's had moved to the latter in the 1890s.[2] For both of them, skills for adaptation, resilience and a determination to succeed in their new countries would have been formative lessons learned from their parents. In addition, the devastating effects of the Great Depression (1929–1939) profoundly influenced their views regarding the importance of a good education and of hard work.

Sydney's upbringing in a South Africa that was undergoing considerable industrial change exposed him to two significant influences that would define his life: his early childhood on a farm in rural Namaqualand, and the qualities of entrepreneurship that his father, Philip Press (1878–1941), demonstrated as an immigrant trader, which influenced Sydney and his brothers Basil (1915–2003) and Hubert (1922–1996) in their future success in the retail business.

Philip had arrived in South Africa during 1894 as a 16-year-old, and began trading in the region of the Western and Northern Cape with his brother.[3] In 1910, he established a trading post and hotel about 300km north of Cape Town at a crossing along the Olifants River. Its establishment in such a remote location was a calculated risk by Philip, who banked on the government's imminent investment in an irrigation scheme in the area, and specifically the train line and station (1915) near his trading post. But the choice of location turned out to be an advantageous one, and by 1920 the infrastructural elements had led to the birth of a town informally called Klaver, though it was finally officially registered as Klawer by 1954. In its early days, Philip Press played a pivotal role establishing this new settlement morphologically, socially and economically. When he moved his family to Cape Town in 1926 to give his children a better education, he sold his trading post and hotel to his cousin but kept his farm, producing prize-winning oranges and enjoying his status in the region as an elder.[4]

05

Sydney Press at Coromandel House in the 1980s

Philip's sons inherited his enterprising character and, thanks to his determination to give them the best possible education in Cape Town, they were able to pursue opportunities that could bring them greater prosperity. Sydney's academic brilliance was confirmed on various occasions. He excelled in English literature, demonstrating that he was "a natural and unobtrusive intellectual",[5] while also showing great athletic skill as a sportsman. By 1935, aged 16, he had earned a bursary to study at the University of Cape Town after graduating from the South African College School with a first-class matric. But with the ripple effects of the Great Depression, his father's declining health and his older brother already attending university, Sydney felt a "certain quality of desperation"[6] and chose to find employment to help support his family and provide them with security once again, while also gaining some independence. He thereby substituted an academic tertiary education for a practical life education. He took on a position in the Edgars retail store, which had been founded in 1929 and was owned by his maternal aunt's brother-in-law, Eli Ross.[7] He described himself later as having "no skill, no knowledge about clothing and less about footwear".[8] After a year, the routine had become tiresome and did not match his need for achievement and independence. Consequently, when Eli Ross offered him the opportunity to open and manage a second Edgars store in a disadvantageously positioned basement shop on Eloff Street in the Johannesburg Central Business District (CBD), the 17-year-old Sydney did not hesitate to take up the risky offer.

By 1938, Sydney had entered into a partnership with Ross, as Edgars Stores Ltd was expanding and becoming increasingly profitable.[9] His perseverance led to the establishment of a chain of stores around the country. Sydney understood the role of people in successful enterprises, both outside of the organisation and within, later claiming that "managers and employees of a business are worth approximately 15 times as much as its physical assets".[10] During the Second World War, Sydney's devotion to Edgars was interrupted by his service as the Executive Secretary of the Defence Force Liaison Office. The toll of the war, combined with overexertion in leading the multi-store Edgars enterprise – which was listed on the Johannesburg Stock Exchange in 1946[11] – led to his decision to move to New York in 1947. There he assumed the role of buyer for Edgars from a more advantageous international location, furthered his education at the New School for Social Research, and pursued a personal interest in psychoanalysis, a burgeoning medical field unknown in South Africa at that time. Exposed to a world of opportunity and innovation, he became acquainted with modern merchandising, retailing and manufacturing methods already prevalent in the United States, and established a lifelong interest in recruiting and cultivating the best (though not necessarily the most acclaimed) professionals in their respective fields to consult for Edgars, as well as for his other projects.[12]

While living in Manhattan he met Victoria, a graduate of the Drexel Institute of Technology[13] in Philadelphia's first work-study programmes in the country. In 1948, Victoria received the second highest honours in a Bachelor of Science degree in Home Economics majoring in fashion design;[14] it was also during this time that she won the "dress of the year prize" for *Mademoiselle*, which she modelled herself in New York City.[15] A passion for design and the broader horizons available in Manhattan made

06

Sydney with his daughter, Suzanne, while revisiting Klawer in the Western Cape

07

Round Hill, c. 1961, designed by Steffen Ahrends for the Press family

06

07

leaving the provincial life in Philadelphia a necessary step for Victoria in pursuing her aspirations.[16] She began working in the studio of the revolutionary American fashion designer Claire McCardell (1905–1958), who specialised in comfortable and stylish ready-to-wear clothes for women who balanced careers and families during and following the Second World War.[17] After hours, Victoria would pursue her passion for art history by reading widely about art and design, and visiting galleries, museums and historic houses.[18] She especially loved the history of art and architecture, antiques and horticulture, and throughout her life she refined her knowledge with further education, complemented by a natural sensitivity to context, bold experimentation and patient observation.[19]

Sydney and Victoria married in New York in 1952 and moved to Johannesburg in 1954, where they settled while continuing to maintain close international ties. Sydney continued to grow and expand Edgars to include new brands like Shelley Shops, Sales House and Jet. His success and enterprising business practices had a significant impact on the retail sector in South Africa. While Sydney was forging new ground in the fashion retail industry and in various non-profit foundations and societies in South Africa,[20] Victoria provided the essential behind-the-scenes support needed to sustain that high level of growth and success. Initially, she used her garment design and construction knowledge as a dress designer at Edgars, and Sydney would consult with her on strategic aspects of the business.[21] Victoria applied her design skills to curate impressive interiors and gardens in all their homes; first in their Sir Herbert Baker (1862–1946) house in Inanda (1902) in Johannesburg, and then in Round Hill (c. 1961), their seaside home in Sedgefield designed by Steffen Ahrends (1907–1992). She cultivated an extensive knowledge of botany, gardening and horticulture, experimenting with novel landscape design ideas and composition, which included the use of indigenous flora. Victoria later applied her horticultural knowledge to founding Lovemore Plants, a hydroponic indoor plant business that she established to encourage the use of plants in office environments, a philosophy that was ahead of its time.[22]

Sydney and Victoria travelled frequently, exposing themselves to international artistic and cultural trends and innovation. On trips to London in particular, their interest in collecting antiques began a lifelong passion for Victoria; later she took a one-year course at The Architectural Association on *The History and Theory of Architecture* in the 1980s.[23] The design skills she refined throughout her life were implemented in her homes, of which 4 Cheyne Walk in London and the Palazzo Giustinian Persico in Venice became revered design masterpieces.[24] Victoria sought to bring visual harmony to her creations in which "beauty was the highest standard for her".[25]

Both Sydney and Victoria's strong individual visions and desire for achievement outside of expectations and established norms led to some unconventional choices. When they encountered someone in whom they saw brilliance regardless of age or experience, they would often hire them over those with established careers. They trusted talent, but were actively engaged throughout the process, sometimes directing, other times learning and observing. Coromandel Farm and particularly Coromandel House are great examples of this process. Their collaboration between a diversity of individuals – which apart from Zanuso included professionals from geologists to audio-visual experts, stonemasons from Sekhukhuneland, furniture designers from the United States, local ceramicists and everything in between – brought to life an architectural artefact that continues to captivate.

●●●

08

Victoria Press with a set of drawings at Coromandel House, c. 1972, overseeing the construction progress

08

ENDNOTES

1 Also known as House Press, Casa Press, African Manor House and the Coromandel Estate Manor House.
2 Dos Santos, J, 2018; Press, D, 2018, p. 58.
3 Press, DS, 2020.
4 Press, DS, *Klawer. How a Town is Born*, USA, 2018, p. 58.
5 Maskew, 1969, pp. 40–41.
6 Personal letter to Margaret Courtney-Clarke.
7 Kaplan, M, 1986, p. 264.
8 Maskew, 1969, pp. 40–41.
9 Dos Santos, J, 2018, p. 129.
10 Maskew, 1969, pp. 40–41.
11 Dos Santos, J, 2018, p. 134.
12 Press, C, Interview, 2020.
13 Now Drexel University.
14 Press, DS, 2020.
15 Press, C, Interview, 2020.
16 Press, DS, 2020.
17 Chia, M, *The New York Times Style Magazine*, April 2015.
18 Press, C, Interview, 2020.
19 Ibid.
20 For example, he founded the South Africa Foundation to further the study and implementation of progressive psychology studies in South Africa.
21 Press, C, Interview, 2020.
22 Katsikakis, D, Interview, 2020.
23 Ibid.
24 Cator, C, "Cheyne Walk – An Interior by Victoria Press", Christie's, London, 2015.
25 Press, C, Interview, 2020.

The genesis of Coromandel House

In their search for originality, their open-mindedness and fascination with the world beyond South Africa, Sydney and Victoria Press discovered in a magazine the twin villas in Sardinia designed by Marco Zanuso in the early 1960s. Casa Arzale became the bridge that connected the architect and clients, and was the starting point for the architecture at Coromandel House

09

At the start of 1969, Marco Zanuso (1916–2001) was at the height of his career as a well-regarded industrial designer and professional architect who was lecturing part-time at the Politecnico di Milano. Little did he know that, some 8,000km away in South Africa, Sydney was about to invite him to travel to Johannesburg for a commission: to design a new house on a remote location at Coromandel Farm. No prior connection existed between them, and the invitation came as a result of chance; an article in an international magazine had so intrigued Sydney and Victoria that the necessary investigations were made to find the architect of the featured project.[26]

Although the role of a magazine feature, which acted as the connection point between the clients and Zanuso, could be dismissed as a happy accident, it merits closer investigation. Firstly, it indicates the high calibre of international publications which Sydney and Victoria were reading. Secondly, the international architect they commissioned did not exclusively specialise in domestic architecture,[27] yet in his design they saw a perfect fit to help them realise their ambitious architectural dreams for their farmhouse. Thirdly, it reveals the clients' affinity for international culture and their responses to local trends,[28] which gave rise to the unique aesthetic of Coromandel House and, later, Edgardale.

As Sydney and Victoria were setting up their home and expanding their business in Southern Africa, they would have experienced two opposing forces: following the Second World War, while the Western world was opening up, in South Africa it seemed to be narrowing. Dramatic post-war social and economic transformations saw a period of optimistic and unprecedented economic growth in the United States, parts of colonialised Africa, Asia and Europe. These changes were echoed in South Africa but limited by its own political extremes. Following the National Party's rise to power in 1948, the nationalistic political policies of racial Apartheid were gaining momentum and entrenched state-sponsored racist restrictions. There was a sense of increasing isolation from mainstream Western progressiveness, with limitations placed on personal expression and access to information. Television was not introduced in South Africa until 1976 and all other media was censored. For those who were able to travel to Europe and the United States, the liberal freedoms they witnessed, which allowed for cultural and ideological expression, would have felt exhilarating.

Sydney had been inspired by his personal experience of American liberalism during the years he spent in New York City from 1947 to 1954. After returning to South Africa, he instituted increasingly multiracial policies in Edgars' workplaces and manufacturing plants, culminating in the integrated, multiracial environment at the Edgardale headquarters. He also supported several foundations that promoted education and environmental stewardship. Through these and other quiet acts of rebellion, including the ongoing invitations to international experts to visit and contribute their knowledge to South Africa, he attempted to push the bar not only in his own personal initiatives, but also for those whom he could directly impact, regardless of race.

While they reached out to international consultants for their business and other interests, Sydney and Victoria remained connected to cultural and scientific innovation, and built up a large frame of reference for contemporary art, architecture and design. They consulted publications

09

Marco Zanuso during one of his visits to Coromandel Farm, with poles in the background that mark the house's future location

such as *The Architectural Forum* and *Architectural Digest*, *Connaissance des Artes*, *Réalités* and the *New Yorker* as sources of inspiration.[29] *Réalités*,[30] for example, used a photo-journalistic approach to documenting contemporary society,[31] while in a more architectural context, *Architectural Forum*[32] would highlight issues arising from increasing urbanisation and its effects on the environment, providing a reliable and insightful exposure to the world beyond. It is not surprising therefore that Sydney would later say that the genesis for Coromandel House came from an article published in *Réalités* that featured "some simple beach houses built [...] on the Costa Smeralda in Sardinia".[33] This was confirmed by an article in *Abitare*, which stated, "The two twin villas built in Sardinia by Marco Zanuso in the early 1960s were the starting point and background for this African architecture."[34] This project, Casa Arzale (1962–1964), would eventually be the catalyst for Zanuso working together with Sydney and Victoria on creating Coromandel House.

Casa Arzale was built in Arzachena on Sardinia's Emerald Coast, and would feature in the March 1967 edition of *Connaissance des Artes*, as well as in the July 1967 edition of *Architectural Forum,* which included a few photographs of spartan-like vacation houses, although the limited accompanying text neglected to mention the name of the architect. Black-and-white photographs of these austere stone "fortresses", which were actually twin vacation houses set into a rugged Arzachena landscape, were sufficiently captivating for Sydney and Victoria to begin a search for the architect responsible among business acquaintances and friends in the design world.[35] Through Cesare Larini at Equatoriale, the Italian buying office for Edgars in Milan, Zanuso was forwarded Sydney's invitation to travel to South Africa. And so, Casa Arzale became both the precedent and architectural starting point for Coromandel House.[36]

Casa Arzale's location on the northern Sardinian coast, with its sandy beaches and the emerald blue-green sea after which it was named, attracted yachting elites away from the overcrowded French Riviera. By 1962, its development was well underway[37] and strict architectural guidelines were set to preserve the coastline's natural beauty, vernacular styles and prevent overcrowding.[38] Although capitalising on the increased interest in the area, Casa Arzale and its twin did not form part of the Emerald Coast property development. Yet their aesthetic and rationale matched and perhaps even exceeded the objective of preserving natural beauty. From a few mid-1960s photographs that circulated at the time, the significance of this highly original design within Zanuso's architectural portfolio is visible: the essence of his modular architectural design planning approach, and direct response to landscape.

Built simultaneously between 1962 and 1964, some 20 metres from the beach, the two houses functioned as summer vacation homes. They were functional and permanent support structures for two Milanese families in Zanuso's extended family, who sought to capture the outdoor feeling while enjoying a seaside holiday. Each house was built within a narrow parcel of land that connected to a local access road to the beach, and consisted of thick granite stone walls enclosing square plans of 15 metres by 15 metres. The walls, which acted like fortifications to protect the internal spaces from the harsh sea winds and hot sun, were placed on site in such a way as to maximise the benefits offered by the natural setting.[39]

10

Courtyard of Casa Arzale in Sardinia

11

Sydney and Victoria discovered Casa Arzale in a magazine. This article, printed in *The Architectural Forum*, vol. 126, no. 5, June 1967, also features the project

10

VACATION FORTRESS ON SARDINIA

On a low promontory along Sardinia's Costa Esmeralda stands a seemingly simple vacation house by Marco Zanuso. In a typically Mediterranean way, the house is both a part of the landscape and an unmistakably man-made form. Its inclined granite walls look almost like natural outcroppings, yet it is square and symmetrical.

The random stone walls are interrupted only by small windows except for a broad entrance opening (photos left), spanned by three archaic-looking blocks —two cantilevered ones and a keystone.

Inside the walls, the house is laid out in a Greek-cross plan (above), with the central cross uncovered as an open living room. The four roofed rooms at the corners, otherwise square and solid, are clipped off diagonally at their inner corners so that all of the spaces open toward the circular table at the center of the cross.

Although it appears to be symmetrical from the entrance, the cross-shaped living space is actually truncated on one side, where a traditional masonry oven is flanked by a bathroom and a kitchen. On the opposite side, a shoulder-high opening offers another view of the sea.

FACTS AND FIGURES
Vacation house, Arzachena, Sardinia. Marco Zanuso, Architect.

64 FORUM—JUNE—1967 65

11

12

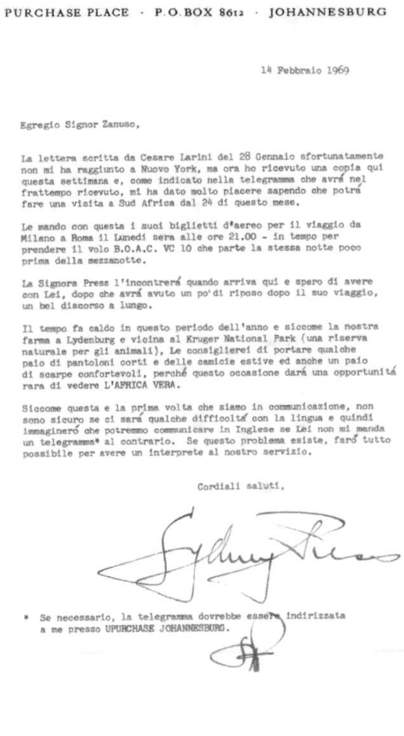

PURCHASE PLACE · P.O. BOX 8612 · JOHANNESBURG

14 Febbraio 1969

Egregio Signor Zanuso,

La lettera scritta da Cesare Larini del 28 Gennaio sfortunatamente non mi ha raggiunto a Nuovo York, ma ora ho ricevuto una copia qui questa settimana e, come indicato nella telegramma che avrá nel frattempo ricevuto, mi ha dato molto piacere sapendo che potrá fare una visita a Sud Africa dal 24 di questo mese.

Le mando con questa i suoi biglietti d'aereo per il viaggio da Milano a Roma il Lunedi sera alle ore 21.00 - in tempo per prendere il volo B.O.A.C. VC 10 che parte la stessa notte poco prima della mezzanotte.

La Signora Press l'incontrerá quando arriva qui e spero di avere con Lei, dopo che avrá avuto un po'di riposo dopo il suo viaggio, un bel discorso a lungo.

Il tempo fa caldo in questo periodo dell'anno e siccome la nostra farma a Lydenburg e vicina al Kruger National Park (una riserva naturale per gli animali), Le consiglierei di portare qualche paio di pantoloni corti e delle camicie estive ed anche un paio di scarpe confortevoli, perché questo occasione dará una opportunitá rara di vedere L'AFRICA VERA.

Siccome questa e la prima volta che siamo in communicazione, non sono sicuro se ci sará qualche difficoltá con la lingua e quindi immagineró che potremmo communicare in Inglese se Lei non mi manda un telegramma* al contrario. Se questo problema esiste, faró tutto possibile per avere un interprete al nostro servizio.

Cordiali saluti,

* Se necessario, la telegramma dovrebbe essere indirizzata a me presso UPURCHASE JOHANNESBURG.

13

12

Sydney and Victoria Press, c. 1969

13

Sydney's invitation letter to Zanuso, written in Italian, sent via Cesare Larini at Equatoriale in Milan, February 1969

They were a place of safety. With their shutters closed, these low-rise vacation "fortresses" may appear to be archaic to the untrained eye, may even seem like unsophisticated sheep-shelters, but their spartan simplicity belies sophistication. They demonstrate a masterful response to placemaking; their existence is a response to untouched nature, the allure of the open landscape in contrast to city life, and the pleasure of quietly relaxing by the sea. This is the truest response of the initial brief that Zanuso received, which was to recreate the experience of camping in this "very simple and wild" place.[40]

Casa Arzale, powerful for its simplicity and sensitivity to *place*, captivated the imaginations of Sydney and Victoria, and their perceptiveness for this project is telling. Zanuso had a novel approach to materialising delightful solutions in a variety of locations – from a compact seaside home to a large corporate office – and harmoniously captured the essence of a building visually freed from the technological complexities that would otherwise clutter the space. Sydney and Victoria's interest in Casa Arzale offers considerable evidence of their search for originality, their open-mindedness and their fascination with the world beyond South Africa. In the development of Coromandel House which followed, it seems that they were propelled to try even harder to make the house not only physically habitable within its site and brief, but more importantly, as Charles Moore suggests, to make it "metaphorically habitable, where we can go beyond where we are to wherever our imaginations will transport us".[41]

The almost decade-long exchange between architect and clients, which started in 1969, and grew to include another building, Edgardale (1978), persisted despite administrative, organisational, geographical and professional difficulties. Their alliance was based on curiosity, continuous creative energy and mutual respect, and fuelled design innovation within the house and its specific characteristics. This international association of like-minded individuals who sought to make a private statement has left its mark on South Africa's landscape and, with quiet resolve, is slowly rippling out into the world, like an archaeological ruin at one with the landscape and revealing its value.

●●●

ENDNOTES

26 Truswell, H, "Spirit of the Veld", *Fair Lady*, 15 May 1985, pp. 54–60.
27 Zanuso designed at the smallest and largest scale and had established his career as an industrial product designer, as well as an accomplished corporate architect and urban planner.
28 Press, C, Interview, 2021.
29 Press, C, Interview, 2020.
30 Founded in Paris 1946; closed 1978.
31 De Mondenard, A, 2018, p. 3.
32 Founded in Boston 1892, closed 1974.
33 Truswell, H, 1985, p. 59.
34 ZM, *Abitare*, vol. 191, 1981, pp. 14–23.
35 Press, C, 2020.
36 Steyn, G, 2016.
37 In the 1960s, Sardinia was in its early stages of development. Among its investors was Prince Shah Karim Al Hussaini, Aga Khan IV (b. 1936), who succeeded his grandfather as the spiritual leader of the Ishmaili Muslims at just 20 years of age. He graduated from Harvard in 1958, around the time when British banker John Duncan Miller saw the potential of the northern Sardinian coastline and assembled investors to buy and develop it.
38 https://robbreport.com/travel/destinations/italian-yachting-aga-khans-2724776
39 Navone, A, "La rivoluzione nell'impianto della casa", in Crespi, L, et al., *Marco Zanuso: architettura e design*, 2020, pp. 53–58.
40 Zanuso, M (Jr.) and Lotus, 2003, p. 96.
41 Moore, C, 1974, p. 49.

The Zanuso method

"When I build my house, I will go to the edge of the city and look for a meadow." With these words, Marco Zanuso summarised his ideal house, the traces of which can be seen in Coromandel. In the evolution of his design thinking, from his earliest houses to those built just before 1969, the ideas, themes and methodologies that mature in complexity at Coromandel House are followed

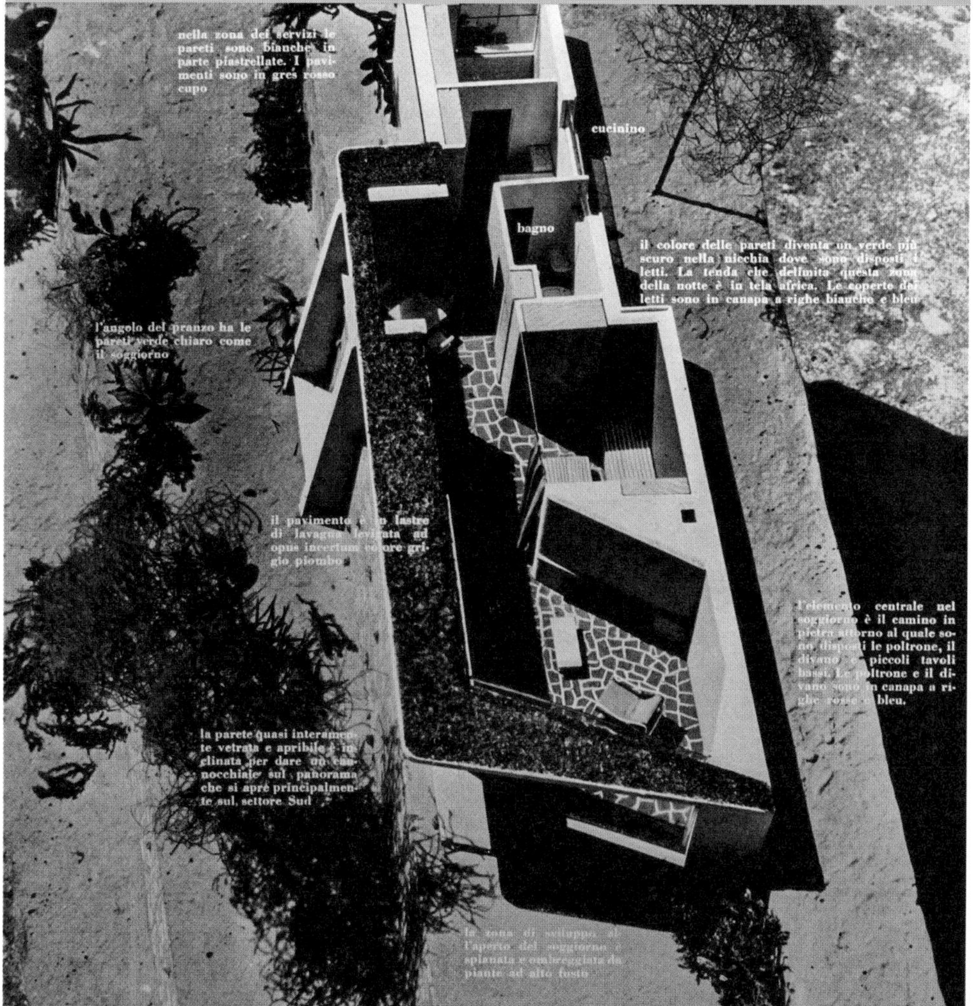
nella zona dei servizi le pareti sono bianche in parte piastrellate. I pavimenti sono in grès rosso cupo
cucinino
bagno
il colore delle pareti diventa un verde più scuro nella nicchia dove sono disposti i letti. La tenda che delimita questa zona della notte è in tela africa. Le coperte dei letti sono in canapa a righe bianche e bleu
l'angolo del pranzo ha le pareti verde chiaro come il soggiorno
il pavimento è in lastre di lavagna levigata ad opus incertum colore grigio piombo
centrale nel è il camino in rno al quale so- i le poltrone, il piccoli tavoli ltrone e il di- canapa a ri- bleu.
la parete quasi interamente vetrata e apribile è inclinata per dare un cannocchiale sul panorama che si apre principalmente sul settore Sud

In 1969, the same year he designed the famously innovative Brionvega Black Box television, Zanuso set off from Milan on 24 February for Lydenburg[42] in South Africa by invitation of Sydney and Victoria. His journey marked the beginning of the Coromandel House project. It unquestionably bears Zanuso's signature forms but, given the size of the brief and the site's particularity, it provided an opportunity for the Milanese architect-designer to advance and refine his theory of living. By tracing a few residential projects that he conceptualised in the three decades between his graduation from the Politecnico di Milano and his arrival in South Africa, it is possible to recognise many of the design themes, architectural theories and other ideas that would later manifest themselves in Coromandel House.

The essence of the Coromandel House concept lies in one of Zanuso's earliest ideas, a text published in *Domus* magazine in August 1942: "I will go to the edge of the city and look for a meadow ...". Yet this would be realised, fully formed, not in Italy, but in the South African veld in 1975. It was in the context of *Domus*, under the direction of Ernesto Nathan Rogers (1909–1969) who introduced the subtitle "The Man's House", that Zanuso defined his point of view on living and his ideal house. But even before that, the architectural principle that later developed in Coromandel was fixed in Zanuso's explanatory text accompanying a conceptual project published by *Domus* in response to an appeal launched by the magazine. "The house and the ideal" was part of a larger initiative promoted under the direction of Massimo Bontempelli (1878–1960)[43], who between 1942 and 1943, during the Second World War and its ensuing professional stasis, launched a "call for projects" in *Domus*, intended to include the most promising young architects who gravitated towards the magazine. When it became clear to everyone that the Second World War would not be a passing event, but was changing the equilibrium of the world, it was decided that the appropriate response to the shortage of commissions and opportunities was to prompt architects to reflect on their idea of living. It was a way to publish idealist hypothetical projects, but also to rally a new generation of architects towards a new, growing cultural elite, for which *Domus* represented its voice.[44] The initiative was promoted from volume 176 onwards, via an editorial essay that defined the context and meaning of each edition:

> *Domus* invited architects to share, with confidence, the ideal project for their dream home. [...] This is how we return, from dreams to proposals that will be very urgent tomorrow, or already are. [...] This race for the ideal is a kind of uprooting. [...] Here they are free from the hooks with which society, slow in taste and intelligence, tries to irremediably stop them, so that they may only serve them instead of save them. [...] The architects' manifestos must be read not only as a guide to their imaginary plans but also as accents of human confession that often transpire [...]. This is a lesson for everyone: not only for the artists I want to save but for us, who are not artists and therefore can only be customers: because we will discover our ideal home, and broaden our horizons for our dream home only by leaving the artist the freedom of his creative imagination.[45]

The *Domus* volumes released during this period placed great emphasis on the ideal house projects submitted by Gian Luigi

14

"House and nature", a project by Zanuso and Gianni Albricci published in *Domus* magazine no. 211, July 1946. This aerial view of the model without a roof shows the internal spaces

Banfi, Enrico Peressutti, Lodovico Barbiano di Belgiojoso – who together with Rogers were founding partners of BBPR architects – Irenio Diotallevi, Franco Marescotti, Cesare Cattaneo, Carlo Mollino, Carlo De Carli, Angelo Bianchetti and Cesare Pea, as well as Marco Zanuso, the youngest participant. The response was extraordinary, especially the way that the architects decided on a theme and its defining potential, and on an ideal client who would then translate the intentions and different points of view into projects accompanied by drawings and texts – sometimes poetic and passionate, other times more technical or programmatic. For Zanuso, the client of his ideal house is a family that grows over time along with their home. Zanuso's idea is that of:

> a nucleus, like a cell, which can grow with the family; that can follow and become part of its elements. Life will take place in large, bright spaces; or contained in limited spaces. In all points you will feel continuity: in the vertical and horizontal planes. The rooms do not exist as limited environments but as spaces that continue without solution in a succession of different sizes. The house is built on one floor. The bridge-built roof is anchored to the vertical structure, made up of stone walls.[46]

In this, Zanuso's first residential project, the principle of a cumulative system of modules that can ideally grow with the family is clearly expressed – conceptually, structurally and constructively – and which he implemented in subsequent projects, not just residential ones. Modularity, the conception of a building as an organism composed of elementary cells that can aggregate to compose sets with their own physiology, constitutes the core of Zanuso's design and construction research. Zanuso's thinking favours attentiveness to the process rather than the formal result, a reason why he is able to control different scales of project designs, from construction to production in the studio workshop, from architecture to industrial design:

> The module of a building, from Vitruvius to the present day, has always been given by a certain measure repeated a number of times to allow the practical realisation of the architectural organism and provide a concrete relationship with reality. The validity of this procedure is not denied, but it can no longer be absolute. If we propose a new architectural dimension, we also need to replace one unit of measurement with another and develop a different method of analysis and synthesis for the given design. The object module, an elementary unit considered complete, in the planimetric as in the altimetric value, on plan and spatially, allows us to establish the new, current and always different limits of architecture. Summarising broadly, we could say that the module of a residential neighbourhood coincides with the typical building typology; an industrial arrangement, with the production unit; a school, with the classroom, etc, that is, for any theme it becomes essential to identify a fundamental nucleus, which circumscribes a specific space and which has an absolute value, such as to guide the development of the entire architectural organism. The thesis of the object module can easily lead to solutions without any limits in space and time. Once the elementary unit capable of satisfying any functional and aesthetic need is identified, the assumption is that all problems are also eliminated. It will be enough to repeat that unit, the number of times necessary to realise the new object. Few words are needed to affirm that an organism always has a form defined in space and time, and however many times its elements may repeat rhythmically, it has a beginning and an end, and above all that, among the infinite possible

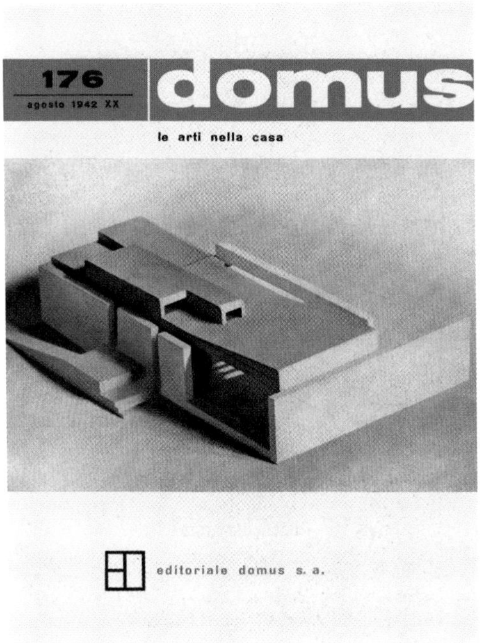

15

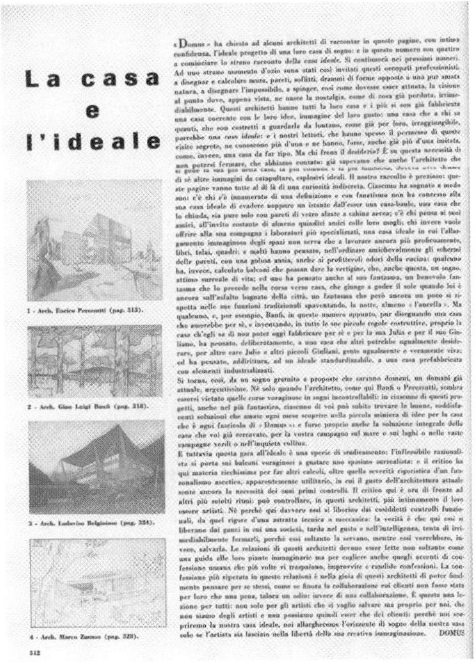

La casa e l'ideale

« Domus » ha chiesto ad alcuni architetti di raccontar in queste pagine, con intima confidenza, l'ideale progetto di una loro casa di sogno: e in questo numero son quattro a cominciare lo *strano racconto* della *casa ideale*. Si continuerà nei prossimi numeri. Ad uno strano momento d'ozio sono stati così invitati questi occupati professionisti, a disegnar e calcolare mura, pareti, soffitti, drammi di forme opposte a una pur amata natura, a disegnare l'impossibile, a spinger, così come dovesse esser attuata, la visione al punto dove, appena vista, ne nasce la nostalgia, come di cosa già perduta, irrimediabilmente. Questi architetti hanno tutti la loro casa e i più si son già fabbricata una casa coerente con le loro idee, immagine del loro gusto: una casa che a chi sa quanti, che son costretti a guardarla da lontano, come già per loro, irraggiungibile, parrebbe una *casa ideale*: e i nostri lettori, che hanno spesso il permesso di queste visite segrete, ne conoscono più d'una e ne hanno, forse, anche già più d'una imitata, come, invece, una casa da far tipo. Ma chi frena il desiderio? È su questa necessità di non potersi fermare, che abbiamo contato: già sapevamo che anche l'architetto che si gode la sua più bella casa, la più comune e la più [illegible] di sè altre immagini da catapultare, esplosivi ideali. Il nostro raccolto è prezioso: queste pagine vanno tutte al di là di una curiosità indiscreta. Ciascuno ha sognato a modo suo: c'è chi s'è innamorato di una definizione e con fanatismo non ha concesso alla sua casa ideale di evadere neppure un istante dall'esser una casa-baule, una casa che lo chiuda, sia pure solo con pareti di vetro alzate a cabina aerea; c'è chi pensa ai suoi amici, all'invito costante di almeno quindici amici colle loro mogli; chi invece vuole offrire alla sua compagna i laboratori più specializzati, una casa ideale in cui l'allargamento immaginoso degli spazi non serva che a lavorare ancora più proficuamente, libri, telai, quadri; e molti hanno pensato, nell'ordinare amichevolmente gli schermi delle pareti, con una golosa ansia, anche ai profittevoli odori della cucina: qualcuno ha, invece, calcolato balconi che possan dare la vertigine, che, anche questa, un sogno, attimo surreale di vita; ed uno ha pensato anche al suo fantasma, un benevolo fantasma che lo precede nella corsa verso casa, che giunge a goder il sole quando lui è ancora sull'asfalto bagnato della città, un fantasma che però ancora un poco si rispetta nelle sue funzioni tradizionali spaventando, la notte, almeno « l'ancella ». Ma qualcuno, e, per esempio, Banfi, in questo numero appunto, pur disegnando una casa che amerebbe per sè, e inventando, in tutte le sue piccole regole costruttive, proprio la casa ch'egli sa di non poter oggi fabbricare per sè e per la sua Julia e per il suo Giuliano, ha pensato, deliberatamente, a una casa che altri potrebbe ugualmente desiderare, per altre care Julie e altri piccoli Giuliani, gente ugualmente e veramente viva; ed ha pensato, addirittura, ad un ideale standardizzabile, a una casa prefabbricata con elementi industrializzati.
Si torna, così, da un sogno gratuito a proposte che saranno domani, un domani già attuale, urgentissime. Nè solo quando l'architetto, come qui Banfi o Peressutti, sembra essersi vietato quelle corse voraginose in sogni incontrollabili: in ciascuno di questi progetti, anche nel più fantastico, ciascuno di voi può subito trovare le buone, soddisfacenti soluzioni che amate ogni mese scoprire nella piccola miniera di idee per la casa che è ogni fascicolo di « Domus »: e forse proprio anche la soluzione integrale della casa che voi già cercavate, per la vostra campagna sul mare o sui laghi o nelle vaste campagne verdi o nell'inquieta collina.
E tuttavia questa gara all'ideale è una specie di sradicamento: l'inflessibile razionalista si porta sui balconi voraginosi a gustare uno spasimo surrealista: e il critico ha qui materia ricchissima per far altri calcoli, oltre quella severità rigoristica d'un funzionalismo ascetico, apparentemente utilitario, in cui il gusto dell'architettura attuale sente ancora la necessità dei suoi primi controlli. Il critico qui è ora di fronte ad altri più sciolti ritmi: può controllare, in questi architetti, più intimamente il loro essere artisti. Nè perchè qui davvero essi si liberino dai cosiddetti controlli funzionali, da quel rigore d'una astratta tecnica o meccanica: la verità è che qui essi si liberano dai ganci in cui una società, tarda nel gusto e nell'intelligenza, tenta di irrimediabilmente fermarli, perchè essi soltanto la servano, mentre essi vorrebbero, invece, salvarla. Le relazioni di questi architetti devono esser lette non soltanto come una guida alle loro piante immaginarie ma per cogliere anche quegli accenti di confessione umana che più volte vi traspaiono, improvvise e candide confessioni. La confessione più ripetuta in queste relazioni è nella gioia di questi architetti di poter finalmente pensare per se stessi, come se finora la collaborazione coi clienti non fosse stata per loro che una pena, talora un odio: invece di una collaborazione. È questa una lezione per tutti: non solo per gli artisti che si voglio salvare ma proprio per noi, che non siamo degli artisti e non possiamo quindi esser che dei clienti: perchè noi scopriremo la nostra casa ideale, noi allargheremo l'orizzonte di sogno della nostra casa solo se l'artista sia lasciato nella libertà della sua creativa immaginazione. DOMUS

1 - Arch. Enrico Peressutti (pag. 313).

2 - Arch. Gian Luigi Banfi (pag. 318).

3 - Arch. Lodovico Belgiojoso (pag. 324).

4 - Arch. Marco Zanuso (pag. 328).

512

16

15

The ideal project for a house by Zanuso, published in *Domus* no. 176, August 1942. The cover shows the model with a clear definition of the walls and the plain roof system

16

Domus no. 176, August 1942. The text "The house and the ideal" launched the call for architects to design their dream home, with their projects to be published in the pages of the magazine during 1942–1943

> compositions of elementary forms, there is one that overcomes all the problems posed. Forms can be repeated, but not infinitely; they determine the size of new organisms, and are not determined by them.[47]

On the other side of the coin, Zanuso's research in those early years explored – theoretically and practically – the possibility of removing the construction of the house from site and taking it to the workshop. In another issue of *Domus*, in which Zanuso describes his thoughts on the industrialisation of construction, Ernesto Nathan Rogers opens with an editorial entitled "Men without a home" dedicated to the theme of post-war reconstruction as an opportunity for a rethinking of ways of living, for a new refounding vision. Rogers opens the magazine with these words:

> This magazine targets people who, almost all of them, have a comfortable enough

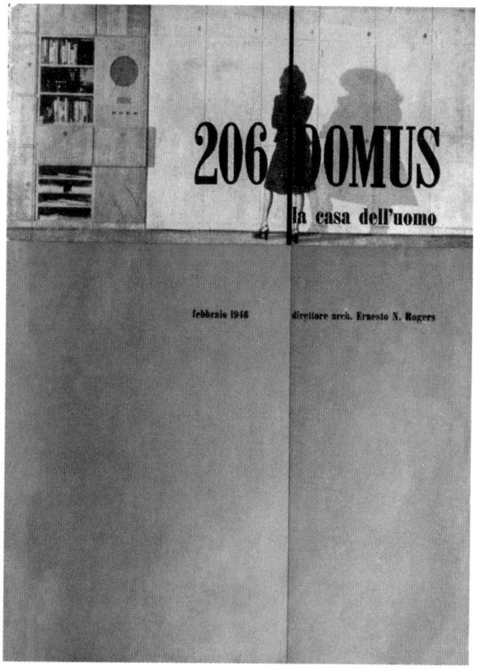
206 DOMUS
la casa dell'uomo
febbraio 1946
direttore arch. Ernesto N. Rogers

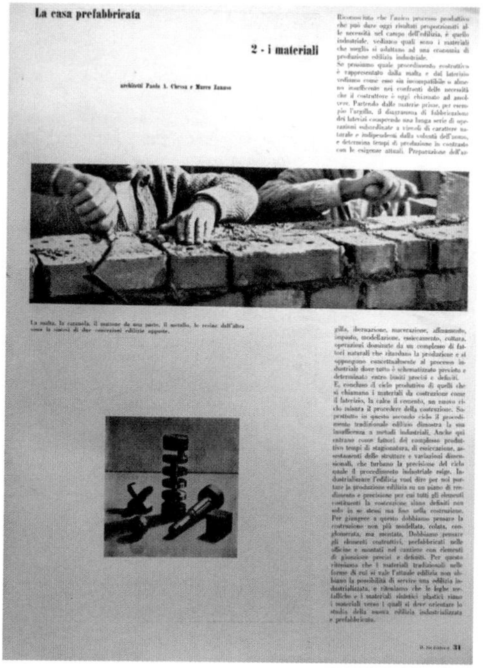
La casa prefabbricata
2 - i materiali

17

207 DOMUS
la casa dell'uomo
marzo 1946

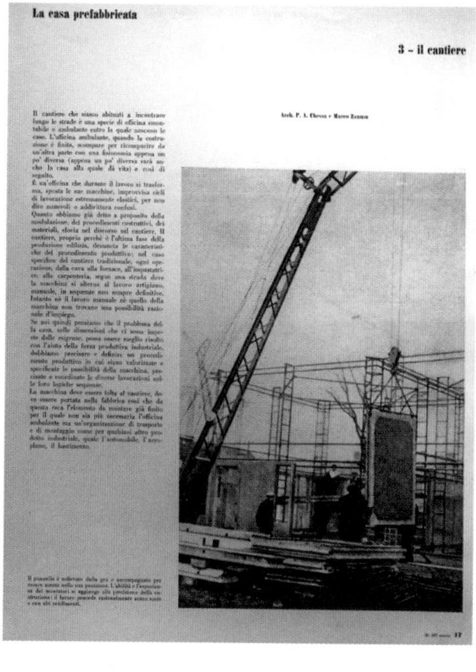
La casa prefabbricata
3 - il cantiere

> home, but I recognise that this is not possible for those who do not even have their own room. [...] Recent experiences have revealed the inconsistencies of our life – especially our bourgeois life – suffocated in the trunk of useless ornaments: those most aware have understood that they lack the most substantial goods, while so many objects that surround them only materialise prejudices, externalities, dross. Those who have the privilege of protecting their family with a roof should aspire to be fully human and, to the extent of these values alone, build their own home: comfortable and beautiful, of course. That the homeless may aim for it, is not an insulting challenge, but reflects the hope of a life, all lawful and possible, even if not yet achievable for everyone.[48]

Implicit in this critique of bourgeois life denounced by Rogers, a vision emerges that initiates from new lifestyle values that inform a reform of the discipline, of construction culture, and the very idea of design. A few pages later, Zanuso tackles how this new construction culture and materiality could unfold:

> If we recognise that the only production process that can fulfil contemporary construction needs lies in the industrial process, let's see which materials are best suited to an economical industrial construction process. [...] Concluding the production cycle of what are called building materials such as brick, lime and cement, a new cycle measures the progress of construction. It is in this regard that traditional building processes prove insufficient for the industial process. [...] Industrialisation of construction means that we can raise construction production to a level of performance and precision whereby all the elements are defined not only in themselves but by the construction process itself. To achieve this we must think of the construction no longer modelled, cast, conglomerated, but assembled. We have to think about construction elements, prefabricated in workshops and assembled on the construction site, with precise and defined joining elements. For this reason, we believe that traditional materials cannot properly serve an industrialised building, and we believe that metal alloys and synthetic plastic materials are the materials upon which the study of new industrialised and prefabricated construction should rest.[49]

Zanuso completes his idea of a prefabricated house and the reasons for its use, namely the appropriate use of technology and the optimisation of resources to streamline processes, in the next issue of *Domus*:

> The construction site we are used to seeing in the streets is a sort of detachable and mobile workshop within which the houses are built [...] that transforms itself while at work, moves its machines, improvises extremely flexible processing cycles, not to mention changeable or even confused schedules. [...] The construction site rejects the characteristics of the construction process, because it is the last phase of building production. So, if we think that the problem of the house [...] can be better solved with the help of the industrial production force, we must define a different production process in

17

Covers and pages of *Domus* no. 206 and no. 207, February and March 1946 respectively, with contributions by Zanuso on the prefabricated house, focusing on the construction materials and the difference between traditional and prefab systems

> which the possibilities of the machine are enhanced and specified, as well as the different processes in their logical consequences. The machine must be removed from the construction site, it must be brought to the factory so that the finished elements to be assembled [...] come out of it [...] as for any other industrial product, such as the car, the airplane, the ship.[50]

Apparently interested more in constructive processes and operational issues than in conceptual motivations, Zanuso here adopts Rogers' refounding vision and it would take a few years before he could follow up on what they both wrote in *Domus*.

For Zanuso, the search for modularity, from which a building organism can grow and be defined through essential functional units, would find its ideal field of application in many projects for production plants. In Italian engineer and entrepreneur Adriano Olivetti (1901–1960), he found the ideal client, and the building process they undertook led to prefabrication as a natural outlet for research on building components. The research towards the standardisation of building components was internalised in his housing projects, pushing Zanuso's research to two extremes: on the one hand, the search for archetypal forms of living, the result of an extreme reduction of the constructive and constituent elements of the house; on the other, the push towards technology, with the aim and result of hiding the complexity behind iconic forms.

Thanks to the introduction of new materials and the possibility of creating prefabricated components, a field of research and experimentation began for Zanuso. This included the design of service rooms, the kitchens, for example, to which he dedicates another essay published in the pages of *Domus*: "Both in the small apartment as in the stately one, in the popular house as in the villa, today there is a tendency to transform the kitchen into a laboratory for the preparation of food where the person assigned to this function works according to an organised work scheme."[51]

In the same way, there are the bathrooms, spaces that – thanks to new technologies but even more to the change in bourgeois taste – transform, changing from service spaces to real environments dedicated to the care of the body and of the person with their own physiology. It is in these environments that Zanuso introjects his idea of an "invisible" technology. He stated:

> If we feel the need to recover a dimension of greater responsibility in our design culture, in which the idea of value is replaced by the idea of gratification, it is necessary that a concept of technocratic culture is replaced by that of cultured technology [...]. The definitive effort is to seek a redefinition of the project in a language, in an operational practice consistent with the technical-scientific evolution, ie, to overcome the dualism of design oscillating between art and technique, culture and practice, expressive and emotional experience and operational practice, without favouring one to the detriment of the other.[52]

It is already clear why Zanuso, through the industrialisation of the construction sector, aims at a reformation of the architectural discipline, from the house to the factory, as a research field parallel to that which is, meantime, defined as industrial product design. The drive towards the extreme simplification of construction methods is the same one that led to research in component standardisation, a crucial step for many architects then. But for Zanuso it is much more than an internal challenge in the construction world. Rather, it is the approach that paves the way for research in the field of industrial design, the high road that holds architecture and design together, a peculiar aspect in Zanuso's entire portfolio.

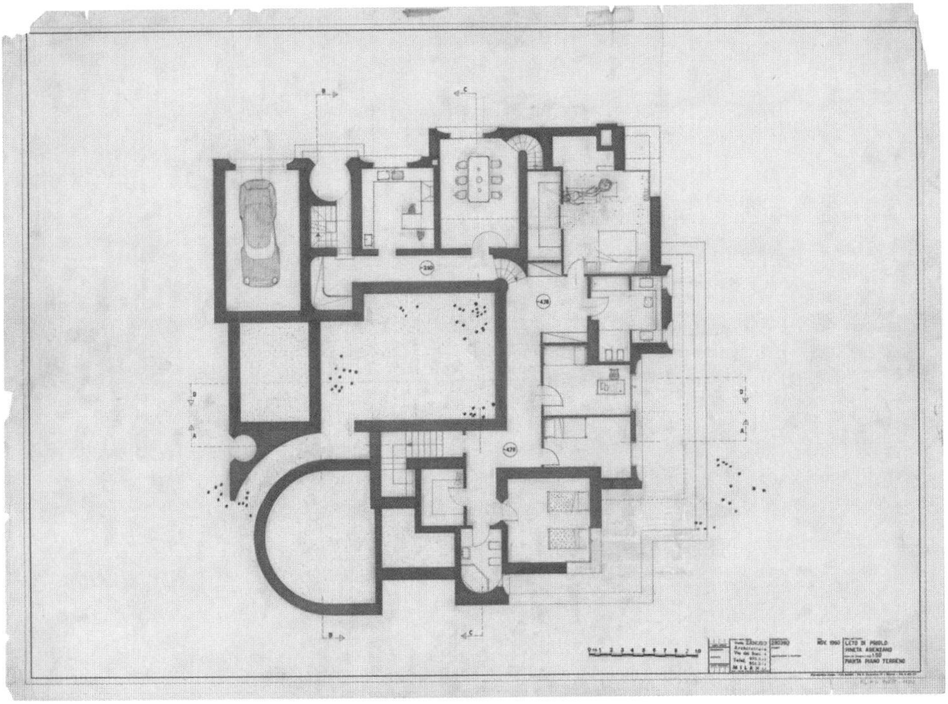

18

19

Much later he reflected on the risks of standardisation, and the subsequent inability to experience truly expectional and customised products:

> The alternative, when customised exceptionally, sometimes still stands out from the norm at the current shows [...] but it is increasingly rare [...]. It has become a specialised machine and no longer exceptional. It was the advent of the monocoque bodywork that shifted the interest of car builders from purely aesthetic-decorative planning to a deeper structural study. The monocoque, the load-bearing bodywork of a car conceived as a stiffened box capable of supporting, as if it were a skeleton, all its organs and organisms: its form therefore coincides with its structural elements [...]. Designers of this typology implement their technique and production experience along with an intuition of formal synthesis, which defines the typical physiognomy of industrial designers.[53]

18

In Casa Leto di Priolo (1960–1962), Arenzano, Zanuso explores the central courtyard design for a family home. In this plan, rooms and service spaces are articulated through the introduction of the curve

19

House on Cavallo Island, Corsica, 1981–1988. Study of the regulatory modular system responding to the geology of the site

20

21

20

"House and nature",
a project by Zanuso and Albricci published in *Domus* no. 211, July 1946. Views of the model show the relationship with the sloped topography and the natural landscape

21

Casa Arzale, one of the twin vacation homes in Arzachena, Sardinia, built between 1962 and 1964

22

Concept sketch of one of the vacation homes clearly showing the nine-square grid and the five-module cross, which represents the open-air spaces

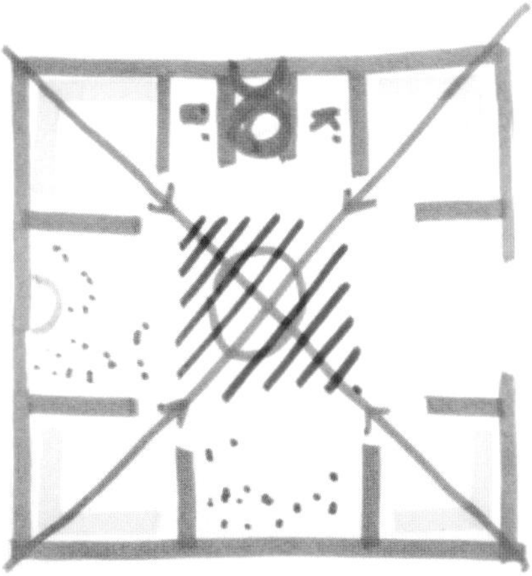

22

A second Zanuso project for a residential house that serves to demonstrate his method appears in the pages of *Domus* in 1946. It is a weekend home of refuge for when the family wants to get away from the metropolis and city life. Even though it is a conceptual project developed for the magazine, the choice of location is significant. Zanuso chooses to place the house in a picturesque, natural context, that of Liguria, in a steeply sloping site to be left as unaltered as possible, defining an innovative settlement method, and opting for distribution and construction practices that respond entirely to the local characteristics. A short description entitled "Home and nature" accompanies the project signed by Marco Zanuso and Gianni Albricci. Here the fulcrum of the search for a direct and nonmediated relationship between architecture and nature appears, only apparently as an antithesis to what he was carrying out on the subject of prefabricated housing:

> A home in nature shouldn't be unusual. For now it represents a vanguard of future urban planning, when we will be able to bring the countryside into the cities. Today, a holiday home is a luxury for the privileged few, and yet it could be provided for quite simply. Those who have a few days available should be able to open their holiday home to find it ready and equipped with the essentials for an organised and comfortable life, and be able to simply close it without long and complicated inventories, winter accommodation, etc. In researching this project, the problem of building economically with traditional construction systems was raised, while adapting the shape and plan to the needs of the selected site. [...] The plan we propose is elongated and the accommodation develops linearly so as to contain the entire building in the maximum depth of approximately 4.5 metres. [...] Given the size of the building, there is no precise distinction between the living rooms and bedrooms; everything is intended to be a living room: behind the fireplace a niche isolates two beds. [...] The structure of the building is very simple: plastered stone walls support a brick roof on which a layer of land cultivated with lawn defends the roof itself from excessive heating in the summer.[54]

It is the long walls, which contain the land and do not just define the spaces, that give shape to this holiday home, which involves extensive use of stone and glass.

> The plan resolves the alignment: different areas find a logical sequence through their natural connection. [...] The composition of the elevation is intentionally very simple, obtained by bringing together rectangular elements linked by mutual proportions. The glazed openings are abundantly shielded by the cantilevered roof, which offers protection from excessive sun exposure in the summer months. Wedged between the buttresses and leaning against them, a stone acts as a bench on the lower terrace floor. [...] The buttresses visually project: they function to support part of the structure that would be excessively burdened by an overturning thrust on the walls that support the terraced land. [...] The contours of the land and the vegetation remain intact: the house fits into them, drawing elements of composition from them.[55]

This is the same reasoning that leads to the modulation of construction components and rational organisation of the architectural form, but in this case, it is a form for human protection in the natural environment and vice versa; it pursues a search for an archetypal form of a shelter in nature, opening up new meanings and developments.

The location of the project was not arbitrary. The young designer saw great potential in the area, a forerunner of the real estate developments that would unfold along the Ligurian coast, harbouring interest from entrepreneurs and the Milanese upper class. Ten years later, the pine forest of Arenzano – a plateau of great landscape value and promontory overlooking the sea, once a Mediterranean forest and hunting reserve – became the subject of a development plan for villas and public amenities for a tourist settlement of about 10,000 inhabitants, and was commissioned in 1956 by Cemadis SPA to Zanuso in collaboration with Ignazio Gardella.

The aim was to create a vacation spot surrounded by greenery, in which the target market of an upper-class Milanese lifestyle could be comfortably transplanted through the domestic architecture and interiors that accommodate family life. Resulting from innovative urban and architectural experimentation, the internal road network builds on existing lanes and paths, newly conceived as pedestrian streets for electric vehicles too, while the years that followed saw the groundbreaking construction of signature villas designed by Luigi Caccia Dominioni, Roberto Menghi, Anna Castelli Ferrieri, Vico Magistretti and Gio Ponti among others.

The first works began in 1957 with the Punta San Martino hotel designed by Gardella and Zanuso, followed by the square designed by Gardella, and Zanuso's Case Rosse (1960). These were followed by three single-family homes designed by Zanuso, with three different approaches to solving the theme of the house with a central plan. In the projects for Casa Cattania (1960–1962), Casa Leto di Priolo (1960–1962), and Casa Valle (1962–1964), the plan of the house is articulated as a cluster of rooms around a central courtyard, first an open-air square space, then gradually more and more articulated but, in all three cases, open on one side to relate to the surrounding landscape in different ways, in relation to the slope of the site. Formally different, the first pavilion has sloping roofs in a compluvium, covered with horizontal courses in bleached slate shingles – which continue beyond the eaves to cover the roof pitches – and windows cut into the building envelope; the second is a stone fortress, with roofs, floors and openings like excavations in the masonry mass; the third is obtained by subtraction in the brick mass around a courtyard that opens in the embrace of two shapes, with circles tipped to open outwards. The plan governs the spaces starting from a square module, gradually more articulated in the thickness of the masonry and along paths that connect different levels and excavate the architectural mass.

But it was the subsequent project in Sardinia, albeit akin to the search for new ways of living, that completely breaks the bourgeois holiday home model, partly the result of an exceptional location that pushed Zanuso to the limits in his search for archaic forms and traditional construction systems. The location was one of the most challenging and evocative, devoid of any architectural reference except the wind and the waves that broke on the coast, less than 20 metres away from the house.

These are the twin houses of Arzachena (1962–1964), one of Zanuso's smaller and yet most iconic projects, linked to the internationally renowned real estate investment that would transform what was then one of Italy's least developed regions. Sardinia represented the new frontier for experimentation by architects of the rich Milanese bourgeoisie, in search of a new "naturalness" of living, in relation to the sweet and harsh Mediterranean coast. But Zanuso's assumptions were completely different from what was beginning to emerge in the rest of the Costa Smeralda, where an invented vernacular completely detached from the context became the prevailing style in which the upper middle class recognised itself:

> In Sardinia I built two twin houses for my brother and a friend. They had the problem of sharing spaces with children. I was inspired by the American missions in California. Here too there is a square wall, both full and empty, which envelops the space to create a seamless experience between closed and open living, in an open space that is very pleasant for living in, capable of protecting from the climate and wind, the beautiful landscape that can be hostile; and the wall is an asset to create different places, light and shadow.[56]

Zanuso seems to be inspired by archaic Nuragic buildings rather than other traditional stone buildings, but the most direct source of inspiration is a spartan model of life, without any comfort, the prevailing way of life there for many years.[57] The twin houses have minimal dimensions – a simple shelter in front of the rugged and rocky coast – built around a square courtyard covered with a pergola, designed for an open-air lifestyle, yet mediating the wild nature of the Sardinian coast beyond. The modular square plan, whose centrepoint is the courtyard, is made up of nine ideal squares, through the usual non-directional central agglomeration nucleus, as if it were a primordial shelter, a completely introverted fortress – although open and permeable to atmospheric events.

The plan begins to resemble a Greek cross, and is an evolution of a cruciform plan in an earlier project seaside villa designed by Zanuso: Casa Cattania (1961) in Pineta di Arenzano.[58] In Arzachena, the plan consists of four squares on each corner filled with rooms or services that lead directly into the cruciform patio made up of the other five squares, which are voids, open to the sky.[59] As with many of Zanuso's designs (industrial projects included), his rationale for hiding complexity within, while keeping the outside of the project clear and iconic, rings true. Further distinguishing features are the dark rooms with small picture windows designed to lessen the impact of the bright sunshine, and three tonnes of granite stones in light grey, yellow, and burnt pink, which together create a colour palette that reflects the tones of the landscape beyond. Fine detailing in the timber shutters, the lintels and waterspouts, as well as the built-in customised furnishings, were designed and made on site without drawings. These houses have been described as "the finest and most evocative work of an architect-designer as eclectic and inventive as Marco Zanuso";[60] an architect searching for an opportunity to immerse himself in nature as a counterpoint to the time he spent in the industrial city and working on industrial designs. They are the architectural response for the soul's yearning to return to nature.

These twin houses in Arzachena enjoyed "a sort of underground celebrity among some admirers in a restricted Milanese circle".[61] Neither stand today in their original form; one was extended by Zanuso himself soon after construction with two well-placed circular volumes and still imbues the ideal of the original design. They bridge what Zanuso had built up to that point and what he would soon be invited to build in the southern hemisphere. The transposition of his research on new forms of living, born in response to commissions from the Milanese upper class, finds an extraordinarily idealised home in the southern tip of Africa. Having recently acquired Coromandel Farm, Sydney and Victoria noted Zanuso's twin houses in Arzachena in a magazine and these defined, without mimesis or allusion, an elementary nucleus of spaces immersed in the rugged landscape. The origin of Coromandel House.

23

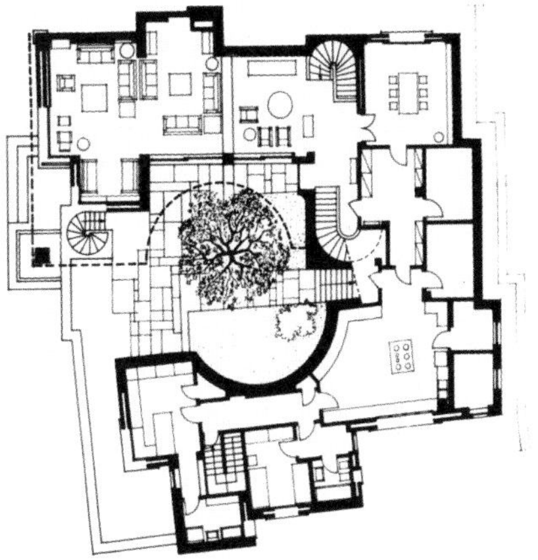

24

23

Casa Cattania (1960–1962), Arenzano, was designed as a single family home made up of rooms clustered around a square courtyard in which the line between the outdoor garden and living spaces begins to fade

24

Casa Valle (1962–1964), Arenzano, sees Zanuso twist and articulate the courtyard even further to acknowledge the terrain, and the presence of a tree in its centre

ENDNOTES

42 Renamed Mashishing for official purposes and located in the easternmost province of Mpumalanga.

43 Renowned journalist and writer of magic realism, who, in 1933, founded the magazine *Quadrante* along with Pietro Maria Bardi (1900–1999) to support Italian Rationalist architecture during the war years.

44 From October 1943, Melchiorre Bega became editor of *Domus*. These were the war years, which forced a continuous change in direction, and the printing of the magazine moved to Bergamo. For the whole of 1944, *Domus* was published monthly, but in 1945 it suspended its publications. Printing resumed in January 1946 with issue no. 205, produced by Ernesto Nathan Rogers and with a new graphic layout, reconnecting a trend of cultural continuity with that of Gio Ponti's direction.

45 "La casa e l'ideale", *Domus*, no. 176, August 1942, p. 312.

46 "Quando costruirò la mia casa andrò alla periferia della città e cercherò un prato", *Domus*, no. 176, August 1942. Zanuso's model is on the cover of this edition.

47 Zanuso, M, "Paesaggio, architettura e design", *Notizie Olivetti*, no. 76, November 1962, pp. 61–68, with E Vittoria, in Grignolo, R, ed., 2013, pp. 177.

48 Rogers E, "Uomini senza casa", *Domus*, no. 206, March 1946, p. 2.

49 Zanuso, M, "La casa prefabbricata. 2 – I materiali", *Domus*, no. 206, February 1946, p. 31.

50 Zanuso, M, "La casa prefabbricata. 3 – Il cantiere", *Domus*, no. 207, March 1946, p. 17.

51 Zanuso, M, "Non dimentichiamo la cucina", *Domus*, no. 197, May 1944, p. 185.

52 Zanuso, "Il dibattito architettonico in Italia nel primo dopoguerra, tra modernismo e ricostruzione", dattiloscritto, 1985, in Grignolo, R, 2013, p. 275.

53 Zanuso, "In piccola serie si fa la fuoriserie", from *Pirelli*, no. 1, 1953, in Grignolo, R, 2013, pp. 111–112.

54 "Casa e natura", accompanying report within the magazine.

55 Ibid.

56 "Si vede che sono distratto", Franco Raggi interviews Marco Zanuso, in Grignolo, R, 2013. Original text *Flare. Architectural Lighting Magazine*, no. 21, September 1999, pp. 80–95.

57 In the same years Aris Konstantinidis (1913–1993) created an equally exemplary house in its simplicity, starting from the same assumptions and with similar formal outcomes. The house in Anávyssos (1962–1964), set on the rock a few metres from the coast on a promontory overlooking the Mediterranean, makes use of a construction system of stone partitions. These define a linear system of parallel walls that are built directly into the soil of the rocky spur, which is exposed to the wind and storm surges along the coast of the Greek island.

58 Zanuso, M (Jr.) and Lotus, 2003, p. 94.

59 http://hicarquitectura.com/2017/06/marco-zanuso-case-di-vacanze-arzachena-sassari-1962-1964

60 Zanuso, M (Jr.) and Lotus, 2003, p. 94.

61 Ibid.

Coromandel Farm

The infrastructure needed to support farming created an opportunity to build three pioneering architectural projects on Coromandel Farm. These have left a testament for future generations and seem to support an earlier statement from Sydney Press that, "I'm not a rich man's son, but a barefoot boy from the fringe of the Namaqualand, who is thinking ahead"

25

Like many iconic twentieth-century houses whose clients sought to arrest the spirit of the landscape within architecture, Coromandel House draws vitality from its vast and impressive setting. The Spitzkop mountaintop, scenic hillsides and golden grasslands are the backdrop for farming activities on Coromandel Farm. Three and a half hours by car from Johannesburg, Coromandel is close to the bustle of South Africa's richest province, and yet far enough away to offer absolute tranquillity.

When Sydney began the search for a farm around 1967, that combination of tranquillity within easy reach of Johannesburg would have helped in his selection process. Whether his intention for buying the farm was to return to his early childhood roots or to start up an agricultural enterprise in parallel to Edgars, the search gained momentum around the time that Edgars underwent a major internal administrative transformation. Perhaps this rendered the opportunity to spend time in a farm setting more appealing.

To find, establish and manage the farm, Sydney looked for professional assistance. On 24 January 1968 he wrote to Alastair Moir (b. 1942) regarding a general manager post for a farm yet to be purchased. Moir had applied for the position after graduating from a beef cattle course at Cornell University. With an undergraduate degree in entomology and farm management from Potchefstroom University and work experience in South Africa and the United States, he was knowledgeable and experienced. Moir must have stated his reservations about the purpose of the farm during his interview, since Sydney replied personally to ease his concerns, stating that his intention was to create a "serious long-term project" and adding, "I'm not a rich man's son, but a barefoot boy from the fringe of the Namaqualand, who is thinking ahead."[62]

For the next few months Moir travelled with Sydney and Victoria to various farms: from the KwaZulu-Natal Midlands, to the Vaal River, and the northern and easternmost areas of Mpumalanga, Victoria would voice aesthetic evaluations while Moir and Sydney would determine suitability for ranch and stud farming. Through an acquaintance, they were informed of the sale of the farm Zwagershoek en-route to Lydenburg, and by 1969, the title deed was registered in their favour. It balanced the needs for productive farming with untouched natural beauty, which included areas with cultural significance: three waterfalls with troops of baboons, and archaeological remnants of the precolonial settlements of the Bokoni people.[63]

They renamed the farm Coromandel, to commemorate the purchase of an antique Chinese Coromandel lacquer room screen, which they acquired around the same time that the purchase of the farm went through.[64] Both purchases symbolised a greatly desired reward after years of persistent hard work to continually expand and improve Edgars.[65] Coromandel Farm offered the family a breakaway from the city. Sydney's commitment to excellence meant a disciplined dedication to everything he undertook, including his interests in art collecting and photography, education, dendrology (he was president of the Tree Society of Southern Africa) and various foundations to promote the study of psychoanalysis, psychology and anthropology in South Africa.[66] In his limited spare time, he turned to strategically coordinating the growth of the farm's vast and often experimental agricultural

25

Coromandel Farm stables (1969–1970) designed by Steffen Ahrends, approached by one of the many avenues of trees planted by Sydney and Victoria

projects. His investment in Coromandel Farm manifested in two distinct aspects: farming itself, and the infrastructure that made it possible.

Sydney's ambition morphed a serious project into an industrious enterprise and he invested enormous resources to distinguish Coromandel as a model-farm for South Africa with the subsequent ripple effects being felt in the growth of Lydenburg itself.[67] As he had done with Edgars, he recruited the best professionals and explored the latest technology and innovation. The farm grew physically, through Moir's management and the purchase of additional neighbouring land parcels, eventually to over 5,800 hectares in size, but also in terms of Sydney's personal esteem. In 1971, he wrote to Zanuso: "The farm itself is developing magnificently now that the extensive irrigation scheme is in full operation."[68] At one point there were 32 managers and their families living on various sections of the farm, and Sydney built two villages with serviced houses and a school for the farm labourers. This process may have revived the formative experiences he had of his father's citrus farm in Klawer, which informed the way he continued – even as an adult – to describe himself as a former "barefoot boy".[69] An emotional association along with an entrepreneurial drive for achievement, risk-taking and independence[70] fuelled this legacy-building project.[71]

With his professional staff, Sydney founded a formidable farming initiative. His quest to create a landmark farm spanned almost three decades with the product of his unprecedented approach being acknowledged through South Africa's "Farm of the Year" commendations. Apart from more conventional crops such as maize, beans, soya, winter wheat, sunflowers and nectarines, it yielded the first blueberry orchard in South Africa for export to Europe, and an olive plantation and tulip-bulb growing projects in collaboration with the Netherlands.[72] The biggest adversary to their successful growth was hail, which resulted in controversial strategies to limit hail by ground-seeding, and masterpieces of shade-net engineering used to protect the fruits. Beef and dairy cattle breeding fetched awards at agricultural shows and the biggest regional Holstein dairy herd was established with a dairy and a butchery. The farm grew different types of clover, hay or grasses to feed the livestock, and a number of irrigation channels and dams secured sufficient water for production even during dry years. This multiproduct response to farming was in part due to the size of the land available, and also in order to boost and diversify food production throughout the year.[73] Sydney adapted his retail experience in merchandising, distribution and sales and applied it to his farming approach, taking into account seasonal changes, distribution networks and diversification.

In May 1970, Italian landscape architect Pietro Porcinai (1910–1986) prepared a layout plan for a vast nursery, including designs for a glasshouse.[74] By January 1971, he had added a detailed report regarding the optimal design and functioning thereof.[75] The nursery was managed by Michael Schurr (1936–2011), who had been recruited because of his training as an arborist and horticulturalist in South Africa[76] and at the Royal Horticultural Society's gardens at Wisley, Surrey, in the United Kingdom. Sydney set Schurr to work on establishing a South African Nursery Association (SANA) registered nursery, in a clearing that measured around 25 hectares,[77] to propagate cuttings and seeds after laying

26

The Coromandel stables designed by Steffen Ahrends, c. 1969

27

Harvesting *Eragrostis curvula* below the house

26

27

28

29

out the mist distribution systems and potting sheds with modern machinery and a team of loyal nursery staff. As a horticulturalist and arborist, Schurr cultivated stock for the farm and sold a variety of surplus fruit trees, including nectarine, blueberry and olive trees grown on the farm, to the public, as well as various indigenous plants. Among the plants propagated, some were used for the landscaping at Coromandel House, Inanda House, and later the Edgardale Headquarters. Sydney also oversaw the propagation of some of his favorite indigenous plants, such as the Natal lily (*Clivia miniate*) and tree ferns (*Alsophila dregei*).

To document these early years on the farm, Sydney commissioned the renowned photographer David Goldblatt (1930–2018), who was then still emerging. In his characteristic documentary style, he quietly observed and captured the social and environmental conditions and exchanges within which Apartheid existed in South Africa. These were often candid portrayals of individuals in their domestic environments or at work, where the contradictions that riddled Apartheid society were brought to light. For example, in his portrayal of domestic life, his photographs reflected the reality that a closeness could and often did exist between black and white individuals in spite of the injustices being perpetrated by the government. Through these provocative yet composed works, Goldblatt used his photography as a medium to communicate the disturbing or touching aspects of the political system in which he was living, without becoming a political activist.

28

A Sussex cattle herd supervised by the first farm manager, Alastair Moir

29

Ablestad, the modernised Coromandel Farmworkers' Village designed by GAPP during the 1980s

In addition to his personal work, in which he pursued his artistic practice, Goldblatt accepted commercial work. His Coromandel Farm series for Sydney conveyed the people and their activities that were "creating Coromandel", day by day. The photographs show an operational farm of some agricultural sophistication, a home for many, juxtapositions in a timeless landscape, a place of instruction and a place in which dreams were being built. Later on, in the early 1980s, together with Margaret Courtney-Clarke (b. 1949), he returned to take photographs of the house for the *Architectural Digest* and *Abitare* magazine features. These later photographs provide a glimpse of Coromandel House as the ideal sought by Sydney, Victoria and Zanuso within the Arcadian setting they had created.

The infrastructure needed to support farming was an opportunity to commission three significant architectural projects on Coromandel Farm. Each was purposefully designed and all have left a testament for future generations to enjoy. In part owing to the family's love of horse-riding, on purchasing the farm Sydney began the construction of a large and impressive stable complex (c. 1969) in which horses were bred and reared, starting with children's ponies with Connemara stock from Ireland, followed by three-day-eventers and, later, prize-winning racing thoroughbreds, some of which came from Argentina.[78] The architect hired to design the stables was Steffen Ahrends, who created Round Hill (c. 1961) for the Press family, a holiday home on the dunes overlooking the Sedgefield beach. Ahrends was born and grew up in Berlin, Germany,[79] where he followed in his father Bruno's footsteps to become an architect and studied at the Bauhaus. Among many intellectual refugees fleeing Nazi Germany, Ahrends emigrated to South Africa in 1937 where he lived for almost 30 years and mentored a number of influential South African architects.[80]

30

30

Blueberry crop adjacent to the natural conservation area

He became renowned for his domestic architecture, which could easily serve any family who moved in, due to its comfort and functionality.[81] Ahrends's projects tended towards a traditional aesthetic but with the exceptional functional planning, proportions and detailing rooted in the Bauhaus method.

The stone-clad Coromandel Stables assumed a traditional European aesthetic, employing local materials and building technologies to transform an everyday functional space into an unforgettable place through detailing and natural light. Stables' manager offices and two open-plan apartments completed the functions. Their stately design marked the presence of the Coromandel stud. Visitors would approach the stables along a tree-lined avenue. Those who moved through the grand archway on horseback found it a memorable experience; meanwhile those in a car or large farm vehicle would experience a transition, from the more agricultural farming activities to the secluded and wilder area of the farm.

During the mid-1980s, after the construction of Coromandel House, Sydney undertook his third architectural legacy project on the farm, this time for the farmworkers: the construction of Abelstad, so named after Abel Manzini, a revered elder and community leader. It was a modernised farmworkers' village with free services, housing and amenities to support the employees and their families living on the farm. He hired Gallagher Aspoas Poplak and Senior (now GAPP) architects and urban designers based in Johannesburg, led by the urban-design expert Glen Gallagher (1935–2010) along with Erky Wood (b. 1954), to design the layout of the village, and Pedro Roos (b. 1954) to design the houses. The architects were briefed to follow the principles of European and Italian villages, albeit appropriately adapted to the African landscape and customs with a town square being the functional, social and communal heart of the village in which the judicial matters were also deliberated on as a group. While the Postmodern architectural style bears little relation to the Ahrends stables or the Zanuso house, the design approach responded to the community's aspirations and needs listed in consultation with the architects. The village was located close to the farm's main entrance with easy access to both the farm and nearby towns. The houses, of which there are three typologies set within a 350–400 square metre site, are clustered in enclaves, with verandas facing a central semi-public space and farming allotments behind each enclave for self-sufficiency. The houses were painted in bright colours and, of the 270 houses projected, the first building phase was completed by 1987.

After Sydney's death in 1997, and with his children living abroad, there was no one in the family who remained to manage the farm. Sociopolitical changes following South Africa's newly established democratic government in 1994 also included land claims and the redistribution of rural land ownership to Blacks who had suffered losses of property or land ownership under Apartheid's racist politics. Coromandel Farm was put up for sale as the new millennium began.[82] Seeing the opportunity presented by the sale, the farm employees mobilised to form the Coromandel Farm Trust and successfully applied to Provincial Land Affairs and Land Bank for financial aid to purchase the estate in 2002, serving as an early case study of an exemplary voluntary land redistribution process. The trust continues to maintain control of the entire estate[83] and this transaction is lauded as a beacon of hope for land reform in South Africa.[84] With this transfer of ownership, it may well be that what has been described as Sydney's "beautiful dream"[85] for Coromandel Farm, has left a living legacy in South African farming.

31

31

View over Coromandel Farm, as seen from the house towards Spitzkop mountain

ENDNOTES

62 Sydney's personal correspondence to Alastair Moir, 1968, Moir Archive.
63 Steyn, G, 2016, p. 47; Maggs, T, 2021.
64 Press, S and E Peres, 2020.
65 Maskew, J, 1969.
66 Schurr, K, Interview, 2021.
67 Press, C and W Press, Interview, 2021.
68 Status letter, Sydney Press to Marco Zanuso, Archivio del Moderno.
69 UJSC B36/4/5: SACS Old Boys Union, Commemorative Brochure on the 150th Anniversary of the founding of the SA College.
70 Dos Santos, J, 2018, p. 223.
71 Press, C and W Press, Interviews, 2021.
72 Da Mosto, J, "Coromandel House and its Legacy", PowerPoint presentation notes.
73 Aucor, "A Dream Goes on Auction", 2011.
74 Drawings available at the Archivio del Moderno and Porcinai archive.
75 Porcinai, letter to Victoria, Archivio del Moderno.
76 He demonstrated extensive knowledge regarding indigenous fynbos, ericas and proteas.
77 Schurr, K, Interview, 2021.
78 Press, S and E Peres, 2020.
79 www.artefacts.co.za, website entry on Ahrends, Steffen.
80 Greig, D, 1971.
81 Schwarz, A, Interview, 2021.
82 www.coromandel.co.za
83 Reeder, M, 2012.
84 www.vukuzenzele.gov.za/workers-restore-farm-land-milk-and-honey
85 Schurr, K, Interview, 2021.

The South African architectural context

The search for authenticity and identity in South African architecture looks to international canons and African architectural vernaculars inspired by the natural context and materials, often resulting in a "Regionalism that has to do with a sense of place and belonging". By importing an Italian architect, Coromandel House bypassed these with a novel response that mediated context and the clients' needs

32

Architecture is always a product of context. Embedded within it are the trends of the time, peculiarities of place, and the dreams, hopes, fears and ideals of the people who created them. Two obvious influences on South African architecture are, firstly, international trends and advancements and, secondly, a preoccupation with notions of reflecting an identity particular to South Africa with decolonisation and diversity being two central themes. Regionalism is one of the ways in which these themes are responded to and which continues to inspire the nation's architectural trajectory, with Coromandel House assuming a prestigious position within a diverse and rich architectural heritage in South Africa.[86]

The social and economic transformations that followed the Second World War were tangible in its built environment. In 1948, as Britain underwent its own internal shifts and loosened its administrative grip over the Commonwealth, the radical National Party tightened control over the South African government and as such impacted its urban morphology. Their race-based political stance of Apartheid promoted their version of Afrikaner-first ideologies and interests, which included total independence from Britain and enhancing discriminatory racist policies put in place in preceding centuries which led to The Natives Land Act of 1913.[87] City planning schemes increased spatial distancing between races in purpose-designed settlements, in which the displaced Black "native" labour force was placed further away from "white" city centres close to industry, which was used as a buffer.

32

Jane Press Da Mosto looks out from the Edgardale construction site towards the Johannesburg skyline, c. 1975

A fast adoption of Western technology, conveniences and industrialisation resulted in a development boom of its major cities and mining towns linked to a period of economic prosperity until the 1980s when international outrage and activism against Apartheid grew and economic sanctions tightened. The domestic, commercial and institutional architectural landscape of the time mirrored these complexities, the foundational scars of which are visible still to this day.

Architects, purposefully or not, played a large part in perpetuating this sociopolitical engineering, often looking abroad to find inspiration. Following the Second World War, Modernism along with all its building technologies and materials – many gained from the mining and local manufacturing industries – caught on,[88] and for the first time architecture became "self-supporting in talent, materials and techniques".[89] There was an increasing desire to create an identity for a young nation that had gained independence from its coloniser in 1961. Yet within fast-developing inner cities, an architectural homogeneity not much different from cities in the United States or Europe was the result. The "placelessness" of the Modernist International Style saw many South African architects shift to engage the ideals of the Modern Movement but adapted to the constraints, needs and opportunities available within the African context. This era of architects balanced the conveniences of the West and the qualities within Africa, and was characterised by "a variety of architectural expression".[90]

The search for authenticity and identity in South African architecture looked to international canons while accommodating an African architectural vernacular that resulted in a "Regionalism that has to do with a sense of place and belonging".[91] Early explorations thereof were a principal concern for Norman Eaton (1902–1966), whose unique designs are lauded for their responsiveness, using the skills of local craftsmen, innovative use of traditional materials and a sensitivity to landscape.[92] His buildings belonged to the African environment and so "his residential architecture draws strongly on the African monumental past, while denoting both a regional and universal consciousness".[93] Owing to South Africa's multicultural identities and the suppression of ethnicity, culturally stylistic responses could often result in cultural misappropriation or superficial aesthetics.

While adapting Modernism to South Africa, Eaton and his contemporaries[94] went on to create their own domestic vernaculars[95] in which houses employed innovative design solutions with low-tech systems, a concern for climatic responsiveness and connection to landscape through glass sliding doors or courtyard patios that could function as extensions of the home.[96] A strong following grew within the Pretoria school of architects, and architecture in the region strongly reflected an approach that required "an empathetic mind and sensitivity to local circumstance".[97] This tradition of contextual responsiveness is detailed in Arthur Barker's essay "Stones that sing".

By the 1960s, discerning clients were appointing architects to design signature houses suited to their context, and made to function as successful dwellings. As Apartheid policies stifled the potential of its multi-racial population to integrate and flourish as equals in a post-colonial period, for some, the architecture of the private home took on an added dimension. It provided an opportunity to express one's own sense of belonging and identity and, inevitably, to make an individual (perhaps even hopeful) statement in an increasingly controlled, uncertain and unjust reality. It was within this environment that Sydney and Victoria practised liberal thinking with regard to architecture and first approached Eaton to design a holiday home for them in Sedgefield (c. 1961), opting, however, for Steffen Ahrends' design instead.

Following their return from New York in 1954, they would have been aware of the local architects distinguishing themselves during the 1950s and '60s. Their Sir Herbert Baker house, initially designed for Wilfred Wybergh in 1902 and set in the rural landscape of Inanda, which later became a suburb on the northern edge of Johannesburg, already merged an adaptation to climate with an aesthetic response that they enhanced through careful renovations. Their interest in horticulture led to botanical gardening experimentations within its 4.45 hectares, with indigenous plants taking priority and contributing to the creation of a landmark garden visited frequently by various horticultural societies and other interest groups.[98] They were actively involved in questions of architectural and landscape design.

Their exposure to international trends, combined with an openness for innovation and design curiosity, would surely have informed their interest in pioneering ideas in architecture and landscaping. Their approach, when designing Coromandel House, was for it to be fit for purpose as well as suited to context. Whether or not they approached local architects in Johannesburg or Pretoria before approaching Zanuso is unknown. In approaching Zanuso, Sydney grafted Italian Rationalism on to South African Regionalism, which has since inspired various iterations of "architectural landscaping".

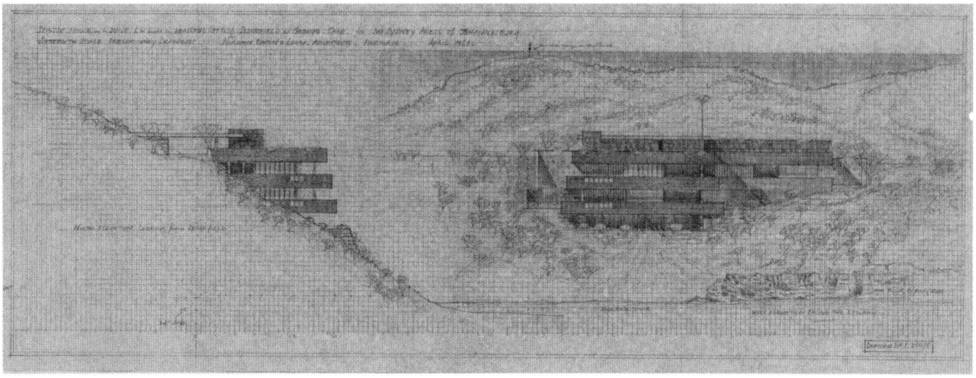

33

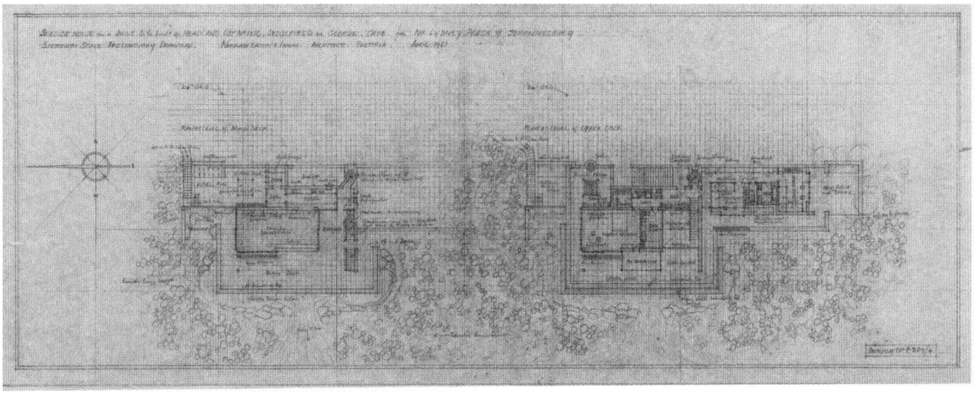

33

A proposal for a new house for Sydney, designed by Eaton & Louw Architects in Sedgefield, 1961. The project was unbuilt, yet it is telling that these drawings were kept in Zanuso's records

ENDNOTES

86 For a full overview, refer to Arthur Barker's essay "Stones that Sing".

87 Blacks were disempowered from owning property and forced into communal tenure in reserves.

88 Grieg, D, 1971, pp. 61–64.

89 Ibid., p. 71.

90 Ibid., p. 66.

91 Peters, W, 1998, p. 187.

92 Fisher, R, et al., 1998.

93 Pienaar, M, 2013, p. 1.

94 Cooke, J, 2000, p. 233; among them John Fassler, Gordon MacIntosh and Norman Hanson.

95 Chipkin, C and M Pienaar, 1993, p. 294.

96 Fisher, R, et al., 1998, pp. 123–147.

97 Ibid., p. 140.

98 Press, C, Interview, 2020; Fassler Kamstra, M, Interview, 2012.

Coromandel Estate

Photographed by David Goldblatt, November 1972 to March 1973

35

34

North facade of Coromandel House with arches under construction and the Girls' wing yet to be clad

35

Feeding the combine harvester

36

Farm road with open irrigation canal engineered to flow uphill

36

37

37

Lunging a pony

38

Coromandel House with the stables in the foreground

38

39

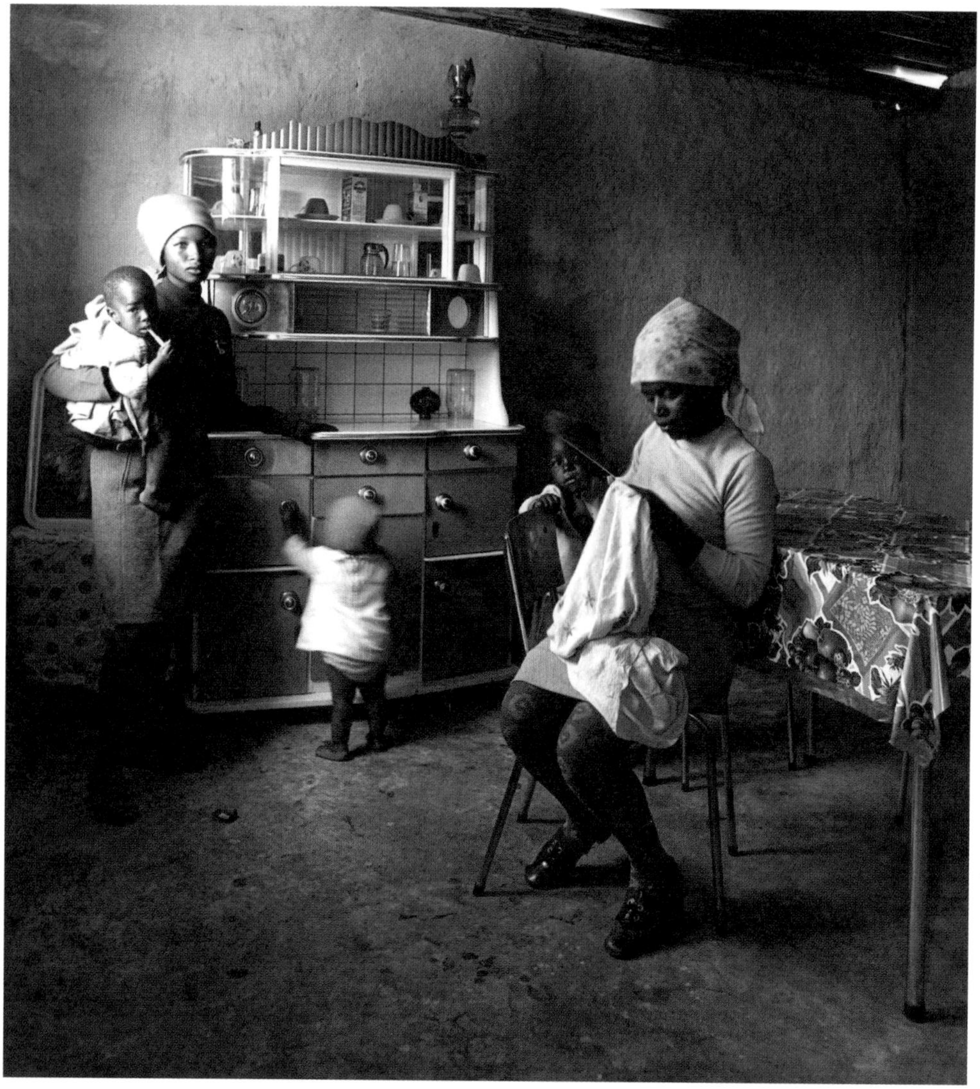

40

39

The stone cladding completed on a linear wall of the house

40

An existing farmworker's home before staff housing was built

41

Tractor and original manor house in the distance

41

42

42

Coromandel School, built for the children on the farm

43

Late-nineteenth-century barn with Friesian calves in the foreground

43

44

44

Herding cattle

45

Stables with pastures and new dam

46

Coromandel House roof viewed from the hillside

45

46

47

48

2. Building

47

Sydney on site during construction of the west wing

48

Zanuso inspects the waterproofing

Construction

"From a small series, the custom series is made", may as well have been Marco Zanuso's motto for the design and construction of Coromandel House. From 1969 until 1975, through the efforts of many people, the house evolved from an idea to a sketch to plans, while the various stages of construction that are embedded within its structure give it its characteristic, timeless form

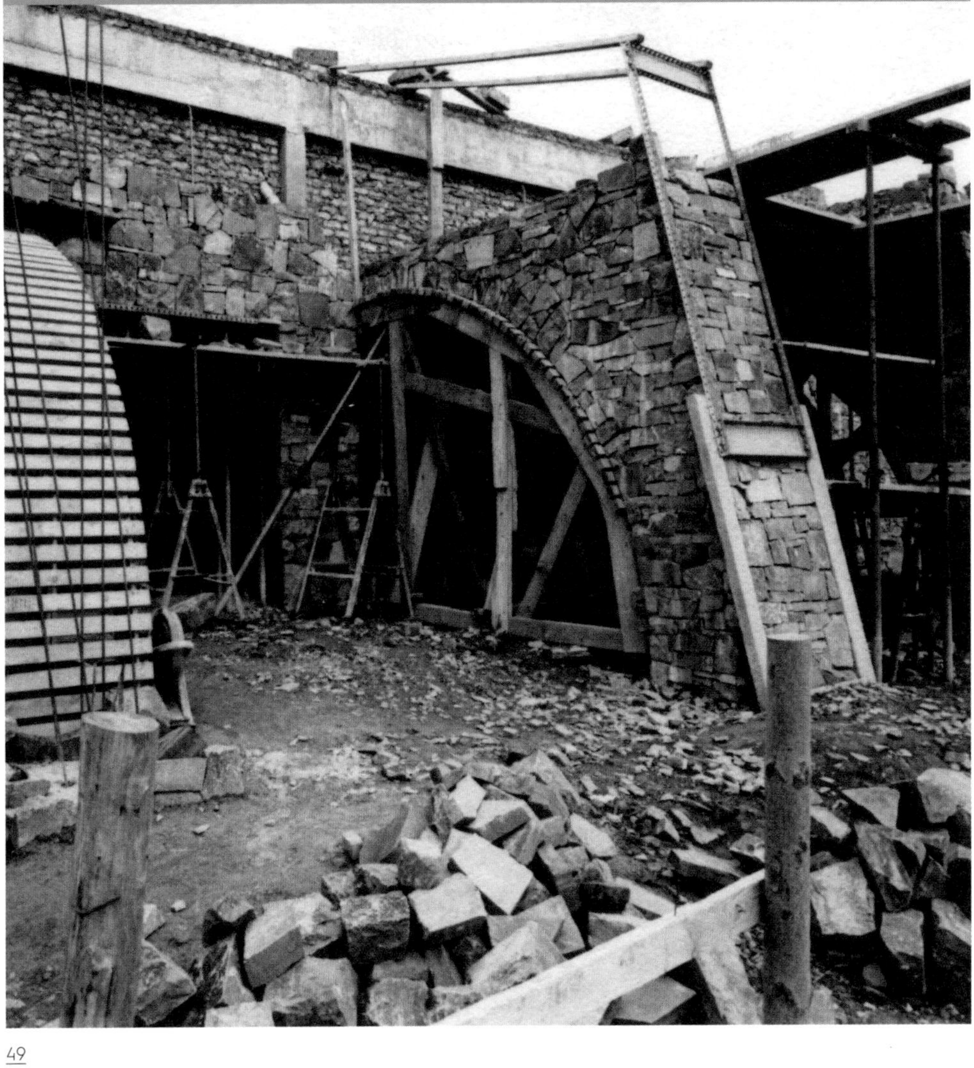

49

Zanuso rarely gave interviews, and in 1999 he consented to one of his last with Franco Raggi (b. 1945). Zanuso spoke about Sydney, whom he described as "a beautiful character, South African [...]. He was a businessman (and I had already designed the [Edgardale] headquarters for him),[99] but his family roots were in farming, the cultivation of large tracts of land, so one day in Johannesburg where he lived, he decided to move 'to the countryside'. He called me to go and see the 'place'. [...] African meadows at 2,000m above sea level, hills, and spruce forests without a living soul."[100]

Zanuso accepted the invitation to travel to South Africa for the first time and conduct a reconnaissance of Coromandel Farm. In February 1969 he departed from Milan via Rome and arrived in Johannesburg, where he was received by Victoria[101] and warmly welcomed into the Press family. After a short stay in Johannesburg, the architect and his clients spent a few days on the farm, during which time a few language barriers did not impede the initial brief and site analysis that needed to occur. Zanuso's first site visit also marked his initiation into the vast African landscape with its golden veld, verdant kloofs and panoramic horizons. His experience was described as being "a sharp spatial sensation from the beginning, similar to the one he had felt years earlier in Sardinia. More than man, of whom only prehistoric ruins remain, here the real protagonist is the natural landscape [...]."[102]

Zanuso's primary task was to choose the ideal location of the farmstead, which he documented with numerous photographs. Within his archive, a photocopy of an enlarged topographical map and some notes on the consistency of the soil show a cross marked in pen. This mark anticipates the founding act of the house, indicating the chosen area on a portion of land that dominates a plateau with a slight slope that preludes the most marked difference in height behind it. From here, the view of the valley below and the entire estate is superb, while on the side you can see a distant waterfall that descends from a crack in the high plateau, perfectly framed. It is a dream place, but also the most logical location to take advantage of the slope and to be elevated, devoid of any element that could obstruct the panoramic view. Zanuso added, "Although the steep site was basically treeless and without cliffs or stone outcrops, it was selected because it was sheltered from the prevailing wind and higher than the perennial mists."[103]

This visit gave Zanuso an opportunity to get a sense of his future clients, their interests as individuals and their needs as a family. Sydney worked tirelessly and Victoria was always interested and curious about ideas and their origins. They both had a large historical frame of reference and enjoyed talking to people. Victoria would ask questions, while saying very little about herself, just listening and prompting to gather information.[104] Sydney similarly was always learning from others, such as the executives from the United States and the United Kingdom whom he recruited to consult for Edgars, and also the distinguished psychoanalysts whom he hired for lecture tours at South African universities.

The novelty of designing a residence in a rural setting in a far-off land for clients with whom he had no previous association meant Zanuso was not bound by local perceptions nor by South African building traditions. This carte blanche, coupled with the geographical distance between his Milan studio and the site, implied a level of sustained objectivity in the years

49

Formwork of an arch under construction

to come between himself, the clients and the rest of the professional team. With the clients' willingness to afford Zanuso every opportunity to realise the ideal architecture needed to capture the *presence* they were trying to seize within the landscape, his design ambitions were allowed to flourish, benefitted by their belief in his ability "to get it right".

Zanuso's well-honed design methodology and architectural maturity, based on decades of experience in Italy and abroad, was also completely foreign. Unburdened by the local dogmas of South African architecture, he imported his own rationale, informed by an architectural lineage of Mediterranean precedents and Italian vernaculars to draw from, as well as a rational approach to designing and problem solving. His observations regarding the climate, landscape, materials and lifestyle in South Africa led to logical responses that expressed modern ideas yet were based on tried-and-tested contextual design principles. Today, these solutions are considered standard practice for "green", "sustainable", "passive", even "environmental" design, but in the early 1970s these trends were just emerging and were not defined stylistically.

BRIEF: A HOUSE THAT DISAPPEARS INTO NATURE

During this initial and formative visit to Coromandel Farm, Zanuso had the opportunity to experience Sydney and Victoria's passion for its landscape, their ambition, and their interest in design and horticulture first-hand. Design and horticulture were certainly the basis of conversations and explorations that evolved into the brief for the future house. Despina Katsikakis (b. 1960), architect and close friend, recalls that plants and flowers were such a strong part of Victoria's personality that it is very likely that her input into the brief of the house would have been to *enhance* nature. Her approach would have been to imagine that a house built there would need to be built from nature, and thereby inclusive of it. In fact, one of the first times Victoria spoke about the house to Katsikakis, she "was intent that the house be one with nature – that nature comes into the house and that the house disappears in nature".[105] In turn, Sydney's passion for horticulture and indigenous flora was complementary to Victoria's fascination with context and trying to recreate an authentic design experience within each of their homes. From an interior design perspective, Coromandel House offered Victoria a fine opportunity to create and shape the architectural context in which she would later decorate the interior rather than respond to an existing house. By being actively involved, she pursued a specific integration and connection between the atmospheric qualities of the architecture and those of the landscape which predominated the design.

Zanuso took this cue to include nature in the design throughout, from the very first design development sketches for Coromandel House until its resolution. An early sketch of a stepped section shows four rooms of equal width each with shrubbery hanging off the edge of a planted roof and various planters at the base of its exterior walls. The flat-planted roof returned the earth, disturbed by construction, to its surface thereby increasing its thermal properties and visually linking with the landscape. On the elevational sketches, various geometric compositions were explored to break up the mass of stone that comprised the main elevation. Ever-present

50

Zanuso explores Coromandel Farm to find the best location for the future home

51

Archaeological remains of a precolonial Bokoni site, showing the system of settlements

50

51

52

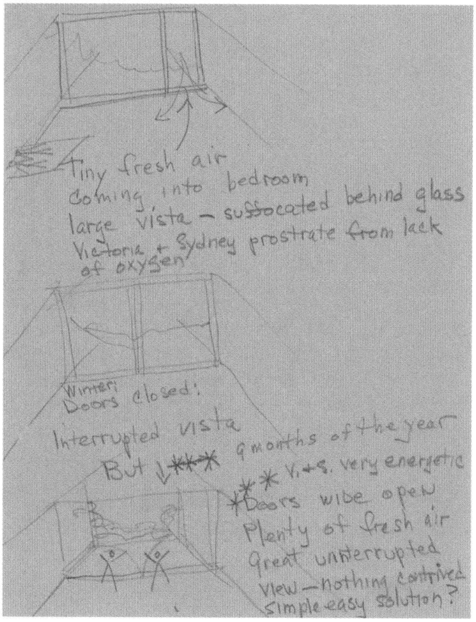

Tiny fresh air
coming into bedroom
large vista – suffocated behind glass
Victoria + Sydney prostrate from lack
of oxygen

Winter!
Doors closed!
Interrupted vista
9 months of the year
But ↓***
** V.+S. very energetic
*Doors wide open
Plenty of fresh air
Great uninterrupted
view—nothing contrived
simple easy solution?

53

54

52

Zanuso reviews the proposed design with Victoria in Johannesburg

53

Correspondence from Victoria to Zanuso, July 1973, detailing her suggestions for the door design

54

Victoria in Milan, in conversation with the professional team

on the renders were shrubs growing off the roof edge and on the walls, and planted just in front of the house. On the many iterations of the plan in this initial concept stage, two themes, which emphasised the qualities of bringing nature into the design, were present in each: long planted courtyards connecting to central gathering spaces and asymmetrical linear internal plans. There was an intention to design a building in which the proximity between architecture and landscape was narrowed, and would merge with time.

This perceptive design of the farmhouse in an archaic aesthetic that interpreted the qualities of the ancient and timeless landscape of Coromandel Farm would have been informed by the numerous explorations and investigations Zanuso undertook there during his visit. Among the features that he photographed were the archaeological, precolonial ruins of a rare type of structure pertaining to the Bokoni people on a hillside to the west of the house. These large circular stone walls defined a system that most likely "were cattle posts shared between several families (hence the large number of individual enclosures) and built well away from the main settlements, being positioned at higher altitude to take advantage of the local grazing. There are several such ruins scattered along the escarpment between Lydenburg and Verlorenkloof".[106] In Zanuso's eyes, these relics from prehistory[107] reflected the archaic values of the ancient Nuragic constructions in Sardinia, which he had referred to in the Arzachena houses, both a primary form of settlement and adaptation to place. Equally inspiring are the prominent natural features of three waterfalls, and the scale of the hills surrounding the valley. During his time in South Africa, his observation of mining structures surrounding Johannesburg and exposure to local vernacular architecture[108] would have been additional references. These included rudimentary timber, steel, and brick or stone farming structures[109] in the immediate area of Coromandel Farm. The predominance of logs and timber supports in mines to prop up cavities and avoid their collapse under the pressure of the ground may have also inspired the system of retaining walls and the measures for reinforcement on the facade of the house. These visual references provided some clues for the concept design in a remote place with few established constructions and references in its immediate vicinity, other than its extraordinary natural beauty and the rich endemic vegetation, which Zanuso discovered and appreciated through Sydney and Victoria's sensitivity. Coromandel Farm provided a source of fascination for Zanuso in a profound and indelible way, as evidenced in numerous photographs where he is happily captured walking or cycling around the estate or, in others, accompanied by children on the farm or on horseback with his clients, always gathering inspiration directly from the South African veld:

> You could go around for days ... You went out at six in the morning on horseback and entered these pine forests, these cathedrals of paradise, which among other things were an economic resource because they supplied the timber for the carpentry of the mines. It was a world, cattle, horses...[110]

Sydney and Victoria requested a house that would be divided into different parts, which Zanuso interpreted as one wing for the parents, one for their four sons, another for their three daughters, a central area to gather communally and entertain guests, and one for the staff involved in running the house. Further insights into initial aesthetic directives or intentions discussed during his first trip to South Africa are unknown, although, in later years, Sydney indicated that the design concept draws inspiration from the precedent principles of Mediterranean town-making and reflects the qualities of an Italian village: a protected public piazza in the middle for gathering in, with narrow roads leading into the more private dormitory spaces.[111] Sydney remarked that anyone having visited Rome would forever be touched by the patina of its cobbled streets and the spaces for living that its piazzas offered, and this appreciation is echoed in the design from the first drafts to the final construction.

Zanuso further observed that "on a South African farm, there is really too much sun, heat and glare. So, the structure must provide copious shade, coolness, greenery and water. The atria should be delicately narrow – like the streets of Rome, always in the shade...."[112] The courtyards provided the multiple purposes of regulating the microclimate by providing morning and afternoon shade and shelter from the wind, allowing for a direct connection to nature in the central gathering spaces, and creating thresholds between the different wings. Even in this larger architectural concept of a traditional Italian village, there is an embedded responsiveness to archaic placemaking, dwelling and gathering, hierarchies of space, to typologies and contextual precedent.

On 12 March 1969, Sydney enclosed photographs along with a personal letter to Zanuso, saying, "It was a very great pleasure for all of us to get to know you during your brief visit to South Africa."[113] With surveys and meteorological measures underway, they looked forward to meeting with Zanuso in May to review his concept design.

DESIGN DEVELOPMENT: MAKE IT RIGHT

Upon his return from South Africa, Zanuso began exploring concept designs. In April he wrote to his clients: "...The project seems to turn out well and become a nice place to live in." In the span of two months, he explored various iterations of a core concept: on plan, a series of interlinked linear wings with courtyards in between; on elevation, an expansive stone wall punctuated by vertical elements, and deep overhangs to shade windows; on section, stepped floor levels to mark the changes in contours. In each, a core idea was replicated and scaled up, much like cells accruing to form the organism.

In early May, Sydney and Zanuso met again in Geneva, Switzerland, after the architect's proposal had been extensively studied by Sydney and Victoria. It was the latter whom Sydney referred to as having "settle[d] down to record her detailed comments"[114] and suggesting a face-to-face meeting in London to review. This level of direct involvement from Sydney and detailed feedback from Victoria would be an ongoing influence in the design and construction process over the next few years. Before their meeting in London, Victoria sent Zanuso a long list of practical concerns and questions preceded by the following declaration: "The house is superb [...] we love the conception, the grand length and the narrowness, very chic and aesthetic [...] it's exactly the feeling we wanted [...] and I could never even have dreamed of it." Her definition of beauty was not stylistic or aesthetic, but rather about belonging: context, scale, and authenticity.[115]

Victoria maintained an active involvement in the design and construction process, asking about methods and researching. She had an affinity for thinking both like an architect and a curator of experiences,[116] and her sense of observation of extraordinary details made her indelibly present in a unique way. Photographs show Victoria in discussion with the designers and builders on the project throughout its construction. Her appreciation and intuition for scale and proportion suggests that "her influence on the design and the aesthetics were probably enormous... [Victoria] and Marco would talk, heads together, in great depth and for long periods and he would surely credit her with being part of the result."[117] She understood what the house needed to be in that context, and Zanuso understood how to materialise it.

In July 1969, Zanuso presented a revised scheme to Victoria in London and this discussion was recorded as having gone very well, with her initial misgivings resolved. In this revision he started from the design module that he used in the houses in Arzachena. However, the extensive site available at Coromandel, combined with the programmatic dimensions and articulation of spaces set out in the brief for the farmstead, led to the linear plan oriented along an east-west axis. It includes five parallel and uninterrupted walls, placed at a regular distance of 3.7 metres and made of irregular basalt stones and a concrete structure. The systems of walls define the individual wings of the house, which are articulated by clusters of continuous rooms, almost forming cells that combine to form longitudinal continuity.

The central part of the plan is contained within four bays that mark the nucleus of the home, from which the spaces requiring increasing intimacy branch off, extending in opposite directions into the landscape and coming to define a unitary body that measures 170 metres in length. This reference back to the archaic typology of the Arzachena houses connecting to landscape echoed what attracted Sydney and Victoria to Zanuso's work in the first place. This archaic timelessness reflected Victoria's appreciation for "the past living in the present, where the world exists as a long superimposition of vivid characters, where even within the landscape there are various features of interest".[118] She saw no distance between the past and the present moment. Zanuso was able to design something that suited the scale, scenery and spirit of an ancient landscape within the modern world in which they lived.

On 27 June 1969, Sydney wrote to Zanuso confirming that he could proceed with developing the final plans for the farmstead. Zanuso's next trip to South Africa was scheduled for the following month together with his colleague, Pietro Porcinai to advise on the landscape architecture. Following their visit, they developed the project always cross-referencing design decisions with each other. By 24 November, Zanuso had sent them his definitive concept plans with material quantities, and indicated that the contractor would have to advise on the foundations. Only at this stage did a detailed contour plan arrive in Zanuso's hands, along with a heartfelt note from Sydney and an accompanying photo of Zanuso on horseback, to reminisce about their memorable day on the farm. A continuous exchange of ideas informed design iterations and refinements – among these, the shade of local dolorite stone to clad the walls, and the most appropriate method to cut them: heavy pointed stone hammers.

By February 1970, the plan had evolved and consolidated into a series of large-format drawings. We can see that the central part is articulated, the service wing extends, the walls extend and the paths are further defined between the double walls within spaces of limited height. This exaggerated extension further into the landscape is likely the result of Victoria's insistence to "make it the right length, it needs to be the right length, I am not interested in big, small or indifferent, I want it *right*".[119] This is evidence of the first peculiarity of the design, in that the horizontality of the house and its four separate wings fearlessly extend into the landscape and create a first line of defence. Victoria also wrote to Zanuso: "It is taking me forever to study your plans, which are not only enormous but very complicated. I also think they are interesting, inspired and the work of nothing less than a genius. I wonder whether it will be fun to live in the house."[120]

The first design solution defined a pergola area with square openings in the outermost wall on the north side of the house and in the central area. In the final version, this evolves in the form of semi-arched buttresses that rest laterally on the outermost wall, connected with the gum poles between them, like those used for mining piling and in local architecture. There are no holes along the north-facing facade that are not

55

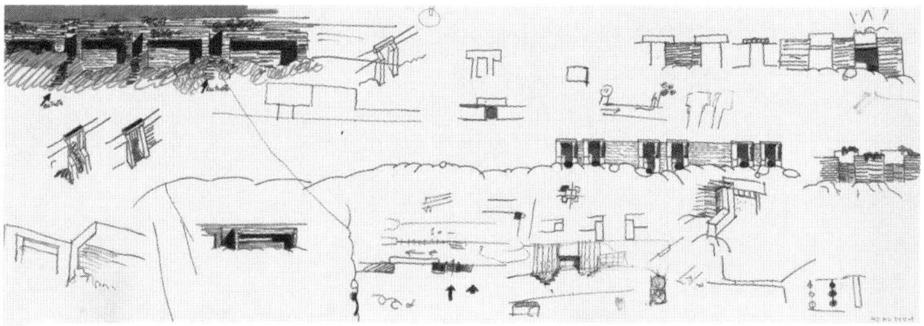

56

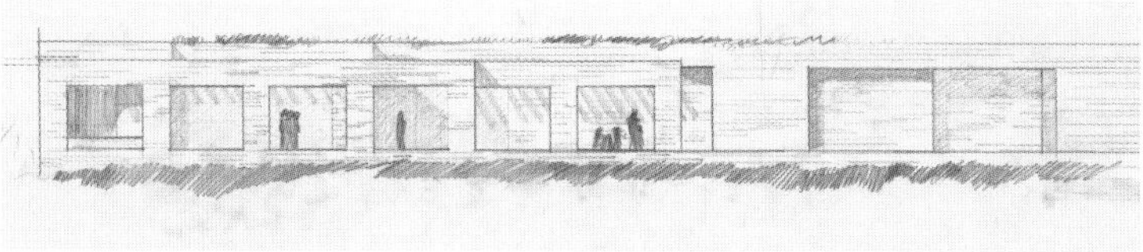

57

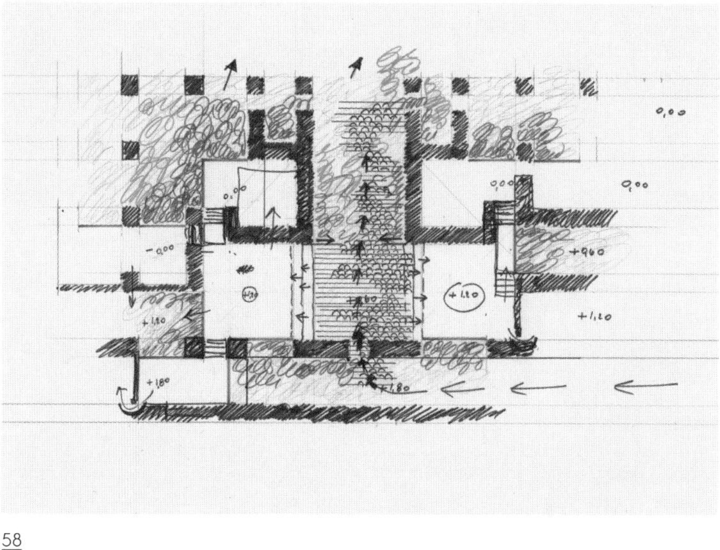

58

55

The initial idea defines a "fortified" system of walls enhancing the sloped topography with loggias and framed openings in the walls

56

Studies of the "fortress" model and the articulation of single parts

57

The evolution of a more linear wall system, including large openings with direct access to the external terraced space in front of the house

58

A detailed study of the central part of the house plan defines the articulation of the walls and pillars, creating a filtered relationship between outside and inside spaces

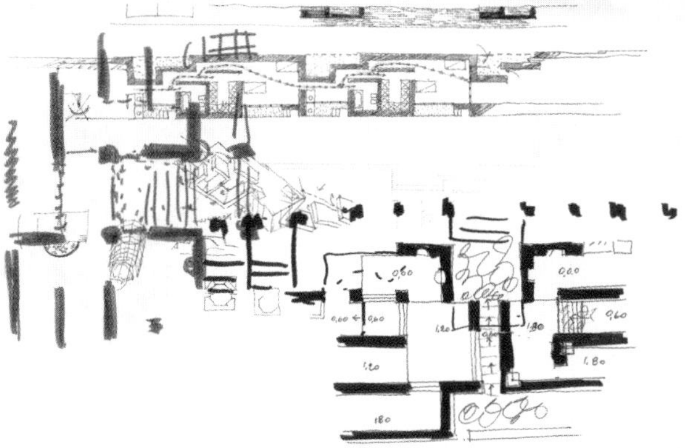

59

A conceptual study of internal spaces without opening holes in the walls, but rather articulating them in order to create sequences of rooms, corridors and openings to the external spaces in a coherent, modular and integral system that carves the spaces out of the walls themselves

60

A study of the section explores the principle of articulating the walls to tackle the differences in height needed to adapt the house to the slope and thereby also separate the different spaces inside the house

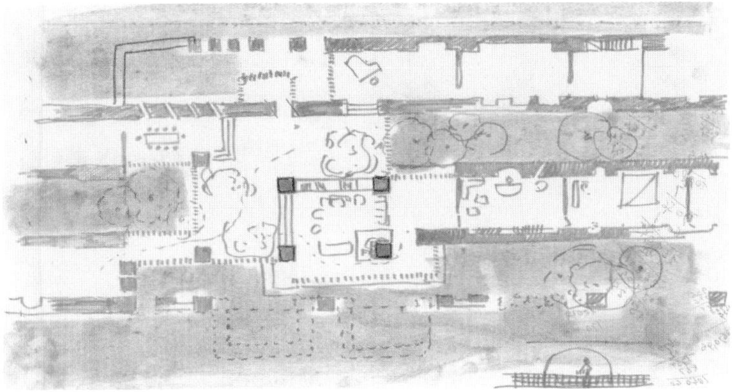

61

A further study in plan of the central part of the house where the walls enter deep into the common area, articulating the width of spaces with steps that correspond to the depth of the walls

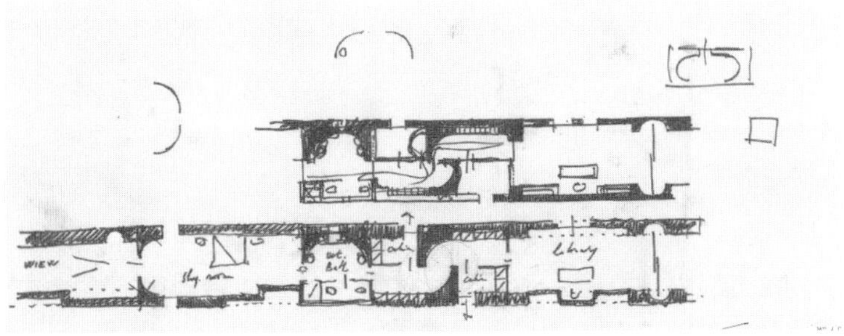

62

A study in the design approach to "carve" the service areas of the bathrooms out of the walls and create intimate spaces shielded by these buttresses. Interstitial spaces all around define external areas, atria and courtyards, where Zanuso responded to heat, solar glare and strong reverberation with "copious shade, coolness, greenery and water" to create microclimates that begin to regulate temperature around the house, further regulated by thick walls within which windows are recessed with shutters.

LAYOUT: A LITTLE OPEN, A LITTLE CLOSED

When Frank Lloyd Wright (1867–1959) surpassed his predecessors in devising a total rethink of room and interior layouts, he did so by dissolving barriers between rooms. The most private bedrooms were still the basic unit, but from there all public rooms flowed one into the next, becoming what now prevails as the "open-plan".[121] Continuing this tradition of organic architecture, Zanuso took the design of the bedrooms one step further, making each bedroom wing a continuity of interleading spaces along a stepped linear gallery corridor of progressively more private spaces that lead you back to the source of the project: nature.

The immediate aesthetic connection to context is achieved through its stone-clad walls which were sourced from local dolerite, chosen for practical reasons and for its extraordinary expressiveness and changeability under different solar conditions. Zanuso remarked:

> In these wonderful African meadows there were beautiful basalt boulders, discoloured by thousands of years of sun and rain. They were there to use and then the house in the project got bigger and longer, the space began to organise itself in a straight line. Like corridors that are a little open and a little closed. [...] Since there were seven children and each wanted an autonomous but integrated space [...] and then there was this landscape that had to penetrate the spaces but also be contemplated [...].[122]

Zanuso's design for Coromandel House carries the same vestiges of core themes that had initiated his preceding domestic projects, but allows them to reach their next logical point in the evolution of his design theories. While Arzachena represents the minimal and rational organisation of four cells around a central space, Coromandel House represents the evolution of a complex organism starting from that nucleus of cells, but extrapolated into the vast horizons of the veld using the modular systems of environmental units that Zanuso applied in his earlier houses and also in his large-scale factories. Just as the walls were inflected like a bulwark in Arzachena, here the heads of the walls incline at the end, reinforcing the impression of buttresses and an interrupted but finished form, reminiscent of an ancestral form or even of Mesoamerican architecture:

> These parallel walls separate yet also unite, like telescopes framing a directional perspective, so that there is a sense that the architecture in this project highlights a point in the landscape. At the end of this view is a waterfall, a gorge, a narrowing of the landscape in the form of a "V", where the vegetation becomes more luxuriant... where you almost see a woman...[123]

These distinctive walls lead one's movement into space, sometimes descending into it as Zanuso did for the Muda-Maè cemetery in Longarone (1967), designed in collaboration with Gianni Avon and Francesco Tentori. This project was completed when Zanuso first visited Coromandel Farm in 1969. Echoes of the project's monumentality and its magnitude are noticeable in the Coromandel House design. Muda-Maè constructs a memory of the Vajont catastrophe (1963) in which a dam burst and obliterated a town, greatly affecting the collective conscience of those years. The design translates the event into a subtraction of the land, symbolising a return of this place to Earth after its natural equilibrium was disrupted by humans. But Muda-Maè is also a form of proto-urban agglomeration generated in the negative, dictated by the emergence of the stone retaining walls among the vegetation that reappropriates the excavation and covers like a veil the memory of the people of the town of Longarone who vanished in the tragedy. This modification of the "injured habitat" is the most plausible form for an operation of "healing" (and not camouflage). But while the Muda-Maè cemetery is dug into the ground like a deep notch and the walls contain its thrusts, Coromandel House is extroverted like an exoskeletal organism or a reclining body in its osteological form.

In a pen study, Zanuso explores the principle to articulate the walls, like cavities in the ancient Masti Gate walls in Lahore, Pakistan, and applies this to tackle the differences in height needed to adapt the house to the slope and thereby also separate the different spaces inside the house. Rooms and service spaces are literally modelled into and in between the thick walls, as if they were carved from their depths. In the more intimate zones, a system of curvilinear cavities is defined, which cocoons these most private spaces and opposes the harshness of the strongly linear basalt walls. This act serves to create the experience of feeling embraced within these intimate spaces, as though they were a welcoming shell that reveals nothing to the outside. Continuous spaces formed by contrasting concave and convex shapes interlink, almost in the way valves do, to define the service areas of the bedrooms, leaving them uncluttered and fit for their purpose.

The succession of service spaces also follows a logic of use, such as the wardrobe, dressing room and bathroom sequence in the master wing tying together the library and the bedroom. All the openings within this sequence of service areas face into the atria or patios as a result of deep wall excavations needed to craft the outer skin. While the cavities and crevices are localised solutions to services where they are needed, the overall layout emerges from the act of excavating the organism, with dug-out corridors that stretch towards the heart of the house.

The second peculiarity of the house, which was touched on in the service spaces, is its extensive open-plan design within each zone of the house, broken only by shifts in views and level differences. These design devices not only accommodate the practical restrictions set up by the slope of the site, but also create important moments in the experiential transition from one space to the next and the definition of space and privacy. An example of this is the lack of doors between the bedrooms. Seven bedrooms for the family are distributed in three wings. Rooms are placed along a long meandering gallery space that is neither corridor nor room, with alternating spaces forming bespoke bedroom or service nooks and crannies, and large private bedrooms marking the end of each wing and the beginning of the landscaping. It is an extreme form of the concept of increasing intimacy that is normally established within a home in the transition from "public" daytime areas to "intimate" ones and private sleeping areas. Normally the bathrooms and other support areas are offshoots in this housing typology; however, in Coromandel House they are part of the system of paths that sequentially cross the house.

The layout was further refined with correspondence verging on the pedantic – from materials, technology, fenestration details and services. Points under discussion were reservations about the durability of the light timber flooring proposed by Zanuso, plus the "cool cave" stone-clad walls being too dark and perhaps needing to be illuminated during the day as well, which was challenging due to the lack

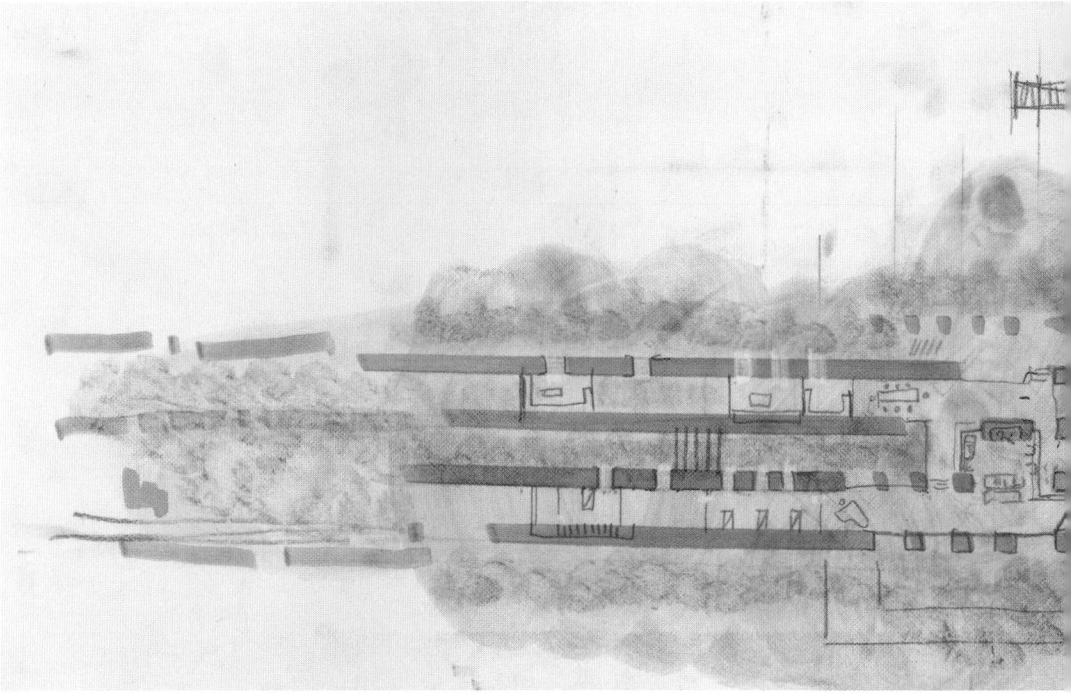

63

64

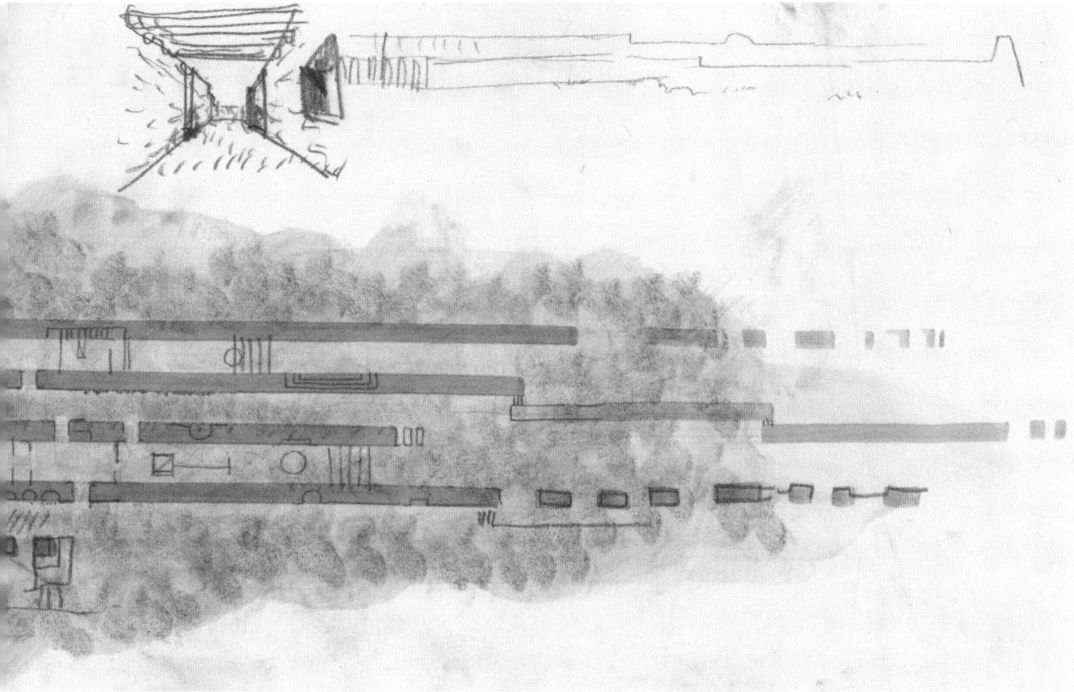

63

A study of the whole plan as a linear system of parallel walls, which extend uninterrupted for the entire length of the house

64

The facade corresponding to the study shows in the central and "public" part of the house a system of pillars that defines the portico as a filter space between the inside and outside

65

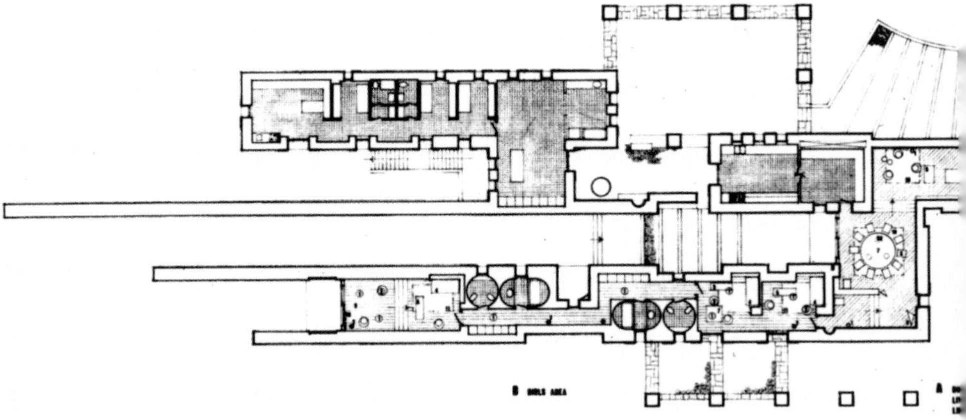

66

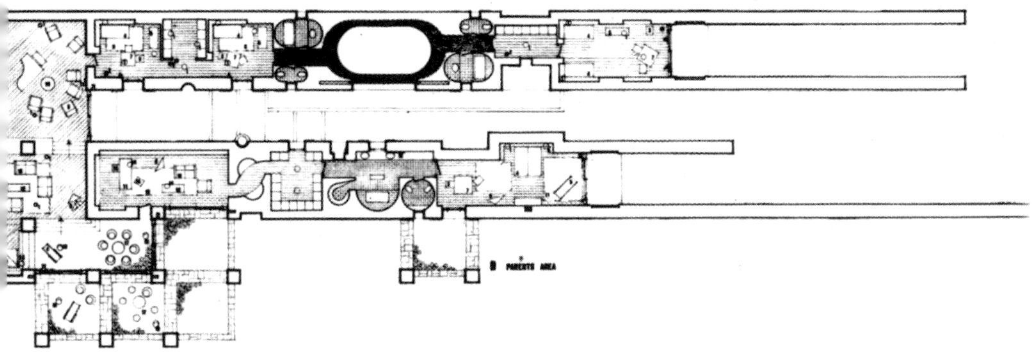

65

The definitive solution of the front facade shows the arches in the central part where they frame the external spaces, protecting them from direct sunlight

66

The plan of the definitive and built solution includes the furniture as an integral part of the internal system of spaces. The bathrooms, wardrobes and gym area define the circular spaces carved out of the walls, which filter access along corridors towards the more intimate areas of the house

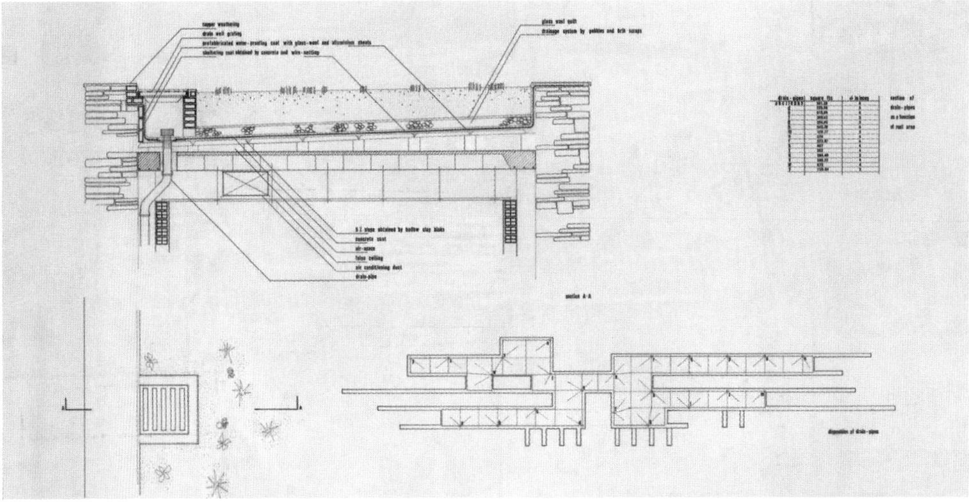

67

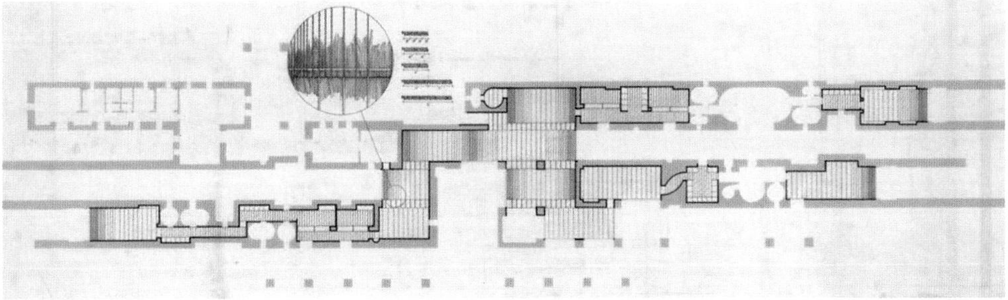

68

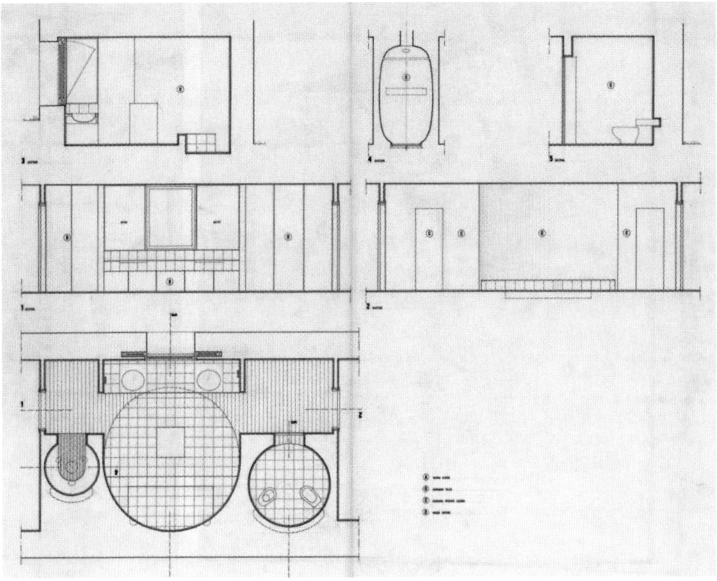

69

67

A construction drawing section shows the roof covered with vegetation and indigenous plants

68

A detailed construction plan shows the false ceiling with compressions and dilations of the scanning of the wooden slats with respect to the modularity of the spaces and the continuity with the walls, contributing to the definition of a coherent and articulated internal system

69

The toilet area in a construction drawing shows the sequence and articulation of single spaces carved out in the walls

of municipal electricity. Some alternative suggestions were made about the floor cover, ranging from cork flooring in the bedrooms to vernacular dung screeded flooring. There were also various exchanges between Victoria and Zanuso regarding the sliding doors at the end of the bedroom suites; Victoria feared the weight of the doors would make it impossible for her to push them open, and so she sketched an alternative, which was implemented,[124] along with a long search for the appropriate material to clad the bathroom walls. By the end of 1973, the acoustic ceiling board had been sourced and the accompanying "white holly" ceiling timber had been prepared by the four-cutter. The position of the speakers, which would connect to a customised music system, had to be determined before installing the ceiling. Plastering was soon to commence, undertaken by Mr. Melan, a building artisan of French origin, who received clear written instructions from Zanuso, in French, regarding the Roman Stucco technique which was to be applied. With the house entering the final stage of detailing and finishes, it was possible to perceive the result of four years' work.

A concise but exhaustive legend at the bottom of the executive drawings lists the materials Zanuso suggested for finishing the entire house, but alterations occurred during construction. The specifications read as follows:

- CEILINGS:
  Plaster finish, white paint, smooth and glossy – all rooms.

- WALLS:
  Stone – all external walls.
  Stone – dining room, living room, porch.
  White roughcast – all bedrooms, library, passages.
  Ceramic tiles – all bathrooms, kitchens, service rooms.[125]
  White pine staves – gymnasium and annexed passages.

- FLOORS:
  Stone – all arcades and porch contours, entrance.
  Pebbles – household staff courtyard.
  Wood deck, oak, diagonal laying – dining room, living room.
  Wood deck, dark wood, lengthwise laying – bedrooms [labelled] B, C, D; passages [labelled] B, C, D.
  Wood logs, radial cut – arcades, porch.
  Ceramic tiles – household staff area, kitchens, all bathrooms, service rooms.
  Coloured rubber – gymnasium contour and annexed passages.
  Cork – gymnasium core.

- WINDOW AND DOOR FRAMES:
  Wood, white paint – all rooms.

CONSTRUCTION: INTERMINABLE

The construction took approximately five years (1970–1975) and is documented by correspondence between Sydney's office and Zanuso's studio. Due to the long distance, Sydney initially approached Stanley Kaplan to supervise the general construction and structural engineering, but he had limited time and so, instead, Henry Joubert of the Johannesburg architectural and planning firm Irvine Smith Joubert & Lennard took over, communicating directly with Zanuso and the building contractor, Tienie Botha.[126] However, for personal reasons, Joubert had to resign from the project in 1972 and Sydney's in-house architect at Edgars, Frantisek (Frank) Kosina (1923–2006), took over the project supervision. Later on, while documenting and managing the Edgardale project, Mallows, Louw, Hoffe and Partners (MLH) provided some construction documentation support to Coromandel. Kosina and MLH closely followed Zanuso's input and orientation. Construction progress was prolonged and Victoria complained, "The rate of building is excessively slow…", a year later stating, "It seems interminable, the building of this house is like a cathedral and it isn't even Blessed!" However, Zanuso also

70

70

Zanuso surveys the land to fix the position of the house, in the presence of Pietro Porcinai, Victoria, a young Roger Press, and others, 1969

71

72

71

Concrete frame structure and earthworks, as seen from the hill, c. 1970

72

Site visits by Zanuso co-ordinated the client and professional teams. Frank Kosina (back left), Tienie Botha (back right) and Zanuso are seen here with Victoria, c. 1974

73

74

73

Stonemasons from Sekhukhuneland clad the north-facing facade, c. 1973

74

The living area under construction prior to installing the music system; hidden ducts within false ceilings and timber flooring are yet to be installed.

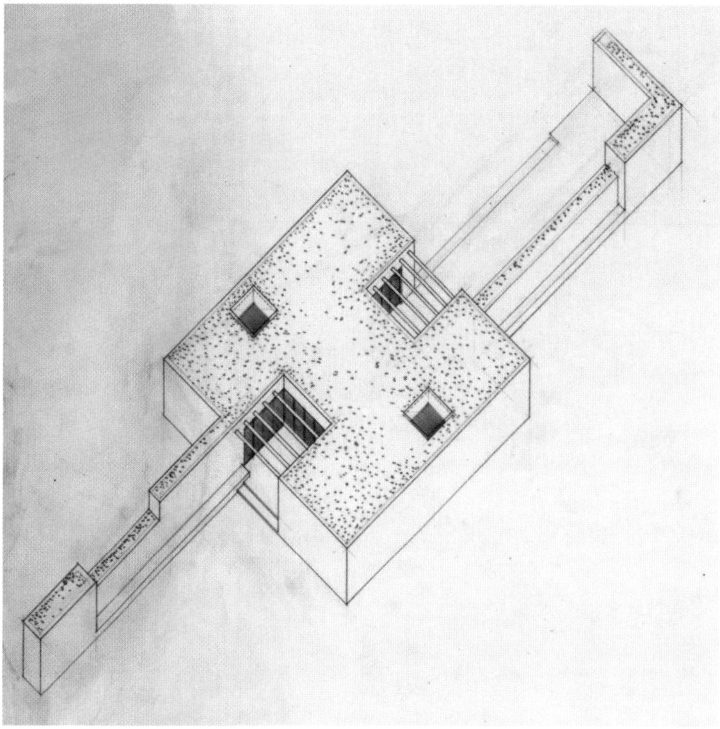

75

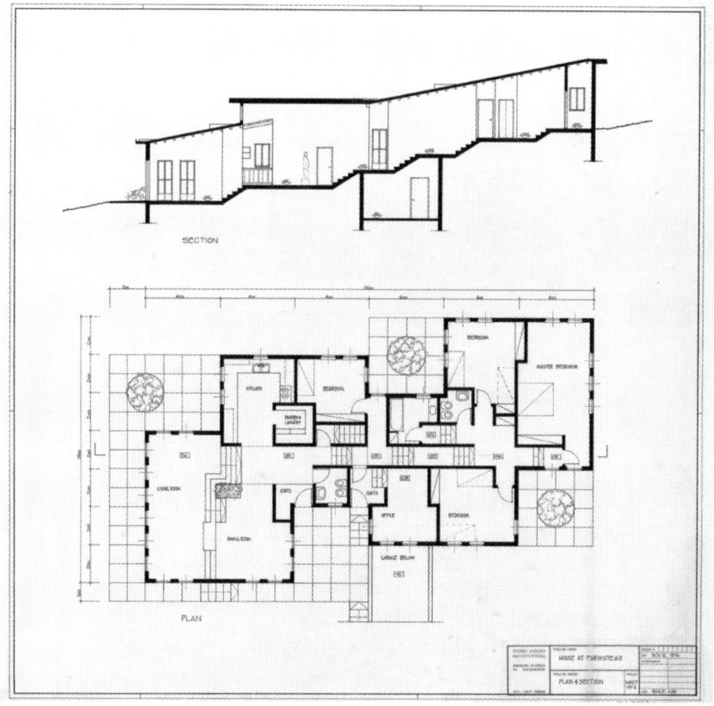

76

75

Unbuilt design for the farm offices and administration areas

76

Unbuilt design for a new homestead, presumably for the farm manager

received additional briefs for the design of farm offices (1971) and another farmstead (1976), neither of which were realised.[127] In any event, while the first arches were being constructed and recorded in a series of impressive photographs, the clients were still exploring a new idea to connect the roof over the kitchen to the hillside. These kinds of alterations proposed by the clients – including big requests for a kitchen redesign, and smaller requests for laundry rooms and doors to the bedrooms of the staff wing – were not uncommon and caused delays. Zanuso would respond with care and command.

The extensive dimensions and scale of the house are visible in photographs which show the vast area of site work undertaken to realise the design, including site preparation and excavation for a service basement. Its footprint (excluding atria but including pergolas) covers an extensive 1,628 square metres of which only 1,018 square metres are usable, due to the thickness of the stone walls, which make up about 30 per cent of the footprint.[128] This design is not that of a house poised upon its columns to rest lightly on the earth and thereby avoid making a mark on the landscape. Instead, the columns are clad and further anchored to the ground purposefully with brick and stone. Coromandel House is designed much like an ancient archaeological monument, to leave a lasting impression *within* the landscape.

Once the foundations from which the walls would grow were defined, and the reinforcing had been specified and inspected by Stanley Kaplan's engineers, the construction of the reinforced concrete frame grid followed, around which the long stone walls were gradually built. All the stoneworks were carried out by hand, without the aid of machines and using material sourced mostly from boulders and a quarry on the farm.[129] In January 1971, Sydney asked Zanuso if he would still like to insert large boulders at intervals along the base of the structure despite Victoria's misgivings. In 1971, the colossal stone walls began to take shape, first with the help of a geologist[130] to find authentic dolerite with the appropriate deep blue hue Zanuso preferred and then under the direction of a British stonemason called John Turner. They were clad over a period of three years by a team of five local stonemasons from Sekhukuneland[131] – Zanuso evaluated photographs that Sydney sent him regarding the colour, size and patterning technique, providing further direction by writing, "in general, the wall texture is good, but in some points the stones are too small all together and this is bad". However, both Sydney and Zanuso later remarked that the finished stonework was excellent. By 1972, it was possible to get a sense of the internal spatial qualities of the house and Victoria wrote, "The house is looking very beautiful. The proportions are divine and the stone is like an Impressionist painting. The feeling is breath-taking and it will be a fantastic house, even if we hardly ever live in it."

The house is held together by an expansive planted roof, covered by 70cm of soil and numerous indigenous grasses and endemic plants. It rests on a reinforced concrete structure on a planning module of approximately 4.5 metres between midlines, with brick infill between the concrete foundations, columns, beams, and stone cladding to complete the wall system. On plan and section, architectural features are asymmetrically placed to avoid predictability and encourage visual intrigue. Zanuso would describe his use of the Golden Ratio to proportion the design for an aesthetically pleasing spatial experience. Openings are sparse, creating the effect of a cool, cave-like interior to contrast with the vast sunny outdoors. Windows are small in relation to the enormity of the stone walls, serving to frame views and specific points in the house, to control solar gain and to increase the archaic fortification aesthetic. Large glazed doors, including a motorised sliding door in the library, serve to visually connect the interiors to the wilderness beyond and, once open, further blur the line between building and nature. Custom-designed timber shutters protect the house from the elements and, like in the houses in Sardinia, close up the envelope of the house to ward off uninvited visits while the family are away.

Two sets of east-west parallel gallery wings are offset from a three-tiered central living area, and extend towards landmarks in the rural landscape – a distant waterfall on one side and hillside on the other. Each wing is framed by 250-metre-long[132] stone walls that partially enclose narrow 4-metre-wide "streets" or densely planted atria, which serve as transitional space and intermediary extensions of the veld.

The 11 buttress arches – 12 if the arch in front of the library is included – serve a number of complementary purposes, which accrue to create the iconic north-facing facade. Although the concrete frame structure of the house was designed to hold the loads from the roof and provide secure footing, the buttress arches contribute to physically anchor the building on the hillside.[133] Aesthetically, as a repetitive architectural element, they provide scale, proportion and rhythm on a long facade that would look excessive without any articulation; their shadows also provide a dramatic show on a bright summer's day. In addition, they form a threshold between the main living spaces and openings towards the vast landscape beyond, making the transition between outside and inside more dynamic and dramatic. Lastly, they mediate solar access and heat gain into the house.

The amount of care and attention to detail spent on the location, layout, form and aesthetic of the exterior of the house was reflected in equal measure within the interiors. One of the young architects in training in MLH during the 1970s was Marcus Holmes (b. 1952), who recalls that the interior was carefully detailed and decisions were purposeful. Sydney had a condition that indigenous timber had to be used for all the joinery for the house. Many timber samples were inspected, including *Dombeya rotundifolia* (wild pear), which was chosen for the distinctive timber entrance door designed by Zanuso and detailed by Marcus Holmes.[134] Australian karee timber logs to be used in the outside patios were shipped from Fremantle and added another layer of texture and grounding to the house. The entire ceiling was made from a continuous suspended ceiling within which elaborate air-conditioning systems[135] and electrical services were hidden.

The works continued until 1975, and the end of construction was marked by the sanctioning of an engraving on the dolerite stone over the main entrance, which reads: "*Hic terminus haeret. Marco Zanuso per Sydney Press. MCMLXXV*".[136] Aerial photographs of the building, taken at the time before the vegetation reclaimed the construction as Zanuso and his clients planned, show the structural form anchored to the ground, like an artefact from a remote period, in which the primary state of the construction and the ultimate state of the ruin co-exist. While the house seems uninhabited and crouched in the ground, its basic shape alludes to the substructures of the mines in the region. Entering and moving through the sequence of rooms to the ends of each wing, is like descending into the ground, much like the experience in Zanuso's Muda-Maè cemetery project. This impression is reinforced by the deep blue dolerite colour of the interior walls, in which one could easily imagine the atmospheric scenes of Plato's "Allegory of the Cave" unfolding. A photographic shot, which can be dated back to this final phase

77

An axonometric view of the cemetery of Muda Maè in Longarone shows the system of open-air spaces, with the burials as "rooms" in sequence or as a village, developing along a longitudinal path dug into the ground and well adapted to the topography of the place

78

"Interesting, even if unfinished". With these words scribbled on a piece of paper attached to this photo, Zanuso summarised the powerful result of the project at its final stages of construction

77

78

79

80

of the construction, portrays the front of the house in black and white at the portico with a strong accentuation of the shadow effect that the buttresses and the pergola generate on the rear wall. A handwritten annotation bears the words "interesting, even if unfinished", unequivocally sanctioning the intrinsic value of this new yet archaic and timeless architectural form. But the writer, Zanuso, also grasps the fact that the specificity of the house is its character of nonfinite, open form, not to be completed, because it is the vegetation that will have to complete the work by regaining possession of the site – which promptly happens.

LIVING: A HOUSE ENHANCES THE WAY WE LIVE

The approach towards Coromandel House has been carefully curated to create a full sensory experience that draws out a sense of awe and wonder at the design of the house, the interiors and the surrounding landscape. A series of memorable moments along this route are the result of many collaborators and include a discreet entrance to the farm, followed by a long avenue of white stinkwood (*Celtis africana*) and yellowwood (*Afrocarpus falcatus*) through to the main stables complex. From there, a carefully positioned winding driveway directs visitors to wonderful views, where thickets of trees conceal and provide glimpses of exquisitely crafted dolerite stone walls – the house eventually being revealed. By pulling back the layers of Coromandel House to see the hidden technologies below, starting with the plants, the stone walls, brick infill and concrete frame, it becomes clear that nothing in this house has happened by chance, or rather, without consideration. Every detail was purposeful, sometimes even agonised over, designed to respond to prompts from the clients, context and landscape, to manifest a collective vision in which the house creates a lingering, unforgettable experience.

Almost three decades after the house was completed, Victoria reflected on a quality of her design methodology that persisted throughout her life, her love for creating atmospheric context. When building, but especially when renovating and decorating a home, she always took her clues, much like an archaeologist, from the architecture and its hidden layers,[137] elaborating in her own words by writing, "my theory of decorations is that the style reflects the date of the house so everything on the walls should reflect that period, anything not attached can be the following period so that it gives the effect of one family collection over generations. I think if a house is undisturbed over generations one leaves the architecture and everything attached to it alone and the middle of the rooms reflect the style of the family of the period."[138]

The interiors that Victoria designed for her different homes varied as much as the architecture that contained them. On one level they were completely different, but on another there is a consistent purity and authentic desire to connect architecture with its interiors to capture the essence of what was happening there. In Coromandel House, the situation offered an added advantage: she was co-creating the architectural context with Sydney and Zanuso from scratch. The new house comfortably paired archaic tectonic elements inspired by the ancient landscape with modern interiors that were furnished to reflect the style of the family. When the home was complete, Victoria took to making it feel lived in and experienced as a series of theatrical moments carefully thought

79

View towards the main bedroom at the end of the parents' wing

80

The living area with the music system by Livio Castiglioni, a key feature of the communal spaces

out to respond to functional purposes and aesthetic delight.[139] Hers was "an innate understanding for the feel of a room, how to make it interesting but with charm, how to let the bones of the room speak, how to give it a mellow gentleness and harmony that immediately made one feel better for being in it".[140]

As a consequence of the state-of-the-art technology that was hidden and installed in the architectural layers – namely the large air-conditioning and central heating systems, but also the media centre and projector system, surround sound, electric doors and an intercom system – Sydney and Victoria commissioned another technological innovation that was custom-made for the house: they approached Livio Castiglioni (1911–1979) to design a music system, part of which was portable. It was installed within custom joinery spanning between two columns in the ledge separating the upper and lower living rooms. Technologically, the house is a luxurious time capsule of international design excellence.

The furniture included Zanuso's Woodline lounge chairs with white upholstery and red lacquer frames built by the furniture company Cassina, as well as a Delfa sofa from Arflex, McGuire's rattan living-room suite and two of Rietveld's Red Blue chairs at the entrance hall near the grand piano. In addition to these furnishings and the Italian design aesthetic that carried the project, Victoria had a local ceramicist make the crockery that would fit with the context of the house and decorated the entrance hall with African masks and a large painting by British abstract artist Albert Irvine (1922–2015). The cushions around the fireplace were covered in African fabrics or painted leather, and the carpets were woven by Coral Stephens.[141] Victoria's approach was about materials and their integration with form and function. She was keen on things having a purpose that enhanced life, so there would be different places to go to sit with two people, or four or 12.[142] Places were adapted to be purposeful and functional, not to be beautiful in themselves. She managed to connect to context, bring totally foreign objects into it and create an intuitive disruption, a juxtaposition in a way that was very harmonious. This innate act was about bringing the house to life while giving it roots that seem to have always been there.[143]

The design and construction processes were the result of a mutual understanding between Zanuso, Victoria and Sydney. Sydney brought the ambition and intention to create a farmhouse that manifested his ongoing quest for excellence; Victoria a sensitivity to context, scale and landscape aesthetic; while Zanuso carried with him a genealogy of design precedents and ideas that had not yet found a suitable place to flourish. Each sought to achieve their own nuanced objective while accomplishing the overall feat of creating a distinctive building, an elegantly poised man-made sculptural shelter in the landscape, capturing the spirit of the veld.

•••

81

Looking outwards from the entrance along the outdoor atrium that frames the view towards the waterfall

82

View of the outdoor dining area overlooking the fishpond and swimming pool

81

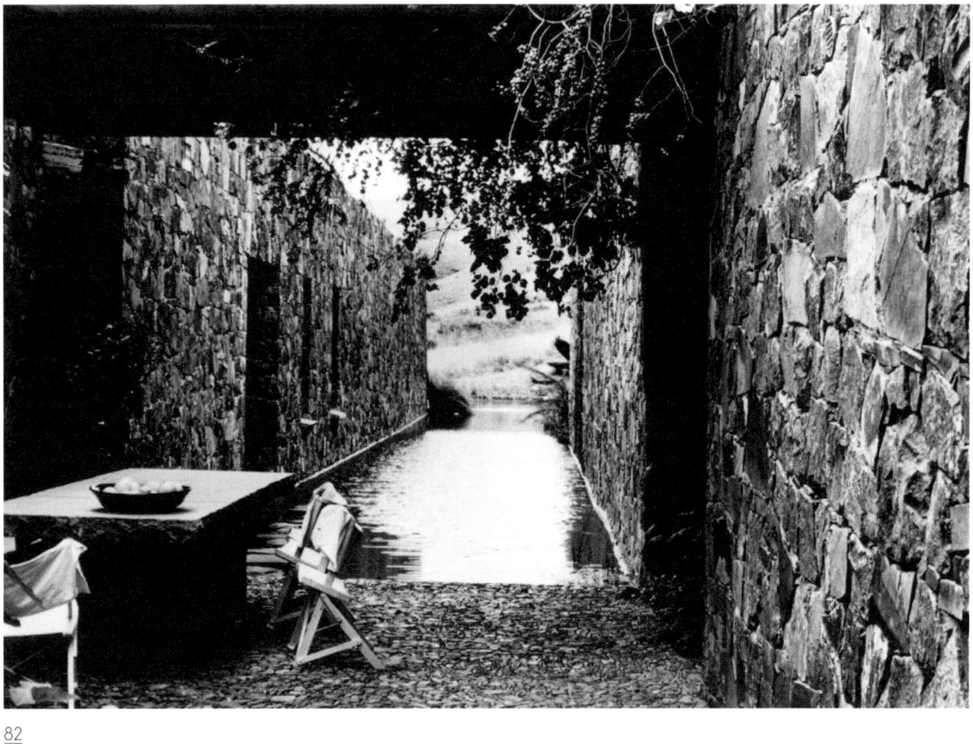

82

ENDNOTES

99 The archival correspondence shows that Coromandel House was first and the invitation to design Edgardale followed shortly after. Both buildings were designed simultaneously with construction overlapping.
100 Grignolo, R, 2013; Raggi interview, 1999.
101 Correspondence from Sydney to Zanuso outlining his travel arrangements, Archivio del Moderno.
102 ZML, *Abitare*, 1981.
103 Ibid.
104 Katsikakis, D, Interview, 2020.
105 Ibid.
106 Maggs, T, 2021; Verlorenkloof is also known as Emakhazeni.
107 Barnes, H, 1980, p. 121.
108 In the Archivio del Moderno, among Zanuso's papers for Casa Press, are complete plans by Norman Eaton for his proposed seaside villa for Sydney Press in Sedgefield, dated 1961.
109 According to Nicholas J. Clarke, the barn's presumably late-nineteenth-century construction places it among the oldest structures on Coromandel Farm, unaffected by the destruction of the Second Boer War (1899–1902), which occurred in the broader area.
110 From "Si vede che sono distratto", Marco Zanuso interviewed by Franco Raggi, in Grignolo, R, ed., *Marco Zanuso: Scritti sulle tecniche di produzione e di progetto*, Milan: Silvana Editoriale and Mendrisio Academy Press, 2013. Original text published in *Flare. Architectural Lighting Magazine*, no. 21, September 1999, pp. 80–95.
111 *Abitare*, 1981, p. 17; *Fair Lady*, 1985, p. 59.
112 Zanuso's conceptual explanation was quoted by Sydney Press in *Fair Lady*, May 1985, p. 59.
113 Correspondence in the Archivio del Moderno, Fondo Zanuso.
114 Letter dated 19 May 1969 in da Mosto, J, PowerPoint presentation.
115 Katsikakis, D, Interview, 2020.
116 Ibid.
117 Press, C, Interview, 2020.
118 Kinmonth, P and T Traeger, Interview, 2020.
119 Ibid.
120 Correspondence from Victoria to Zanuso, dated 21 February 1970, Archivio del Moderno.
121 Moore, C, 1974, p. 73.
122 From "Si vede che sono distratto", Marco Zanuso interviewed by Franco Raggi, in Grignolo, R, ed., *Marco Zanuso: Scritti sulle tecniche di produzione e di progetto*, Milan: Silvana Editoriale and Mendrisio Academy Press, 2013. Original text published in *Flare. Architectural Lighting Magazine*, no. 21, September 1999, pp. 80–95.
123 Ibid.
124 Letter and sketches from Victoria to Zanuso, Archivio del Moderno.
125 Small mosaic ceramic tiles.
126 Joubert's wife, Erna, was an Italian language lecturer at the University of South Africa and translated their correspondence.
127 In the Mendrisio archive under House Press are drawings attributed to the house that belong to another project drawn up by Zanuso in parallel to drafting the final construction drawings for Coromandel House. Dated 1971, they bear the words "Office Building Farm Swagershoek Transvaal" and represent typological variants of a small complex consisting of two single-storey pavilions. These twin pavilions intended for laboratories and offices connect in an elongated and unified shape, and are typologically inspired by the houses of Arzachena. Both pavilions centre on a square courtyard, connected by long stone walls that stretch in both directions and end at small technical service volumes, with vegetation that emerges from the flat roofs, from the profile of the long and low building and, finally, above the terminal volumes on both sides. The construction system, with stone-clad walls and limited openings facing the central courtyard, refers directly to the construction of the farmstead. Only the drawings remain of this unbuilt project, preserved together with those of the house.
128 Steyn, G, The Coromandel Manor House, 2016, p. 41.
129 Steyn, G, 2016, p. 47.
130 At Anglo-Gold.
131 These artisans were hired from the Rustenburg Platinum Mines following cut-backs in production. Due to Apartheid controls, they likely substituted the Portuguese building artisans, who had been recruited from Portugal but for whom immigration formalities were lagging.
132 The May 1985 *Fair Lady* article incorrectly cites the walls as being 100 metres long.
133 As with the air-conditioning system, this may have been over-engineered.
134 Interviews were conducted during 2011 and 2012 with surviving architects at MLH in order to understand their role as supervision architects, as well as record their memories of working with Zanuso. Marcus Holmes was an apprentice during this time.
135 The outlets were continuous bands on the edge of the floor where it meets the ceiling and wall.
136 From Latin, this literally means, "Here stays the end" or more poetically,

83

"Here is your journey's end". This implies something akin to an ephemeral boundary, the end of a process, but not The End. In Virgil's *Aeneid*, it takes on a more dramatic meaning with its contextual reference to the Aeneid's fate of taking on the Trojans in Italy and to fulfil an immovable destiny. More in Part 3: "Coromandel House in Zanuso's Portfolio".

137 Katsikakis, D, Interview, 2020.

138 Press, V, 2004.

139 Kinmonth, P and T Traeger, Interview, 2020.

140 Cator, C, 2015, p. 9.

141 Da Mosto, J, PowerPoint presentation; handwoven carpets from Swaziland, now Eswatini.

142 Kinmonth, P and T Traeger, 2020.

143 Katsikakis, D, Interview, 2020.

83

Sydney beyond the buttresses on the north side of the house

Building the landscape

Sydney Press wrote to Marco Zanuso for help finding "a landscape architect for this project who is not, repeat not, committed to formal patterns, but rather one whose designs are likely to blend with the character of the farm". With this brief, various professionals advised on the landscape design for Coromandel, where the natural, indigenous garden became almost indistinguishable from the architecture

84

On 9 July 1969, Sydney set in motion the next important design process at Coromandel House: the natural garden. He wrote to Cesare Larini at Equatorial to ascertain from Zanuso whether he could bring along "his friend the landscape architect" to settle the landscape design while in Zanuso's presence, adding "we would of course prefer a landscape architect for this project who is not, repeat not, committed to formal patterns, but rather one whose designs are likely to blend with the character of the farm".[144] Two days later, Zanuso confirmed by telex that Pietro Porcinai (1910–1986) would be able to accompany him on his return trip to South Africa. The clients intuited the need to design a landscape that suited the natural context. Zanuso provided the means to achieve this, both through the architectural design and through his professional association with Porcinai.[145] Zanuso would frequently collaborate with some of the most important contemporary consultants and designers in his projects and on construction sites, who would assist him in completing his vision and make important contributions to the overall design. Porcinai was one such frequent collaborator: he was considered to be one of the most important Italian landscape architects of the last century. Pinocchio Park (1962) built in Collodi is one example of their collaboration.

As a living system, the landscaping at Coromandel House has significantly altered over the past five decades. Trees have matured, tastes have changed and now it appears as a forested oasis in the veld where nature has taken over. Traces of the wild garden envisioned by Sydney and Victoria, and the design initiated by Porcinai, are still visible and it maintains three key qualities. Firstly, the wild aesthetic with an understanding of local flora and habitat to create a continuation of the grassland biome, with self-seeding endemic veld plants in each of the courtyards propagated from kloofs on the farm – an approach well ahead of its time and which has now grown in popularity. Secondly, the landscaping is inseparable from the architecture and not limited to the ground plane – the walls and roof are areas for planting so that the building itself becomes a habitat for new life to take hold. Thirdly, the garden emphasised the *genius loci,* the ancient *spirit of the place,* which the architecture complemented, and as such the design was not always gentle, but involved earthworks, planting large trees, redirecting water, and uprooting, planting and replanting endemic flora to emphasise the sensory experience. The garden design reached its peak in the early 1980s, before gradual changes and the introduction of exotics began to change the aesthetic.

As with a classical symphony, the landscape was the result of many contributions orchestrated principally by Victoria. She sought skills and talent from the people around her to realise the vision she and Sydney had for a wild garden. The first contributor was, naturally, Zanuso's architecture. Although he did not direct the botanical or ecological aspect of landscaping, at the crux of his Coromandel House design was the relationship between architecture and nature, which advanced a lineage of Modern Movement architectural thinking, and in 1973 Victoria wrote, "The grass is growing on the roof where it is already tall and falls over the top and it is spectacular. Sydney said it was an 'inspired idea'." Although critics point to his commercial architecture and fail to see the connection to nature, Zanuso's position was that "architecture originates as the relationship towards landscape"[146] and Coromandel House

84

Pietro Porcinai and Zanuso during a visit to Coromandel House, 1969

is evidence of that. As for his residential architecture, particularly in his twin houses in Arzachena, Sardinia, his own holiday home in Paxos, and the house he designed in Cavallo Island, he pushes this relationship to the essence of what it means to *inhabit* a place – in the most sensitively phenomenological sense of the word.[147]

Coromandel House serves as another example in this architectural lineage of dwelling in the presence of a *genius loci.* His design responded to site morphology and the clues it offered to create wild or wonderful spaces. It further catered to exisiting cultural traditions yet allowed the family to construct new rituals from their interactions with the architecture. This broad environmentalist approach, bolstered by a "precise understanding of the habitat, which is not limited to physical and formal aspects, revealing immaterial influences on the project that aim to environmental and social-economical sustainability, preluding environmental governance", opened the path to a real restructuring of architecture schools in Italy.[148] In the 1960s and 1970s, "environmental" architectural approaches are visible in his projects. His Case Feal (1961–1963) apartment buildings in Milan and the Arzachena vacation houses in Sardinia, explore themes of recreated or contained habitat now prevalent in environmental design. Similar to what was accomplished in Coromandel House by incorporating planting within the building fabric, in the case of Case Feal this was done within the walls with recesses through which vegetation could "peek out and over" the edges of the building, while in Coromandel House, the shallow soil covering the roof and the rock-clad walls became habitats. In the houses in Arzachena in Sardinia, the exteriors appear to be blocked up, while inside, the buildings open up to the sky, and when the shutters are open, they frame splendid views that connect to the raw beauty of the landscape beyond. This approach is similarly experienced in Coromandel House where fortress-like arches anchor the structure in a vast landscape almost resembling a dam wall or a defensible edge, all the while enclosing cave-like interior spaces that in turn delicately reconnect to the landscape through well-placed doors and windows that regulate the climate through shutters. The missing element now is the "wild" effect created by the plants, because for Victoria, especially, the way they interacted with the architecture was absolutely essential to the form and experience of the house.[149]

The second contributor to the landscape design of Coromandel House – and also the network of interconnected landscaped areas on the farm, consisting of the stables, the dams and canals, and the nursery – was Porcinai, who was famed for designing gardens that appeared untouched by human hands. From the middle of 1969 until the middle of 1971, he provided the guidance and plans for a myriad of projects on the farm, and advised on the landscaping at Edgardale and Inanda House in Johannesburg. He also planned an extensive tour of important gardens in Italy for Sydney and Victoria to visit during 1970, though this was never realised. Apart from landscaping masterplans that included the house and stables, with a pathway along a series of dams and canals linking the two, Porcinai also prepared extensive planting lists that were based on indigenous flora such as *Sparrmannia africana*. He provided reports regarding the optimal design of the nursery, the design of a house for the nurseryman, the greenhouse design and suggestions for design features at the waterfalls which could

85

A photo Zanuso took of Coromandel House shortly after construction, c. 1975

86

Coromandel House fulfilling the intention to blend in with the landscape, c. 1980

85

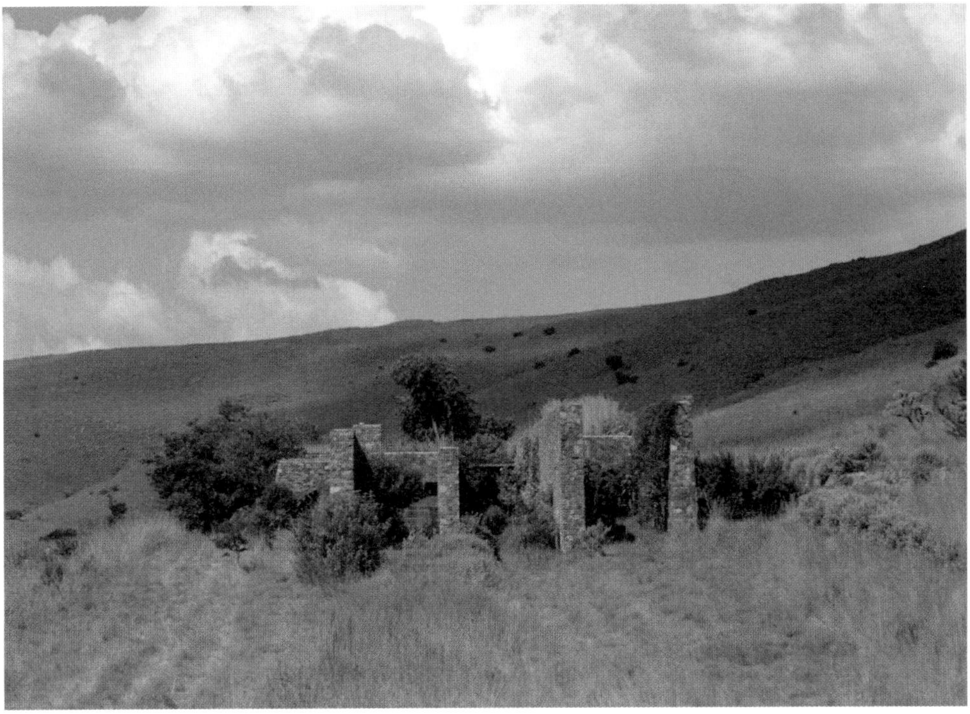

86

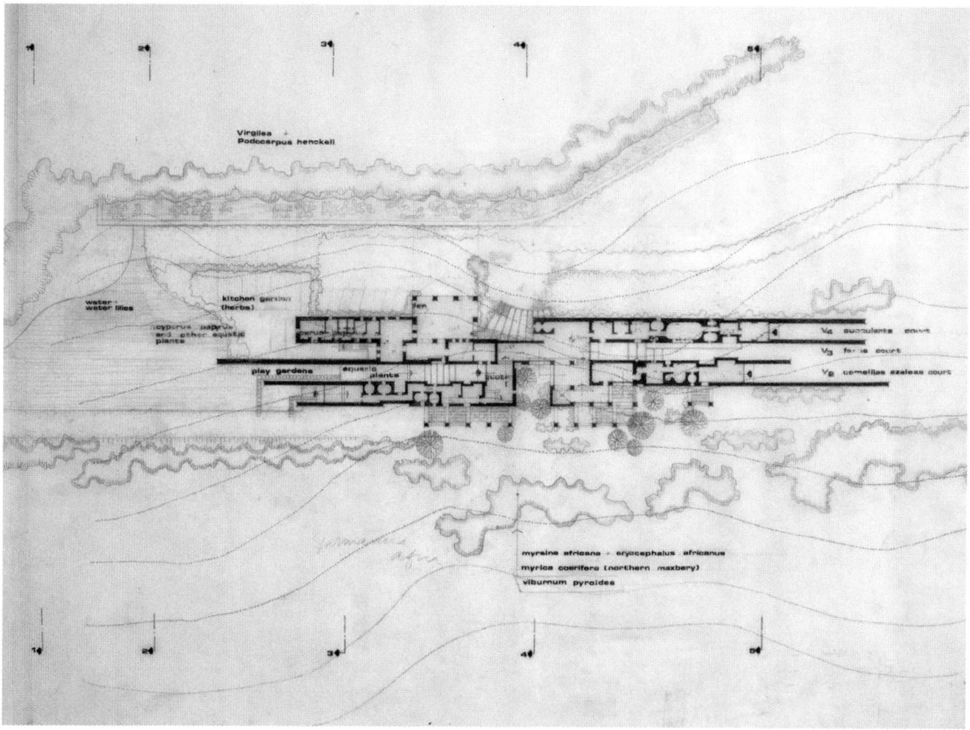
Virgilea +
Podocarpus henckeli
water -
water lilies
kitchen garden
(herbs)
cyperus papyrus
and other aquatic
plants
play gardens
aquatic
plants
V4 succulents court
V3 ferns court
V2 camellias azaleas court
myrsine africana + erycephalus africanus
myrica cerifera (northern maxbery)
viburnum pyroides

87

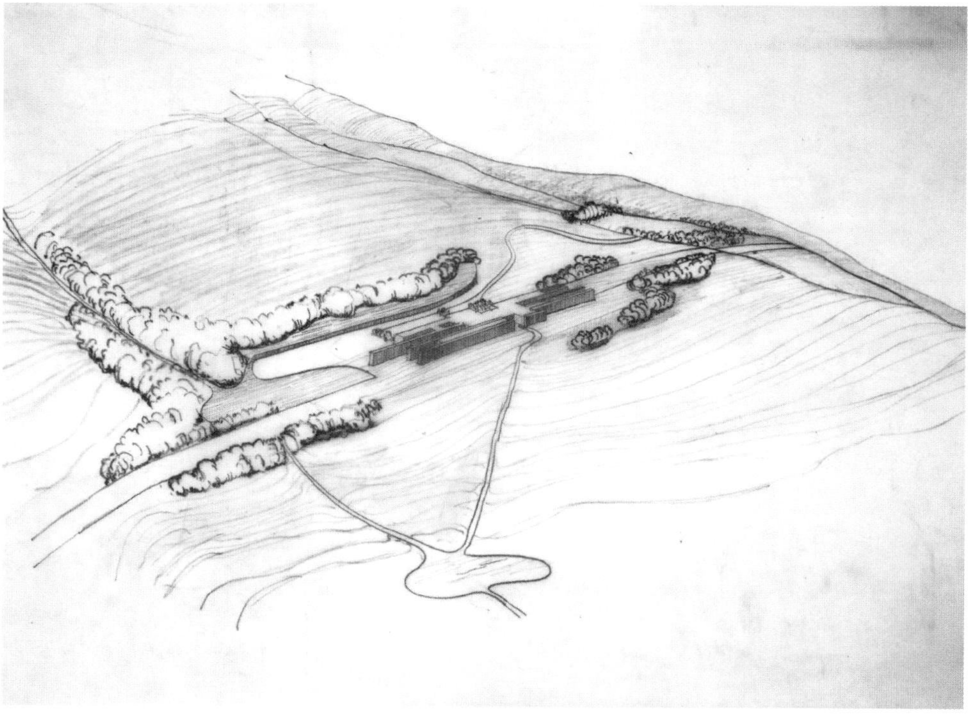

88

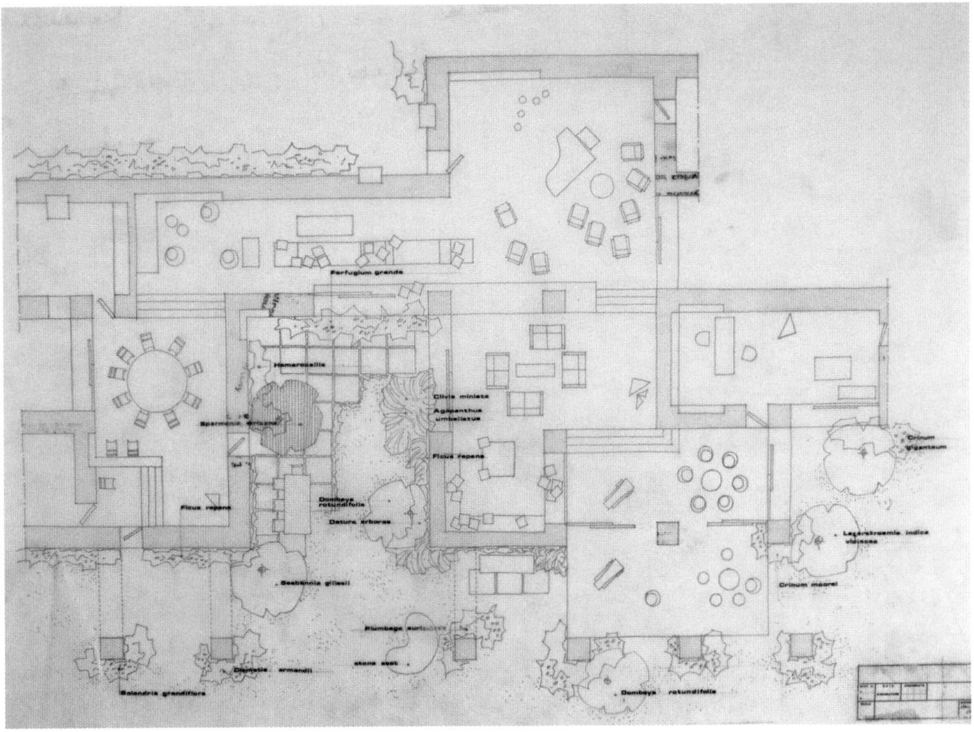

89

87

Porcinai's proposal for the indigenous landscaping plant palette around the house

88

Porcinai's perspective study of the landscaping around the house, with pockets of vegetation and water

89

Detailed planting scheme made up of indigenous species to be planted close to the house

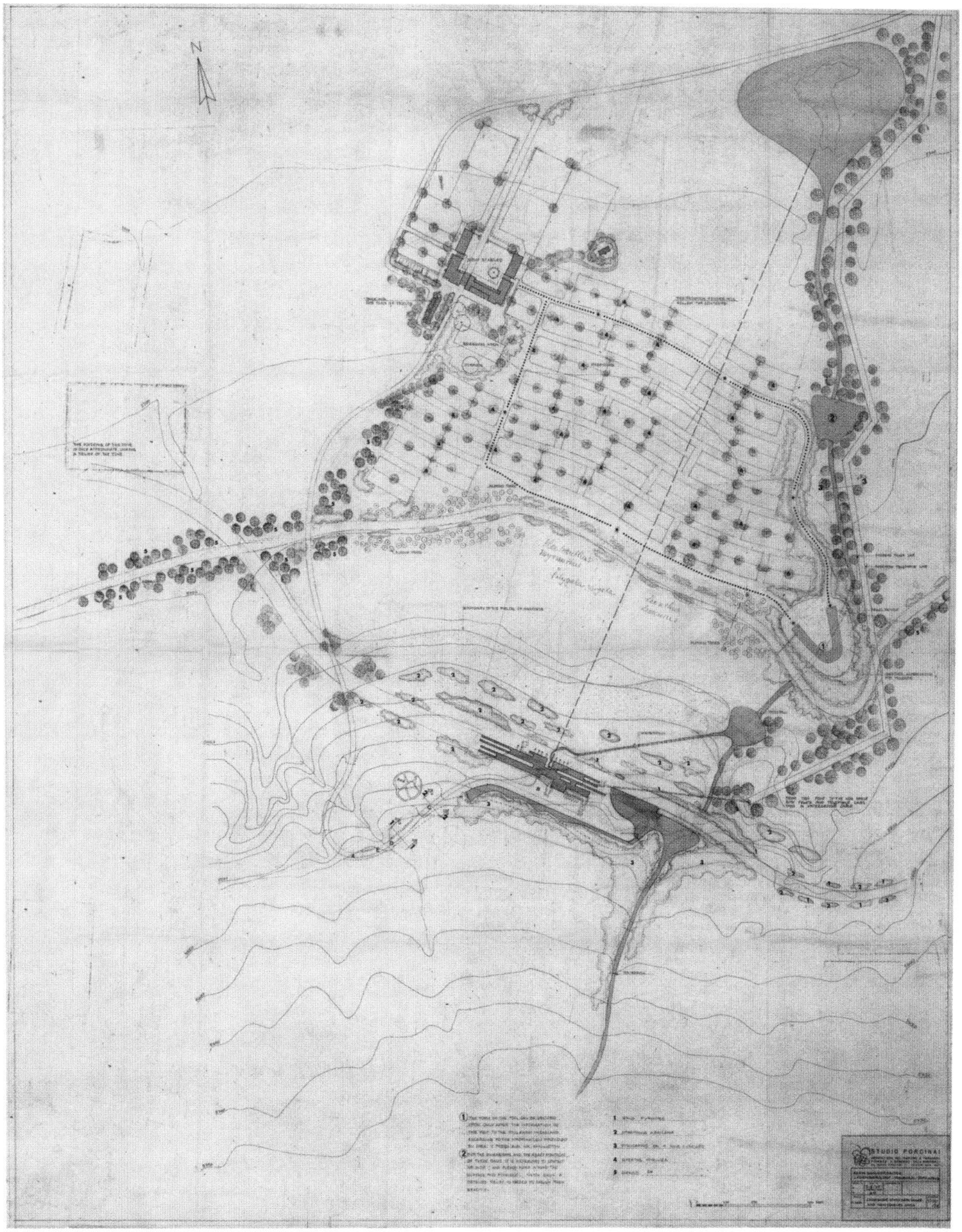

90

91

90

Porcinai's masterplan proposal links the house with the stables by a meandering driveway, proposed horse meadows and pond

91

Indigenous vegetation creates a meadow aesthetic

improve convenience there (parking, a bar with refrigerator and dressing rooms). In addition, he provided extensive guidance on the construction of the meandering driveway that connected the stables to the house and which included small bridges over furrows in the veld. This element was present from the first concept design and, together with one of the smaller dams and canal, was one of the few elements that were implemented – albeit with construction challenges. Due to the lack of detailed survey drawings, the contractor found himself having to dig a trench through portions of the road, which concerned Victoria. However, Porcinai insisted that the effect of grading the road above and below the datum of the natural ground line would enhance the dramatic effect of moving through the veld to create a sense of arrival more interesting than "a continuous movement along an untouched hillside".[150]

By March 1971, despite numerous requests from Porcinai for the appointment of someone on the ground with sufficient botanical knowledge and experience to oversee planting growth and provide regular bi-weekly updates to him so he could supervise the works on all projects, there had been no progress. The next piece of correspondence dates from as late as 1973, referring to a trip Victoria had undertaken to visit a few gardens with Porcinai and his daughter Anna. Victoria later mentioned how influential Porcinai was in establishing the native gardening strategy that has become so integral to the Coromandel House experience[151] – whose intention was to create a wild natural garden that suited the archaic architecture, but more importantly, the context of the farm and veld beyond. Porcinai's biography lists the Coromandel House project (Villa Transvaal 1969–1971) as unbuilt, but his input cemented Victoria and Sydney's intentions for an indigenous natural garden.

The next contributor arrived around 1970. As chairman of the Tree Society, Sydney contacted Michael Schurr and invited him to meet him in Johannesburg, after which they would visit Coromandel Farm to look at Sydney's various landscaping projects, including the farm itself, Inanda House and the future Edgars Headquarters. Schurr became plantsman, put in charge of propagating many of the plants and endemic species on the farm which would be planted around the house. A few years later, he also met and provided input to the planting scheme in the design proposal from Roberto Burle Marx (1909–1994), which led him to go to Brazil to study his work. Another of Schurr's collaborators would be Zanuso – at Coromandel House, Schurr would grow and supply the plants that would be used in its landscaping to blend in with the natural scenery, and Zanuso was very curious about the plants and knowledgeable in his field.[152] But Schurr preferred to be a plantsman and not dabble in design. In addition, his role on the farm involved removing the pine plantations and propagating and planting indigenous trees along the farm roads to create shade and wind breaks. The main road leading to the stables was planted with yellowwood and dubbed "Yellowwood Avenue". Later on, Sydney's interest in *Clivia* led to Schurr ordering *Clivia miniata* seeds from which the highly regarded orange Coromandel *Clivia cultivar* was propagated at the nursery. The Coromandel nursery became well regarded for selling indigenous and other plants to nurseries all over the country.

In 1970, the fourth and most enduring contributor to the garden was introduced to Victoria. Patrick Watson (b. 1947), now a revered natural landscape architect in South Africa, was a self-taught botanist and horticulturalist. Victoria later described Watson to Zanuso as "a divine young man who will be in charge of the plantings and is very enthusiastic..."[153] She would meet Watson after encountering his childhood friend, the professional architect and garden design connoisseur Mira Fassler Kamstra (b. 1938) at an outing to the landmark garden

92

93

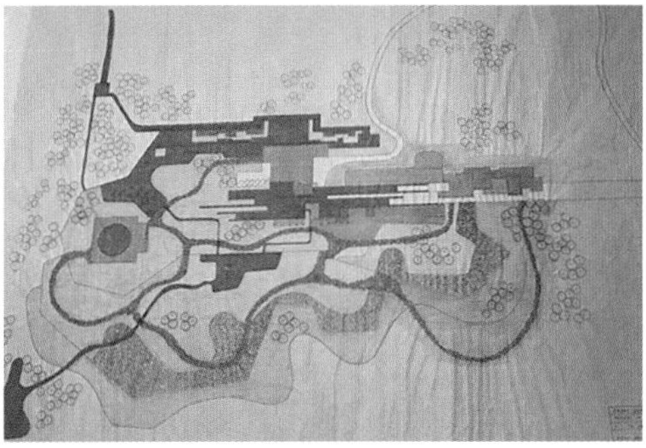

94

92

Victoria speaks to a resident gardener while Patrick Watson (far right) waters the garden

93

Zanuso and Roberto Burle Marx meet during a visit to Coromandel House, 1973

94

Unbuilt landscaping concept proposal designed by Burle Marx for Coromandel House

at Inanda House, originally designed by Joane Pim (1904–1974). Victoria was hosting the event for the Wits University Women's Society, and Mira – finding the landscaping to be exceptional – suggested a follow-up visit where she would introduce Watson to Victoria.

Victoria had an affinity with Watson's approach towards landscaping and horticulture and began collaborating with him on the design of sections of the garden at Inanda, using more indigenous species and a natural aesthetic. He recalls, "Victoria Press was really a garden genius at the time. The combination of Sydney, who was a poet, and Victoria, who had real genius, I think [was] fantastic. And she always was a fantastic gardener. Inanda House was very beautiful. [...] She did that in an Arts and Crafts [style] I would say." When Victoria introduced Watson to Coromandel House, construction was well underway. In Watson's words: "I came when it was half built [...] almost to the roof height. By then they had already brought [...] out Porcinai. [...] What was envisaged was just a wild garden, natural to the site so that it looked like the cliffs in the background."[154] The strategy was always to make house and garden a part of the hill: "natural". The roof already had veld grass on it, as Zanuso intended for the architecture to become part of the hill, and so Watson took over to help bring the garden to life.

Watson was influenced by ecological landscaping ideals, but in 1973 the Coromandel House landscaping could have followed a very different course. Roberto Burle Marx, whose sculptural Postmodern tropical gardens were synonymous with many of the iconic boulevards and modern architectural masterpieces in Brazil, travelled to Pretoria in South Africa to take part as guest speaker at the Institute of Landscape Architecture of Southern Africa (ILASA) congress titled "Planning for Environmental Conservation", which left a major impact on the landscaping profession there.[155]

The event took place at the University of Pretoria's Landscape Architecture Department. Burle Marx was accompanied by Ian McHarg (1920–2001), the Scottish landscape architect based in the United States. McHarg had shifted away from the dogmas of the Modern Movement towards its ideals, allowing him to envision a methodology for *design with nature*, based on a contextual knowledge of ecology, geography and systems thinking. His

95

95

Architecture and the landscaping begin to merge a few years after construction

96

97

96

The swimming pool and fishpond integrate into the natural landscaping. The multiple tree ferns were planted to mimic those found at the farm's waterfall

97

The water atrium, as seen from the al fresco dining area, where the landscaping merges with the architecture

1969 publication, also entitled *Design with Nature*, continues to influence designers aiming to integrate their projects within natural systems. All this related to what was emerging in Coromandel House, and in the packed audience at the University of Pretoria was Watson, who met Burle Marx and described the ensuing events as follows: "Roberto Burle Marx came out to South Africa for a conference and he asked me to take him round South Africa, so then I took him to northern Transvaal and flew from Durban to East London, to Port Elizabeth, to Cape Town, and Sydney got on the flight from – I think – East London to Port Elizabeth, and I said, 'This is Roberto Burle Marx', and he said, 'Oh, that's great, won't you design our garden in Lydenburg?'"[156]

In September 1973, Sydney wrote the following to Zanuso: "During an international ecological conference here, I met Roberto Burle Marx – and he is interested in providing planting plans for both the Farmhouse (where he favours sculptural effects to go with your architecture) and the new Corporate Headquarters. Victoria and I hurriedly set aside a day to travel to the farm with Roberto and his assistant and are hoping that what he has in mind will work."[157]

Burle Marx appears in a photograph taken during November 1973 at an advanced stage of construction on site and in the presence of Zanuso and Watson. Burle Marx's drawings for "Farm Swagershoek" date to February 1974 and reflect the graphic style and composition typical of his work. While Sydney may have welcomed the prospect of assigning another prominent international designer to the project, Victoria was less enthusiastic; she deemed the Burle Marx design utterly unsuitable by failing to capture the desired essential contextual responsiveness – that of blending into the veld.[158] She proceeded to orchestrate the garden design herself.

The resultant landscape flourished and rooted Zanuso's architecture into the veld. Schurr, Watson and Zanuso exchanged ideas on how to enhance the natural system of plants and to achieve the aesthetic Victoria composed. She was an exceptional garden designer in her own right, yet she would draw on experts in the field to constantly improve her gardens and build her knowledge. She later wrote, "My idea of a perfect garden would be to have all the plants of interesting horticultural distinction arranged in a very beautiful form."[159] Her aesthetic proficiency was especially useful in her garden designs and she was described as being "visually fine-tuned to seeing how different plant patterns and colours could come together [... being able to] visualise the landscape like a canvas from which the raw material of plants created an artistic flurry of colour and pattern that enabled her to create impressive gardens in formal styles, such as at her historic home in Inanda, as well as wild gardens in her modern home at Coromandel Farm".[160] Indeed, the "wild" garden was, in fact, a curated composition of purposefully planted bulbs, flowers, grasses, shrubs and trees *en masse* that enhanced an experience of beauty.

Perhaps encouraged by their experience of the landscaping at Coromandel House, Sydney and Victoria maintained their enthusiasm for bringing plants and nature into cities and buildings as a means of serenity and wellbeing. Around 1983, Sydney led an initiative within the Sandton Committee to create a green verge of indigenous species along one of the main highways cutting through Johannesburg, for which he consulted with French landscapers and Burle Marx, along with Watson in order to propose a scheme.[161] He also encouraged initiatives to plant trees in Soweto and other suburbs and sidewalks of Johannesburg,[162] contributing to what is claimed to be one of the largest urban forests in the world. Likewise, Victoria's interest in plants was not simply aesthetic. She started Lovemore Plants, an indoor plant business, during the 1970s, where she promoted the use of plants within buildings, especially in offices and workspaces to improve wellness, a philosophy now readily understood under the ambit of biophilic architecture. Victoria explained her fascination for including plants in architecture, stating that she had had "the most marvellous house built with grasses growing over the top and it was just blending into the landscape".[163] Her understanding of landscape, however, touched on a sensitivity towards its important role as a functional ecology.

If Victoria tended to object to more of Watson's ideas at Inanda, the pair cooperated and worked in unison while at Coromandel House. Watson and often Victoria herself sourced wild flowers and ferns from the veld to bring the wilderness closer to the home, in a considered way. Watson managed to reintegrate the house with nature while allowing the architecture to remain visible, saying:

> I don't want to hide it [...] that house [Coromandel] is monumentally beautiful and I would prune it [...] so that you are more aware of the walls. What he [Zanuso] wanted was it to be part of the landscape [...]. I think he had very urbane courtyards and things [in mind] and in fact when I first started, he didn't like it. He didn't like the earthworks going up like that. He took me down to show me what he didn't like and then he did like it when he saw it from the bottom. This [the meadow garden approach] was like an English garden in that way with different plants and things... [we were] plant collectors. So Zanuso may only have put hedges in, but he saw the sense of the [wild] garden and he loved it so he went that way.[164]

Watson extended the 15ft (4.5 metre) module used in the architecture into the landscape. Victoria loved the view towards the waterfall and chose to emphasise the axis of the house through the landscaping leading towards it, which she achieved by creating a foreshortening of the view on the west "to take one's eye up to the waterfall".[165] As he recalls, site visits were regular:

> We all used to go once a month, the whole family in a big bus and I would spend the weekend [landscaping]. We grew plants and dug them out of the veld to propagate and plant and put all the wild flowers in the garden and indigenous trees. So it is indigenous to that site. Even then that is what I did. On the roof are *Aloe arborescens* and *Greyia sutherlandii* (Natal bottlebrush), things that grow on shallow soil and bulbs that grow on shallow soil and in the kloofs, like *Rothmannia capensis* and the wild fig at the back, which went up a wall and which I now see has seeded itself all over the house [...]. I did all the earthworks around the house and I modulated all the landscape [...], and the big retaining wall. I actually had it closer, 4.5 metres, and then Sydney pushed it back and then I moved it two modules, so it is a bit boring now I think, because the tension has gone.[166]

Watson's recollections, as the only landscaper on the project who is still around, offer a glimpse into the energy, innovation and exchange that went into making a "wild" garden. With his extensive botanical knowledge and propagation experience, he would create projects in the garden, relying less on drawings and more on physically engaging with design while on site. Those projects requiring drawings – for example the rock wall at the back of the driveway with room for little plants to be planted into it like an English countryside drywall, an idea put forward by Victoria[167] – would be drafted by the architect Frank Kosina. He also supervised the installation of the stone pebble paving, the swimming pool and connected fishpond with stepping stones inside it, which had not originally been designed by Zanuso in the first proposal,[168] but while the house was being built, emerged naturally as an extension of the eastern courtyard. He continued in this way to tend to the Coromandel garden for about 15 years, while building up his career as one of the foremost indigenous- and wild-garden designers in South Africa.

While the philosophical approach to Coromandel House's landscaping emerged from observing the natural world and aimed for a deeply contextual reconstruction of natural habitats, Zanuso's approach to architecture and industrial design is similarly interested in the interpretation of context, which is also echoed in Victoria's approach to interior design. In Zanuso's perspective, the object functions best within its *context* and for its intended use.[169] His methodology establishes a conceptual standpoint of archetypes and typologies of families of objects in modern culture. Through this process, "modernness" is rejected as a style in favour of a contemporary response to the "tensions of a society undergoing profound structural transformations".[170] Construction materialises the image and spatial concept of an object into its environment, replacing the laws of nature with technical operations. Zanuso would add that architectonic experience is always one where organised space can condition human experience. Given this perspective, Coromandel House can be described as a dramatic manipulation of the landscape that responds to context by offering practical, periodic shelter within its organised spaces and rational lines. Deeply rooted in Zanuso's architectural ethos, his regard for context, typology, image, spatial organisation and rational technical construction is revealed in all layers of design, and extends to the landscape.

Through his exploration of typologies, Zanuso considered a home for the South African setting that has been fittingly adapted to local conditions, despite his unfamiliarity with such surroundings for designing or building. Sydney and Victoria went further in visually rooting the house so that their landscaping could blend in with the surroundings. In its prime, the balance between architecture, interior and landscape carefully orchestrated an experience that heightened the senses and has left a lasting impression, even to this day.

●●●

ENDNOTES

144 Letter Sydney Press to Cesare Larini, 9 July 1969, Archivio del Moderno.
145 Numerous drawings relating to the project are preserved in the archive: Farm Swagershoek, Lydenburg District, Transvaal, South Africa – from the 1970s for Sydney and Victoria Press. From file no. 126, no. 130 and no. 208, different materials were collected, including copies of drawings from Studio Zanuso.
146 Calgarotto, A, 2014, p. 186.
147 Ibid.
148 Schiaffonati, F, F Mussinelli and E Gambaro, 2011, p. 49.
149 Katsikakis, D, Interview, 2020.
150 Letter from Porcinai to Victoria, 1971, Archivio del Moderno.
151 Chia, M, *The New York Times Style Magazine*, April 2015.
152 Schurr, K, Interview, 2021.
153 Letter from Victoria to Zanuso, Archivio del Moderno.
154 Watson, P, Interview, 2020.
155 Pienaar, M, 2013; ILASA Brochure.
156 Watson, P, Interview, 2020.
157 Letter from Sydney to Zanuso, 1973, Archivio del Moderno.
158 Fassler Kamstra suggests that this plan was later adapted to be built in Vargem Grande, Areias, Brazil.
159 Press, V, 2004.
160 Katsikakis, D, Interview, 2020.
161 Watson, P, 2020.
162 Press, C, Interview, 2020.
163 Katsikakis, D, Interview, 2020.
164 Watson, P, 2020.
165 Achieved through major earthworks.
166 Watson, P, Interview, 2020.
167 Press, S, in Kinmonth, P and T Traeger, Interview, 2020.
168 Not by Porcinai nor Burle-Marx; both located the swimming pool further away from the house.
169 Burkhardt, 1994, p. 20.
170 Ibid., p. 8.

Innovation

In his design approach, Marco Zanuso advocated for a shift from a mechanistic towards an organic method represented by a complex relationship of all the elements of a project. In Coromandel House, as in all his design, innovation arises from the integration of technological aspects with the form of the artefact and its environment: like an organism in which the sum of the whole is greater than the parts

In 1965, Zanuso contributed a somewhat visionary and unusually utopian essay to *Pianeta* magazine. Entitled "The House. Megastructures, habitable cells, caves of the 21st century", it featured his depiction of a futuristic lifestyle in which humans progressively liberated from physical constraints would hypothetically experience a parallel human evolution – an unlikely consideration then but topical today. This evolution followed the refinement of technology in liberating humanity from their elementary needs, in order to concentrate on higher, more cultural needs. Finally freed from such restrictions, Zanuso imagined how the house could finally be at the total disposal of the highest, constitutive, irrepressible and even cultural needs of the human being as a thinking and feeling being:

> Man lives enclosed in an architectural envelope; despite new communication tools we still use our senses to communicate and gather together physically; man exists where he lives [...], his life cycle can be summarised in a series of facts and functions that firmly link to physical structures: man is born, eats, expels, sleeps, makes love, works, dies, and each of these facts is linked to well-defined places and spaces.[171]

This vision matches the spirit of emancipation unleashed by the social and cultural revolution of 1968, but, in practical terms, for Zanuso it corresponds to precise choices in the internal configuration of a home that reflects progress in terms of functionality and flexibility.

> The ability to use the house completely, will significantly reduce its overall volume; the functional spaces, according to existing trends, will be specifically sized: they will only be used for sleeping, loving and eating, consistent with the uses handed down by the fathers. None of the usual furnishing elements of the home should be distinct: everything disappears and flattens into the walls, which become fully equipped surfaces; the integral modular coordination will ensure the interchangeability and redistribution of the parts according to the uses and comfort of the family.[172]

This revolution of the home offers a liberation from inconveniences, allowing for the embrace of contemporary aspirations; the significance of this technological advance is evidently for Zanuso the product of a cultural – and ultimately also biological – change of our complex relationship towards nature, a change that he expresses even more clearly in a subsequent passage of the same text:

> This new house and this new organic city will constitute the first act of regression and return, at least formally, man to nature; the city will resume the behaviour of the natural landscape; through the new technology of organic structures, man will paradoxically come to rediscover and reproduce the totality of natural organic species, conditioning them in form and behaviour: an entirely artificial Arcadia will be built. At this stage, the cycle of instrumental civilisation will have ended, initiated by man, who dared to act against nature: the first civil act. Man's estrangement from nature will then be complete and total, both the human-nature confrontation and human evolution. The environment will have undergone its evolutionary process. However, for humans, the final act of this technological trajectory concerns artificially constructing himself at the height of his physical and intellectual

98

The recently mowed veld on the roof reveals the shape of the habitable "caves" and "cells" of Coromandel

> performance. The consequence will be the mechanisation of man together with the formal regression of his confrontation with nature: prehistoric man was at the disposal of nature through subjection, the man of the future will re-propose his availability towards nature in terms of total emancipation. The sense and dimension of nature will be completely changed.[173]

Coromandel House translates this into architectural form: the perfect emblem of Zanuso's fundamental design philosophy, in which the technological aspects are an integral part of the architectural and environmental ones. The latter translate into iconic forms that hide technological complexity behind an elementary and articulated form – not exhibitionistic but rather suitably hidden away in the most recessed and discreet parts of the building, like an organism in which the sum of the whole is greater than the parts. This aspect was of particular concern to Zanuso, who critiqued polarity, writing:

> Today, cognitive and scientific activity investigates reality to explain its complexity by making use of organic thought models derived from the study of sciences and disciplines such as biology, history and human sciences [...]. The development of these sciences has led us to believe that the mechanistic scheme is in the process of being overcome. [...] The organic scheme replaces it, taking the organism as a metaphor for cognitive activity. The phenomenon is something more than the sum of its parts, the process grows and evolves within it, rediscovering, in its very nature, the energy of its own self-regulation. Hence systemic thinking, the meaning of appropriate technology (cultured technology) could emerge [...] We should then speak not so much of appropriate design but rather of design reappropriation.[174]

The architectural form of Coromandel House derives from precise research, well documented by sketches, which demonstrate the options Zanuso explored before reaching a definitive solution. This solution incorporates the idea of a hollow body, a space defined by thick walls that are carved into and articulated to generate well-defined sequential rooms with different forms, as though it were a modern cave.

The goal is not only to create welcoming rooms that suit their uses, but also to eliminate anything that could disturb their optimal use, which is achieved by eliminating all technological elements from view. An example is the heating and air-conditioning system, which, hidden conveniently in the cavity behind the wooden slatted ceiling and floors, serves every room. It is visible to the most attentive eyes only through a narrow metal grid that runs along the length of the walls, separating them from the edge of the wooden floor. The machine room, from which the air-conditioning conduits branch off, is located in the basement corresponding on plan to the main entrance, but perfectly hidden from view and accessible via a discreetly positioned staircase located in the service wing. Just as the house looks hermetic and rugged from the outside, on the inside it is comfortable and innovative, "carefully detailed, with furniture and accessories".[175]

Equally illustrative is the sound and amplification system, for which Zanuso involved Livio Castiglioni's innovative cable radio expertise. Castiglioni was commissioned at Zanuso's suggestion to custom-design a mobile and multi-format music station within the central living area opposite the fireplace: it was the only visibly highlighted technological system throughout the house, and took the form of a dark-coloured prism comfortably coexisting with the wooden floor and ceiling as well as the stone walls. With Castiglioni and Zanuso in attendance, numerous photographs document the quality control testing conducted in Italy before shipping and

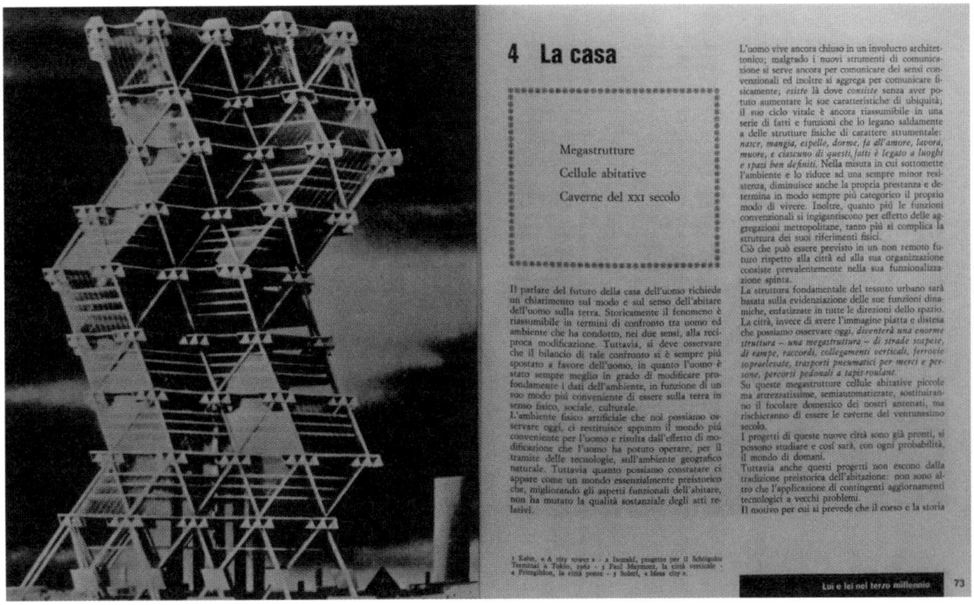

4 La casa

Megastrutture

Cellule abitative

Caverne del XXI secolo

Il parlare del futuro della casa dell'uomo richiede un chiarimento sul modo e sul senso dell'abitare dell'uomo sulla terra. Storicamente il fenomeno è riassumibile in termini di confronto tra uomo ed ambiente che ha condotto, nei due sensi, alla reciproca modificazione. Tuttavia, si deve osservare che il bilancio di tale confronto si è sempre più spostato a favore dell'uomo, in quanto l'uomo è stato sempre meglio in grado di modificare profondamente i dati dell'ambiente, in funzione di un suo modo più conveniente di essere sulla terra in senso fisico, sociale, culturale.
L'ambiente fisico artificiale che noi possiamo osservare oggi, ci restituisce appunto il mondo più conveniente per l'uomo e risulta dall'effetto di modificazione che l'uomo ha potuto operare, per il tramite delle tecnologie, sull'ambiente geografico naturale. Tuttavia quanto possiamo constatare ci appare come un mondo essenzialmente preistorico che, migliorando gli aspetti funzionali dell'abitare, non ha mutato la qualità sostanziale degli atti relativi.

L'uomo vive ancora chiuso in un involucro architettonico; malgrado i nuovi strumenti di comunicazione si serve ancora per comunicare dei sensi convenzionali ed inoltre si aggrega per comunicare fisicamente; *esiste* là dove *consiste* senza aver potuto aumentare le sue caratteristiche di ubiquità; il suo ciclo vitale è ancora riassumibile in una serie di fatti e funzioni che lo legano saldamente a delle strutture fisiche di carattere strumentale: *nasce, mangia, espelle, dorme, fa all'amore, lavora, muore, e ciascuno di questi fatti è legato a luoghi e spazi ben definiti.* Nella misura in cui sottomette l'ambiente e lo riduce ad una sempre minor resistenza, diminuisce anche la propria prestanza e determina in modo sempre più categorico il proprio modo di vivere. Inoltre, quanto più le funzioni convenzionali si ingigantiscono per effetto delle aggregazioni metropolitane, tanto più si complica la struttura dei suoi riferimenti fisici.
Ciò che può essere previsto in un non remoto futuro rispetto alla città ed alla sua organizzazione consiste prevalentemente nella sua funzionalizzazione spinta.
La struttura fondamentale del tessuto urbano sarà basata sulla evidenziazione delle sue funzioni dinamiche, enfatizzate in tutte le direzioni dello spazio.
La città, invece di avere l'immagine piatta e distesa che possiamo osservare oggi, *diventerà una enorme struttura – una megastruttura – di strade sospese, di rampe, raccordi, collegamenti verticali, ferrovie sopraelevate, trasporti pneumatici per merci e persone, percorsi pedonali a tapis roulant.*
Su queste megastrutture cellule abitative piccole ma attrezzatissime, semiautomatizzate, sostituiranno il focolare domestico dei nostri antenati, ma rischieranno di essere le caverne del ventunesimo secolo.
I progetti di queste nuove città sono già pronti, si possono studiare e così sarà, con ogni probabilità, il mondo di domani.
Tuttavia anche questi progetti non escono dalla tradizione preistorica dell'abitazione: non sono altro che l'applicazione di contingenti aggiornamenti tecnologici a vecchi problemi.
Il motivo per cui si prevede che il corso e la storia

1 Kahn, « A city tower » - 2 Isozaki, progetto per il [illegible] Terminal a Tokio, 1962 - 3 Paul Maymont, la città verticale - 4 [illegible], la città ponte - 5 Soleri, « Mesa city ».

Lui e lei nel terzo millennio 73

99

99

Pages from *Pianeta* magazine, no. 8, June/August 1965, with text by Zanuso and an image of "A City Tower", a project by Louis Kahn and Anne Tyng with a modular tetrahedron structure of utopian proportion, including the notion of growth. It was designed for Philadelphia in the late 1950s and included in the 1960 exhibition Visionary Architecture at the Museum of Modern Art.Referring to this project, Kahn wrote, "In Gothic times, architects built in solid stones. Now we can build with hollow stones. The spaces defined by the members of a structure are as important as the members. These spaces range in scale from the voids of an insulation panel, voids for air, lighting and heat to circulate, to spaces big enough to walk through and live in. The desire to express voids positively in the design of the structure is evidenced by the growing interest and work in the development of space frames."

installing this extraordinary technological appliance in Coromandel House, where it came to characterise the heart of the house.

All the mundane functions of the house are hidden in the crevices of the walls, in cavities, in the false ceiling and under the floor, optimising the numerous spaces defined by the planimetric and altimetric system. The entire house can be traced back to the notion of a large hollow volume dug out longitudinally and articulated in a transverse direction.

The principles that guide the design of Coromandel House are the same ones that Zanuso used to develop the design of the Black Box ST201 Brionvega television (1969), or previously the TS502 radio (1962), whose hermetic and enigmatic shells act as streamlined user interfaces that conceal an innovative and technologically advanced internal operational system, perceptible only through carvings, cracks, excavations, or opening the devices to discover their complexity.

In all these technological objects – televisions, radios, turntables, many of which had been designed for Brionvega, but not

100

101

exclusively – the iconic form comes from concealing the technology, emphasising the object in its direct relationship with the user, to build confidence with the technology itself. It is an extraordinarily contemporary vision, one capable of placing industrial design and architecture on the same level, or rather a vision which places the human user of the design at the centre of both disciplines.

When Zanuso was interviewed by architect and historian Vittorio Magnano Lampugnani (b. 1951) on what an adequate professional and university-level basis for architecture and industrial design (history, construction science, ergonomics) could be, he replied:

> Technology, in Italian universities and perhaps in general, is understood as a mere technical mechanism [...], ways that reveal an approach to the project in which legislation, unification, applied components, mechanics, geometric modulation are dominant. These elements, taken in isolation, ignore the real question. That is, that necessary passage, in the field of technology, from the mechanistic to the organic vision. This does not only represent a vision of scientific enrichment, but above all means leaving the Cartesian dimension to introduce a more complex, more difficult, more problematic but perhaps even more adventurous system of relationships. The true vice of the historical period in which we live is not, in my opinion, the technology in itself. It is, technology not brought to its final consequences – which are the liberating ones, a return to nature and humanity. What I think I have clearly identified, in these years of teaching, is that the approach to halved technology is a devastating approach [...]. I'm not talking about a technological formalism, which is nothing but the representation of technology halved and certainly not the right way to respond, in architectural terms, to the world and the moment in which we live. [...] When we say organicism, we mean that at a certain point we must also keep in mind other design possibilities. This organicism gives us different and more complex liberations, more open to a conception not so much of form as an aesthetic feature of the object, but as a form of the environment in its widest dimension. [...] I confirm, with few contradictions, my curiosity about the motives of the Modern Movement. I believe that the Modern Movement is still full of messages and solicitations, also considering the fact that it posed revolutionary problems, much more revolutionary and unexplored than what is said and seen. What was posed as a theme was the passage from the dimension of the architectural object to the dimension of the volumetric city, a somewhat phantom and crazy idea. It was looking for something that would attempt a comparison between artifice and nature. The artifice problem is a serious one that opens up great opportunities for response. In fact, the only possibility of giving salvation to nature, and guaranteeing the survival of the terrestrial globe and humanity, is to bring the artifice to its extreme consequences. It is a great adventure, with inexhaustible suggestions and curiosities; it is a very difficult and very tiring commitment.[176]

100

Installation of the air ventilation ducting

101

Zanuso seen here with Castiglioni testing the new music amplification system, designed and manufactured in Italy

The construction documentation of Coromandel House provides evidence of the adventurous implementation of this vision: in its remote setting where it rises to take shape and bear witness to the idea of artifice when brought to its extreme consequences. In this case it exists as a return to nature that continues to evolve and be admired for its innovative yet timeless appearance.

In 1969, the same year in which Zanuso was commissioned to design Coromandel House, *The Architecture of the Well-tempered Environment* was published, the volume-manifesto by Reyner Banham that draws attention to ducts, technical shafts, air flows and all those aspects removed, like foreign bodies, by the critics and the "high" culture of the project. The Olivetti plant built by Zanuso near Buenos Aires, characterised by an ingenious modular system of hollow structural members for the air ducts, is included in the volume as an innovative and pioneering realisation of an integrated approach and the desired return to a cultured design that brings together form and technique, artifice and nature, man and environment.

Also published in 1969 was the Italian edition of the volume *On Growth and Form. An Abridged Edition* (1961), which was retitled *Growth and Shape. The Geometry of Nature* (Bollati Boringhieri). This was an expanded version of the famous 1917 essay by the biologist and mathematician D'Arcy Wentworth Thomson, which, by tracing the philosophical foundations of biology to the relationships between the shape of organisms, lays the foundations for the study of morphology of living beings from an innovative and more extensive point of view. It was highly regarded by Zanuso, since it defines the principles that establish how an organism is a mechanical and natural whole – the core of the research and the ground on which the designer is moving explore how the technological, the constructive and the environmental are parts of the same whole.

Coromandel House combines the thoughtful study of comfort with environmental adaptation factors, common sense and low-tech solutions. The thick and uninterrupted walls, the extended and elongated shape and the single-storey construction exploit the natural conditioning of the ground and the recirculation of air. The fully grassed roof, covered by 70cm of earth and an abundance of indigenous plants, takes advantage of the same thermal inertia of the soil, the cheapest and most natural insulation, just as the water in the outdoor tanks reduces the thermal inversion and promotes the exchange of air in the interstitial spaces. The few openings, and only at the ends of the walls, reduce the accumulation or dispersion of heat, while the buttresses shadow the walls. The appearance of a fortress is inspired by the idea of an impenetrable barrier against sudden changes in temperature, generating a natural and self-regulated air conditioning of the rooms. Coromandel House is intrinsically innovative and extraordinarily current, an example of a project that combined all aspects of architecture, before design, technology and environmental planning all took independent paths with respect to architectural design, and in so doing, losing the integral vision that Zanuso knew how to control with great consistency and effectiveness.

●●●

102

102

In its remote setting, the relationship between Coromandel House and nature demonstrates artifice brought to its extreme consequences

ENDNOTES

171 Zanuso, M, *Pianeta. Planete*, no. 8, June/August 1965, pp. 73–77.
172 Ibid.
173 Ibid.
174 Zanuso, "La cultura del progetto: dal meccanicismo all'organicismo", 1987, in Grignolo, R, 2013, pp. 286–288.
175 Peres, E, 2013.
176 Un'idea di tecnologia – excerpts from "*Portare l'artificio alle sue conseguenza estreme*", Vittorio Magnago Lampugnani interviewing Marco Zanuso, *Domus*, no. 690, January 1988.

Edgardale

After Marco Zanuso's visit to South Africa in 1969, Sydney Press invited him to design a headquarters for Edgars in Johannesburg. As a result, over the next decade, Zanuso resolved complex projects at extremes of scale: residential and corporate. In its location and office landscape design, Edgardale pushed the bar as "an 'integrated system' [...] 'new type of spatial ordering' for a corporate headquarters."[177]

103

When interviewed by Raggi, Zanuso explained how, occasionally, his relationships with his clients sometimes went beyond the details of the brief and began to assume the qualities of "falling in love" as though it were an "amorous relationship. [...] you have to be careful when a woman tells you she is falling in love with you; you would have to automatically understand what is behind those behaviours and realise what is essential and what is useful." In this description, he was referring to Olivetti and their collaborations, elaborating that "among the various clients I met in my life, Adriano Olivetti was the one who recalls more than any other Filarete's saying: 'Architecture has a father and a mother; the architect is only the mother, the father is the client.'"[178] Zanuso cited a number of projects that still left an impression upon him as among the most exciting and challenging in his career. Among those was Edgardale (1969–1978), the new head office and merchandise distribution centre for Edgars. The intensity of the Coromandel House and Edgardale projects established a bond between Zanuso and Sydney in which Zanuso was able to interpret his aspirations architecturally, in both domestic and corporate ways.

Sydney had tasked a frequent collaborator, civil engineer Stanley Kaplan (1926–2019), with supervising a scheme for the Edgars Headquarters that would consolidate various offices and allow for future expansion, but progress was slow, due to the large amount of design discussions among the project team. Sydney was advised to explore other options and it is likely that he regarded Zanuso – an experienced architect with "great aesthetic sense"[179] and a successful reputation for designing innovative industrial buildings for Olivetti – as the ideal person to help bring his vision to fruition and establish an image and a space to lead Edgars into the future.

During the 1960s and '70s in South Africa, local businesses had the opportunity to assert their success in the developed world by hiring overseas architects. A prominent example of this was the Carlton Centre (1967–1973), the tallest skyscraper in the Johannesburg CBD, designed by Skidmore, Owings and Merrill (SOM) for Anglo American Properties. There were also strong associations between the local architectural schools and the Congrès Internationaux d'Architecture Moderne (CIAM) symposiums held in Europe, and students from the University of the Witwatersrand, for example, followed (and replicated) international trends in design and architecture, of which the Italian architecture and design of the 1960s was particularly admired for its debate – it energised a new era of design, called "The Next Step".[180] Therefore, an affinity and interest for imported architectural ideas already existed.

On 27 June 1969, only a few months after their first meeting, Sydney wrote to Zanuso confirming that he could proceed with developing the final plans for the Coromandel Farmstead. He also wrote: "Your cable of the twenty-fifth indicating your availability for our new corporate headquarters and merchandise centre, was also much appreciated." A visit scheduled for 24 July set in motion his involvement in designing the new Edgars head office and distribution centre, to be completed in time to commemorate their 50th anniversary in 1979.

Within Edgars, Sydney was assembling a team of managers to help him expand the company. Among these was Adrian Bellamy

103

Sydney, Zanuso and Victoria on site at Edgardale, constructed on a former mining area

(b. 1944), whose administrative practicality and vision was highly regarded by Sydney. Around 1968, Sydney identified the need for a new corporate headquarters to centralise the group's operations, but there were few buildings large enough to accommodate their needs within the CBD and immediate surrounds,[181] so Sydney sent Bellamy to Europe and the United States to investigate the latest trends in corporate headquarters. His quest was to understand where the company was headed strategically and how they planned for it to grow so that the state-of-the-art headquarters would answer those needs.[182]

In keeping with the tradition of establishing distinguished businesses within the CBD, the initial plan was to build the Edgars' Headquarters and the distribution warehouse in Selby at the corner of Westex and Trump streets. By October 1969, Zanuso had prepared a feasibility study and arrived at a board meeting with an exquisite wooden model of a first proposal for a strikingly large tower scheme that would dominate the Johannesburg skyline. It joined the trend of high-rises being developed in the city centre; however, to accommodate the brief, Zanuso had to exceed site boundaries, building lines, and town planning regulations, and the site could not allow for future expansion. The board conceded that it would not be feasible to house the entire enterprise within the CBD.

Bellamy had conducted extensive research on new headquarters internationally and proposed that they might consider, following an emerging trend, relocating "offices away from the pollution, bustle and inaccessibility of down-town to pleasant, quiet, rural surroundings, well located for freeways and a pleasure for staff to work in".[183] Following a suggestion from the architect and professor Edward Mallows (1905–2003),[184] a site was identified 2.5km south-west of the CBD in the Crown Mines district, a defunct gold-mining site which was rezoned as an extension of Selby, and which was well serviced by the motorways being developed around the CBD. This new location offered ample space to tailor buildings to the business's needs. The symbolic significance of the site, with mine residue stockpiles[185] in view as the origin of the South African economy's growth, was that Edgars was "poised to continue the tradition",[186] and the decision to move out of the CBD to unknown terrain impressed upon everyone the maverick vision and legacy-building intentions that Edgars had. Zanuso undertook the challenge to completely revise the scheme.

By February 1970, various meetings had been held between Zanuso and Edgars' representatives in London and Milan. Sydney's team had identified Swiss expert Raoul Illig, who had worked on this type of office design for Volvo's headquarters, to join the team to lead the interior office landscape planning.[187] The Bürolandschaft or office landscaping methodology focused on the individual and the natural by creating egalitarian and interactive workspaces where desks were grouped informally and separated by curved screens and plants. Zanuso revised the design from the initial tower block to a campus with separate buildings positioned in relation to each other and their functions as independent structures within the site. The office block became an "environmental structure"[188] following the Bürolandschaft open-plan office design concept developed by Illig's team,[189] and had to assemble a large and complex programme within seven core functional areas with varying security access levels ranging from public to restricted. The scheme, which elaborated on earlier industrial architecture innovations that Zanuso had designed, such as Olivetti (1955) and the Merlo factory (1964), was accepted by the Edgars board of directors; it offered an opportunity for the campus to house the entire enterprise (then around 2,000 staff in 16 different buildings), to grow and to incorporate the latest ideas and advances of high efficiency for minimal energy.

Zanuso reflected on the nature of these industrial campuses, stating:

> The exciting theme of these years is by now a unanimous judgement, the determination of a new scale of urban architecture. The building, in the Renaissance sense of the word, no longer exhausts the architectural "fact": every day we find ourselves faced with ever more enormous surfaces to cover, ever larger spaces to enclose, ever larger natural lands to transform and to be included in the environment built for human life. [...] We can articulate these ideas in five points, namely: architectural expressiveness in an urbanistic function; the definition of the elementary form and the replacement of the measure-module with the object-module; the essentiality of the architectural organism; the technical invention as a function of architectural expression; representativeness as the organism's compliance with the proposed theme.[190]

Towards the end of 1970, architects Mallows, Louw, Hoffe and Partners were officially appointed to lead and coordinate the project through senior partner Harry Hoffe, consulting closely with Zanuso at all times.[191] The project was financed by a third party, Sanlam, on a long-term lease-back[192] and phased into three parts: the warehouse and distribution centre in two phases (22,000 square metres) were built first (1974–1975) and included a handling system designed by a consultant from New York to handle 250,000 units per day via overhead conveyors, followed by two phases of the office block (1975–1978).[193] During 1974, Zanuso also conceptualised a convention centre for Edgardale and provided input for a flagship Edgars department store in Johannesburg, the latter to complement proposals from Milwaukee-based firm Miller, Waltz & Diedrich Architects, as well as the Johannesburg firm Abramovich, Schneider, Sacks and Associates, led by Monty Sack (1924–2009).

Regarding his approach to Edgardale's design, Zanuso recalled:

> The resolution of problems posed by the needs of the new Edgars Headquarters involves a very specific architectural and methodological approach; between functional and dimensional needs (and related spatial consequences) resulted a complex organisation that has forced us to carry out a systemic investigation from the origins of the project process. As our rigorous development of this design approach began to formalise into more concrete concepts for Edgardale, we realised that we were dealing not so much with a "building" as an "environmental structure": this concept seemed to satisfy the need for a dynamic structure capable of responding to continuous transformations and evolutions in the relationships between functions and spatial organisation. The final result is a system of "artificial territories" that answers the present and foreseeable organisational needs of the Edgars Store, while at the same time ensuring a balance at every point of the dynamic process of development and an optimal relationship between function, space and environmental conditions at the level of the individual workspace. The design process followed our usual methodology aimed at guaranteeing a complete integration of the structural, mechanical and architectural design, in order to maximise the functional versatility necessary to achieve a type of flexible environmental structure we intended as our goal at the outset. The site chosen for the construction of the new Edgars Headquarters is adjacent to an urban motorway junction of particular interest and complexity from which Edgardale can be viewed in a number of perspectives. These environmental characteristics have given rise to a building with a volumetric

104

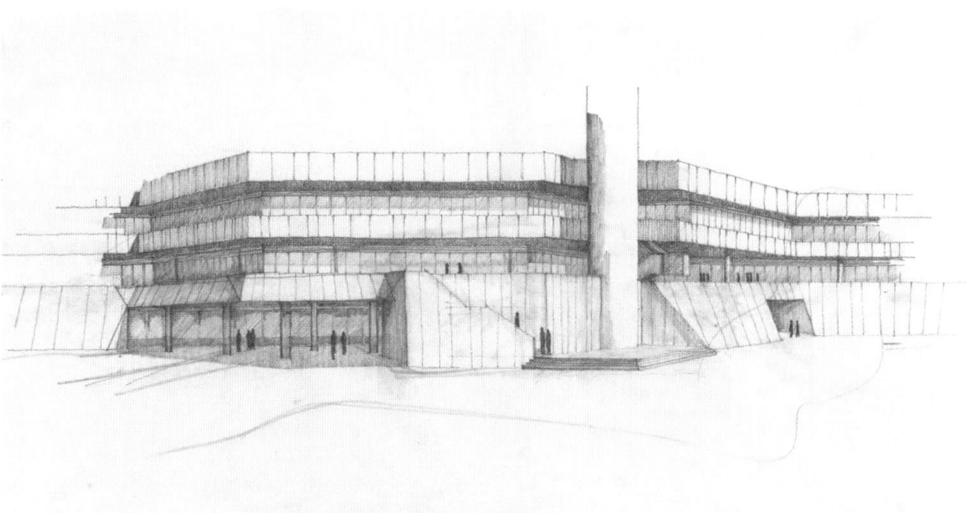

105

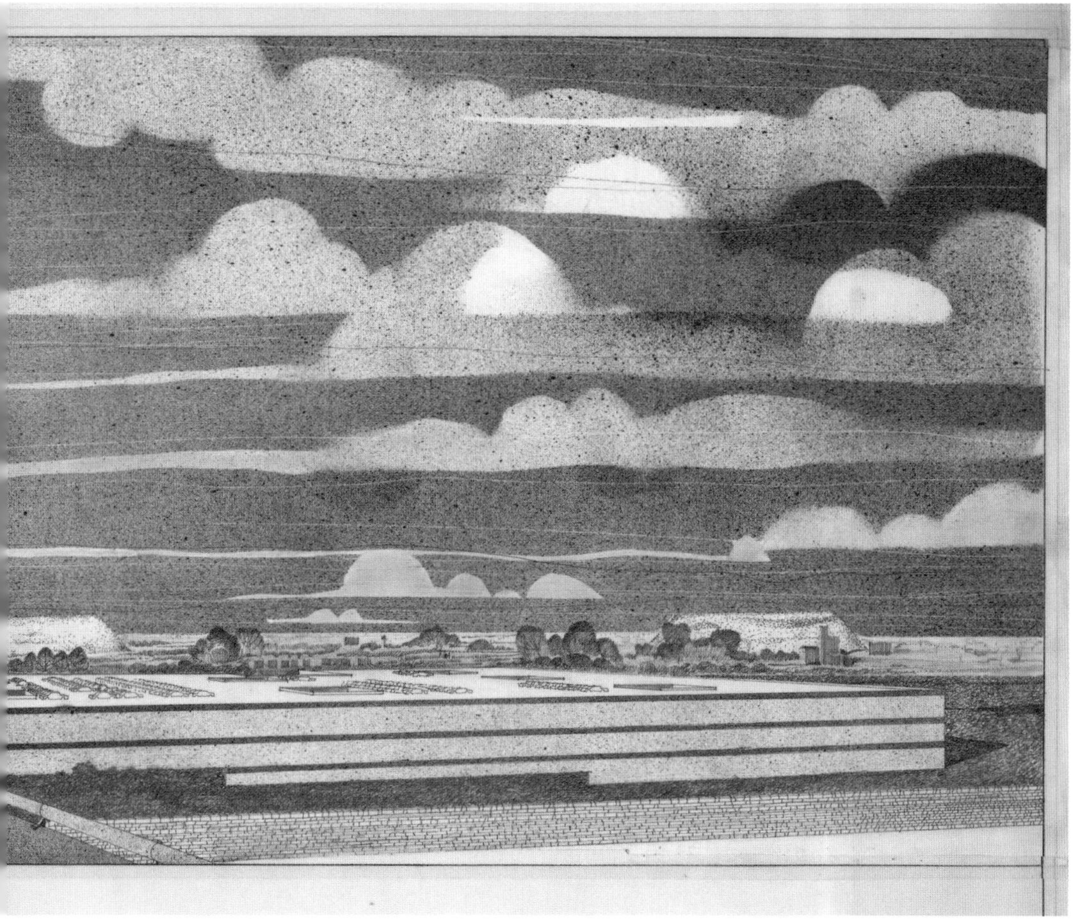

104

The first concept design for a skyscraper presented to the Edgars board for a site located in Selby, Johannesburg, 1969

105

A new scheme designed for a new site in Crown Mines, and future location of the Edgardale corporate office park, 1970

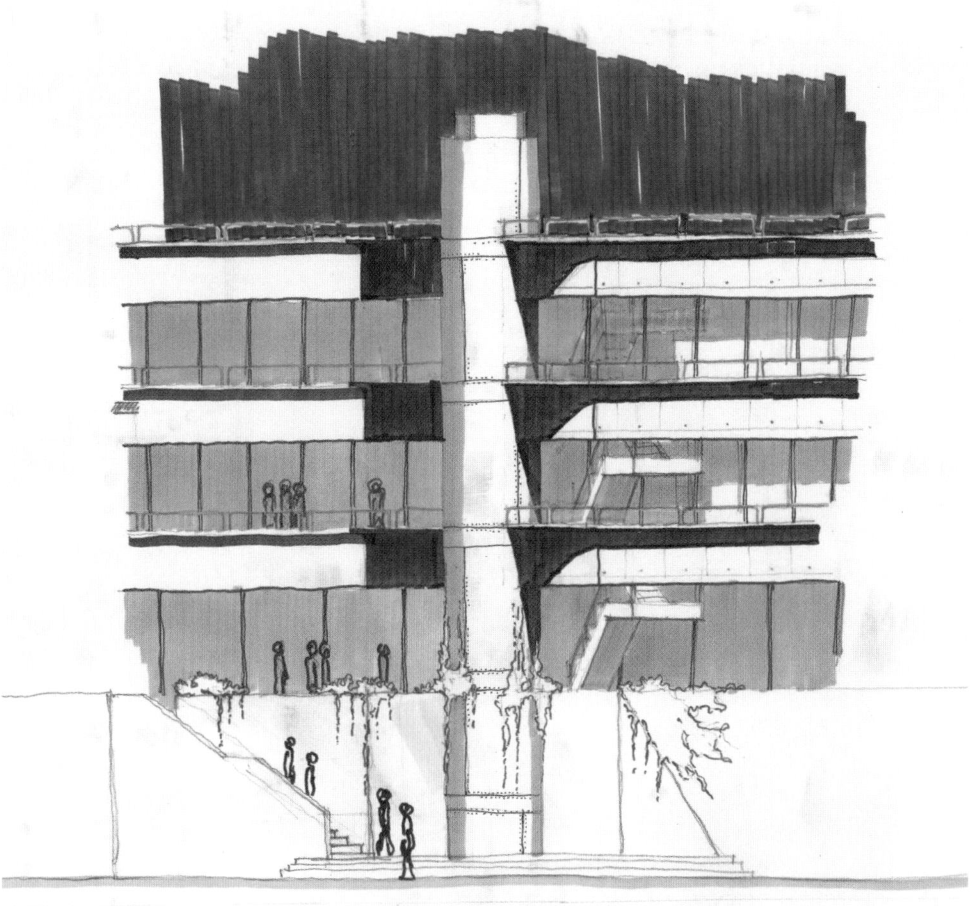

106

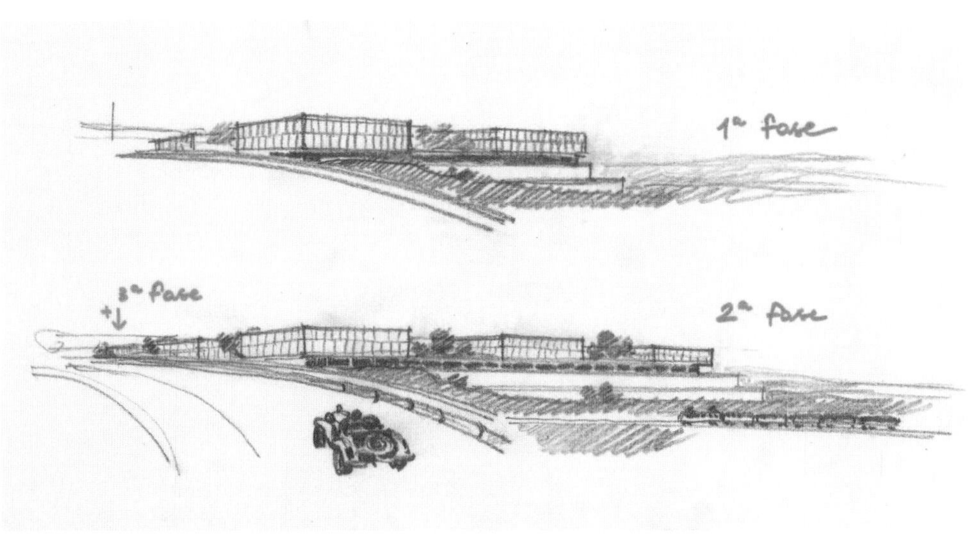

107

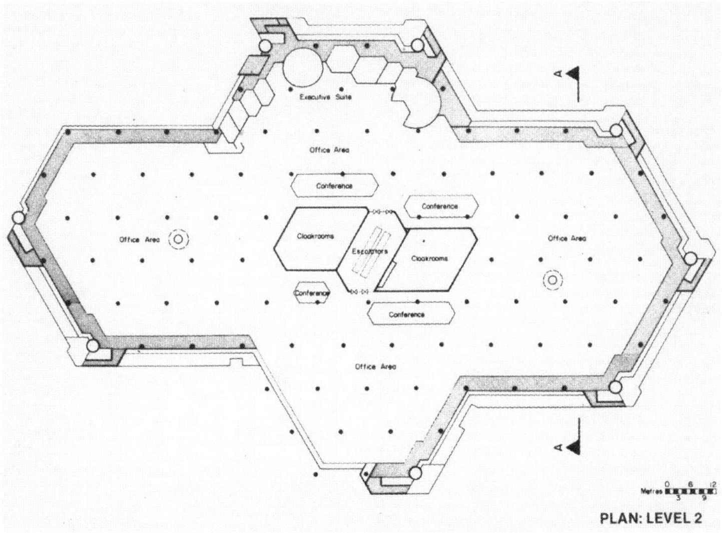

108

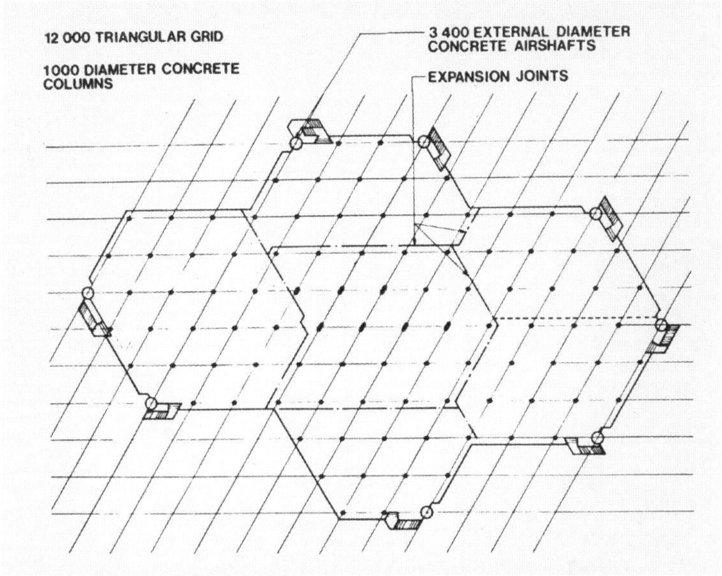

109

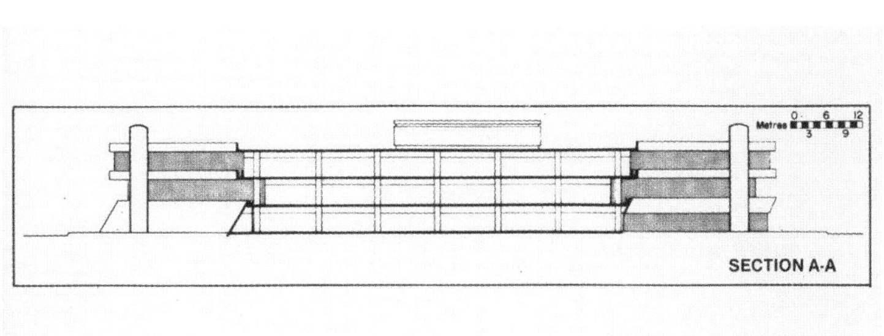

110

106

Elevation study, which recalls elements of the fortification language in the walls at Coromandel

107

Development sketches showing the future phases of the Edgardale office park as seen from the highway

108

The office landscaping on plan shows the flexibility for the office departments to be rearranged and evolve with the company. A service core forms the central node of the "beehive", alluding to the possibility for the entire structure to "grow".

109

The triangular grid, used by Zanuso previously, with descriptions of the columns and slab

110

A section showing the chamfered walls alludes to Coromandel House

111

112

113

114

111

Pre-manufactured components are assembled on site

112

Under construction, with the city skyline and mining landscape in the background

113

The first phase of the office building after completion, 1978

114

The "monumentalisation" of the inclined walls on the Edgardale facade

fragment on the facade oriented in different directions and connected internally by strongly articulated "visual hinges". The resulting structural system – based on the triangle module – accommodates the organisation in the hexagonal module chosen for the individual workspaces. Thus, the compositional whole of Edgardale, with its development of modulated and dynamic internal and external spaces, forms an "integrated system", which, starting from the individual workspace up to the organisational needs of the entire production structure, is organised in an environment with a strong urban connotation and suggests a "new type of spatial ordering" for a corporate headquarters.[194]

As for the work spaces:

> It answers to the functions provided for in the organisation chart, which must be carried out in a certain workplace. But each individual recognises himself as such, and so a discourse on proximity opens up: what is the territorial area of this individual? How does he relate to others, etc? On the one hand, there are the functions; on the other, the conditions of the person. We have provided a starting plan, indicating the degrees of variability, interpretation and management. [...] It is not a question of delimiting properties, but territorial spaces of action that each person must respect and see respected. Evidently in a community of this size, every single movement affects others.[195]

This hypothesis of "environmental structure" and office landscape encourages the phenomenon of coexistence between work groups with differentiated relationships and, given the particularity of South African politics, bridges the racial divide.

According to Italian sociologist Fausto Colombo:

> Relating this hypothesis to the complex and contradictory reality of South Africa means triggering – in the use of organised space – one of the (possible) processes of social "re-composition" of the group and intergroup. The Edgars experiment should be considered one of the first attempts at racial integration in the workplace.[196]

> If Zanuso's architectural research tends "constitutively" to a refusal to recognise oneself in a pre-established linguistic order or formal code (and the non-apparent diversity of image, as the comparison between the IBM offices (1972–1975) and the Edgars Headquarters further confirm), a distinctive and constant feature is found in the non-mimetic relationship between architecture and landscape. The link between form and nature is realised in the Johannesburg project, using and enhancing the primary figurative elements – the ventilation columns, the base-bastion, the ribbon windows, the external stairs, etc – of the architectural organism and arranging them according to a formal arrangement by "hinge points" – the vertices of the polygon, which define an articulated structure with a centrifugal sign. The environment and pre-existing buildings – the artificial hill, the motorway junction, the city skyline – are a pretext and comparison, background, horizon, dynamic observation points that signal, without absorbing, the characteristics of a new urban presence.[197]

This new landmark presence featured sloping walls that outlined the limits of a geometrically defined but expandable hexagonal modular system and conveyed an aesthetic of fortification reminiscent of Coromandel House. Once again, Zanuso organised the system for which he was designing into various functions and flows: an environmental structure that responds "to the transformations inherent in the vitality of an organism", which modify over time. This organisational model repeats from the design considerations taken at an individual's work area right through to the entire organisation. The structure was built upon concrete piles, above which one finds a triangular grid of 92 columns with floors above of areas that average an impressive 12,000 square metres; a service core in the middle contains the main circulation escalators that were surrounded by four zones. Three floors were completed by 1978 and there was provision for a fourth floor to be built at a later date. Sketches in Zanuso's archive dated 1982 show that expansion concepts were in progress to extend the building into the parking area, but with the unexpected change of management at Edgars in 1982, resulting in Sydney's retirement, these were never realised.[198]

The sheer scale of the project required innovation to maintain human comfort, including adaptability and liveability. The facade utilised suspended precast concrete panels made of washed aggregate, to create a colour and material palette that "fits" into the surroundings. The 92 columns resting on their own bearings, along with special structural steel vertical and horizontal movement joints between the deck slab, were designed by Ove Arup engineers. This provided the durability to accommodate for ground subsidence, due to mining of the main reef, without causing structural collapse – a solution that opened up this underutilised area for further development.

Part of the concern was in creating comfortable acoustics indoors within open-plan environments, resulting in carpeted floors, sound-absorptive ceilings and the introduction of "pink noise" to mask the transfer of sound.[199] Services drawn from the baffle-type ceiling were located within delicately constructed chrome tubes that hid wires within, thereby connecting service ducts in the ceiling through to individual tables and allowing for technological adaptation when necessary. The reception lounge, including the circular reception desk, was finished off with travertine marble imported from Italy, with panelling using yellowwood from Knysna in the Western Cape, while the rest of the flooring featured carpeting for sound absorption. A ramp for inclusive access was embedded in the design, and ergonomic furnishings were chosen to add comfort to the individual's experience in an open office setting, assisted by detailed design in the workstations and colour-coding in various zones of the building.[200] Plant and fabric screens supplied by Lovemore Plants were placed around workstations to create privacy and soften the space.

Edgardale is significant for at least three aspects, which have had consequences for corporate architecture in South Africa. The first is its contribution towards the slow but steady decentralisation away from the Johannesburg CBD by big business and investors, which began during the late 1950s but gained momentum during the 1970s following the construction of new motorways in the late 1960s, with 602 non-retail firms indicating a desire to decentralise,[201] and which increasingly did so following the success of the Sandton City development to the north in becoming "an edge city".[202] During the 1980s, with the pressure of the international community objecting against Apartheid policy in South Africa, the inner city began to undergo its own changes. The peripheries began to suffer from "crime and grime", and as Apartheid

115

Sydney's office, one of a few spaces that are private and not part of the open-plan office design

116

The open-plan office, with informal and adaptable meeting spaces to provide an efficient work environment enhanced by natural plants

115

116

restrictions gradually lifted, the 1990s saw a period of "white flight" from the inner city, which saw a collapse in the number of big businesses operating from the CBD in favour of decentralisation into the suburbs and various nodes therein.

Its second contribution was towards the South African corporate office park trend. This followed the American model, and was dependent on private vehicle and motorway access to rezoned former farmland or industrial zones on the edge of town that were cheaper or larger than what might be obtained in established areas. The campus design had the added benefit of being able to create "defensible and identifiable" space, reflecting the company's identity. Lastly, campus design created the opportunity to customise design to the needs of the business, and also to include elements of nature and landscaping within the design. Although the intention for "greening" of these early campus projects as essential in promoting human wellbeing was further removed from what is practised today through biophilia and ecological design, the desire to connect to nature was effective in promoting landscape architecture as a profession in South Africa, and in Edgardale in particular, it was a foremost interest.

In this, the involvement of Pietro Porcinai in the early proposals was crucial. In November 1970, he wrote to Sydney, "In the past days we discussed with Marco and the team that collaborates on the headquarters project, the design of the green areas [...]. The proposed solution foresees the formation of vegetation consisting predominantly of *Phytolecca dioica* and the evergreen *Quercus retusa* and *Quercus ilex*, in order to obtain isolation from the surrounding environment and provide an exotic note to the space around the various buildings." Given the ecologically deteriorated conditions on the site following almost a century of mining, Porcinai's unrealised proposal to create the green landscaping was to harmonise while also be "distinct from that which can be observed in Johannesburg". For this, he proposed using the non-indigenous *Phytolecca dioica*, both due to its ability to thrive in the soil conditions present on site and also for being a fast-growing impressively sculptural tree for the local climate. He also proposed planting schemes for the rest of the campus: trees, shrubs and flowers; shading trees for the parking area that was reserved for future expansion, which would in future be easily transplanted or felled, as well as screening plants for the (unbuilt) roof parking. Under Porcinai's supervision, the campus would have been turned into a forested green island with 555 trees and 1,800 shrubs; however, it is unclear which parts were implemented. Later on, Sydney sent Schurr to the United States to learn the art of balling and burlapping large trees so as to transplant mature *Vachellia sieberiana* trees[203] from the lowveld to Edgardale in order to create "green ribbons" in the vast parking areas, which included open-block grassed parking areas and fast-stormwater-drainage into the soil.[204]

The last contribution worth highlighting here is the adoption of the "free plan", one of the major characteristics of modern architecture. By freeing the interior plan of walls and structure, the building yields a lot more usable space and has the potential to adapt to changing needs within the organisation, future growth and changes in technology, staff or management requirements. Socially, it also created an inclusive workspace in which there were no "better" offices and where there was limited distinction between departments and employees – lounge chairs around tables were placed in different zones to encourage informal meetings among staff of any department. The project did not provide for the separation between races propagated during Apartheid, instead creating a democratic space for all employees, regardless of their culture, creed or race, to work side by side as a part of the enterprise. The rapid extent with which the open-landscape – or rather open-plan – office design spread through corporate South Africa was a major change in the interior design trajectory within the country. However, whereas Edgardale invested a great deal in creating conditions within which its employees would feel comfortable and at ease working in an open environment, many other projects that copied the idea for its pragmatism did not follow through on the systems of comfort, greening and screening.[205]

The Edgardale project was the most publicly "visible" of the two architectural collaborations between Zanuso and Sydney in South Africa. Its critics alleged it was a "personal monument to Sydney Press"; however, during Edgars' 50th Anniversary dinner, at which Zanuso was a VIP guest, Sydney retorted, "Such disdain was easy to withstand because I knew that our real aim was to produce a working environment in which our people could perform at their best. Indeed, Edgardale is a visible expression, a prefiguration of what has become possible for our company despite its ignominious beginnings."[206] The atmosphere at Edgardale during those initial years fostered an infectious "merchant mentality" derived from a kaleidoscope of behind-the-scenes activities, like bees in a hive, that would result in the retailing experiences that Edgars became known for.[207]

●●●

ENDNOTES

177 Zanuso, M, project description in *L'architettura cronache e storia*, no. 12, December 1982, p. 879; and Zanuso, M, 1978, p. 5.

178 Zanuso, M, "Progettare fabbriche per Adriano Olivetti", 1976, in Grignolo, R, 2013, p. 297.

179 Bellamy, A, 2021.

180 Chipkin, C, Interview, 2011.

181 Dos Santos, J, 2018, p. 318.

182 Ibid., p. 302.

183 Ibid., p. 319.

184 Professional architect and head of the Town and Regional Planning Department at the University of the Witwatersrand; adviser and consultant to significant real-estate developments in the CBD.

185 Colloquially termed mine dumps.

186 Edgars Stores Limited, 1979, p. 7.

187 Bellamy, A, 2021.

188 "An Intricate Beehive: Edgardale", *Planning*, vol. 33, 1978, pp. 31–90.

189 Chipkin, C, Interview, 2011.

190 Zanuso, M, "Paesaggio, architettura e design", *Notizie Olivetti*, no. 76, November 1962, pp. 61–68, with E Vittoria, in Grignolo, R, 2013, pp. 175–176. The text refers to the industrial complex design in Scarmagno for Olivetti.

191 Holmes, M, Interview, 2011.

192 Edgars Stores Limited, 1979, p. 5.

193 Dos Santos, J, 2018, p. 320.

194 Zanuso, M, describing the design in "L'architettura cronache e storia", no. 12, December 1982, p. 879; and Zanuso, M, 1978, p. 5.

195 Taken from a conversation with Fausto Colombo and Marco Zanuso, who talks about the IBM Italia headquarters in Segrate, created with Pietro Crescini and published together with the Edgardale project in *L'architettura cronache e storia*, no. 12, December 1982, p. 874.

196 Fausto Colombo, in *L'architettura cronache e storia*, no. 12, December 1982, p. 883.

197 Ibid., p. 884.

198 Later additions and renovations by other firms were not in keeping with the open office design and architectural systems.

199 ArchSA, 1978, and Dos Santos, J, 2018.

200 Edgars Stores Limited, 1979, pp. 9–12.

201 Beavon, K, 2014, p. 378.

202 Chipkin, C, "The Great Apartheid Building Boom", in Judin, et al., *Blank: Architecture Apartheid and After*, 1998, pp. 248–267.

203 Until recently known as *Acacia sieberiana*.

204 Schurr, K, Interview, 2021.

205 Sydney would have been aware of the latest research into the relationship between architecture and human comfort, now well documented as Environmental Psychology.

206 Press, S, 1979.

207 Edgars Stores Limited, 1979, p. 29.

Coromandel House

Photographed by Dewald van Helsdingen, 2014

118

117

View over Coromandel Farm with the house walls in the foreground

118

East wing walls partially concealing the swimming pool beyond

119

The narrow courtyard between the west wings where mature trees provide shade in the summer

121

120

A stone pebble threshold to the western courtyard, planted with Coromandel *Clivia cultivar*

121

Gum poles provide screening above openings, and *Ficus sur* tree roots have made a natural home in the walls, as intended

122

Window shutter detail

123

Pattern and patina of the dolerite stone cladding

122

123

125

124

Forecourt between the carport and service wing, with access by stairs to the turfed roof

125

Arches form a threshold between the living spaces and main openings on the northern facade

126

The planted roof visually merges with the vegetation surrounding the house

127

Acacia sieberiana grow along the linear wall on the northern facade of the parents' wing

126

127

129

128

Mature trees in the western courtyard are now integral to the experience of place

129

Communal living areas, which connect the kitchen and entrance

130

The recreational room in the western wing. The door detailing matches the main entrance door

131

132

3. Legacy

131

Zanuso experiencing Coromandel Farm on his first site visit, and the start of his contribution to the South African architectural landscape

132

An aerial photo shows the mature vegetation around Coromandel House, 40 years after Zanuso's first visit

Zanuso's South African legacy

Marco Zanuso once said, "Designing a space for contemporary people becomes the design of possibility, a modification of reality." Through his work in South Africa, he modified reality not only through two buildings, but also by demonstrating new possibilities. In particular, Coromandel House became a model for boundary-pushing design and has influenced a new generation of South African architects

133

Ironic though it may be, Zanuso's imported architecture is a source of inspiration for architects contributing to an evolving contemporary South African vernacular aesthetic. Of the two complex and sophisticated buildings Zanuso materialised for Sydney, it is interesting that the domestic project, rather than the corporate headquarters, has sustained a greater level of appreciation over time. Curiosity for the project seems to grow from its private status and unconventionality. Built during a period during which Sydney and Zanuso were undertaking a number of large projects in their respective careers, the lag in schedule afforded Coromandel House the luxury of maturing into a long-term design experiment that encompassed the clients' ideals and interests, overlapping them with the experienced methods of the architect and other professionals. A private statement envisioned to capture the clients' aspirations within the beauty and timelessness of the setting, became a model for boundary-pushing design.

When referring to Zanuso's legacy in South Africa as boundary-pushing, the presumption is not that it is flawless. However, for many architects Coromandel House answers the question of what contextually responsive architecture might be if it were to disregard stylistic traditions and follow a new course. Mostly unfamiliar with Zanuso's portfolio and design approach, they infer clues from its architectural responses to nature and technology. As Zanuso was initiating the design for Coromandel House, he wrote about technology and nature as elements of architectural innovation. Perhaps the presence lingered in his mind, for he added to these the passage of time, precedent and the search for new forms of architectural expression. He explained that, as things age, "we demand new forms, new images: designing a space for contemporary persons, becomes the design of possibility, a modification of reality".[208] For this modification of reality and expectations, a change of mindset is required. We see examples of this break with the domestic traditions in Coromandel House's open-plan bedroom wings and the number of possible "main" doors subtly positioned in the building's shell. A further modification is the house's relationship to the landscape, where the disruptive effects of construction are hidden by its subsequent merger with nature. Zanuso's motivation is to change the substance of architecture to "transform our surroundings" through architecture and, therefore, to encircle all the other things of which the world in motion is made (science, technology, production, etc) and which form a whole that we call human civilisation".[209] Coromandel House suggests what a domestic environment *might* be if it disassociates from the expectations of what a house *should* be. Zanuso's design methodology combined the needs of the clients, site and technology to create innovation, and yet remain relevant even with the passage of time.

The continued contribution of Coromandel House towards South African architecture is twofold. Firstly, the appointment of Zanuso gave him the opportunity to apply his rationale and methodology to an unfamiliar context, to develop a fresh and inventive artefact in South Africa, and also within his portfolio, which has stood its ground as an unusually powerful piece of architecture in both form and substance. It includes the architectural framework onto which indigenous landscaping takes possession of the building, rendering the "architectural landscape" aesthetic possible. Secondly, its interesting history, picturesqueness, and its exciting proposition for an alternative domestic architecture, have made it a site

133

Margaret Courtney-Clarke captured the archaic quality of the Coromandel House site at the foot of a scenic hillside for its international debut in *The Architectural Digest*, June 1980

of architectural pilgrimage. Proof of its influence is seen in its use as a precedent in numerous award-winning South African projects over the past 20 years.

By examining five award-winning South African architects who refer to Coromandel in a specific project or in their approach to architecture in general, it is possible to track their interpretations of Zanuso's design for Coromandel and the lessons they have extracted.[210] These have been absorbed and adopted within this new homegrown architectural generation's contextually responsive designs. While each of them extracts different nuances from Coromandel, they overlap at five points, which lend themselves to an aesthetic lineage of contemporary South African architecture. First, locally sourced or natural materials for cladding; second, an active integration of architectural form with nature and appropriate siting and scale within the landscape; third, the building as part of a designed ecological system; fourth, linearity emphasised on the plan and open flow between spaces; and lastly, a degree of fortification mediated through purposefully placed openings and thresholds.

We begin with the award-winning architect whose formative exposure as an adolescent to Zanuso's architecture occurred when he happened to visit Coromandel House while Sydney was there. The young man was Pierre Swanepoel (b. 1965) and the subsequent tour of the house was a revelation into the possibilities of architecture. He recalls how the experience shifted his perceptions:

> I always enjoyed the idea of making and designing structures. At the time of growing up I thought of buildings merely as structures (including buildings, sheds, bridges, roads and dams). It was only when I was first exposed to the Coromandel House [...that] the notion of "design of buildings" as architecture somehow more than structure came to mind. Meeting Sydney Press and learning the expressions of architecture was a realisation, it changed my life forever![211]

Sydney's tour of the house revealed to Swanepoel the potential of design to unlock phenomenological qualities. He made specific reference to a new tree planted close to the structure with a surrounding wall, which intended to make people in the future wonder which came first – the wall or the tree. Swanepoel later graduated *cum-laude* with a postgraduate degree in architecture from the University of Pretoria, and founded studioMAS Architecture & Urban Design, where he would work on a formidable residential estate on the hillside of the historic Westcliff suburb in Johannesburg for businessman and art collector Gordon Schachat (b. 1952). Westcliff Estate (2002) received a South African Institute of Architecture Award of Excellence in 2004, and in Swanepoel's description of the concept he cites Coromandel House as a primary precedent, and his opportunity to interpret that exceptional first exposure to architecture that lingered in his consciousness. For Westcliff Estate's design, "the long stone walls, interleading rooms, the way the garden and building were integrated, the long house idea, the integration of hill and house, all was adapted observing Coromandel. Even the idea of a waterfall as the termination of the long view was borrowed, it was my way of paying homage to the house that started it all for me."[212] The Coromandel House concept was so influential on the Westcliff Estate design that Swanepoel took his client to visit it in the late 1990s. Swanepoel adapted Zanuso's residential typological ideas to the Highveld and the social and urban context, and in later projects his evolution of the long house typology underlines his interpretation of a contextually refined building that reflects a progressive South African architectural ethos.

For architect Nicholas Plewman (b. 1963), Coromandel House has had a profound influence on his private practice, which designs homes and lodges in ecologically sensitive landscapes, from his first lodge in Sandibe Okavango to over 35 projects he has embarked upon throughout Africa. Of significance to him is how Coromandel House lies low on the landscape, how it creates an interpretation of landscape through architecture, and how it creatively fuses ideas on the edge of architecture, art and landscape. His first exposure to Coromandel came around 1985 during his architectural studies at the University of Cape Town via one of the few South African articles that were published on the subject of the house in its heyday. He marvelled at how the buttress arches appeared to echo a deep human need to connect with nature and explains that "they imprinted themselves in my design ethos and have inspired my work".[213] Years later, while flying over the Mpumalanga hills with their magnificent remnants of the Bokoni society's circular stone kraal ruins, the unmistakable linear form of Coromandel House revealed itself to Plewman in stark contrast, and it was his first "real" encounter with the building. He only gained access into the house well after it was sold in 2002, unoccupied for almost 20 years and unfurnished, exuding a melancholic air of "dreams unfulfilled". Yet in the time he was able to observe its detailing, materials and iconoclastic and uncompromising design, he was able to perceive its power as a "monument to an ideal that mankind's search for immortality can be reconciled with the infinite patience of the earth". Although its formal design is strange and peculiar, Plewman suggests that its design approach, particularly at the time, was so brave that it created a "legacy building" in that Zanuso's least known building has "quite possibly become South Africa's greatest piece of landscape architecture". In 2011, almost 30 years after the publication of the definitive *Fair Lady* article he read, he wrote an article for South African design magazine *Visi*, not only documenting its significance in South African architecture, but also urging for its preservation and re-use.[214]

After the Press family sold the farm to the Coromandel Farmers Trust and the house was no longer used as a private residence, it created an opportunity for the architectural public to gain access to visit it directly, and so its sphere of influence as a design precedent increased. It was during this time that architect Karlien Thomashoff (b. 1968) received an invitation from a friend who loved finding "hidden architectural gems" to visit Coromandel House. While she did not get to experience the house on that occasion, the photographs he later showed her encouraged her to do so later on. The experience was defining. Coromandel House along with Allan Konya's St Peter's Seminary in Hammanskraal are Thomashoff's preferred design precedents; their linear plans and how they negotiate a relationship with a vast landscape beyond are themes that can be traced in her design approach at various scales and contexts. She describes Zanuso's architecture at Coromandel as "dissolving into and incorporating the landscape" with transitions between space and levels marked by "poetic" building elements such as stairs, steps and platforms. She describes this approach to balancing building and landscape as being subtle yet purposeful, forcing one to take in and appreciate the views framed by the long courtyards and picture windows, and allowing the silence outside to take over inside too. Moving from the central gathering places in the heart of the home through a series of meandering corridors in each wing adds to the dramatic experience of the home – you are forced to disconnect and prepare to let go into the landscape as you reach the end of each bedroom wing with its fully glazed and openable terminal wall.

The linearity and functional layout of the plan at Coromandel House has featured in many subsequent award-winning buildings designed by Thomashoff in collaboration with her husband and business partner, Fritz Thomashoff (b. 1966), including Vygenhoek Spa (2008) and House Rooke (2011). They ascribe much of the success of the house to its architect and client being comfortable with being "outsiders" to preconceived ideas; they are demanding and persistent in achieving

134

135

136

137

134

House of the Big Arch by Frankie Pappas, in Waterberg

135

Arijuju Retreat by Nicholas Plewman Architects, Kenya

136

17 Glen by studioMAS, in Cape Town

137

Vygenhoek Day Spa by Thomashoff + Partner, in Dullstroom

their ideals. The result of this is a building that sculpts spaces from the earth that synthesise craftsmanship, materials, and the elements in a way that continue to captivate with their creativity.[215]

The idea of constructing an architectural landscape to merge nature and building by effectively blurring out the boundary between them was the design target at 17 Glen (2012) in Cape Town, conceived by studioMAS's Cape Town office. Its director, Sean Mahoney (b. 1964), learned about Coromandel House through a lecture presented to his class during his architectural studies at the then University of Natal. He describes the eventual actual engagement – a result of his friendship and business partnership with Swanepoel – as "even better in real life". It allowed him to experience first-hand how nature can be integrated with architecture and how there need not be a divide. This has become a central theme in various design strategies employed by his studio over the past two decades; another is how plants can be used like a building material when assembling architecture. This is visible in House Letschert (2010), but the manner in which Coromandel House has been "claimed" by nature as its own is the inspiration behind the award-winning design of 17 Glen. It is an ongoing architectural experiment and a homage to "architectural landscaping" in the grandest sense. The romanticised relationship between the house and nature is described as "about a natural devolution of the building form into nothingness, where nature is allowed to evolve and take over in time" and this is achieved by combining the essential materials and forms without losing the poetic qualities that turn it into a philosophical study of the potentialities of architecture.[216] And even though the form of 17 Glen references the magnificent Great Zimbabwe ruins, the use of biophilic design principles and the understanding that the architecture can be constructed like a habitat to stimulate new ecological systems and boost biodiversity, trace back to Sean Mahoney's experience at Coromandel House. His interpretation of the strong contrast between the permanence of the thick-walled kloof-like courtyards curating fleeting views towards the waterfall, set far away in the distance among a varying landscape, is the cornerstone of the experiential architecture he describes Coromandel to be. He imagines that the exaggerated heaviness, solidity and strength give it a timeless character easily mistaken to be a few centuries old and surely one "which will look as good in 1,000 years".[217]

The dissolution between the boundaries of architecture, landscape and gardening, is the crux of international award-winning design the House of the Big Arch (2019) along with its guest house the House of the Tall Chimneys (2019) by maverick Johannesburg-based architectural collective Frankie Pappas. The collective exists to enhance the remarkable world they see around themselves and fulfil their deep reverence for the future by building dreamers' legacies, which they summarise as "an absurd desire to create a utopic future". They learn from and keep company with "the dreamers, the believers, the courageous, the cheerful, the planners, the doers, the people with their heads in the clouds and their feet on the ground", and it is this prescient energy that they experience at Coromandel House. To them, "Sydney and Victoria and Marco and Patrick seemed intent on building the Elysian Fields right here in South Africa. They succeeded."[218]

Frankie Pappas' Ant Vervoort (b. 1990) recalls being introduced to Coromandel House in his youth while accompanying his father on business trips in the area. He parallels the experience of Coromandel House with those he had at the Matobo Hills or Great Zimbabwe ruins. It seemed to him that there was nothing excessive in the design – it was like a ruin. This idea of a building that is allowed to ruin gracefully is an aspect that carries through to his Houses of the Big Arch and Tall Chimneys. Set in the midst of a nature reserve in the Waterberg, their design is specifically moulded to the clients, the site and its topography, flora and fauna, and to the constraints of building and sourcing materials in such a remote location. The buildings were placed to leave a minimal footprint on the ground, camouflaged among the canopy of marulas and saringas, with the building structure composed of simple materials and systems that create habitat for vervet monkeys and baboons and can eventually break down into nature.

Creating an architectural landscape that could eventually disintegrate into nature was not likely Zanuso's intention for Coromandel House. However, his proposal, so particular to the place and time in which it was envisaged and to its clients, lends itself to an architectural habitat that today appears to be more a part of the landscape than an object set within it. This landscaping legacy was the result of the direct exchange between Zanuso, Victoria's vision to develop the Coromandel garden following a "natural" aesthetic and, of course, the landscape architects who were involved in the project. The "natural" design initiated by Porcinai, Zanuso's contemporary and long-time collaborator, complemented the architecture that deliberately engaged and manipulated the landform and the building mass that was designed to fortify the human habitat within the building yet blur the line between architecture and landscape. Zanuso would sometimes hike through the farm with Watson while he observed the principles of the wild habitats, from which he identified endemic flora to plant into the recreated habitats of the house's "cliff-like" walls or "valley-like" courtyards. The landscaping that was successfully layered over the architectural skeleton was not intended to be as overgrown as it is now. The plants have reseeded and appropriated the building, returning it to the veld.

Yet it is this overgrown oasis that captivates the imagination of so many designers and dreamers and propagates its allure as a beacon in South African architecture and landscape design. Coromandel House is said to serve as an example of the tradition of Critical Regionalism in South African architecture, a term which was only coined almost a decade after the house was completed.[219] This accolade is a tribute to Zanuso's proficiency as an architect and his ability to adapt to different geographies and societies, while still maintaining his clear methodology. His was a design that used local stone, emphasising the rustic qualities of the natural palette; deep, shaded verandahs and windows, a response to harsh climatic variations; and a deep sensitivity to the grasslands, farming landscape and natural features.

His design was not without critique. Aspiring architects in South Africa during the 1960s and '70s, many under the direct influence of Louis Kahn, were pushing for a "new brutalism" within residential and commercial projects, and would class Coromandel House as overly decorative, nostalgic and romantic, not honest in its reflection of materials and structure.[220] By understanding Zanuso's design rationale in response to contemporary lifestyle, production process and qualities of the natural setting, its palette and resources all demonstrate that his visual contextual design response was not purely aesthetic, but also reflected a deep connection to a holistic response to technology, which included the interpretation of the *genius loci* or the archaic spirit of the veld.[221] The phenomenological qualities of Coromandel House are so rooted in the making of *place* that an authentic architecture in which man can "be" in the world is the result. Zanuso may have imported his fascination with holistic technology based on a rational typology of modules or families of "cells" into a remote South African farm, but he adapted his ideas for living to the clients' love for the *nature* of the site. This fusion is embodied within the architecture of *place*, resulting in the timeless qualities of the project. Coromandel House now stands as a noteworthy example among the innovative and varied architectural works of the South African architectural landscape, and its quiet influence has inspired a new generation of architects.

138

138

Coromandel House is almost indistinguishable from the surrounding veld in winter, 2021

ENDNOTES

208 Zanuso, M, "I nuovi atteggiamenti della progettazione in rapporto al cambiamento delle condizioni tecnologiche", from *L'industria del Mobile. Rivista di arte, tecnica, industria, artigianato e commercio del mobile*, no. 103, 1969, pp. 530–531, in Grignolo, R, 2013, pp. 235–239.

209 Ibid.

210 The selection is not exhaustive. The criteria of award-winning projects since 2000, or architects who have published about the house, are by no means a true reflection of all the architects who have been inspired by the house.

211 Swanepoel, P, Interview, 2011.

212 Ibid.

213 Plewman, N, "Paradise Lost" in *Visi* magazine.

214 Plewman, N, Interview, Google Meet, 2021.

215 Thomashoff, K and Thomashoff, F, Interview, Google Meet, 21 April 2021.

216 Louw, M, "The Craft of Memory and Forgetting", *SAJAH,* vol. 32, no. 2, pp. 93–106.

217 Mahoney, S, Interview, 2020.

218 Vervoort, A, Interview and email, 2021.

219 www.artefacts.co.za, entry on House Press.

220 Watson, P, Interview, 2020.

221 Norberg-Schulz, C, 2000, pp. 19–20.

Growing interest

The unexpected public interest that has grown for Coromandel House has cast light on Marco Zanuso's work in South Africa. The house that was in many ways ahead of its time could be referred to as a "best-kept secret" in that its prestige and influence have taken their time to reach a wider audience. Now, though, its valuable contributions and experimentations in design have become popular themes

139

Another curiosity about Coromandel House concerns how the story of its existence has followed an almost mythical trajectory. By word of mouth, its unusual design with its Arcadian backdrop began to gain a following of mesmerised architects shortly after its completion. While the unorthodox structure left locals bemused, this very deliberate design with its breakaway from norms accrued an influential place within niche architectural and design circles in South Africa. As already established, Mira Fassler Kamstra was among the first to inspire others with her testimony of the radical design, and she accompanied Patrick Watson on site visits to photograph the house and its landscaping. These photographs and design descriptions shared with close colleagues and friends created a network of designers who knew about the existence of the private house, long before the public did. By the 1980s, when Postmodernism raged through South Africa's architectural circles, a handful of university lecturers were exposing their students to projects such as Coromandel House in design lectures at architectural schools in the Cape, the Free State, KwaZulu-Natal and Gauteng – what seemed like a revolutionary architecture resonated with many budding architects.[222]

Five years after its completion, the house was unveiled to the international public via two well-placed articles: *The Architectural Digest* in 1980 and *Abitare* in 1981, photographed by the esteemed Margaret Courtney-Clarke and David Goldblatt. Their depiction of the house, after it had been lived in for a while and gained a patina of time as well as a mature indigenous landscape, added to the allure of the project. Whether these articles made a mark internationally, though, is unlikely. There were many reasons for this, not just the clients' desire for discretion. For one thing, outside of Italy, Zanuso was not a household name, although his professional work was regarded among architectural, academic and industrial design peers after being mentioned in Reyner Banham's acclaimed *Age of the Masters,*[223] and he had been invited to lecture such tours as his Industrial Design lectures in Australia in 1971, while in 1972 he contributed to the Museum of Modern Art's 'Italy: The New Domestic Landscape' exhibition, which today exhibits many of his industrial design products. But there are other likely reasons for the project languishing in relative international obscurity. During the 1970s and '80s, architecture was dominated by Postmodernism, and Critical Regionalism was only starting to materialise – Coromandel House was not "trendy". Added to this was the growing disdain for Apartheid in South Africa within the media, resulting in political sanctions that provoked public consciousness about its discriminatory and highly racialised society. Therefore, an article that featured a home for the White "elite" in South Africa may have been overshadowed by civil rights violations occurring there at the time.

During the mid-1980s, though, two South African monthlies featured articles on Coromandel House, one of which was seminal in dispersing knowledge about the house within South Africa itself, even though they provided no plans, sections or details of the architecture. The first was a *Style* magazine exclusive published in 1984, which tracked Sydney's initiatives after Edgars. It featured Coromandel Farm and the stud enterprise, and only briefly mentioned the House as being "a little out of context on the side of a Transvaal hill".[224] In the following year, a more architecturally sensitive feature, written by Heloise Truswell and photographed by Pieter de Ras, appeared in the *Fair Lady* magazine and traced the origins of the design and the

139

View from the hillside behind the house. Margaret Courtney-Clarke returned to Coromandel, c. 1989, to document the house for an unpublished feature in *Town and Country* magazine.

project, which was described as capturing the "spirit of the veld".[225] Both magazines interviewed Sydney directly, and they provide rare public first-person testimonials of his intentions and ideals. While sparse on details, they further galvanised the house's standing among the architectural community in South Africa, who now had something other than word of mouth to refer to.

A smattering of newspaper articles about the farm or the house were subsequently published in South Africa, especially before and after its purchase in 2002 by the Coromandel Farmers Trust as part of the land reform and land redistribution process. As the internet has grown during the 2000s, short pieces in popular design websites such as *Architzer, Hidden Architecture, Visi* and *Lifestyling* have surfaced and increased its public accessibility. However, it was in François Burkhardt's comprehensive publication on Zanuso's portfolio, *Marco Zanuso: Design,* the first of its kind with sections in English, where we see the house's significance placed in context, documented as part of Zanuso's work in South Africa and his international architectural oeuvre. Slowly, the house's place in Zanuso's versatile career has been further revealed, beginning with contributions by Prina and Trabucco in *Marco Zanuso: Architettura, Design e la Costruzione del Benessere* (2007), Manolo de Giorgio's Mendrisio Academy Press and Silvana Editoriale publication (2013), and most recently within the comprehensive record of Zanuso's architecture and design edited by Crespi et al. (2020). Through a series of articles in design and architecture journals, Coromandel House's influence has begun to be properly traced: by de Giorgio in *Inventario* (2011), Peres in the *Journal of the South African Institute of Architects* (2013), Steyn in the *South African Journal of Art History* (2016) and Zamboni in *Domus* (2017).[226]

For the past few years, the house has also been a site of architectural pilgrimage. Within South Africa, its influence within local architecture has been a source of inspiration for topographical architectures, as explained in the essay "Stones that Sing" by Arthur Barker. This is an additional feature at the end of this publication, as is a second specially written annexed essay on the documentation and valorisation of the architecture of Coromandel in South Africa. The latter contribution expands our knowledge of Coromandel House, whose architecture was merged into the landscape and assimilated by it so powerfully that it captured the attention of academics carrying out a survey of the archaeological Bokoni remains. They have subsequently continued to document the house over several years.

Coromandel House could be referred to as a "best kept secret" in that its prestige and influence have taken their time to reach a wider audience – now, though, its valuable contributions and experimentations in design are popular themes. Despite initial obscurity, a combination of a need for maintaining privacy and the repressive Apartheid politics, which limited its exposure in architectural and design publications, the house is now open to the public. Since then, Zanuso's adaptability as an architect-designer, capable of solving design problems at various scales and multiple disciplines, has gained ground. Perhaps another reason for the house's past obscurity, however, is that it was built a few decades before mainstream design thinking could catch up with it. With hindsight, we can see lineages in design that allude to the advancement of modern architecture through "Good Design" principles, as well as its role in the evolution of Zanuso's architectural portfolio, acknowledged regionally and internationally as a source of inspiration and interest in the establishment of a contemporary South African aesthetic. That such a project, never intended for a public following and for which so little has been published, has gained and maintained local and even international interest over time, is a sign of its distinction and novelty.

140

140

Stepping stones in the fishpond, here seen empty, lead to the east wing

ENDNOTES

222 Some of these include Barker, A, S Mahoney, N Plewman, F Thomashoff.

223 Banham, R, 1975.

224 *Style* magazine, 1984.

225 Truswell, H, 1985.

226 These publications are fully cited in the reference list.

Coromandel House in Zanuso's portfolio

"Hic terminus haeret". With Virgil's words inscribed above the entrance, Marco Zanuso marked the end of the project and a crossing of a border between his research on living and its construction. And for Sydney and Victoria Press, it marked the start of a new journey in their home. For the rest of us, it notes a point in a lineage of architectural ideas that extend from archaic times into the future

141

In this extraordinary story, characters and elements have gradually revealed themselves and, like pieces in a mosaic, have created the picture of Coromandel House's complex design and construction narrative. There is a symbiotic relationship between its clients and architect, nurtured in the creation of a unique project, with universal characteristics that make it inseparable from its place and context.

The profound rapport established between Zanuso, Sydney and Victoria, evidenced by intense correspondence and the way in which the construction site was documented during all phases, also testifies to the particular challenges posed by its exceptional conditions – even for the designer himself. But it allowed him the opportunity to manifest his own vision of living. Coromandel House represents the maxim of Zanuso's architectural methodology, and this publication has explored how he translated his thinking into an exemplary form. Equally, it is also true that this project would have been unthinkable without Sydney and Victoria's perceptiveness to imagine something more novel than the mere construction of a house, creating, realising and occupying it by putting into play all the resources and determination to bring it to completion.

Zanuso declared that Coromandel House was the result of "falling in love", on the one hand with the clients' esteem for his work, and, on the other, by the manner with which he was struck by the uniqueness of the place and his clients' bold vision. Together the three of them shaped something substantial that we can still admire today. In 1975, the end of the project was sanctioned with a stone engraving above the entrance door of "Casa Press": a verse by Virgil taken from the fourth book of the *Aeneid* along with a tribute. It reads: *"Hic terminus haeret. Marco Zanuso per Sydney Press. MCMLXXV".*

Hic terminus haeret, which literally translates as "here the term is fixed" or "here stays the end", evokes the idea of the threshold where "boundaries adhere" between two worlds. The aim is to immutably and literally mark, recalling through Virgil[227] the epic act of the founding of Rome, the end of an enterprise that has the characteristics of the extraordinary. But there is certainly a more hidden meaning as well:

> *Sol, qui terrarum flammis opera omnia lustras, tuque harum interpres curarum et conscia Iuno,nocturnisque Hecate triviis ululata per urbes,et Dirae ultrices, et di morientis Elissae,accipite haec, meritumque malis advertite numen,et nostras audite preces. Si tangere portusinfandum caput ac terris adnare necesse est, et sic fata Iovis poscunt, hic terminus haeret:at bello audacis populi vexatus et armis,finibus extorris, complexu avulsus Iuli,auxilium imploret, videatque indigna suorum funera; nec, cum se sub leges pacis iniquae tradiderit, regno aut optata luce fruatur, sed cadat ante diem, mediaque inhumatus harena.*[228]

> O Sun, whose rays survey all that is done on earth; and Juno, agent and witness of unhappy love; Hecate, whose name is wailed by night in city streets; and Avenging Furies and gods of dying Elissa: hear me now; turn your anger upon the sins that merit it, and listen to my prayers! If that accursed wretch must reach harbour and come to shore, if Jove's ordinances so demand and this is the outcome fixed: yet even so, harassed in war by the arms of a fearless nation, expelled from his territory and torn from Iulus' embrace, let him plead for aid and see his friends cruelly slaughtered![229]

141

Model of final and built version of Cavallo House

Hic terminus haeret is an expression that evokes an eternal quality, indicating both a temporal limit and a physical boundary that is immutably marked by the will of Jupiter. But the verb *haeret* has several meanings, including that of hesitating or lingering. That is, it refers to the idea of the limit as an open border and a threshold towards the unknown. For Sydney and Victoria this threshold represents a point of arrival – the point of contact between nature and artifice, ideally represented on the threshold of the front door of the house. Meanwhile, for Zanuso, this work represents the fulfilment of an idea and the opportunity to achieve it.

Zanuso himself defined the exceptional characteristics of this story: "This house was so isolated in a place without architecture that it was almost obligatory to find material as it was there. [...] If you make sure to design so that you smell the scents and see the hippos [...] If you make architecture like that, where you can ride a horse almost into the living room, I think something happens."[230] To achieve this phenomenological architecture, he added light as a building element, greatly reduced within the interior to contrast the exterior: "Light, a light that changes its colour, in the hour of the day and in the time of the year, on the majestic and ancient nature and immerses its forms in an atmospheric temperature, which vibrates with tonal incidences on the planes and edges of buildings and softens in the soft pervasiveness of plant forms." He constituted the architecture around not only its functional needs and self-referential interests but also the direct relationship to nature which required "an adequate resonance to the landscape and the surrounding environment", which, he argued, created "the spatial idea of a refined structural and expressive dialogue between the ancient landscape and the new activity". He referred to these themes in later projects too, in which Virgil's influence once again emerged: "The 'natural' image of the surrounding landscape and its related reflection in the advanced and technologically soft character of the [production] form that is housed there reminds us of the Virgilian element that pervades the works of Claude Lorrain; that anxious feeling of a golden age expressed in images of perfect harmony between man and nature may perhaps allude to the dream of a general structure of production and reproduction of life that is both innovative and composed with the rhythms of nature. It is appropriate to close with the response of Apollo Delio to Aeneas uncertain of his goal: '*Antiquam exquirite matrem*' – 'Look for the ancient mother'."[231]

Given the size of the brief and the particularity of the place, Coromandel House goes beyond its entity and peculiar characteristics to establish a surprising leap with respect to the idea of living that Zanuso was pursuing in other areas of his work. In this project, incidentally the only villa built by Zanuso outside the geographical and cultural context of the Mediterranean,[232] we see not so much a synthesis in the progression of his housing research, but more so passing the threshold, beyond which the house blends more into the landscape, towards open environmental systems of architecture. It is a principle inherent in the twin houses of Arzachena. Starting from their minimal modularity of environmental units, Zanuso's homes progressively become open systems, not indeterminate but unfinished – or rather unfinished because they are immersed in the landscape and completed by it:

> Looking at the plan you can see how the architecture and landscape blend. The stone walls, which stretch out over the land, becoming part of it, lead into an intermediate space that is no longer exterior but not yet interior: in the background they open into the heart of the house. [...] This building is not conventional, shaped like traditional homes, but it suggests memories and cultural references from various sources

> and manages to be very modern and ancient at the same time. At first, within the plan, [...] I thought I saw an urban layout: a square in the centre, a public place for meetings, and roads leading out at the sides, with private spaces too. A Mayan votive construction or a petrified spaceship. Someone called it a huge chameleon, capable of changing skin colour with the seasons: a sort of changing architecture. Reading the house as a mimetic object is essential, but only partially so. From the front, it appears like a linear mark anchored amidst green rolling hills, and from far away this precise horizontal outline can be perceived. Military fortifications, walls and Roman aqueducts are perhaps implied here; but there is a strong and layered human presence that feels as though it has existed here for ages. The equilibrium of this architecture lies in Zanuso contrasting predominant natural forces with an equally strong-willed and necessary "humanity".[233]

Even in extreme cases such as Coromandel House, the architectural form as an articulated organism is defined by the modular system of structurally, architecturally, functionally complete units. But it is precisely the "open form" of the organism that, at the expense of its potential growth, unquestionably determines the agglomeration of modules and the complete form resulting from its position on the ground and its adaptation to the place.

Coromandel House is likened to the image of a body lying on the ground, an osteological form, reduced to its supporting "bone" structure, an organism reduced to its constitutive and primary components. But it overcomes this state, by exaggeratedly tapering the walls into the landscape, to fuse artefact and nature. From this point of view, the house succeeds in transitioning from closed modular systems towards "open environmental systems", a challenge that Zanuso pursued throughout his design production.

But integration in the landscape of such extraordinary beauty – that always seems to be present in Zanuso's choice of *place* – undergoes a further acceleration after Coromandel House, determined by two inseparable factors. On the one hand, there is the search for elementary and ancestral forms of "occupation" in a place; on the other, the construction of "archaeological" markers in the soil, fragments that do not seek recomposition but find a balance in the character of nonfinite or, on the contrary, of forms about to return to ruin, assimilated by the site. One could venture a parallel with the geoglyphs, such is the iconic and ancestral strength of these "bodies" in the landscape, for their ability to mark a place without contaminating it with the presence of man, and without upsetting its balance.

If this kind of progression, places with extreme environmental characteristics, begins at Arzachena and finds its most successful expression in Coromandel House, the house on the island of Cavallo in Corsica (1981–1988) marks its ultimate, most extreme point. Located on a site constantly beaten by waves and wind, in an exposed position and leaning towards the Strait of Bonifacio, this home is a system of marks in the landscape of the wild Corsican coast. Devised as a holiday retreat for the businessman, lover of sailing and collector of racing cars Jack J. Setton and his family, it could have been one of Zanuso's most impressive creations, but its construction was beset by various problems and resulted in it being downscaled.[234]

As at Coromandel House, Zanuso starts his design for the Cavallo home with a site reconnaissance in a context devoid of "cultural" holds, studying its characters and drawing inspiration from topographical and natural forms, the large boulders scattered on the inaccessible promontory. He takes inspiration from aerial photographs for the precise mapping of the boulders in the profile of the coastal stretch, treating them as archaeological reliefs within which to generate a system of walls capable of adapting to the topography without changing anything. A first plan follows that "strongly influences this suggestion of an archaeological habitat: oriented north-south for the entire extension of a peninsula [...], the project consists of a splendid dissolution between walls of a path along an axis, more like a large public space of Roman architecture than a building organism."[235]

The plan evokes the archaeological relief of the Ventotene ruins of the Imperial Villa Giulia, residence of the daughter of Augustus, while introducing open curvilinear elements and other diagonals of a Wrightian matrix, to complete a sequence of longitudinal walls dilated for the entire width of the hillock. The origin of this precedent emerges in an early text by Zanuso in which he explains his interest in the Roman villa model: "In this regard, a letter from Plinio describing a Roman villa is very interesting: it speaks of the exact orientation of the rooms, with those facing south protected from excessive insolation by means of arcades and walls raised to defend the house from wind; even the plants, the flowers in the garden are arranged in the most appropriate points for their needs."[236]

The project is resized in a second design draft and simplified on two axes, cardo and decumanus, punctuated by large hollow columns to determine the paths that extend away from several central nuclei where the pavilions that make up the home are situated. The downsizing is the result of building regulations, which ultimately lead to a more compact scheme around a single central core in which the 7.5 metre x 7.5 metre module defines both the living volumes and the covered parts. This design solution is implemented, but only partially retains the original spirit of the project of an extreme fusion with the place, giving shape to a large coastal house that is exposed to the natural elements, yet appears to be minimally touched by the hand of man.

Spread out in the ground, as though creating a "mineral continuum" with the large boulders, hollow columns contain the only vegetation present and define the axes of an agglomeration of pavilions invisible from the sea, of which the wall eaves emerge beyond lowered vaults; this house contains both ancestral and classic references in the pursuit of mediation with nature, where ultimately, it is man who submits to the rules of nature, stripping himself of all trappings.

The project is an extreme outcome of Zanuso's desire to "bring the artifice to its extreme consequences", definitively overcoming the mechanistic vision towards the organic one, where man finds through living with nature the point of contact between mechanical civilisation and the natural elements (*hic terminus haeret*). It thereby closed a circle that had opened for him several years earlier at Coromandel House.

Today, architecture students visit a Coromandel House that is engulfed by vegetation, a sort of African Taliesin West, where they admire the equilibrium between artifice and nature, and experience a link between Italy and Africa that Zanuso interpreted and pioneered. It concretises ideals of living that are as topical as ever, established in Italy but which find new humus in the far south of Africa to take root in unprecedented and fruitful developments that continue to be explored in their "extreme consequences".

On his first trip to Coromandel Farm in 1969, Zanuso was developing a project for a nautical club on the Olona river together with the then young architect Renzo Piano (b. 1937), his assistant (between 1964 and 1967) in the industrial design course at the Milan Polytechnic.[237] A couple of years earlier a publication signed by Zanuso, Piano and Roberto Lucci, the result of research carried out at the Milan Polytechnic, was entitled

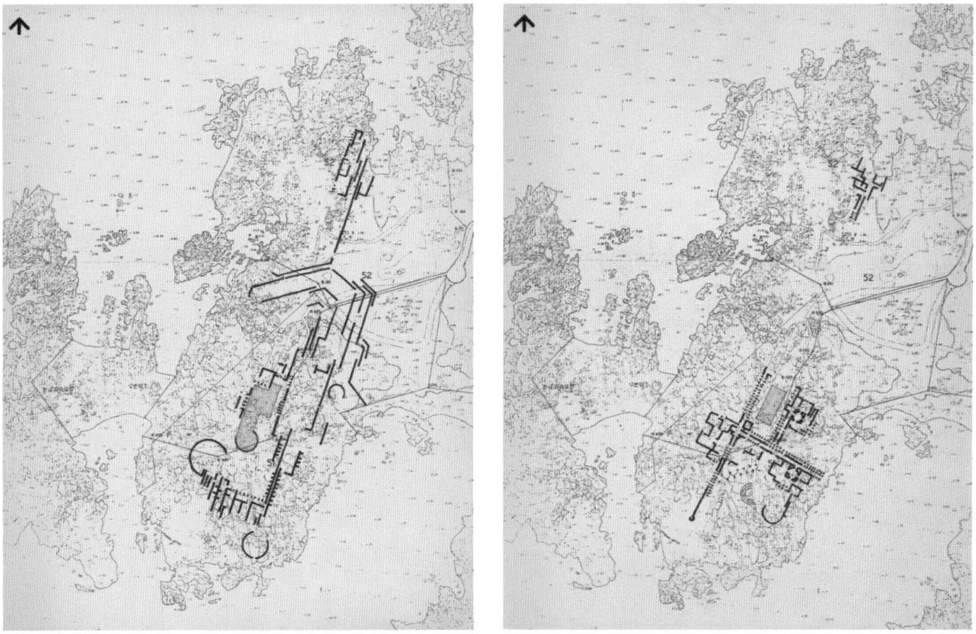

142

142

Plans of Cavallo House, the final evolution of ideas that came to the fore at Coromandel House

Elements of Technology of Materials as an Introduction to the Study of Design.[238] In the same period, Piano's studio collaborated with Zanuso and Eduardo Vittoria on the construction of the roofing system for the Olivetti factory in Scarmagno (1967–1968).

Also working in Zanuso's studio, between 1956 and 1963, was Aldo Rossi (1931–1997), who left a year before Renzo Piano's arrival, in a hypothetical "passing of the baton", shortly before being appointed professor at the Polytechnic of Milan,[239] and publishing *The Architecture of the City* (1966), a volume of enormous importance that changed the face of Italian and international architecture.

In an ideal genealogical lineage of Italian architecture, it is significant that the two most influential Italian architects of the twentieth century – the only Italian Pritzker Architecture Prize winners – have both passed "through the workshop" of Zanuso. The subsequent path undertaken by Rossi was to design only from within the parameters set by the architectural discipline. Piano, in strong continuity with Zanuso's philosophy, followed the experimental path oriented towards research on technology and materials, drawing on the very act of building to clarify the form of the project.

For Piano the idea of the building as an organism – in its growth intrinsically linked to the *place* – runs through all its realisations; meanwhile for Rossi the key is not so much organic as it is osteological – less topological than typological – and therefore it is translated into ancestral, primary forms, such as the horse's skeleton, his formal obsession. What is striking is not so much the chronology of Rossi then Piano working alongside Zanuso, but Zanuso's approach, which contains both positions in a non-contradictory way, embracing the core of both, in the spirit of the research best synthesised by Coromandel House.

143

ENDNOTES

227 Sydney was well versed with the classics and would quote Virgil's *Aeneid.*

228 *Eneide* (IV; vv. 615–620).

229 https://www.theoi.com/Text/VirgilAeneid4.html, translated by HR Fairclough.

230 From "Si vede che sono distratto", Marco Zanuso interviewed by Franco Raggi, in Grignolo, R, ed., *Marco Zanuso: Scritti sulle tecniche di produzione e di progetto*, Milan: Silvana Editoriale and Mendrisio Academy Press, 2013. Original text published in *Flare. Architectural Lighting Magazine*, no. 21, September 1999, pp. 80–95.

231 Zanuso, M, "Costruire lo spazio aperto: un esempio di dialogo tra architettura e natura", typescript, 1985, in Grignolo, R, 2013, pp. 300–301. These quotations refer to the IBM di Santa Palomba complex (1979–1984).

232 An example is Zanuso's holiday home on the Greek island of Paxos (1972), which recovered and reconstructed three stone-walled huts originally used as a refuge for farmers, generating an agglomeration of pavilions for outdoor living immersed in the landscape of olive trees and in contact with nature "scattered and broken up for a total of just over 110 square metres" (Manolo de Giorgi, SKIRA, pp. 284–287).

233 ZML, *Abitare*, 1981, pp. 16–17.

234 Navone, A, "La rivoluzione nell'impianto della casa. Un approccio genetico al progetto di due case in riva al mare", in Crespi, L, et al., "*Marco Zanuso. Architettura e design*", Archivio del Moderno, Officina Libraria, Rome, 2020, pp. 61–74.

235 De Giorgi, M, Skira, pp. 304–309.

236 Marco Zanuso's "La Casa", from "Libro e moschetto. Settimanale dei fascisti universitari", 1939 (AdM, Fondo Marco Zanuso), in Grignolo, R, 2013, p. 76.

237 Unbuilt Project. In the volume edited by Lorenzo Ciccarelli, "Renzo Piano prima di Renzo Piano. I maestri e gli esordi", Fondazione Renzo Piano, Quodlibet, 2017, pp. 153–155.

238 Tamburini Editore, Milan, 1967.

239 Aldo Rossi was assistant to Ludovico Quaroni at the school of urban planning in Arezzo (1963) and later to Carlo Aymonino at the Institute of Architecture in Venice.

143

"Hic terminus haeret", written above the main entrance to Coromandel House, marks the end of the journey for Zanuso, but the start of Sydney and Victoria's at Coromandel House. For the visitor, it signals the importance of the place and preludes the experience therein, which will linger within their memory long after their departure

Lessons for today and tomorrow

This study reminds us to mould the present moment from the best ideas that are rooted in past traditions and to incorporate progressive innovations from varied sources that can improve human experience. The house's outlandish design demonstrates possibilities to new generations of architects, but as this study shows, its value lies in prioritising the design process as a means of problem solving

144

To well-trained or even intuitive architects and designers, the lessons that Coromandel House offers may seem obvious. During the 1970s, a few local architects thought the stone-clad walls of Coromandel House appeared "too romantic", with uncomfortably European interiors.[240] To the layman the house was a conundrum – and strange. Echoes of these opinions persist to this day, but with hindsight, the knowledge we have today removes the project from obscurity, revealing its formidable qualities. To those with an open mind, the house is a portal to a timeless dream place. To architects searching for an integrated method with which to problem-solve complexity, modularity, organicism, technology and nature, it offers principles and strategies. And so, the clearest lesson to be drawn from this project is one which repeats in many iconic projects: in order to leave a mark, to make a legacy, one must push boundaries that are not always comfortable nor easily understood at the time. Indigenous landscaping, biophilic design and passive green building strategies, today considered essential, were novelties back then.

Another lesson is that ideas have precedents as well as antecedents, which architect and writer Roger Fisher (b. 1951) has referred to as a "genealogy of ideas". For Coromandel House, the design intention found its genesis at Casa Arzale in Sardinia – although it evolved into a much greater level of complexity in Coromandel House, and later reached its finality in Zanuso's Cavallo House, while diverging with a new South African lineage at Westcliff Estate. Next, the fusion of ideas to incorporate the best of both most often results in novel interpretations of the status quo that lead to new solutions. The fusion of ideas occurs not only though geographical and social transplants, but also through the collaboration between individuals: Coromandel House was not the result of a single man's vision. It *is*, however, the cumulative product of the combined visions of the clients, their professional team and the labourers, who made it real. Lastly, its aesthetic and form derive from "method" and not from a composite of images taken from other buildings. Its design can therefore not be replicated successfully since the specificities that led to its creation – those of context, time and place, clients and professionals, technology, materials and brief – were the parts that make the whole. It is these qualities that make it unique.

At the time of writing this book, 20 years after Zanuso passed away, we have come to admire his design versatility. His design methodology provided the structure to find solutions for the smallest and largest design problems. During his own lifetime, architects have been taught increasingly specialised programmes with set parameters and deliverables, and substituting methods with pre-determined outputs. While we are not in the same position as Zanuso – who was rethinking the role of architecture in a post-war world – we are facing our own global-scale economic, environmental and social challenges that pose uncomfortable questions about the future, which are especially challenging for architects in particular to tackle. Zanuso's portfolio inspires us to think about design that lasts for the long term and can adapt over time; design that integrates, innovates and experiments; and design that works across scales to build resilience for the future.

144

Coromandel House in 2021 – architectural landscape archaeology or the remains of Modernism "with an ancient heart", 2021

Coromandel House serves to inspire and remind all of us about *being* in place and *placemaking* in an increasingly fleeting, image-saturated global culture in which method, meaning and purpose are most often forgotten. This study reminds us to mould the present moment from the best ideas that are rooted in past traditions and to incorporate progressive innovations that improve human experiences. The house's outlandish design has demonstrated possibilities to later generations of architects, some of which relate to siting, materiality, scale, proportion, rhythm, texture and surprise. But there are lessons beyond Zanuso's design methodology – to practise in a way that helps to find order in complexity, to quietly pursue excellence, and by doing so, leave a legacy.

ENDNOTES

240 Watson, P, Interview, 2020.

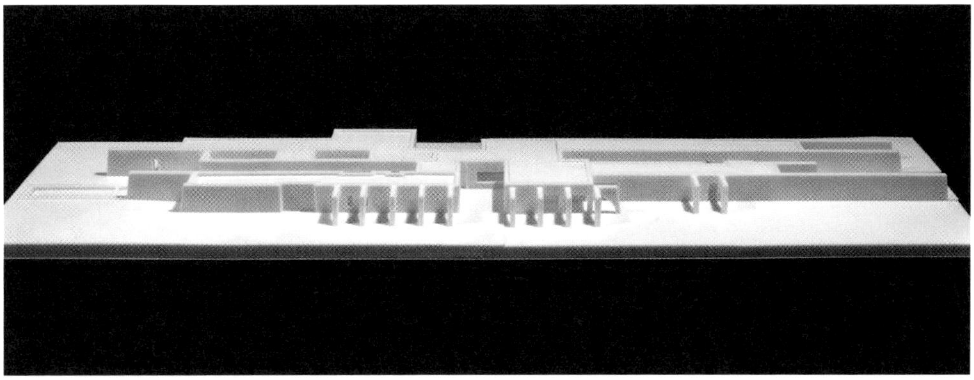

145

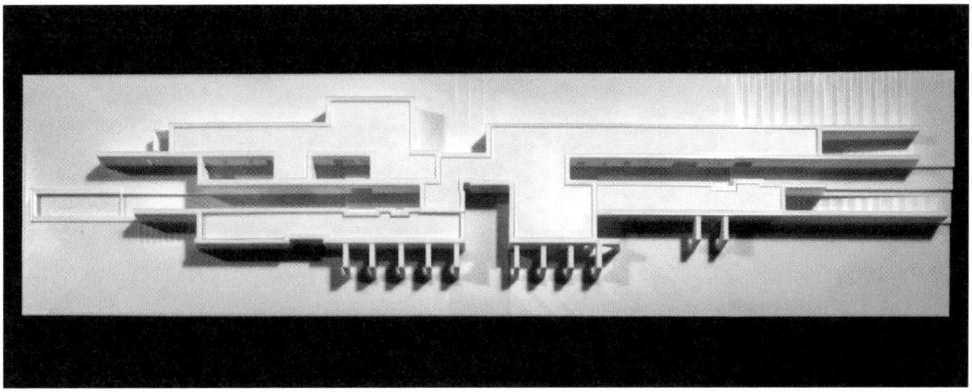

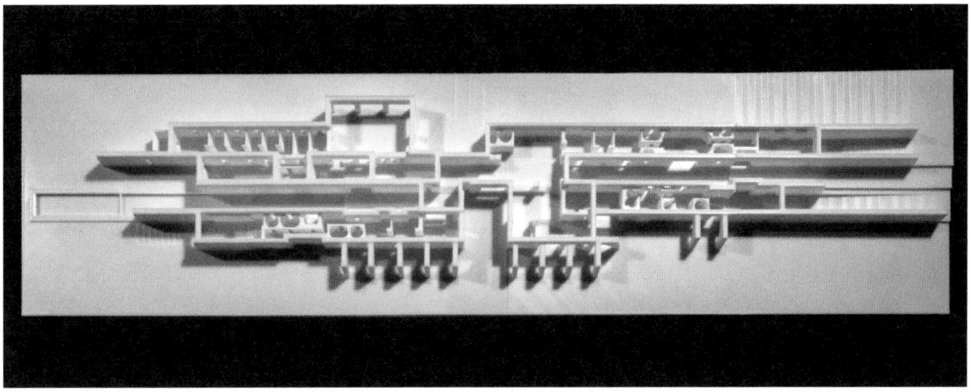

145

A 3D printed model of Coromandel House created by Zamboni Associati Architettura. It is reproduced at a scale of 1:100 and measures 90cm in length

146

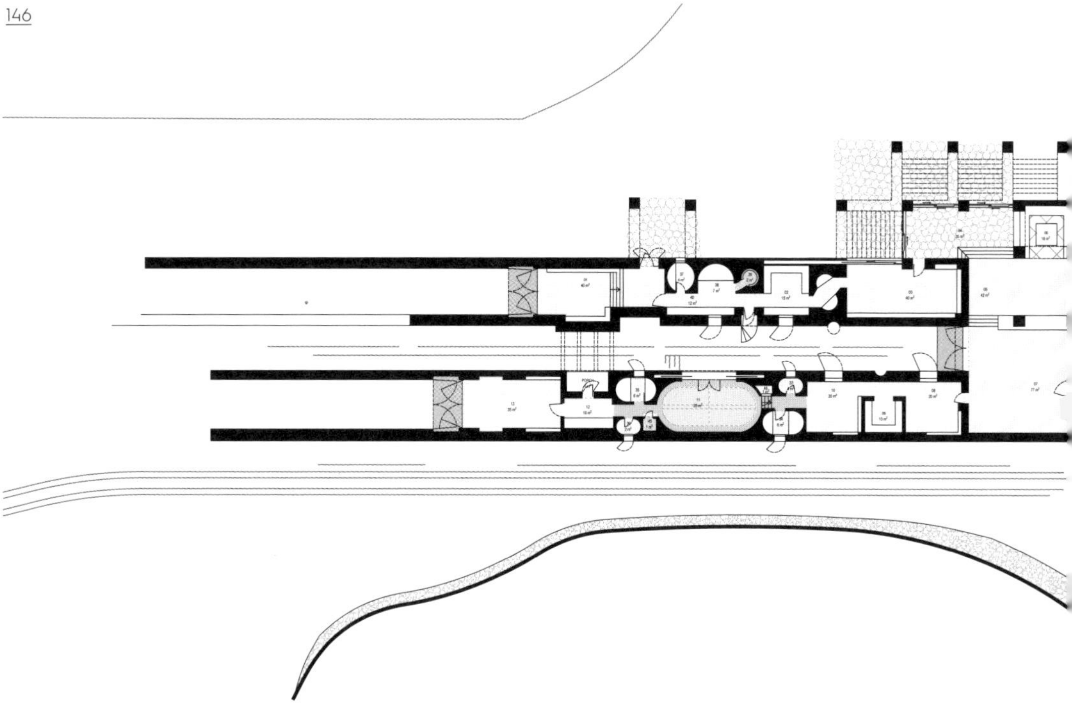

147

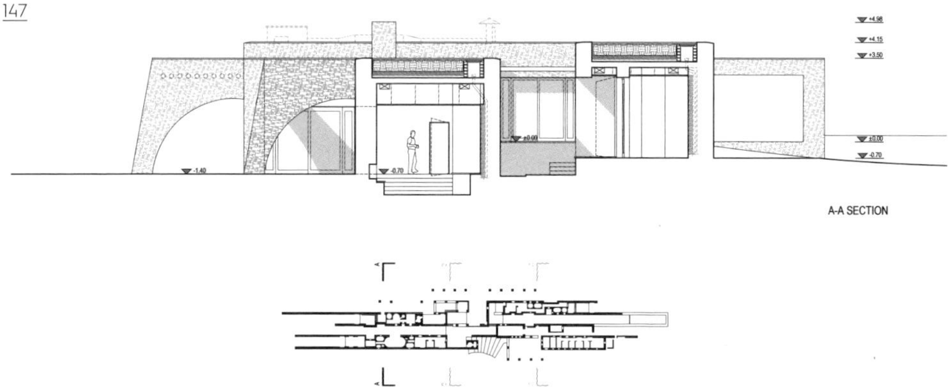

A-A SECTION

148

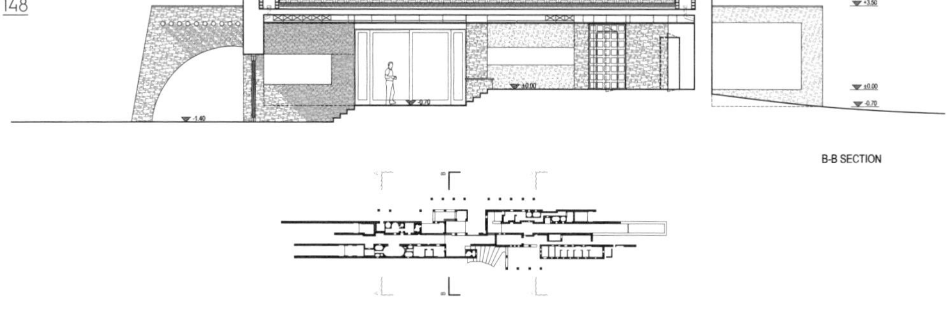

B-B SECTION

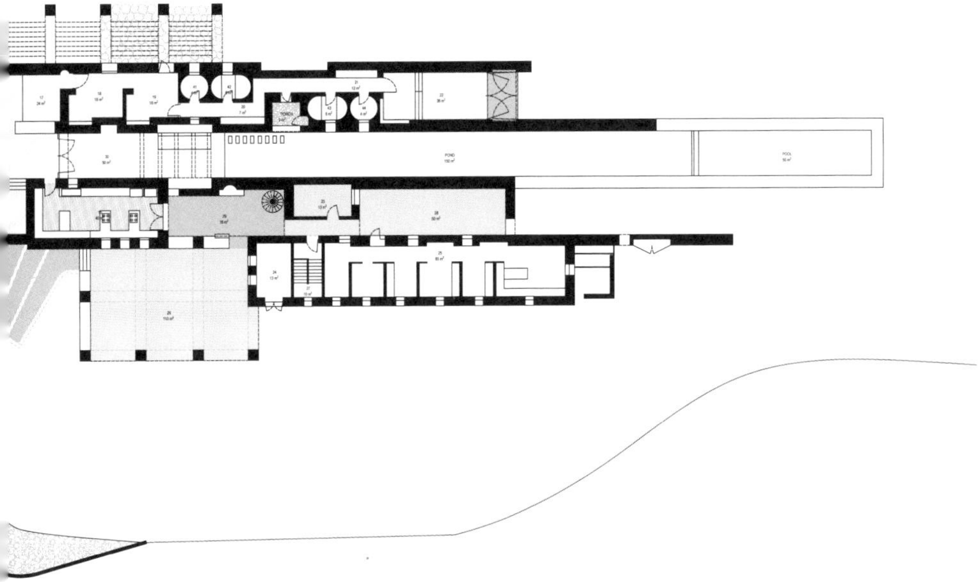

149

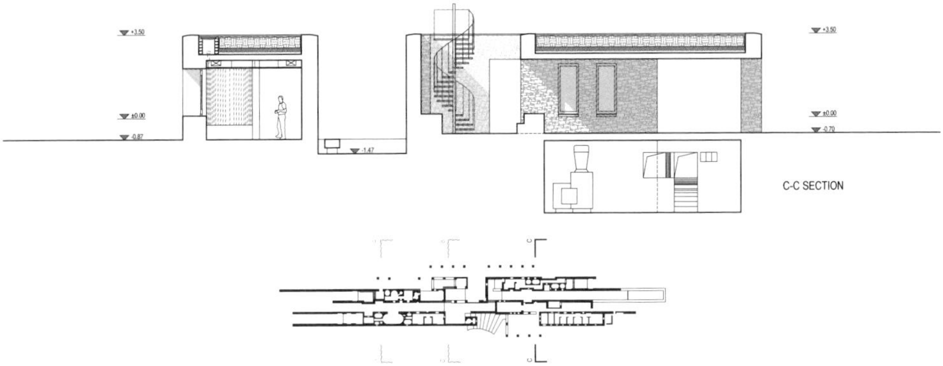

146

The original plans of Coromandel House were reproduced by Zamboni Associati Architettura into a digital 3D model, which provides an opportunity to draw new section lines and perspectival views

147

Section AA – The narrow courtyard creates a vegetated threshold between the two western wings

148

Section BB – The central living areas are stepped in three levels to follow the topography between the main entrance and the arches

149

Section CC – The eastern wing, fish pond and kitchen courtyard, with its spiral staircase, which diverts attention from the entrance to the “hidden” basement service space next to the covered parking

150

150

Coromandel House, with its characteristic arches, linear walls and "camouflaged" stone walls

Essays

Stones that sing

by Arthur Barker

This essay tracks the trajectory of Regionalism in South African architecture with Coromandel House as an example. It covers a middle-ground approach to Regionalism, a Relative Regionalism, with Zanuso's work here highlighting the fine balance between responding comfortably to the local context while including technological innovation and international architectural influences

BUILDING THE LANDSCAPE – A SOUTH AFRICAN RELATIVE REGIONALISM

A stone's throw from a pine plantation on Coromandel Farm, and on the Mpumalanga escarpment of South Africa, lie numerous kraals[241] and terraced stone walls built by the Bokoni people, from around 1500 until the 1820s. The terraces were used for agriculture, but they represent only a smattering of the stone walls, circles, mazes and ridges, spanning 150km from Ohrigstad to Carolina[242] and connecting over 10,000 square kilometres of land.[243] These largely unprotected artefacts represent a unique vernacular response to the landscape as the existing topography was manipulated to suit cultural and economic practices. These approaches were conscious exploits, passed down through the generations. They represent habits of thought, repetitions of construction technology and local ways of living. While these efforts promote the local, and are regional, they are unlike self-conscious responses to place, referred to by theorists and historians as Regionalism. Coromandel House is the result of an architect making critical choices from the local and international options available to him. Although Zanuso was not South African, his approach to Regionalist design complemented approaches that were already underway in South Africa.

Regionalist architectures in South Africa range from conservative, often eclectic, solutions such as those from the colonial Dutch and English traditions to radical reactions influenced by the Modern Movement or universalist influences from Europe and Brazil. Coromandel House is an example of a middle-ground approach where global influences met local traditions. Zanuso synthesised the self-conscious influences of his education and training, the principles of Italian Rationalism, with conscious approaches to local stone building traditions, climate and topography.

CAST IN STONE – CONSERVATIVE REGIONALIST BEGINNINGS

The eminent South African architect Gawie Fagan (1925–2020) once defined Regionalism as "a return to basic values, and an enabling architecture adapted to our climes and cultures [which] above all, [can] restore the self-esteem of our nation"[244]. Unfortunately, the approach can easily result in a conservative or unhealthy[245] Regionalism, bordering on nationalism. Here, history is used selectively or politically, experience dominates, old ways of living are accepted and new technologies largely ignored.

Arguably, the first conservative Regionalism, but oldest surviving building in South Africa, was the Cape Town Castle, built between 1666 and 1679. With its five iconic bastions and battered, dressed, stone walls of Malmesbury Group slate, it recalled the form of Dutch forts in other parts of the world. Between 1893 and 1913, the English architect Herbert Baker (1862–1946) created a unique but rather conservative Regionalism through his translation of the English Arts and Crafts style, particularly in his houses in the Cape region of South Africa but also through his most renowned architectural contribution, the 1910 sandstone-clad Union Buildings in Pretoria. Later, his protégé Gordon Leith (1886–1965) revised local building materials and practices[246] to reproduce Castelli Romana in his own house in Houghton, near Johannesburg, in 1952.[247] Here a reconstruction of the site and the use of local stone resulted in a romantic, but rather foreign neo-Renaissance architecture. Later, the Arts and Crafts inspired work of the Bauhaus-trained Steffen Ahrends presented a "congenial vernacular"[248] and it is telling that the Presses would approach him to design the stone-walled[249] stables on the Coromandel Farm, as well as a Spanish-style inspired house on Round Hill, in Sedgefield in the Southern Cape, in the early 1960s.

LEAVING NO STONE UNTURNED – RADICAL REGIONALIST REACTIONS

Radical Regionalisms are politically and ideologically driven. They are consciously critical of sentimental relationships with place, while being more accepting of universalist principles and the possibilities of progress through the use of new technologies. Unfortunately, these rational approaches can often lead to an abstraction of local traditions and, in so doing, can sever the link between context, architecture and the inhabitant.[250]

The first Radical Regionalism in South Africa was that of Gerard Moerdijk (1890–1958), who rejected English and Dutch architectural inheritances, replacing them with an Art Deco style in his granite-clad Voortrekker Monument of 1938.[251] The Radical Regionalism of the Transvaal Group[252] in South Africa, in the 1930s, attempted to get rid of the "eclectic, reiterative and tired"[253] neo-Renaissance[254] architecture of the period, by using Modern Movement principles inspired by Le Corbusier (1887–1965). Unfortunately for the Transvaal Group, the public showed little interest in

01

02

03

01

Photo of the Bokoni remains on Coromandel Farm, 2021

02

Gordon Leith's Houghton House (1952), Johannesburg

03

Painting by James Reeves of Steffen Ahrends' Round Hill House (c. 1961), Sedgefield

their creations,[255] while the buildings often leaked and overheated in the harsh climate. More importantly, the buildings demonstrated little connection to local architectural traditions.

Fortunately, Rex Martienssen's (1905–1942) contemporaries, such as the South African-born, but English-trained, architect Douglas Cowin (1911–2000), dealt with the more practical problems by fusing the Bauhaus planning principles of Ludwig Mies van der Rohe (1886–1969) with those of Frank Lloyd Wright (1867–1959) inspired roof forms, particularly in his house, Bedo, in Johannesburg in 1936. The design of the house was also a unique response to the topography of the site, as part of it was a suspended structure over painted brick walls that formed a partially subterranean entrance, emulated in 1966 by Gawie Fagan in House Bertie-Roberts in Camps Bay, Cape Town.

KILLING TWO BIRDS WITH ONE STONE – A RELATIVE REGIONALISM

A middle-ground approach to Regionalism is, as Lewis Mumford (1895–1990) argued,[256] critical of both global and local influences. Experience of place and tradition are still important aspects but equally important are changes: a close link to the site and its topography, a combination of new and old building technologies and an understanding of new living requirements. An early example of this approach was presented in the March issue of the 1938 *South African Architectural Record*, where Le Corbusier's Mathes house (1935) was shown with its rough stone walls and timber substructure, similar to Maison Errázuriz in Chile (1930). These projects reinforced Le Corbusier's belief that "the rusticity of the materials is in no way a hindrance to the expression of a clear plan and a modern aesthetic"[257] and preceded the advent

04

05

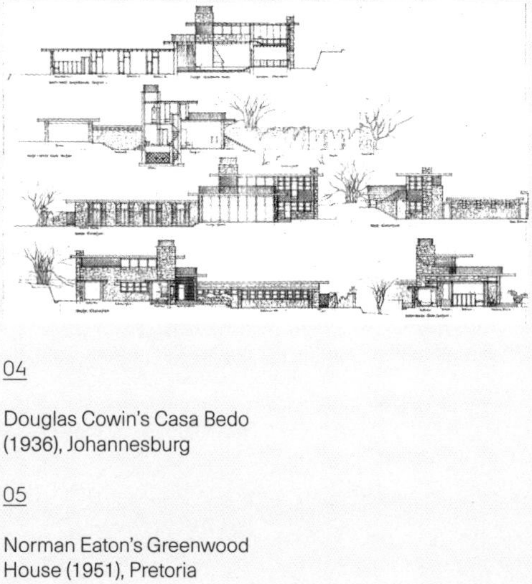

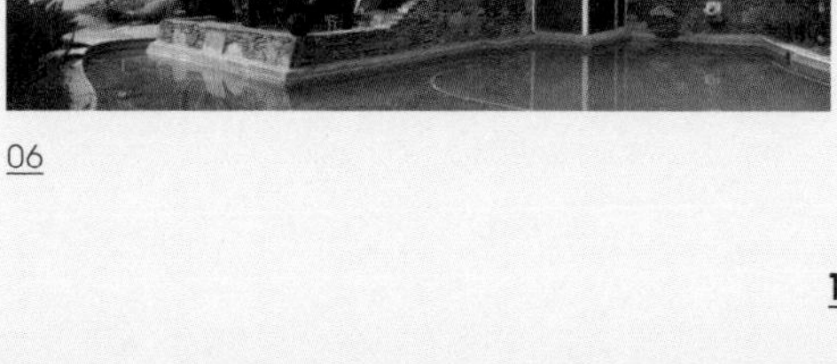

06

04

Douglas Cowin's Casa Bedo (1936), Johannesburg

05

Norman Eaton's Greenwood House (1951), Pretoria

06

Hellmut Stauch's Hakahana House (1952), Pretoria

of a Modern Regionalism,[258] particularly in places outside of Europe.

In 1981, the architectural historians and theorists Liane Lefaivre (b. 1949) and Alexander Tzonis (b. 1937) described later developments of this middle-ground approach as Critical Regionalism.[259] Kenneth Frampton (b. 1930) added to the definition through his ten binary oppositions[260] such as typology and topography. However, Lefaivre and Tzonis[261] were adamant that the original introduction of the term Critical Regionalism referred to architects who were providing an alternative to Postmodern Historicism. As the latter style had not seriously impacted on South Africa before the 1980s, it can be argued that the Regionalist responses here were not "critical" but rather *relative* in their various articulations. That is, they alternated between the extremes of acceptance and resistance to global influences while selectively reacting to local architectural traditions, the need to incorporate new ways of living and the possibilities of new building technologies. These relative, middle-ground, regional responses were also "not so much a collective effort [but] ... the output of ... talented individual[s] working with commitment towards some sort of rooted expression".[262]

This approach was evident in the architecture of some post-Second World War architects in South Africa such as Norman Eaton (1902–1966) and Hellmut Stauch (1910–1970), but as Tzonis reminds us, "with few exceptions their idea of amelioration and quality, addressed physical aspects rather than aspects of culture, community, identity, or individual self-respect ... South African Regionalists of the 1940s and 1950s centred [their] attention mainly on advancing efficiency of construction and enhancing comfort".[263]

Eaton, an employee of Leith, was, however, influenced by the traditions of African architecture, together with that of the Brazilian Modern Movement, and he assimilated these influences with new ways of living, responses to climate and place, and an often-used Frank Lloyd Wright Prairie-style and Richard Neutra (1892–1970)[264] approach to the making of form. This partially topographical approach was reinforced by the use of rustic materials, most often face brick, which was used to suit the colour of the site, but in a few houses such as Greenwood (c. 1951), Anderssen (1949–1950) in The Willows, and Holsboer (1955) in Waterkloof, Pretoria, the use of horizontally shaped stone indirectly connects the houses to their context. In 1961, the Presses approached Eaton (and his partner Tobie Louw) to design their Sedgefield house in the Southern Cape. Here Eaton designed a series of elongated brick-clad platforms and roofs reminiscent of Frank Lloyd Wright's Fallingwater residence (1936–1939) which, itself, was the result of a unique reinterpretation of the topography of the site at Bear Run in Pennsylvania. Eaton's proposal was never built as the Press family preferred Ahrends' "congenial vernacular" Spanish-styled residence.

Hellmut Stauch merged the universal principles of his German *Ittenschule* training with structural and spatial efficiencies and a direct reaction to the local climate and topography. In his own house Hakahana (1959), to the west of Pretoria, he used the natural slope of the ground to root the house into its site through a continuous stepped movement route through the house, paved with slate and lined with other stone from the site, ending in a Brazilian-Modernist inspired swimming pool.

In the 1950s and '60s, a number of Cape-based architects used the stepping stones of an already well-established Relative Regionalism to forge new but more traditionally connected architectures. The Cape Town-trained architect Revel Fox's (1924–2004) houses in Worcester were a unique synergy of Scandinavian Modern Movement influences (through his experience under Arne Jacobsen) and the Cape Dutch vernacular. Pius Pahl (1909–2003) merged the principles of his Bauhaus education with the

Cape Dutch vernacular, designing a number of seminal houses in the Stellenbosch area in the 1950s and '60s. In his last design, House Van der Horst (1994–1998) in Betty's Bay, his career-long philosophy of merging local and Bauhaus architectural traditions, through an interpretation of place and technology, culminated in a unique topographical response situated between mountain, lake and sea. Gawie Fagan's synthesis of the Cape Dutch vernacular and his Modern Movement training, completed the Relative Regionalist approaches in the Cape, reinforced by similar approaches in Natal by Barrie Biermann (1924–1991), Hans Hallen (b. 1930) and Danie Theron (1936–2011).

In 1960, the Dutch-born architect John van de Werke (1913–1980) began building a house for his family in Kameeldrift, east of Pretoria. The sprawling dwelling, in the savannah bushveld, recalls the cross-axial planning and chimneys of Frank Lloyd Wright's Prairie-style houses and Eaton's similar interpretations. The house was constructed of stone directly sourced from the site, as the architect put it,[265] in such a way that none of the stones were ever "hurt" in the 14-year construction process. The dwelling is a tour de force of a hands-on construction process with internal and external walls, floors and ceilings all constructed in varying shapes and sizes of local stone. The planted roof was never completed but would have increased the connection between building and site. Van de Werke merged vernacular building methods with new technologies, all suited to the local climate, while modern ways of living were accommodated through a delicate balance of open-plan living spaces and cave-like bedrooms.

In the early 1970s, the Relative Regionalist approach was further developed by architects

07

08

09

07

Pius Pahl's House Van der Horst (1994–1998), Western Cape

08

Gawie Fagan's own house, Die Es (1963–1968), Cape Town

09

Van de Werke House (1960–1974), Kameeldrift, Pretoria

such as Karl Jooste (1925–1971), who, together with Carl (Gus) Gerneke (b. 1930), designed the highly functional, and climatically responsive, Tshilidzini Hospital in Tzaneen[266] using a combination of industrial materials such as steel roof sheeting, set against rough face brick walls that rooted the buildings to their site.

Thereafter, a limited number of architects continued to explore the possibilities of a Relative yet topographically influenced Regionalism. Using the site as inspiration, Stan Field's Miller House (1975), on Khyber Rock in Johannesburg, established a unique architectural relationship between place and dwelling through the contrast of the suspended and tinted reinforced concrete structure over the rocks that formed the hill. In 1976, Allan Konya (1935–2021) used the steep topography of a site in Waterkloof as a series of platforms to organise the functions of House Carpenter-Kling, using rough dark-coloured brick for the walls, slate roofs and a Frank Lloyd Wright aesthetic.

Stanley Saitowitz's (b. 1949) House Brebnor (1978) in Midrand, midway between Pretoria and Johannesburg, represents the construction of a new topography through its direct relationship with the surrounding rocky outcrops. As the architect explains, "the house extends the original most habitable part of the site, the rocks. The house is a process of making the rocks habitable. The house is a hollow rock".[267] These approaches were enhanced by the internal and external slate floors, with channels that echo the contours and the movement of water across the site.

THE FOUNDATION STONES OF COROMANDEL HOUSE

By 1976, Zanuso's Coromandel House, for the Press family, in the Mpumalanga landscape had been completed. The existing grasslands

10

11

10

Stan Field's Miller House (1975), Johannesburg

11

Allan Konya's Carpenter-Kling House (1975-1976), Waterkloof, Pretoria

and adjoining hill were reconfigured through the addition of new stone walls, and a grass-covered reinforced concrete roof, to form a new topography. On the one hand, Zanuso's approach borrowed from local traditions through his understanding of place, arguably influenced by the horseback visits to Bokoni kraals on the Coromandel Estate by himself and Press.[268] On the other hand, the highly engineered stone cladding, hidden reinforced concrete structure and manicured interior reflect a Rationalist and industrial design response, almost in antithesis of the former, more romantic intentions. Through Zanuso's education and experience, his Rationalist European architectural inheritances were self-consciously merged with the vernacular responses of indigenous peoples and the natural qualities and properties of the surrounding hills, valleys and waterfalls.

In 1938, Zanuso's unbuilt project, designed with Giovanni Albricci and titled "Albergo Rifiugio",[269] had already forged a connection between history and the present. The constructional rationality[270] of buttress-like columns, separated at times from the substantial stone walls, recall Roman architectural traditions, setting the scene for the approach at the Coromandel House.

Zanuso's association with Ernesto Nathan Rogers (1909–1969) in the 1950s, while serving as assistant editor to him at *Domus* (from 1946–1947) and later at *Casabella,* alerted Zanuso to the importance of historical responses in architecture after Rogers renamed the journal *Casabella-continuità*, pursuing the theme of "continuity", which encouraged new architecture to maintain close ties with its past.[271] This Rationalist approach was at the core of Zanuso's education and philosophy as he clearly articulated around 1946: "I admit my Rationalist formation and no longer run away from it. What I do not want to say, but is often said about Rationalism, is that it was a limitation. It is a bit like speaking of the Enlightenment, or the French Revolution, as a limitation. It is just a cultural formation that leads one to confront problems in a certain way."[272] Zanuso's admission was confirmed in 1957 by Vittorio Gregotti (1927–2020), who, as assistant editor of *Casabella-continuità,* described Zanuso as being part of the second generation of modern architects influenced by Rationalist ideals.[273]

By the mid-1970s, the mainstream Modern Movement was considered to have lost its way, witnessed through publications such as Brent Bolin's (b. 1940) *The Failure of Modern Architecture* (1976) and Charles Jencks's (1939–2019) *The Language of Post-Modern Architecture* (1977).[274] A plethora of architectural responses ensued, ranging from conservative historicist examples to Jurgen Habermas's (b. 1929) later definition of "modernity as an incomplete project".[275] The Italian neo-Rationalists sought to continue the intentions of the Rationalist project through a synthesis of the "nationalistic values of Italian Classicism and structural logic of the machine age"[276] but also to "save architecture and the city from being overrun by the all-pervasive forces of megapolitan consumerism".[277]

During the construction of Coromandel House, a number of seminal neo-Rationalist buildings were built in Italy, such as Aldo Rossi's (1931–1997) structurally ordered, and urbanistically responsive, Gallaratese in 1973. Mario Botta's (b. 1943) house at Riva San Vitale (1971) exemplified the idea of "building the landscape" with compensation for the loss of an urban context by buildings being "cities in miniature".[278] This was an approach that Zanuso had already used in 1964, in the design of the centralised courtyard of his fortress-like house, built in granite, at Arzachena in Sardinia[279] and, later, through narrow courtyards that separated the elongated wings of Coromandel House.

More importantly, for Zanuso, was the possible influence of Gregotti, who believed that "[t]he origin of architecture is not the primitive hut or the cave of the mythical Adam's 'House in Paradise'. Before transforming a support into a column, a roof into a tympanum, before placing stone on stone, man placed the stone on the ground to recognise a site in the midst of an unknown universe: in order to take account of it and modify it."[280]

CONCLUSION – THE KEYSTONE

Zanuso's topographical construction of Coromandel House has forever entrenched its architecture into the annals of seminal South African and international buildings, through its Relative Regionalism that built a new landscape. The middle-ground approach to Regionalism resisted a conservative understanding of local traditions while recognising the importance of new technologies and ways of living. This was the result of the education and practice experience of the Italian architect and the clearly articulated desires and expectations of the client. The resultant architecture is a unique synthesis of technological progress, and local and international architectural-historical traditions.

Coromandel House is also part of a consistent development of a centuries-old building tradition, with a close relationship with topography. It has inspired many other South African architects since its completion, fostering further Relative Regionalisms. May future Regionalist developments allow the stones of the Bokoni, and other local traditions, to continue singing through different, nuanced and even more critical tones, so as to further Claude Monet's dictum of "everything changes, *even* stone".

●●●

ENDNOTES

241 Maggs, T, 2021.
242 Delius, P, et al., 2012, p. 399.
243 Delius, P, 2020.
244 Fagan, GT, 1996, p. 10.
245 Van Schaik, L, 1980, p. 19.
246 Chipkin, CM, 1993, p. 132.
247 Anon, 1952, p. 272.
248 Chipkin, CM, 1993, p. 306.
249 Zanuso suggested the use of a slate roof covering during construction (Press, 1969).
250 Barker, 2012, pp. 112–113.
251 Ibid., p. 89.
252 A group of young graduates who, under the leadership of Rex Martienssen (1905–1942) from the Department of Architecture at the University of the Witwatersrand, drew up a manifesto in 1933 titled "Zerohour" in which they published a number of Modern Movement-inspired houses in South Africa. A copy was sent to Le Corbusier.
253 Herbert, G, 1975, p. 1.
254 Cooke, BS, 1960, p. 21.
255 Connell, P, 1945, p. 164.
256 Lefaivre, L and A Tzonis, 2003, p. 19.
257 Frampton, K, 2001, p. 133.
258 Tzonis, A, 2006/2007, p. 216.
259 Lefaivre, L and A Tzonis, 1981.
260 Frampton, K, 1983.
261 Lefaivre, L and A Tzonis, 2003, p. 10.
262 Frampton, K, 1983, p. 156.
263 Tzonis, A, 2006/2007, p. 216.
264 Eaton visited Neutra at his office in Los Angeles on 27 September 1945 (Eaton, 1945).
265 Van de Werke, I, 2021.
266 Fisher, RC, 1998, p. 143.
267 Beck, H, 1985, pp. 24–25.
268 Refer to Part 1: "The Genesis of Coromandel House" for photos of his initial site visit.
269 Blakely, S, 2011, p. 333.
270 This was a recurring feature of Zanuso's work even in his timber-framed-and-clad house on Lake Como (Anon, 1979).
271 Blakely, S, 2011, p. 5.
272 Ibid., p. 15.
273 Ibid., p. 3.
274 Prinsloo, I, 2000, p. 65.
275 D'Entrèves, PM and S Benhabib, 1996.
276 Frampton, K, 1992, p. 203.
277 Ibid., p. 294.
278 Prinsloo, 2000, p. 66.
279 Anon, 1981, p. 17; Anon, 2003; De Giorgi, 1993, p. 93.
280 Frampton, 2019.

Documentation and appreciation of Coromandel

by Salvatore Barba, Anna Sanseverino and Carla Ferreyra

The following essay serves to expand the knowledge of Coromandel House. However, its deeper meaning lies in recognising how this extraordinary work of architecture, so merged into the landscape and assimilated by it, captured the attention of those carrying out a survey of Bokoni archaeological remains, which, by coincidence, had inspired Zanuso in one of his surveys of the site

INTRODUCTION

This essay collects, mainly for dissemination purposes, some reflections resulting from the fruitful International Cooperation Agreement between the Università degli Studi di Salerno in Italy and the Universidad Nacional de Córdoba in Argentina. This collaboration was subsequently extended to the African continent with the participation of colleagues from the Tshwane University of Technology, and it culminated in the signing, in 2016, of a Memorandum of Understanding between the Department of Civil Engineering of Salerno and the Faculty of Engineering and Built Environment of Pretoria. By involving lecturers, researchers and students from the three universities, the didactic-cultural activities represent a real intercollegiate southern triangulation: "South Italy-South America-South Africa".

The educational journey organised by the Tshwane University of Technology, with the contribution of the Italian Institute of Culture and the Italian Embassy in Pretoria, as part of the Summer School on Architectural Surveying, can be considered the natural continuation of the workshop held in Salerno in July 2015. At the campus of the University of Salerno, it was our pleasure to host a delegation of students and professors of Building Engineering-Architecture and Architecture from the Tshwane University of Technology and the Universidad Nacional de Córdoba.

The Summer School consisted of two integrated modules, one on "analogical surveying"; the other on "digital surveying", with laboratory activities supervised by the late Professor Vito Cardone. The main objectives, defined with Professor Jacques Laubscher, were to represent the different architectural-archaeological scenarios of the province of Mpumalanga, and then to explore them using a digital approach, applying photogrammetric techniques such as Structure from Motion (SFM) and Terrestrial Laser Scanning (TLS) 3D technologies. The aim was to develop and strategically exercise critical-selective skills aimed at identifying, depending on the specific case, the most appropriate surveying technique. The sites chosen for the training activities were Coromandel House on Coromandel Farm (Mashishing), by Italian architect, designer and urban planner Marco Zanuso, and the stone terraces built by the Bokoni people on the Verlorenkloof Estate (Emakhazeni).

The collaboration led to a co-funded Joint Mobility Projects – New Technologies for Social Science, as part of the Italy-South Africa Joint Research Programme, extending the range of investigation to the Moxomatsi village, also in the Mpumalanga province. The original span of the agreement covered a period from 2018 to 2020 – postponed to 2021 due to the COVID-19 emergency – and included four projects eligible for the Youth Exchanges programme set up by the Italian

Ministry of Foreign Affairs and International Cooperation, the last of which was named in memory of Professor Roberto Vanacore.

The present work, leading back to Coromandel House, was then intended to test the potentialities and, possibly, the limits of distance learning, following the experience acquired, over the years, through the surveys and digital restitutions. Firstly, we worked on a Building Information Modelling (BIM) of Coromandel House, chosen because of its structural peculiarities and the well-known architectural value; secondly, we decided to further explore the area of enquiry, focusing on the near archeological ruins of a Bokoni settlement, employing an experimental remote photogrammetric survey.

AN APPROACH THAT COMPLIES WITH A BIM TECHNICAL METHODOLOGY

In designing Coromandel House, Zanuso succeeded in interpreting the South African landscape, climate and local constructive technology of the Mpumalanga region, by means of research and exploration of different typological solutions, to transform his project in a proposal that included both the built environment and the surroundings. By combining the environment with the clients' requests, he managed to ingeniously and efficiently deal with the topic of private residence, so the product became a masterful example of South African Regional architecture.

Coromandel House constitutes a suitable case study to analyse the results produced by a mixture of different cultures and to test the proposed approach. This study aims at analysing masonry structures belonging to the local, traditional constructive technology, with the support of modern investigation tools. Moreover, this academic exercise confirmed the importance of group work of an interdisciplinary approach, and of the benefits of using the BIM methodology as an analysis and research tool.

The proposed graphical method involved a simplified approach, directly starting with the modelling of the artefact in a SketchUp environment. A first informative layer was added to the geometric model by texturising the constructive elements using the Enscape plug-in. The resulting graphic drawings were included – together with the pre-existing written, graphic, photographic, public and unpublished documentation regarding the site – in an informative system linked to the three-dimensional model, thus operating in compliance with the BIM technology.

Given the peculiar characteristics of the case study, its structural irregularities, high anisotropy of internal spaces and materiality that seems to both emerge from and blend with the environment, it became objectively convenient to employ a "user-friendly" and "low-cost" software such as SketchUp. It was indeed easy to model the complex geometries that the built environment and site represent.

The collaborative approach undoubtedly followed the principles of the BIM methodology: an object-oriented, parametric and informative modelling process. To this purpose, the constitutive elements of the house were discretised and organised in components, according to the object-oriented paradigm. Free tools were employed to parametrically model finishing elements because of the higher level of detail required in, for example, window frames and the helicoidal staircase. These were easily resizeable later.

The first piece of information added to the model was the geo-referencing, by directly accessing from SketchUp the available Google map: thus, in the contextualisation stage, it digitally reproduced, albeit in simplified form, the topography of the site. Further detailed information regarded the constructive and material characteristics of the asset. Having then the chance to request educational licences, the real-time-rendering and virtual-reality plug-in Enscape, by Enscape GmbH, was chosen as a tool to develop photorealistic reconstructive hypotheses of the actual and past materiality of Coromandel House.

Keeping in mind the informative paradigm, which properly distinguishes a Building Information Model from a simple three-dimensional one, the digital artefact was then organised into constructive "components" in accordance with the IFC 2 x 3 classification standard. This procedure is propaedeutic to export the geometric model to IFC – which is a standard developed by Building Smart and universally accepted for the Open BIM applications: this kind of conversion will let anyone examine the model just by employing a free viewer among the ones available online. An Open BIM standard lays the foundation for reaching the desired interoperability: the exchange of information based on shared languages and formats is key in order to optimise each work phase, aiming at a transparent and fully collaborative process.

The rendered images were then incorporated into an online shared repository that was made available for everyone; they were then linked to the model by making specific adjustments to the textual code of the IFC file. For the implementation of the elaborated data, it was necessary to edit the script of the IFC file, which is usually structured according to the logic of the Express G data modelling language. Human-shaped Elements were used to place, throughout the architectural artefact, privileged Point of View, while the Info Points had the purpose of giving access to the external documentation, including both the one produced at the end of the present application and the one already available online but not yet organised as a structured database for the dissemination of Zanuso's work. The Google Earth Coordinates and the related KML for the localisation project were added, too.

By editing the script of the IFC file, it was therefore possible to properly redefine the pre-existing properties, so as to complete their descriptions as necessary and improve the associated LOI (Level of Information). The result produced by this didactic experience was a number of geometric models that qualify as LOD (Level of Development) 300, according to the American Institute of Architects classification, or LOD C, in compliance with the Italian regulation. Detailed internal and external images were produced, taking care to accurately define the texture of the structural elements, the graphic rendering, the lighting, the photographic exposure and to add furnishing and human figures; for example, those elements used to accomplish the contextualisation and to serve as a metric reference. An informative repository for harvesting newly produced data was set up; said data, together with data that was already available, were subsequently linked to the model. The resulting interactive model, which can be inspected using an online platform (Autodesk Viewer) or a downloadable application for IFC visualisation (BIM Vision), served to disseminate knowledge about Coromandel House.

Specifically, the online images (Corresponding property: "WebImage"), gathered under the "Links" identification, were each attached to the constructive elements represented in them, hence the related descriptions were completed. The rendered images were linked to anthropomorphic elements distributed across the model and oriented in accordance with the points of view from where said images were taken (Property: "Render"). The documents and the photographs taken during the educational trips jointly organised by all three of the universities involved were linked to modelled info points (Property: "A travel journal", "Paper" and "Web Site"), which were evenly placed around the architectural asset. A pair of textual-volumetric info points ("Real-time rendered model") were eventually laid to provide access to two inspectable and navigable versions of the model realised with the Enscape plug-in.

AN EXPERIMENTAL REMOTE "PHOTOGRAMMETRIC SURVEY"

Following on, to fully define the object of study, the territorial context in which the estate is located could not be disregarded, focusing firstly on the archaeological area corresponding to a previous Bokoni settlement, located north-west of the house at an approximate distance of 1.5km as the crow flies. Using remote sensing techniques, although within the limitations induced by the current situation, the objective was to obtain an initial reconstruction of an area of approximately 0.1 square kilometres, using the Google Earth Pro application in combination with Agisoft Metashape, a well-known software for the development of a photogrammetric pipeline.

Using Google Earth Pro, which recently became free, it was therefore possible to record a tour simulating a drone flight in a virtual environment, taking special care to move the camera slowly and constantly. The same application then allows the tour to be exported by rendering the frames according to a predefined time interval. A total of 346 "virtual photogrammetric captures" of the area of study were then produced for subsequent processing in the Metashape environment. The processing phase involved the creation of an initial *sparse* cloud of 664 699 Tie Points, a subsequent *dense* cloud of 16 719 784 points and a final mesh of 11 987 725 faces and 5 995 927 vertices. The terrain model thus reconstructed was then appropriately georeferenced and scaled by inserting the three values of latitude, longitude and altitude, of six marked points, once again, digitally measured.

The resulting Orthophotos and the Digital Elevation Model (DEM) have respectively a ground sample distance of 3.96cm/px and 7.92cm/px, propaedeutic to finally export contour lines with an interval of 50cm starting from a minimum elevation of 1,752 metres to a maximum of 1,824 metres asl.

The results obtained, although far from being considered definitive, are proposed as a geometric reference of first approximation for the survey of the ruins, to be validated with an *in situ* accurate survey when the research activities restart. To complete the remote sensing acquisition, having also in mind an initial verification of the results

01

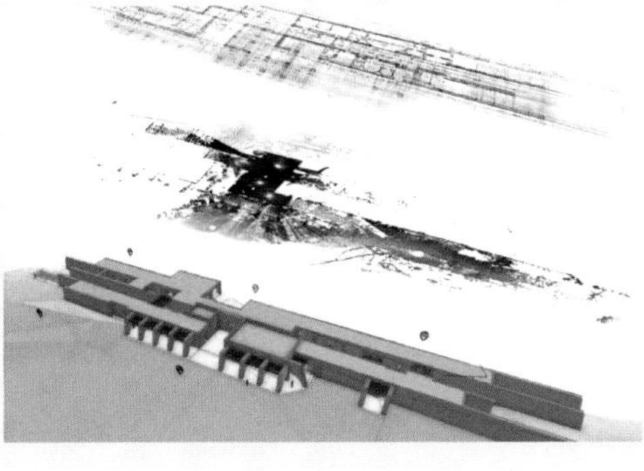

01

Building Information Modelling (BIM) highlights, starting from archive documentation and TLS survey

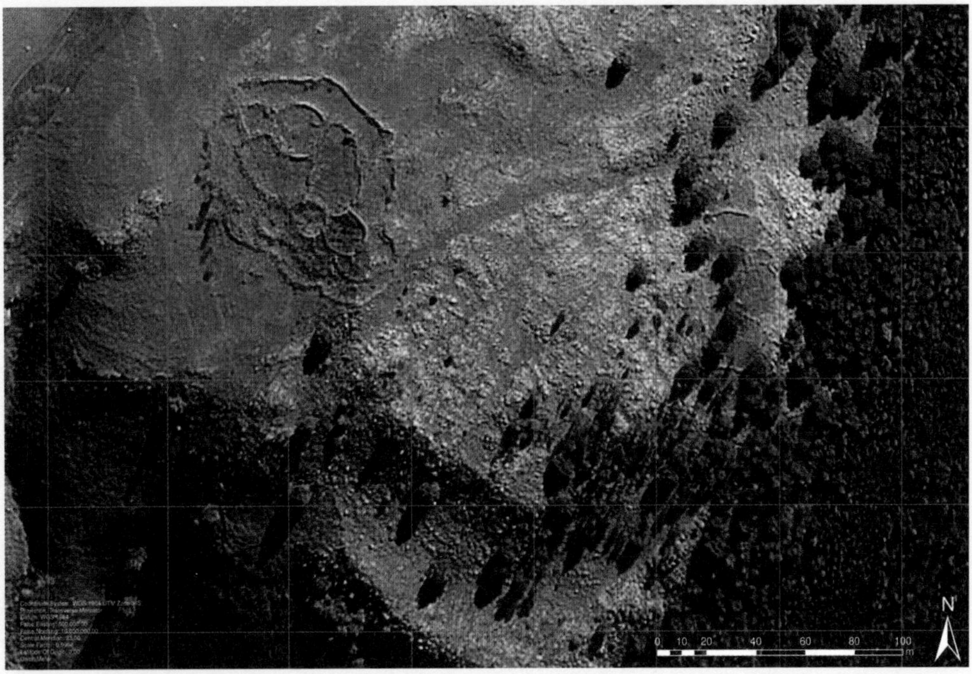

02

02

Satellite imagery showing
the Bokoni ruins

obtained, an archival satellite image (July 2017), with a resolution of 50cm (Ground Sample Distance), which covers a larger area of about 25 square kilometres and includes both the site of the ruins and the estate, produced by the Pléiades sensor with the Gram-Schmidt method, was finally acquired.

CONCLUSION

It becomes clear, on the one hand, that the employment of accessible technologies allowed all the stakeholders, including professors, researchers, students, architects and engineers, to profitably interact, so as to encourage a continuous cultural and educational exchange. On the other hand, only through close international intercollegiate co-operation and the shared memory of those who, in the recent past, had the opportunity to visit the site was it possible to collect and organise the available documentation inherent to the object of study, thus managing to propose a systematisation. Data collected was incorporated into a model which, by means of an Open BIM approach, acts as a "repository", with the aim of contributing, in a broader perspective, to the appreciation of the architectural and archaeological heritage that is unjustly considered minor.

The leitmotif of the activities was to gain knowledge of the sites by employing fast and practical tools, with the ease of information gathered aimed at supporting future initiatives for creating awareness among national and international heritage protection organisations. Moreover, the aim was to encourage the dissemination of specialist knowledge, together with the implementation of advanced equipment, if possible at low cost, in developing countries and within the limits imposed by the health emergency, with the main objective of documenting the past to pass it on to future generations.

Bibliography

CREATING COROMANDEL: PARTS 1–3

Artefacts, "House Press (Coromandel)". *Artefacts.co.za*, http://artefacts.co.za/main/Buildings/bldgframes.php?bldgid=7588, accessed 19 August 2011.

Artefacts, "Steffen Ahrends". *Artefacts.co.za*, http://artefacts.co.za/main/Buildings/archframes.php?archid=7, accessed 10 July 2020.

Aucor, "A Dream Goes on Auction", https://docest.com/a-dream-goes-on-auction, accessed 4 September 2021.

Banham, R, *Age of the Masters*, Architectural Press, 1975.

Bassi, A and L Tedeschi, *MZ Progetto integrato. Marco Zanuso. Design, tecnica e industria*, Milan: Mendrisio Academy Press and Silvana Editoriale (Collection directed by Letizia Tedeschi), 2013.

Beavon, K and P Larsen, "Sandton Central, 1969–2013: From Open Veld to New CBD?", in P Harrison, G Gotz, A Todes and C Wray, eds., *Changing Space, Changing City: Johannesburg After Apartheid* – Open Access selection, Johannesburg, Wits University Press, 2014, pp. 370–394, https://doi.org/10.18772/22014107656.22

Bellamy, A, (Former MD Edgars) Email: Zanuso, 13 July 2021.

Bellamy, A, (Former MD Edgars) Interview: Edgardale and Zanuso, 23 July 2021.

Burkhardt, F, *Design: Marco Zanuso*, Milan: Realizzazione Editoriale, 1994.

Calgarotto, A, "The Sky in the Room: Marco Zanuso: Holiday Houses", *House and Site: Rudofsky, Lewerentz, Zanuso, Sert, Rainer*, Firenze University Press, 2014, pp. 186–237.

Cator, C, "Cheyne Walk – An Interior by Victoria Press", London: Christie's, 2015.

Chia, M, "Victoria Press's Blithe Spirit", *The New York Times Style Magazine*, April 2015.

Chipkin, C, "The Great Apartheid Building Boom", in H Judin, et al., *Blank: Architecture Apartheid and After*, Rotterdam: NAi publishers, 1998, pp. 248–267.

Chipkin, C, (Architect and Architectural Historian) Interview: Zanuso in South Africa and his business relationship with Press. Parkview, Johannesburg, 17 August 2011.

Cooke, J, "Revisions of the Modern", in R Fisher, et al., *Architecture of the Transvaal*, Pretoria: Unisa Press, 1998, pp. 231–251.

Crespi, L, et al., *Marco Zanuso: architettura e design*, Rome: Officina Libraria, 2020.

De Giorgi, M, "Casa Press/Press House Marco Zanuso", *Inventario*, vol. 1, 2011, pp. 156–159.

De Giorgi, M, *Marco Zanuso architetto*, Milan: Skira, 1999.

De Mondenard, A, "Exposer une revue: l'exemple de *Réalités* (1946–1964). Maison européenne de la photographie (Paris), 16 janvier–30 mars 2008", *In Situ*, vol. 36, 18 October 2018, http://journals.openedition.org/insitu/18482, accessed 3 May 2019.

Dos Santos, J, "Entrepreneurship in the fashion retail industry: Sydney Press and the rise of Edgars 1929–1982", PhD thesis. Johannesburg: University of Johannesburg, 2018.

Fassler Kamstra, M (Architect) Interview: Watson's work on House Press, his introduction to Victoria Press; the Burle Marx connection, Killarney, Johannesburg, 26 January 2012.

Fisher, R, "The Third Vernacular: Pretoria Regionalism – Aspects of an Emergence", in R Fisher, et al., *Architecture of the Transvaal*, Pretoria: Unisa Press, 1998, pp. 123–147.

Fisher, R, "Coromandel", *Clivia News*, vol. 15, no. 1, 2006, p. 4.

Fisher, R, "On-reflection – A Re-look at the Future of the Past", *Journal of the South African Institute of Architects*, Cape Town, vol. 53, January/February, 2012, pp. 6–7.

Grieg, D, *A Guide to Architecture in South Africa*, Cape Town, Howard Timmins, 1971.

Grignolo R, *Marco Zanuso: Scritti sulle tecniche di produzione e di progretto*, Milan: Mendrisio Academy Press and Silvana Editoriale (Collection directed by Letizia Tedeschi), 2013.

Hoffe, H, (Architect, former director MLH) Interview: Association with Press and working relationship with Zanuso, House Press and Edgardale, Waverly, Johannesburg, 29 March 2012.

Holmes, M, (Architect) Interview: Working on House Press while interning at MLH, Forest Town, Johannesburg, 25 January 2012.

Joubert, O, ed., *10 Years + 100 Buildings: Architecture in a Democratic South Africa*, Cape Town: Bell-Roberts, 2009, p. 22.

Kaplan, M, *Jewish Roots in the South African Economy*, Cape Town: Struik, 1986.

Katsikakis, D, (Architect) Interview: Victoria's course at the AA, her design knowledge and approach to Coromandel, Zoom, 7 August 2020.

Kinmonth, P and T Traeger, (Opera director and designer, writer, editor, filmmaker, photographer) Interview: Victoria Press's design approach and recollections about Coromandel discussions, Zoom, 3 August 2020.

Le Roux, G, (Architect) Interview: MLH association with Press and memories of Zanuso, House Press and Edgardale, Randburg, Johannesburg, 6 March 2011.

Louw, M, "The Craft of Memory and Forgetting", *South African Journal of Art History*, vol. 32, no. 2, 2017, pp. 93–106.

Maggs, T, (Archaeologist), Email: Bokoni, 11 May 2021.

Mahoney, S, (Architect) Interview: Inspired by Coromandel, Google Meet, 11 December 2020.

Maskew, J, "Press (and Priorities) at Edgars", *News/Check*, 11 July 1969, pp. 40–41.

Moir, A and M Moir, (First farm manager and his wife) Interview: Establishing Coromandel Farm and construction developments, Google Meet, 23 May 2021.

Moore, C, *The Place of Houses*, New York: Holt, Rinehart and Winston, 1974, p. 49.

Morgan, A and C Naylor, eds., *Contemporary Architects*, Chicago: St James Press, 1987, pp. 1025–1026.

Norberg-Schulz, C, *Principles of Modern Architecture*, London: Andreas Papadakis, 2000, pp. 89–95.

Peres, E, "The Coromandel Estate Manor House: A 'Ruin'

of a Landscape", *Journal of the South African Institute of Architects*, no. 62, July/August 2013, pp. 32–37.

Peters, W, "Houses for Pretoria", in R Fisher, et al., *Architecture of the Transvaal*, Pretoria: Unisa Press, 1998, pp. 175–195.

Pienaar, M, The Norman Eaton Legacy (Unpublished dissertation), University of Pretoria, 2013, http://hdl.handle.net/2263/41017

Pienaar, M, "Eaton for Africa", *Journal of the South African Institute of Architects,* vol. 87, September/October 2017, pp. 38–49.

Piva, A and V Prina, *Marco Zanuso: architettura, design e la costruzione del benessere*, Rome: Gangemi Editore, 2007.

Plewman, N, "Paradise Lost", *Visi* magazine, 2011.

Plewman, N, (Architect) Interview: The influence of Coromandel, Google Meet, 25 March 2021.

Press, C, (Daughter) Interview: Sydney and Victoria Press's design interests and professional rigour, Zoom, 2 July 2020.

Press, C, (Son) Interview: Coromandel House and Farm, and Edgardale, Zoom, 29 April, 6 May 2021.

Press, DS, *Klawer: How a Town is Born* [s.l.]:[s.n.], 2018.

Press, DS, *The House of Benjamin – A Family History*, New York, Manuscript in preparation, 2020.

Press, S, (Daughter) Interview: Victoria Press's design approach and Coromandel, Zoom, 3 August 2020.

Press, S and Peres, E, "The Story of Coromandel", Information document for visitors to the farmstead, 2020.

Press, V, No. 4 Cheyne Walk. Annotated photo album for Suzanne Press, 2004.

Press, W, (Son) Interview: Construction of Coromandel House and Farm, Zoom, 4 May 2021.

Reeder, M, "Coromandel: A Beacon of Hope for Land Reform", *Mail & Guardian*, 3 February 2012, pp. 1–4.

Rogers, E, "Uomini senza casa", *Domus*, no. 206, March 1946, p. 2.

Rogers, E, et al., "Quindici anni di architettura italiana: Architettura italiana 6 domande", *Casabella*, no. 5, May 1961, pp. 33–34.

Schiaffonati, F, E Mussinelli and E Gambaro, "Tecnologia dell'architettura per la progettazione ambientale", *Techne: Journal of Technology for Architecture and Environment*, vol. 1, 2011, pp. 49–53.

Schurr, K, (Nursery manager's wife and co-administrator) Interview: Coromandel Farm nursery. Telephonic interview conducted by C Deacon, 25 June 2021.

Schwarz, A, (Architect) Interview: Steffen Ahrends. Romeira, Portugal, 19 April 2021.

Steyn, G, "The Coromandel Manor House (1975): Marco Zanuso's Encounter with an African Site", *South African Journal of Art History*, vol. 31, 2016, pp. 38–54.

Swanepoel, P, (Architect, urban designer) Interview: Coromandel and its influence on his career. Forest Town, Johannesburg, 5 October 2011.

Thomashoff, K, and F Thomashoff, (Architects) Interview: Influence of Coromandel, Google Meet, 21 April 2021.

Truswell, H, "Spirit of the Veld", *Fair Lady*, 15 May 1985, pp. 54–60.

Unknown, "Vacation Fortress on Sardinia", *The Architectural Forum*, New York, vol. 126, no. 5, June 1967, pp. 64-65.

Unknown, Sydney Press feature, *Style* magazine, Johannesburg, 1984.

Various, "Edgardale", *Architecture SA*, December 1978, pp. 23–29.

Various, "An Intricate Beehive: Edgardale", *Planning*, vol. 33, 1978, pp. 31–90.

Various, "Inside Edgardale. Corporate Headquarters of the Edgars Group of Companies", Brochure: Edgars, 1980.

Vervoort, A, (Architect) Interview: Coromandel influence, Google Meet, 10 December 2020.

Viviers, A, "To Save or Not to Save?", *Visi*, accessed 12 August 2011.

Watson, P, (Landscaper) Interview: Process and vision; experience and memories of working with the Presses and Zanuso, Greenside, Johannesburg, 18 August 2011.

Watson, P, (Landscaper) Interview: Coromandel landscaping, Zoom, 15 September 2020.

Wood, E, (Urban designer, town planner) Interview: Design and construction of the Coromandel farmworkers' village, and working with Press, Melville, Johannesburg, 1 September 2011.

Zamboni, A, "Casa Press, Lydenburg, Sudafrica", *Domus* no. 1015, July/August 2017, pp. 71–83.

Zanuso, M, "La casa e l'ideale", *Domus*, no. 176, August 1942, p. 312.

Zanuso, M, "Non dimentichiamo la cucina", *Domus*, no. 197, May 1944, p. 185.

Zanuso, M, "La casa prefabbricata. 3 – Il cantiere", *Domus*, no. 207, March 1946, p.17.

Zanuso, M, "Architettura e pittura", *Edilizia Moderna*, no. 47, December 1951, p. 43.

Zanuso, M, "Paesaggio, architettura e design", *Notizie Olivetti*, no. 76, November 1962, pp. 61–68, with E Vittoria.

Zanuso, M, "La casa. Megastrutture, cellule abitative, caverne del XXI secolo", *Pianeta. Planète*, no. 8, June/August 1965, pp. 73–77.

Zanuso, M, Un'idea di tecnologia – excerpts from "portare l'artificio alle sue conseguenza estreme", Vittorio Magnago Lampugnani interviewing Marco Zanuso, *Domus*, no. 690, January 1988.

Zanuso, M (Jr.) and Lotus, "Casa ad Arzachena", *The Modern Inside Out*, Lotus, vol. 119, 2003, pp. 90–105.

ZML, "Un segno nella natura; Lydenburg Sudafrica", *Abitare*, vol. 191, 1981, pp. 14–23.

Bibliography

STONES THAT SING

Anon, "House Leith, Houghton", *South African Architectural Record*, vol. 37, 1952, pp. 272–275.

Anon, "House on Lake Como; Architect: Marco Zanuso", *Architectural Review*, vol. 166, no. 992, October 1979, pp. 225–228.

Anon, "Un segno nella natura; Lydenburg Sudafrica", *Abitare*, vol. 191, 1981, pp. 14–23.

Anon, "Casa ad Arzachena, Marco Zanuso 1962–64: Vacanze Spartane", *Lotus International*, no. 119, 2003, pp. 90–105.

Barker, AAJ, "Heterotrophic Syntheses. Mediation in the Domestic Architecture of Gabriel (Gawie) Fagan", Unpublished PhD, University of Pretoria, Pretoria, 2012.

Beck, H, ed., "UIA International Architect: Southern Africa (Issue 8)", London: International Architect, 1985, pp. 24–25.

Blakely, S, "The Responsibilities of the Architect: Mass Production and Modernism in the Work of Marco Zanuso 1936–1972", Unpublished PhD, University of Columbia, 2011, https://academiccommons.columbia.edu/doi/10.7916/D86Q245S, accessed 26 April 2021.

Chipkin, C, *Johannesburg Style: Architecture and Society 1880s–1960s*, Cape Town: David Philip, 1993.

Connell, P, 1945, A review of "The Architectural Review, October 1944. Special number devoted to South Africa", *South African Architectural Record*, vol. 30, pp. 162–165.

Cooke, BS, "The Emergence of Contemporary Architecture in South Africa 1927–1939", *South African Architectural Record*, March 1960, pp. 21–22.

D'Entrèves, PM and S Benhabib, eds., *Habermas and the Unfinished Project of Modernity: Critical Essays on the Philosophical Discourse of Modernity*, Cambridge, UK: Polity Press, 1996.

De Giorgi, M, "Marco Paesaggi 1949–1988", *Ottagono*, vol. 33, no. 129, December/February 1999, pp. 87–103.

Delius, P, "South Africa Risks Losing Rich Insights into an Ancient Farming Society", 2020, verlorenkloof.co.za, https://verlorenkloof.co.za/south-africa-risks-losing-rich-insights-into-an-ancient-farming-society, accessed 28 April 2021.

Delius, P, T Maggs and M Schoeman, "Bokoni: Old Structures, New Paradigms? Rethinking Pre-colonial Society from the Perspective of the Stone-walled Sites in Mpumalanga", in "Rethinking South Africa's Past: Essays in History and Archaeology", *Journal of Southern African Studies*, vol. 38, no. 2, June 2012, pp. 399–414.

Fagan, GT, *An Enabling Architecture*. Eaton Memorial Lecture, Pretoria, Unpublished, Fagan archive, 1996.

Fisher, RC, "The Third Vernacular: Pretoria Regionalism – Aspects of an Emergence", *Architecture of the Transvaal*, RC Fisher, S le Roux and E Maré, eds., Pretoria: University of South Africa, 1998, pp. 123–147.

Frampton, K, "Prospects for a Critical Regionalism", *Perspecta*, vol. 20, 1983, pp. 147–162, http://www.jstor.org/stable/1567071, accessed 23 July 2008.

Frampton, K, *Modern Architecture: A Critical History*, Thames and Hudson, 1992.

Frampton, K, *Le Corbusier*, London: Thames & Hudson, 2001.

Frampton, K, "The Unfinished Modern Project at the End of Modernity: Tectonic Form and the Space of Public Appearance – Soane Medal Lecture", Sir John Soane's Museum, 2019, https://arquitecturaviva.com/assets/old_media/Documentos/the_unfinished_modern_project_.pdf, accessed 30 April 2021.

Herbert, G, *Martienssen and the International Style: The Modern Movement in South African Architecture*, Cape Town: AA Balkema, 1975.

Lefaivre, L and A Tzonis, *Critical Regionalism: Architecture and Identity in a Globalised World*, Munich, London: Prestel, 2003.

Maggs, T, Personal email communication with the archaeologist, 11 May 2021.

Martienssen, R, "The Golden Road: Impressions of an Architectural Pilgrimage to the Cape", 1928, wiredspace.wits.ac.za/bitstream/handle/10539/7403/June%201928.doc, accessed 8 July 2011.

Press, S, *Letter to Zanuso*, Mendrisio Archivio del Moderno, Balerna, Switzerland, 23 March 1969.

Pretorius, et al., eds., *25 Sophia Gray. Memorial Lectures and Exhibitions 1989–2013*, Department of Architecture, University of the Free State, 2014.

Prinsloo, I, ed., *Architecture 2000: A Review of South African Architecture*, Johannesburg: Picasso Headline, 2000.

Tzonis, A, "Thoughts on South African Architecture Today", *Digest of South African Architecture*, Cape Town, 2006–2007, pp. 216–218.

Tzonis, A and L Lefaivre, "The Grid and the Pathway. An Introduction to the Work of Dimitris and Suzana Antonakakis", *Architecture in Greece*, vol. 15, 1981.

Van de Werke, I, Interview with the author, Kameeldrift, Pretoria, 25 April 2021.

Van Schaik L, "Against Regionalism", *Architecture South Africa*, March/April 1980, pp. 19–23.

Banfi, F, L Barazzetti, M Previtali and F Roncoroni, "Historic BIM: A New Repository for Structural Health Monitoring", *ISPRS – International Archives of the Photogrammetry, Remote Sensing and Spatial Information Sciences*, vol. XLII-5/W1, 2017, pp. 269–274.

Barba, S, C Ferreyra and J Laubscher, "Documentazione e valorizzazione del paesaggio culturale di Mpumalanga in Sudafrica", in R Ferraris, ed., *Atti del VI Congreso Internacional de Expresión Gráfica en Ingeniería, Arquitectura y Carreras afines*, Córdoba (Argentina), 22–24 September 2016, pp. 536–542.

Barba, S, M Limongiello and M van Schoor, SSIMM. Italy-South Africa Joint Research Project. The surveys, *Patrimoni Culturali, Architettura, Paesaggio e Design tra ricerca e sperimentazione didattica*, didapress, Dipartimento di Architettura – Università degli Studi di Firenze, 2019, pp. 284–289.

Calvano, M and F Guadagnoli, "3D Reconstruction of the City of Amatrice. An 'Instant Modeling' Operation", *DisegnareCON*, vol. 9, no. 17, 2016, pp. 7.1–7.9.

Comisión es.BIM. *Guía para la elaboración del Plan de Ejecución BIM (BEP)*, España: Gobierno de España, 2018.

Lo Turco, M, "Il Building Information Modeling, tra ricerca, didattica e professione", *DisegnareCON*, vol. 4, no. 7, 2011, pp. 42–51.

Osello, A, *Il futuro del disegno con il BIM per ingegneri e architetti/The Future of Drawing with BIM for Engineers and Architects*, Palermo: Dario Flaccovio Editore, 2012.

Peres, E, "The Coromandel Estate Manor House: A 'Ruin' of the Landscape", *Architecture South Africa*, no. 62, 2013, pp. 32–37.

Steyn, G, "The Coromandel Manor House (1975): Marco Zanuso's Encounter with an African Site", *South African Journal of Art History – SAJAH*, vol. 31, no. 1, 2016, pp. 38–54.

Rossi, A and U Palmieri, "LOD per il patrimonio architettonico: la modellazione BIM per la fabbrica Solimene", *Diségno*, 2019, pp. 213–224.

Sacchi, L, "Il punto sul BIM", *DisegnareCON*, vol. 9, no. 16, ISSN: 1828-5961, 2016.

Sacks, R, C Eastman, G Lee and P Teicholz, *BIM Handbook: A Guide to Building Information Modeling for Owners, Designers, Engineers, Contractors, and Facility Managers*, 3rd Edition. Hoboken, New Jersey: John Wiley & Sons, Inc, 2018.

Tchouangouem, JF, P Pauwels, HA Fonbeyin, C Magniont, MH Karray and B Kamsu-Foguem, "Integration of Environmental Data in BIM Tool & Linked Building Data", in Poveda Villalon, M, P Pauwels, R De Klerk and A Roxin, eds., "Proceedings of the 7th Linked Data in Architecture and Construction Workshop, LDAC 2019", Lisbon, 17–21 June 2019, pp. 78–91.

Yousefzadeh, S, JP Spillane, L Lamont, J McFadden and JPB Lim, "Building Information Modelling (BIM) Software Interoperability: A Review of the Construction Sector", in Raiden, AB and E Aboagye-Nimo, eds., "Proceedings of the 31st Annual ARCOM Conference, ARCOM, 2015", Lincoln, UK, Association of Researchers in Construction Management, 7–9 September 2015, pp. 711–720.

Zhang, C, J Beetz and M Weise, "Model View Checking: Automated Validation for IFC Building Models", in Mahdavi, A, B Martens, R Scherer, "eWork and eBusiness in Architecture, Engineering and Construction – Proceedings of the 10th European Conference on Product and Process Modelling, ECPPM 2014", Vienna, Boca Raton, CRC Press, 17–19 September 2014, pp. 123–128.

WEB REFERENCES

https://architizer.com/projects/coromandel-estate-manor-house, accessed 4 June 2021.

http://hiddenarchitecture.net/coromandel-estate-manor-https://technical.buildingsmart.org, accessed 4 June 2021.

Photography Credits

CREATING COROMANDEL: PARTS 1–3

© Photographs courtesy of:

Christian Sumi, 2021: Image 02

Christoffel J. Mentz, December 2019: Front Cover, Image 132; July 2021: Images 138, 144, 150

David Goldblatt Legacy Trust, Photographs by David Goldblatt, 1972–1973: Images 04, 25, 34, 35, 36, 37, 38, 39, 40, 41, 42, 43, 44, 45, 46

Dewald Van Helsdingen, July 2014: Images 117, 118, 119, 120, 121, 122, 123, 124, 125, 126, 127, 128, 129, 130, 140

Domus magazine nos. 176, 206, 207, 211: Images 14, 15, 16, 17, 20

Frankie Pappas, 2019: Image 134

Giorgio Mastinu: Image 94

Justin S. Coetzee, 2015: Image 143

Margaret Courtney-Clarke, 1980: Images 01, 79, 83, 102, 133, 139; 1989: Image 05

Mendrisio Academy Balerna, Archivio del Moderno, Fondo Marco Zanuso: Images 10, 13, 18, 19, 21, 22, 23, 24, 33, 50, 51, 53, 55, 56, 57, 58, 59, 60, 61, 62, 63, 64, 65, 66, 67, 68, 69, 71, 74, 75, 76, 77, 78, 80, 82, 85, 98, 100, 101, 104, 105, 106, 107, 108, 109, 110, 111, 112, 113, 114, 115, 116, 131, 141, 142

Moir Family Archive, 1969: Image 28

Nicholas Plewman Architects + Associates, Photograph by Dook: Image 135

Pianeta. Planète, no. 8, June/August 1965: Image 99

Pietro Porcinai Archive: Images 87, 88, 89, 90

studioMAS Architecture & Urban Design: Image 136

Sydney and Victoria Press Family Archive: Images 03, 06, 07, 08, 09, 12, 26, 27, 29, 30, 31, 32, 47, 48, 49, 52, 54, 70, 72, 73, 81, 84, 86, 91, 92, 93, 95, 96, 97, 103

The Architectural Forum, vol. 125, no. 5, June 1967: Image 11

Thomashoff + Partner Architects, Photograph by Renante Le Roux, 2009: Image 137

Zamboni Associati Architettura, 2021: Images 145, 146, 147, 148, 149

STONES THAT SING

Arthur Barker, 2008: Images 08, 11; 2015: Image 06; 2020: Image 07; 2021: Image 09

Catherine Deacon, 2021: Image 01

Sydney and Victoria Press Family Archive, Watercolour by James Reeves: Image 03

University of Cape Town Libraries, Thornton-White papers, Photograph by Leonard Thornton-White: Image 04 (https://www.artefacts.co.za/main/Buildings/bldg_images.php?bldgid=310#19602)

University of Pretoria Repository, Norman Eaton Collection: Image 05 (https://repository.up.ac.za/bitstream/handle/2263/7648/ar001pap_etn.0045.pdf?sequence=2&isAllowed=y)

University of the Free State, 25 Sophia Gray Memorial Lectures and Exhibitions, 1989–2013, Pretorius, et al., eds., p. 96, 2014: Image 10

South African Architectural Record, no. 37, 1952, pp. 272–275: Image 02

DOCUMENTATION AND APPRECIATION OF COROMANDEL

Joint Mobility Projects – New Technologies for Social Science, as part of the Italy-South Africa Joint Research Programme led by Salvatore Barba: Image 01

Pléiades Data: Image 02

Acknowledgements

CREATING COROMANDEL: PARTS 1–3

Our deepest thanks to Suzanne Press for her unwavering support in documenting this history and her generosity of spirit, and to Caroline Press for her editing support and direction. We also thank the children of Victoria and Sydney Press, for recognising the value of this complex and layered architectural history as a source of inspiration and learning for the next generation of designers and architects.

For their financial support, we give our thanks to Suzanne, Caroline, Jane, Clifford, Roger, Gregory and William Press, as well as Oppenheimer Generations. We also thank Letizia Tedeschi, Nicola Navone and Elena Triunveri from the Archivio del Moderno for their invaluable assistance in making this publication possible; Salvatore Barba for promoting the project to receive financial support from the University of Salerno and the Italian Ministry of Foreign Affairs and International Cooperation (Project: "Missione Roberto Vanacore: documentazione e valorizzazione dell'architettura e del territorio di Coromandel in Sudafrica"); Alessandro Molesini, Omar Ben Hamed and Giulia lotti from Zamboni Associati Architettura; Gianluca Grassi, International Relations, Reggio Emilia Municipality; as well as Catherine Deacon, Oupa Makgana and Mark Wright for going a few extra miles for this project. And lastly, we thank all the individuals who contributed to the making of this book – fellow authors, interviewees and Coromandel's many friends, who have become our friends along the way.

DOCUMENTATION AND APPRECIATION OF COROMANDEL

We would like to thank Jacques Laubscher (Dean of the Architectural Department), Mostert Van Schoor (Professor of Survey) and Marinda Bolt (Professor of Design II) at Tshwane University of Technology, Pretoria, and Victoria Ferraris (Professor of Architecture) at the National University of Córdoba, Argentina, for their cooperation and prompt sharing of documents in their possession. Lastly, it is important to mention that the Italian-South African collaboration also took place thanks to Pierguido Sarti – Scientific and Technological Attaché at the Embassy of Italy in Pretoria.

PEER REVIEW

In accordance with academic practice, this book has undergone a double-blind peer review in which the accuracy, novelty and contribution of the research has been verified by academics or researchers who are specialists in this field.

This book is dedicated to all those who dare to pursue excellence.

Ministero degli Affari Esteri e della Cooperazione Internazion

UNIVERSITÀ DEGLI STUDI DI SALERNO

Dipartimento di *Ingegneria Civile*

This book is published by Artifice Press Limited, a company registered in England and Wales with company number 11182108. Artifice Press Limited is an imprint within the SJH Group. Copyright is owned by the SJH Group.

Artifice Press Limited
The Maple Building
39–51 Highgate Road
London NW5 1RT
United Kingdom
—
+44 (0)20 8371 4047
office@artificeonline.com
www.artificeonline.com

Creative direction and design by Anton Jacques
Printed in Lithuania by Kopa

ISBN 978-1-911339-47-2

British Library in Cataloguing Data. A CIP record for this book is available from the British Library.

Artifice